Stone Cold Fox

Stone Cold Fox

Rachel Koller Croft

THORNDIKE PRESS
A part of Gale, a Cengage Company

GALE
A Cengage Company

GALE
A Cengage Company

Thorndike Press, a part of Gale, a Cengage Company.

Thorndike Press® Large Print Thriller, Adventure, and Suspense.
The text of this Large Print edition is unabridged.
Other aspects of the book may vary from the original edition.
Set in 16 pt. Plantin.

LIBRARY OF CONGRESS CIP DATA ON FILE.
CATALOGUING IN PUBLICATION FOR THIS BOOK
IS AVAILABLE FROM THE LIBRARY OF CONGRESS.

ISBN-13: 979-8-88579-294-3 (hardcover alk. paper)

Published in 2023 by arrangement with Berkley, an imprint of Penguin Publishing Group, a division of Penguin Random House LLC.

Printed in Mexico
Printed Number: 1 Print Year: 2024

for my favorite foxes,
Henny, Ratty & Smithy

Chapter 1

I decided that I would marry Collin Case after the fifth time we fucked. His performance had been consistently adequate, both in the bedroom and while we were out socially. We had been on seven dates, each more lavish than the one before it, raising the stakes suitably during our early courtship. Collin always selected an upscale bar or restaurant in a desirable neighborhood where people made no mistake about who he was, and therefore we were treated appropriately. He didn't tip like a Rockefeller, but I'd wager Rockefeller didn't even tip like a Rockefeller. Old money is old money for a reason and it's not to brighten some downtrodden server's day. So I didn't really care about Collin's standard 20 percent, since it was neither overtly cheap nor blatantly embarrassing. There was nothing blatantly embarrassing about Collin. Don't get me wrong, there was nothing terribly exciting about him either, but I knew that taking up with a man like Collin Case wouldn't exactly lead me down a path of intrigue and excitement and hot sex, which was precisely the point.

I didn't come this far only to get swept away by some narcissistic playboy in a McLaren who made his fortune via white-collar crime, an indictment forever looming, assets ultimately seized in the night, leaving me with nothing. Absolutely not. There would be room for only one criminal in my partnerships, *ahem,* and I was sincerely looking for the right man so I could finally leave that life behind for good.

That was probably not the intended takeaway from *her* lesson plan, but a good teacher inspires the student to discover their own meaning from any given lecture or text. And she was admittedly one of my best teachers, especially at her worst.

Despite the low to medium levels of charisma he exuded, Collin Case obviously had plenty going for him or I wouldn't have even considered our first date. He was attractive in a standard sort of way, admittedly more so when his mouth was closed due to his aggressively white and enormous teeth that would probably look wonderful if his head were slightly larger to accommodate their immense size. Alas, his head was on the narrow side and his short, albeit very expensive, haircuts didn't help matters. I wasn't worried about it in the long term, as he did nearly everything I asked him to do, so surely he would agree to grow out those chestnut locks at my behest, particularly since it would be to his physical benefit. As for the unfortunate dental situation, I always suspected veneers, since they were a luxury item, but my goodness, the dentist very much overshot it. Perhaps we could get those amended as well in due time.

Collin performed well enough in his career and had quickly risen through the ranks to Chief Marketing Officer at a huge consumer packaged goods company. Sure, it was the Case Company and his family had owned it for a hundred years or so, but I found it moderately impressive, since he was only in his early thirties and didn't really have to work. He was a homeowner. Bequeathed, but still. His town house in Chelsea was clean and upmarket. Real estate's always a turn-on. Neutral tones with tasteful splashes of color, modern lines, plush pillows and inoffensive yet thought-provoking art on the walls. The designer he hired possessed forward-thinking taste and made him look cooler than he actually was. A testament to Collin's talent at outsourcing whatever he happened to lack, which wasn't much, at least materially. Collin Case came from supreme wealth, which was the initial attraction for me. Priority number one. Sorry not sorry.

Truthfully, I thought I would ultimately snag myself a divorced and upwardly mobile hedge fund manager with a well-done hair transplant, about ten to fifteen years my senior, in want of a younger trophy wife who could actually hold a conversation and acquiesce to anal on anniversaries, but that whole plan turned out to be much more of a slog for me than I imagined.

By the time I happened upon Collin Case, I had already dated more than my fair share of New York "somebodies" with middling personalities and big-enough bank accounts. They were relatively easy to find when you looked like me. I spent hundreds of my hard-earned dollars on fresh highlights every four to six weeks. I mastered an authentic feminine titter for jokes that weren't remotely amusing as I grazed nearly nonexistent biceps with my perfectly manicured hands, an almond shape on each nail. And I choked down liquid meals with organic ingredients on the regular to stave off a bloated belly and thighs that touch. I did everything I had observed as a child because ultimately it works. I watched her do it for years. But what I learned rather quickly is that dating men in that particular orbit is no picnic at all.

They truly believe the entire universe revolves around them and their underwhelming penises and that everything they do all the time is just so fucking great. It's exhausting having to exalt those types of men, day in and day out, just to secure a Harry Winston diamond; a generous allowance for fillers, Botox and other miscellaneous body maintenance; and most importantly, a life of true leisure without a care in the world. The ultimate safety net. Impenetrable. Though many of my attempts were ill-fated, I stayed the course because I believed wholeheartedly that it would be well worth it, due to a past I never wanted to relive, and I had to make my future different from hers. But none of those relationships with the so-called alphas of New York City panned out in the way I had hoped.

Philip Hartley, an Ed Harris dupe with a Cialis prescription, dumped me after I deigned to ask his sister-in-law about the family trust when we were blitzed on rosé at their vacation home in Palm Beach. Like we were competitors on *The Bachelor,* that "recovering" bulimic with a benzo problem told him I was there for "the wrong reasons." Busted.

That's what I got for trusting a woman. Sloppy work on my part. Deserving of the scathing critique *she* definitely would have given me. I could just hear her, but I always heard her, even when I didn't want to. The words floating out of her mouth, in that light and airy tone of hers, nearly always in complete juxtaposition to the dark and deprecatory language launched in my direction. A verbal lashing disguised as care or concern to anyone else's ear but my own.

Dan Felix was a high-profile litigator who'd had previously court-appointed anger management classes, and he flat out smacked me across the face when I got a text from a male coworker after midnight asking for my dealer's info. Dan didn't actually care about the content of the message — *he* was the one with the coke problem, whereas my own usage was rather infrequent and purely recreational in cases where I thought it could bond me with someone useful — and Dan wrongly assumed I was cheating on him. As if I would waste my time on some junior account executive who shared his place with three roommates in

Dumbo. Please.

But I was learning. An angry man simply would not do.

Speaking of cheating, Morris Haley III, a real estate developer, chronically cheated on me, which I knew would happen on occasion, and the act didn't outright bother me, but there was nothing discreet about his dalliances. I didn't take kindly to openly looking like a fool in front of others, even though he was outrageously handsome — a rarity — and had one of those Kohler shower rooms with seemingly endless streams of water shooting out from all angles. Pure luxury.

She would have approved of Morris, but my reputation mattered too much to me to carry on with him. Meanwhile, that woman had no concept of a reputation at all. Why would she? Her endgame was not like mine. For her, it was about the count. One after another after another after *another,* for as long as she could. But I wanted something different. I relished any differences between us; truth be told I craved them. Clung to every last one.

I had rarely dated men my own age, or thereabouts, because I wrongly assumed it would be a fruitless pursuit of true affluence. But when Collin Case asked me out, I decided to give the notion of inherited wealth an earnest whirl.

I had successfully pitched the Case Company, killing it in the room with all of Collin's underlings, roughly three to five midlevel hires without any real say in the matter but who enthusiastically nodded at me as I performed flawlessly all the while. It was this combination of total self-possession, self-confidence and the wherewithal to weave utter bullshit like a magic wand that got me the job in the first place. It's not like anyone in HR actually checks a university transcript, and providing faux references isn't exactly difficult, is it? It's just advertising, for God's sake; you simply have to roll in and dominate, that's all that really matters, and that's exactly what I did. For example, by the time I wrapped up the pitch for the Case Company, Collin wanted to close the deal in the room. *Naturally.* Shortly after, he crept into my office exuding almost zero confidence and delivered a small knock accompanied by a nervous laugh. I knew immediately what he was after, so I made it easy on both of us.

"You have my card." I smiled. "It has my office line. And my cell."

"Great," he said. "So I'll call you?"

"Looks like it."

"Cool." He grinned, like an oaf, proud of himself for taking the leap even though I had basically operated the safety harness for him. He wasn't the first client, current or prospective, to ask me out, but he was the first I actually considered. After perusing some online literature about the Family Case, I correctly estimated that Collin could more than afford me. Everything in the public record all but confirmed it, but so did my foray into more extensive research, which ended up being a hollow quest. I was undeterred. In fact, I was more confident than ever he was the one.

See, most people have plenty of private things out in the open if you know where and how to look, and I do — thanks to her — but a family like the Cases? You only see what they want you to see. Everything else is in the vault. And that was the crux of pursuing a man like Collin Case. The true challenge would likely not be obtaining Collin's eternal love and devotion but securing my acceptance into his world.

As an added and unexpected perk, I quickly learned that another major difference between Collin and my exes, aside from him being considerably younger than them, was that he was actually nice to me. Her men were nice, too. Easy targets and easy to live with. Easy to gain their trust and their loyalty. Easy to maneuver and manipulate, among other things.

But the types of brash, ambitious men I had been wasting prime husband-hunting years on were angry and dominant and focused purely on their self-made success. I yearned to end the game, and soon, but not at the cost of keeping such brutal company for a life sentence.

With someone like Collin, I realized there was another way.

Collin had had just about everything handed to him, so naturally it made him soft. Some might say malleable. Impressionable. Qualities that were much to the chagrin of the family patriarch, but I didn't see how that was Collin's fault. Sure, he bumbled around at work, practically playing dress-up in his father's clothes, but he saw an opportunity with me where he could actually be himself and I would respond kindly. He wanted to be coddled and praised and adored. In return, he would do the same for me. Boring, sure, but safe, if it went my way. Perfect for me. And he was right there for the taking.

Men like him were rarely accessible, even to tens like me, dating in the same moneyed domains for decades, outsiders deemed too messy to bring into the fold. They don't understand the proclivities and problems of the rich. Keep it in the circle. It's just easier that way, for everybody. But Collin opened a window for me, and I wanted to leap right through it. There would be many obstacles and absolutely no guarantees I'd get what I wanted, but she wouldn't even try for someone like Collin Case. That's how big of a challenge I was up against.

And that settled it. I had to have him.

It would take the ultimate social finesse, but I believed I was up to the task. I had done it before so many times, albeit not on this scale, but all the more reason to trust myself and test my skills and just truly go for it with everything I had.

I was never one to parade my relationships around at work, but I took particular care to keep my relationship with Collin Case quiet at the office. He was officially a client of the agency, and I knew that the optics wouldn't be great for me, professionally speaking. I was a senior business development director at one of the biggest advertising agencies in New York, where most of the men pretended to be Don Draper and Roger Sterling, tossing back bourbon in their offices when the clock struck five, taking prospectives and currents out to Gramercy Tavern, where they could all act like they were more attractive than they were due to the generous low lighting. As for the women I worked with, they largely resented me for ascending to a senior role relatively quickly, at least compared to their own moderate trajectories. I knew they all thought it was because of how beautiful I was, and while I'm under no delusion that didn't factor in as an element of my success, I'm also excellent at my job because of my skillful play of the corporate game.

Yet another difference between her and me — and an important one. I devoured all of those bullshit businesswomen bibles by the likes of Sheryl Sandberg, Ivanka Trump and Dr. Lois P. Frankel, applying their strategies with a deft hand so I could use them to my advantage. I also read all the strategy books aimed at the C-suite, written for men in power, so I was aware of what was going on in their feeble minds. Unlike her, I could actually apply myself in a multitude of ways. I could succeed in business *and* in dating. I earned a salary. I had benefits. I had an expense account. I enjoyed my work, commanding the room, closing deals, counting my money that I had earned.

As if she ever had a real job. She could never.

Soon enough, I knew exactly how and when to lean in, always just enough, but never crossing any perceived boundaries that would label me a bitch or ballbuster by the male powers that be. In truth, I found it all rather entertaining and supremely rewarding when I would unlock another achievement at work, whether it was in the form of a promotion or an opportunity to collaborate on a challenging pitch.

I learned the rules so I could win.

I always knew what men wanted to hear, the setting never mattered, and specifically in business, the playbook was so abundantly clear. Sexism goes in and out of vogue depending on the year or damning article making the rounds in the press, but the deep-seated sentiments never change. So Miss Jessica McCabe could speak ill of me in her cube all she liked, languishing for years on end in an entry-level position, but it was hardly my fault she didn't get her head in the game so she could snag an actual office with a door that shuts. Address the bags under your eyes and seek out a reliable silhouette to flatter your wide-set hips, *Jessica,* and just watch what career wonders could unfold for you. Didn't her mother teach her anything? Looking good is perpetually a transferable skill.

See, it's not really about if *you* personally subscribe to these "girl boss" ideologies when they've already permeated their way into the corporate psyche. It's your responsibility as a member of the capitalistic workforce to acknowledge the game, learn it backward and forward and then manipulate the rules in your favor. Remember: It's not personal. It's business.

And while I'm loath to give her any credit for my success at anything, I'm certain I could attribute my natural aptitude for all things manipulation to Mother.

Her influence was largely a curse, but once in a while a blessing. Safe to say that I wouldn't be where I was, or who I was, without her. It's like she gave me a map that only I knew how to read, and I'd have to force myself to go in the opposite direction of nearly every path she took. A lifelong challenge.

I mostly enjoyed Collin Case's company. As much as I could enjoy a man who believed that boat shoes and colorful polos under a quarter-zip sweater were the height of men's weekend fashion. He adored listening to me talk, and I had plenty of entertaining things to say. Whatever he said to me was typically bookended between lovely compliments about my appearance or my sparkling personality. I could get used to such a winning relationship dynamic. Coupled with the constant extravagance of running around town with his drivers and helicopters and multiple homes, it was a no-brainer to set my sights on marriage.

Getting Collin Case to *want* to marry me would be simple given how smitten he was, but with his elevated stature in society, I knew he would not be the sole decision-maker. Even so, I believed my forged identity would still fly with Collin in my crosshairs. I had conjured up a solid backstory for myself as Beatrice.

But please, call me Bea.

A working woman in New York, the perfect balance of prestigious and plausible. I couldn't quite risk flaunting an Ivy League degree without considerable risk of being found out as a fraud, which was unfortunate, as that type of connection would have all but sealed the deal.

The Case men were Harvard men, along with his mother at Radcliffe, but the family tree often branched out to Yale, Princeton and Brown over the years. Never Cornell. Please. And I *knew* that these people all ran in the same social circles, no matter the institute of higher learning, and would begin to ask me very specific questions. What year did I graduate, did I know so-and-so professor, what house did I live in, what family do I come from and so on and so forth. Even if I copped to being on scholarship over legacy, an embarrassment in their eyes, the due diligence would inevitably be done. It's who they were. We're talking about grown adults who still started conversations with strangers about where they went to school, so I had to play my cards accordingly.

I told Collin that I grew up in Wilmington, North Carolina — a charming and well-to-do port city by Southern standards — and attended Duke, just like my father. I shared that I was an only child my parents had later in life. Bob and Alice's little miracle, both dead now, but everything I did was all to make them proud of me, even in death. I tacked on a couple tears at the back end of this yarn to really hammer things home.

It was always key to mention to anyone that my faux family were deceased when the opportunity presented itself because it tends to shut people right up, cutting short any further probing into the reality of my checkered past. Sure, the story I concocted was a little folksy, but that was the point, as it was historically well received and unassuming. Collin even got a real kick out of the very slight Southern lilt I cultivated as part of the persona. I just needed his family to get on board, then I could be this woman for the remainder of my life.

As if I could tell anyone the truth about where I really came from. I don't come from anywhere. Only from her. Mother dragged me all over the country, forcing me to take part in her sordid schemes and dark dreams, and I could never figure out what she was looking for until I finally realized she wasn't looking for anything. She was just addicted to the shake-up for the sake of the thrill.

So I avoided thrills as best I could as an adult. For my own good.

Making Collin the perfect fit.

If I had to hitch my wagon to some mediocre man with a lukewarm personality for the rest of my life, just to get some well-deserved repose, why not aspire to the 1 percent? For someone like me, the only way was by association. The Cases didn't work for their empire; that's called inherited wealth and, for all intents and purposes, it makes one infallible. I worked my entire life to meet someone like Collin Case. I was ripe and ready.

So yes, I thought I could handle a historic family of WASPs who never had to really work a day in their goddamned lives, because, frankly, I deserved it.

It could all end with Collin.

One last round for all the money on the table.

Chapter 2

When Collin wanted to introduce me to his friends, I wasn't worried about my reception at all. He had talked about them often and with true affection. They all grew up together, since filthy rich families tend to socialize with others in the same tax bracket. Even the friends he claimed to have made at college "in the Boston area" were already familiar to him throughout the years because he was a Case. His social circle likely never experienced much variation at all until I got into the mix, and I knew Collin was excited by that so I was ready to shine. It couldn't be hard. Men adored me almost without fail so I was sure his friends would fall in line, too, especially since I had looked into their own wives and girlfriends via their social media, objectively none of whom came even close to my startling level of beauty. A bunch of sixes and sevens, and frankly, that's being generous.

It would be so easy to win over the guys, but I didn't know what to expect when Collin told me about his "best friend." First of all, it's very alarming when adults identify other adults as "best friends," a term that ought to be a relic from junior high. Second of all, Collin's best friend was a woman.

Gale Wallace-Leicester.

The Wallace-Leicesters — descendants of railroad tycoons, *naturally* — were lifelong friends of the Cases. Gale had been Collin's unrequited admirer since their charmed childhoods. From being banished to boarding school during their formative years to family summer vacations at a luxury resort or ranch or aboard yet another yacht, Collin and Gale had an undeniable history together. As an adult, she looked exactly as one might picture. A rather bookish brunette with strikingly broad shoulders for her average height, dressed head to toe in an online-only clothing brand, like a student of library science instead of an actual heiress who could easily engage a personal stylist to evoke elegance with a custom-tailored wardrobe. Instead, she chose to roam the earth in ill-fitting basics that did absolutely nothing for her figure, all in the name of faux sustainability. Her skin-care regimen must have been similarly underwhelming, since she was only a few years older than me but her pronounced crow's feet and pink undertones went completely unaddressed, all suggesting that she was on the wrong side of thirty-five when she was still on the right side of thirty.

Well, *just.*

Like Collin, she didn't have to work for a living but subjected herself to the corporate grind regardless. Gale was an editor at Spartina, a modern art book publisher, a vanity career if I ever heard of one, and something I was certain she'd be ill-suited for considering she didn't seem to possess any taste whatsoever. She couldn't have been making considerable money from such an endeavor, but she had a generous trust to dip into at any time and thus could afford to take a low-paying job with perceived prestige.

Collin invited me to his friends' weekly trivia night at an Irish bar downtown — it doesn't really matter which one, they're all the same — and I was instantly turned off, not by the bar but by their chosen activity. Collin and his ilk thought they were so cheeky and clever and cool for associating with the plebes like that, all out in the open, over happy hour pints of Guinness and red baskets of french fries and potato skins dripping in cheese and sour cream, topped off with bacon bits from a plastic cylinder. They exchanged brief glances when a guy their age would walk by the table, sporting a Timex instead of a Rolex. They chuckled when the waitress asked if she should keep track of their orders by seat, in case they wanted separate checks later. They raised an eyebrow after sipping a cocktail made from the well, shrugging their shoulders with a smile, continuing to drink it anyway. What the hell! Down the hatch! When in Rome!

I noticed that Collin participated, too, but never initiated anything himself, which offered some relief. He was just fitting in, and how could I fault him for that, since I was guilty of doing the same? So Collin's loathsome friends thought it was entertaining to pretend they were just like everyone else in a humdrum bar, all while knowing they had the kind of access and money the others knew absolutely nothing about, and probably never would. Was it gross? Sure. But what kind of behavior did I expect? There wasn't anything normal about them. Besides, having to suck it up being with them would always be preferable to being with anyone else. Follow the money.

Henry Ogilvy's mother was literal Spanish

royalty, disgraced after an exposed affair, unfaithful to her first husband with a much younger footballer, but still a princess all the same, now married into the Ogilvy American banking empire. Evan Burkhart was to inherit the storied candy throne from his family, well-known in the continental United States for their classic varieties, especially favored at Christmastime, but often joked about how he didn't touch the stuff, since the only chocolate worth its salt was imported from foreign lands, not to mention he also had a well-known problem with the candy of the nose. Recreationally and generally harmless, unlike Marty Knox, whose ancestors essentially invented the framework for modern American publishing, and he went to rehab three times on their dime, which must have been the charm because now he and his wife were regularly lauded in the society pages for their philanthropic efforts, like rehab never even happened.

These were people with a family net worth in the actual billions of dollars.

That said, most of Collin's friends were innocuous enough on a personal level, never having to really cultivate strong personalities in any singular direction. Sure, I suffered daggers from the eyes of their respective romantic partners, but that was par for the course in my experience with women. Hannah Ogilvy, Elizabeth Scott and Paisley Cooper-Knox were completely interchangeable as far as I was concerned, all vacant eyes peering out of their sunken faces, bird-like bodies clad in Ralph Lauren and Tory Burch for such a casual outing, but with Birkins slung on the interior of their elbows, making the obvious social statement no matter how objectively hideous the bags actually were. Despite their palpable disdain for me, I pressed on with the introductions alongside Collin, smiling sincerely and kissing their cheeks adorably, ready to speak their stupid language that would win them over just enough to keep me there without any fuss. They didn't smile back at me, they sneered. They didn't embrace me, they held out a flaccid hand. They didn't say my name, they just called me *Collin's girlfriend,* because I was an outsider. To those women, I didn't deserve to congregate at the same table, much less have them address me directly. Why wasn't Collin keeping it in the club, they must have wondered, and certainly discussed amongst themselves later. But when they watched their partners take me in with their eyes that night, it made them sit up straighter. More aloof, yes, but also more alert. Good. I'd just have to be sweet as pie to make their chilly behavior toward me look even worse. I wanted those men to do missionary to those shrews that night with their eyes closed, thinking of me. All of them.

"It's so lovely to finally meet the group." I beamed at Collin's friends after he announced my presence.

"We've heard so much about you, Bea." Gale Wallace-Leicester smirked openly, unlike the other women, who barely spoke and at least had the decency to take a sip of their drinks when they wanted to purse their lips at me in disapproval. Gale did not seem bothered to keep up appearances, not even for Collin's sake.

"Only good things, I hope." I chuckled in a way that chilled my bones, expertly mimicking the type of woman expected to be alongside Collin Case.

"Collin tells us you're an ad woman. What's *that* like?" Gale put a hand up to her face, playing at fascination, when she was actually condescending to me. She wasn't wearing any polish at all, and a set of gels would have made a world of difference on those hooves of hers. Squat fingers. Short nails. Unfortunate. A pale pink or nude would have offered the illusion of extension, but I wasn't about to give her an unsolicited beauty tip in mixed company. In fact, all of the women had underwhelming manicures with little in the way of length. Men love a long nail with a French tip. Surely their mothers told them so or at least made a passive-aggressive comment about it once or twice. Nothing outrageous, just enough to deliver the right amount of scratch during sex. How silly they all were to not put in the effort. It's not like they worked with their hands. Didn't they want to keep their husbands?

"I find it to be an exciting career," I answered Gale. "We have a lot of fun at the office, all sorts of clients, which keeps things interesting. And, obviously, it led me to Collin, which is nothing to sniff at either." I grinned at my boyfriend, going in for the sweet and obligatory peck on his thin lips, to make the men in our company jealous and the women internally groan. Collin gazed at me like I was the queen to his king, visibly proud that I belonged to him.

At the same moment, Gale noticeably flinched, showing her hand.

So she *was* still in love with Collin.

Oh, now my ears were up, my heart was aflutter. Some recreational sport presenting itself? Excellent.

"That's right," Gale continued. "Collin is your client, isn't he?" She took a sip of dark beer. A curious poison for a woman, considering the physical ramifications. Mother would say something about beer being the kind of libation that could settle on a woman's thighs until the end of time if she was not careful with the frequency. I could hear her voice again and needed to snap out of it. *Focus.*

"Correct. One of many clients."

"But the only one you're sleeping with, I hope."

"Gale, stop!" Collin reprimanded her jovially with a good-natured scoff, and the table laughed, including me. What else could I do? It was all but necessary to be deemed affable, which was the whole purpose of the charade. Collin would be getting reviews by the end of the evening, and these were the people he cared about, so I wanted raves.

"Yes, Collin is the only client I'm currently bedding," I said, careful to use tasteful yet evocative language in Gale's presence to further twist the knife. "But that's because he was special. Most of my clients are bald and boring with little imagination, which tends to be why they hire the agency. Nothing like you, babe."

I ruffled Collin's hair playfully and then

swept it back out of his face so we could exchange an intimate look for all to see. His tresses were finally getting longer, so he was getting better-looking.

"Oh, Gale, on that note, I could set you up with one of them, if you like? I hear you're still single. How could that possibly be?"

Even the wives and girlfriend clearly appreciated my wily burn disguised as good-natured jest. Hannah squeezed Elizabeth's knee under the table while Paisley stifled a small laugh. Their bony shoulders shook to keep laughter inside, their buoyant medium-length blowouts bobbing up and down, all but giving it away. They glanced at Gale for her reaction and then quickly looked elsewhere — clearly she wasn't part of their little gaggle of gal pals. Gale didn't even acknowledge their poorly repressed reactions at her expense because she knew the truth, too. Their forced camaraderie was only a technicality based on proximity. She took another sip of her beer, buying herself a moment to decide what to say next.

"Thanks, Bea, but I'm actually seeing someone," Gale said, surprising all of us at the table. Satisfied, she pushed her hair back behind her ears. It was far too long and a muted brown, in definite need of some highlights for dimension if she actually cared, which she obviously didn't. Must be nice to not have any of your self-worth wrapped up in appearances. So much space for so many other things. Intriguing if not altogether confounding to someone like me, whose priority of the physical was always nonnegotiable.

"Who?" Collin was the first to inquire. A little *too* quickly. In fact, he seemed to be the only one present with a true affection for Gale. A character flaw I'd just have to overlook, much like his narrow shoulders.

"A coworker introduced us a little while ago. We've been on a few dates and it's going pretty well." Gale searched his face for even a modicum of jealousy but came up short. In fact, Collin looked delighted by the news.

"That's an exciting development. Do we know the guy?" Collin asked, and I knew what he meant. Was this alleged boyfriend of Gale's one of *them*?

"No, probably not, but Bea might." Gale's eyes narrowed at me, a predator closing in on her prey, as if I were some other girl she could reasonably dangle about for fun. "He went to Duke."

"Oh, is that right?" My hackles were only moderately raised, since I was prepared for such a discussion. I was not at all surprised that the subject of where we attended university came up so immediately into our carousing. This crowd touted their distinguished degrees like they'd been earned as opposed to being purchased by their respective legacies, alongside libraries and laboratories emblazoned with the family name.

"Mm-hmm." She nodded, animated. Hannah, Elizabeth and Paisley were watching us go back and forth, each of them rapt, with white wine in hand, one leg primly crossed over the other. "But the funny thing was that he said he wasn't familiar with you. That's a little strange, isn't it? Being such a small school?" Her eyes narrowed even further as she smiled at me, smug, her top lip all but disappearing into her teeth.

"I wouldn't call Duke small," I replied. "I mean, yes, there's a community, but I can't say I know every person that waltzed through campus during my tenure."

"Well, he recognized your name, but not your face."

Someone had done her research. My back arched in anticipation. Chest up, ears perked, fully captivated.

"You showed your new boyfriend a photo of me before we even met?" I asked coolly. "Gale, I'm so flattered. Clearly, we're destined to be the greatest of friends, just like Collin said we would be." Collin had said nothing of the sort.

"No, I just —" she carried on, despite looking positively obsessed with me. "I just found it a little weird, that's all. Like you said, Duke has a close community as well. You know, like *we* do."

"We don't know everyone from our graduating class, Gale," Collin said, a soft attempt at standing up for me, but an attempt nonetheless.

"Sure, maybe not personally, but through chatter. Though Duke could be very different. Sometimes I think everyone's university experience must have been like ours, when that's probably not the case." Gale smiled at me as if I were a peasant. She was very good at this, commendable, but I could be better.

"I'm sure there are plenty of differences, and not just in the geography. Duke has a national sports presence, for example." I winked at the men slyly, believing they would enjoy a basketball reference from the beautiful woman at the table, but it seemed to go over their heads. Did they have any interests outside of their stock portfolios? For all its fortunes and finery, this blue-blooded bubble I was trying to burst into also seemed rather dim at times. I surmised we would not be gathering for a March Madness tournament viewing anytime in the future. Fine by me. One less thing to pretend to care about.

"I will say that it does seem crazy how a guy on campus could not know you. I mean, look at you!" Collin admired me openly, and I basked in it, taking the opportunity to extrapolate on his very well-made point.

"Okay. I didn't want to say anything, but I actually was known for being something of a pageant queen. Cotillions and deb balls and all that hullabaloo when I was young. I know it's all so silly in the grand scheme of things, though I had a good time." Gale openly snickered at me as I spoke of such nonsense. No matter. Truthfully, I wish I could have done the same, but I had to stick to my script. "But anyway, Gale, it's possible your new companion didn't admit knowing me to spare your feelings. You know how men are — they always think the worst of us, as if we're all jealous crows. So tell us more about him. What's his name?" I was beginning to enjoy the bandying between us.

"L-lu—" she stammered, racking her brain, unable to roll anything off her tongue, ill-prepared for cross-examination. "Luke

Dunne."

Oh, for God's sake, she might as well have said George Glass. Faltering so soon? Tsk-tsk.

"Luke from Duke." I smiled, baring my teeth. If she was interested in creating such a dynamic, I would gladly assume the role of a predator, too. "It doesn't ring a bell, but I look forward to meeting him in person soon so we can reminisce about campus life."

The bar trivia began before Gale could get another word in, and the group took it quite seriously, so there would be no more time for barbs or banter when we'd all have to be paying close attention to the emcee. They were fierce competitors — the Bulging Veritaffles, an inside Harvard joke I didn't really care to have explained to me — all pretending to be in it for the glory and the comped round of Jameson shots, but I suspected it must have been a superiority thing. The rest of the crowd in the bar looked just like them, more or less, all young adults looking to blow off some steam after work with their buddies in a dark bar, but I knew that was not the case for Collin and his friends. The majority of the others would ultimately go home to undesirable roommates in small apartments that cost small fortunes, at least a healthy percentage of their monthly take-home pay, a futile attempt at building a sustainable life in a city they couldn't actually afford and would probably never be able to without lifelong sacrifice.

Collin and company would never know anything about that.

As the night came to a close, I excused myself to the restroom so Collin would get a chance to receive instant feedback about my performance and appearance, but it was also an unsaid extended invitation to Gale Wallace-Leicester to join me, if she dared. I stood in front of the mirror, finally shedding the phony smile, my face at rest. I rolled my head from side to side slowly, loosening my neck, at long last able to relax.

And I waited.

Waited for her.

I should have kept Gale at arm's length. Even after I had proved myself in possession of a brain that evening, in addition to my beauty, it was quite clear she would never welcome my presence, since she loved Collin. I could never really gain her affection. I could keep an eye on the situation as it pertained to Collin, since his opinion of me was what truly mattered to get what I wanted, but still, I yearned to fan the flames with Gale for the sake of the fire in me.

I was competitive by nature, and a worthy adversary would certainly lighten up my day-to-day. Unlike Collin's friends, I had no interest in competing against people beneath me for a quick hit of feeling superior, much less with the stakes as low and meaningless as bar trivia. No, I craved something I could really chew on. Some pleasure for pleasure's sake. I didn't believe she could really jeopardize anything I had with Collin, but it would be amusing to watch her try.

Perhaps Gale Wallace-Leicester could whet my appetite for fun.

I gazed at myself in the mirror, taken aback by the pronounced venom in my eyes at the thought. Large and round in front of everybody else, they took on Mother's shape in private moments like these. Our shape. At rest, the eyelids lounged just a little bit lower, hovering delicately above a bright blue iris. "RBF" at its absolute finest, particularly when prey was in sight. I admit my desire to find trouble for trouble's sake was not my most sterling personality trait, but some urges I could not suppress so easily. They were inherited from her. It was a near-constant battle in my mind — be good or have a good time — but perhaps this one with Gale would be for naught. Maybe she wouldn't show after all, staying behind with the rest of the women to deliver subtle derision of me behind my back like normal people, relieving me from my propensity to sin.

I was applying a dash of lip gloss in the mirror when Gale appeared through the swinging door, an irresistible treat, revealing the boldness I suspected was dwelling inside her frumpy frame the whole time. The type of moxie that women like Hannah, Elizabeth and Paisley could only dream of. Without saying a word, I offered my lip gloss to her with a small smile. She shook her head as she came closer to me.

"Not my color," she said, not wholly incorrect, as it would have washed her out.

"Fun game," I replied, turning to face her head-on. "You do this every week, I hear?"

"More or less, depending on the guys' schedules." Gale jutted her chin out at me like a barracuda. Effective body language for aggression, but not remotely flattering. Another subtle flex about how she didn't have to care about such things?

"Not yours?" I asked her.

"My schedule is my own. They don't have the same luxury."

That did sound luxurious. Rich *and* single,

left to her own devices each day, answering to nobody but herself. The grass is always greener. She looked at her phone instead of me. Dismissive on purpose. I ate it up.

"So," I said, not wasting any more time, "what do you think?"

"Of you?" Gale almost laughed, setting her gaze upon me again. "Doesn't really matter what I think, does it?"

"You obviously want to tell me. You followed me here."

"Followed you?" She laughed this time. I noticed her teeth were in dire need of whitening. "You wanted me to."

So she knew.

"You're very pretty," Gale dully declared, as if it were an insult.

"Oh, well, thank you," I replied, well aware it was not a compliment.

"Collin always has pretty girlfriends." She leaned back now with her bottom on the sink, almost childlike, with an impish grin. "And you're not the first from the fringe."

"The fringe?" I asked innocently, fully aware of what she meant, but I wanted to hear her explain it. How would she explain this venom of her own?

Gale got up from the sink and inched closer to me, taking small steps.

"Bea, you're smart, you know what I

mean. Perhaps what you don't know is that this is kind of his *thing* with relationships. You're one of many. Collin's been searching for something for as long as I can remember. How to best put it?" She paused, thinking. "It's like he's looking for an identity outside of his own."

"How admirable," I said, maintaining my position. She could bump right into me if she wanted to, I wasn't going to move. "Collin and I have that in common."

"I bet you do," she said, closer still, now looking up at me. I had a good five inches on her, but she was undeterred.

"It's a more compelling way to date, allowing for lifelong discovery. It's easy to get bored when you know what's coming," I said. "And who wants to be bored?"

"I hear you. Such thrills were overlooked when we were all young and foolish. Credited to curiosity, getting it out of the system, experimentation. But we're all getting older now, Bea, we're older than they were when they settled down, our parents' generation, and now with Henry and Marty married off, Elizabeth's expecting the ring from Evan at any moment, and Collin will be well on his way soon enough. The timing is right, which I'm sure you know, but they won't allow it to progress much further than where you are right now. And I'm sure you want much more than that, and by the looks of you, I have no doubt you'll get it. Just not from Collin Case or anyone like him. So I thought I'd give you a fair warning, woman to woman. And by *they,* I mean —"

"His family. I understand. And while I appreciate you looking out for me, Gale, woman to woman, I can assure you that Collin and I are very serious about each other and that will be communicated to the Cases in due time. So you can take your very considerate, but very misguided, concern for me off your plate."

"I just don't want you to get hurt, Bea. That's all," she lied, touching my shoulder.

"You're sweet," I said, placing my hand atop hers, electrified by our duel. Then I sidled out from her grasp and swung open the door to exit. "We will see you soon, I'm sure."

The door closed behind me before I could watch her shudder at my pointed use of *we.* I should have deployed it sooner for my own amusement. I took a deep breath, smiling to myself, before catching Collin's eye by the entrance. I waved at him. All was well. I was sure of it.

My innocent jousting with Gale was different from Mother's because I actually enjoyed keeping a female nemesis, whereas Mother largely maintained a safe distance from other women, finding them far too unpredictable. So true, and the tragic cornerstone of the appeal for me. See, men are so much simpler to bat about like a cat does a mouse; it's not difficult to decipher what they really want — generally power, money and sex — but women and their ambitions are much more complex, more layered. I found it all very fascinating, especially from someone like Gale Wallace-Leicester, who easily could have rested atop her laurels, but instead, she challenged me directly in the women's restroom of a shithole bar like a fucking cowboy.

Fantastic.

I took Collin's arm jubilantly as we shuffled out the door. He wouldn't pick up on it, would he? A harmless hobby just for me? I've always told myself I wouldn't be like her. I couldn't be like Mother. But engaging with Gale was actually for the good of my relationship with Collin. She needed to know where I stood *and* where Collin stood. He would never do it, so I'd have to be the representative for our family. The game had a tangible end goal — get Gale out of our business — and it didn't mean that I couldn't have a little fun along the way.

After all, it had been so long. Collin was basically on lock. Stable. Exactly where I wanted him. I deserved a last hurrah with someone like Gale Wallace-Leicester to take the edge off. Besides, based on her warm welcome of me that evening, she all but deserved to be knocked down a peg or two. I would never do anything to seriously hurt her or put her in harm's way.

That's what Mother would do. Not me.

Yes, I could see this through with Gale. No problem. I couldn't back down from such a challenge, especially when I was so confident that I would be the victor. Sure, Collin could play both sides, but for how long until he had to choose? And what did Gale have to offer him, really? Of course he would choose me. I didn't want to underestimate her, but it was difficult considering her lovely lot in life. What hardships did she have to overcome? What skills did she have to hone? What senses did she have to sharpen? The list had to be short based on her sheltered upbringing alone, with little stake in anything of consequence beyond her obsession with Collin, and while I commended her active attempt to throw me off course, *welcomed* it even, she would never actually succeed.

The most fun games are the ones you

already know you're going to win.

And winning this game would be to the benefit of all three of us, if I was really being honest. So, yes, I would be doing this for myself, to scratch a dubious itch, but also for Collin, since he wouldn't be able to cut her off himself, and even for Gale! After I was done with her, she would finally be set free to find some equally bland billionaire bozo who might actually want to bone her. Putting it that way, my behavior was positively saintly.

All of us were outside the Irish bar now, bidding adieu for the evening, exchanging half-hearted hugs and nice-to-meetyous and let's-do-this-again-soons, and I made it a point to pop a swift kiss on Gale's ruddy cheek before Collin and I took off for the evening.

A physical mark on my target. She winced, the poor dear.

Then one of Collin's arms was raised in the air, hailing a taxi for us, and the other was wrapped possessively around my tiny waist. I glanced over my shoulder at Gale once more with a knowing grin, inviting the bitch to do her worst.

Richard

ATLANTA, GEORGIA

I am Rebecca but I know that isn't true. Mother tells me that most people are a sucker for destiny. I don't know exactly what she means, but I pretend I do so she likes me. All I know is that's why my name is Rebecca, hers is Rosemary and we live with a man named Richard. She tells me once that her real name begins with the letter *B*. It makes me want to ask her more questions about who she is, who we are, but I know better than to upset Mother.

She makes me call her Mommy in front of other people, but I'm not allowed to call her that when we're alone. It makes me nervous because if I mess up, I know that she won't talk to me for hours. Sometimes days. I hate when Mother is mad at me, so I make extra sure to think about where I am and who we're with before I call out for her. I always want her attention, so I try not to do anything that will make her take it away from me. I just want her to like me.

Richard's house has white bricks, a black door and a swimming pool. It seems to always be hot in Atlanta, even in the fall. Richard teaches me how to swim and it's my favorite thing. Mother watches us, saying nothing. I like how it feels being underwater. Like *The Little Mermaid.*

I sing down there.

I'm quiet at the surface.

The pool water feels like a warm bath from the heat. Richard wears bright blue swim trunks that stop just above his knees. He usually takes the steps to go into the pool, but sometimes he'll jump in with me if I ask nicely. We hold hands and count to three.

"Rosie, come in the pool with us!" Richard shouts to Mother. She's in a black bikini with black sunglasses and bright red lips. Her pretty lips, like a bright bow, are even prettier when she smiles, but she never smiles with her teeth. Maybe because then she'd be too pretty, too shiny for anyone to be around her, and I always want to be around her. Richard does, too. Even though she always says no about the pool, Richard always asks anyway. "Come on, Rosie! Please?" She shakes her head and smiles at him. He'll ask her again. Beg her. Mother knows this and enjoys it because she says it's exactly how it should be.

Mother tells me that Richard is the ideal man for us right now. She needs a rest and he's easy. Richard's a very tall person with weak shoulders. That's what Mother calls them. She says his chin is weak, too. His eyes, nose and mouth are all bunched in the middle of his face with the ends of each falling down like a melted candle. His cheeks droop, too. He's not handsome, but he has a good voice. Deep, but kind. He has the voice of a handsome man. He hangs my report card on the refrigerator like he's proud of me. Mother laughs about it.

"How could he be proud of you? He doesn't even know you. I'm the only one you need to worry about. Make *me* proud of you."

Maybe Richard could get to know me, I think.

And I don't think I could make Mother do anything.

We go to Mass on Sundays at Christ the King with Richard's mother, Lois. She likes me and tells me to call her Grandma. She says Richard is lucky to have a new wife with such an adorable little girl. She tells the people at church that I'm her granddaughter and I like when we shake hands with them. We say *peace be with you.* Lois always dresses up for church and wears a colorful scarf, either around her neck or over her hair. We pick her up from assisted living on the way to Mass, but we never go inside her place. She meets us at Richard's Cadillac and he always opens the door for her. She sits in the front seat and I can tell Mother doesn't like that, but she allows it. Grandma Lois is Richard's only family, except for us now. Mother and Grandma Lois never say much to each other, unless it's about me.

"Becky is just the cutest little thing, Rosemary. You really should be taking her to auditions. She's a star, I know it," Grandma Lois says. "The next Shirley Temple. Do you know who Shirley Temple is, honey?"

"No, ma'am," I say.

"But she should smile more. Why don't you smile more, honey?"

"She smiles plenty," Mother responds for me, her voice low, and I know instantly that I had better start smiling more. Mother tells me later that everyone trusts a smiler. It's important to be a genuine smiler. She makes me practice until my cheeks hurt. I do whatever she asks so she likes me.

"Rebecca needs to concentrate on school,"

Mother says in a way that ends the conversation about auditions. Grandma Lois scoffs.

"I'd take you myself," she whispers to me through the gap between the front seat and the back seat. "But I've already been put out to pasture." Then she speaks a little louder. "Maybe you can come over and watch a Shirley Temple movie with me sometime?"

"We'll see you next Sunday, Lois," Mother says.

Mother takes me on an audition for a kids' variety show and doesn't explain to me what that means. She doesn't tell Richard about it. It makes me nervous but I am already enjoying the extra time alone with her so I am excited to go if it will make her happy. She dresses me in a nautical jumper with polka dots and curls my hair and does my makeup. A bright red lipstick pops out of its gold case. She holds my chin and I feel her nails press into my skin ever so slightly. She has a French manicure like always. Quick little swipes on my little lips.

I love having her so close to me.

"Blot," she says, holding up a Kleenex to my face. "Well, bunny, you're no JonBenét, but you're pretty damn cute."

I smile at her. Really. I'm not practicing. I feel the smile all the way to my toes.

She doesn't smile back at me, but when she calls me *bunny,* I know she likes me, at least a little bit, and that's good enough for me.

The room is empty except for a long table with two women and one man behind it; all of them grin at me when I come inside. I can't seem to smile back. I'm alone. Parents aren't allowed. There's an *X* on the floor in tape. I am supposed to stand on it. So I do. The room is very cold. Now I just want to get this over with and I hope I do a good job for Mother. I wonder if they can see the goose bumps on my legs. I'm freezing.

"Sing 'Mary Had a Little Lamb' for us, sweet pea," the man says to me.

I shake my head.

"You don't know that one?" one of the women asks.

I shake my head again. No. I don't know that song.

"Okay, honey, why don't you sing a song you do know?" the other woman says.

I'm still so cold and it feels like I've been quiet for hours. I make fists with my feet in my Mary Janes and I want to throw up because I can't think of a song.

"Why don't you just sing the ABCs?" the

man says. I can tell he's annoyed with me. I start to sing and I don't know how I'm doing it. I know they can barely hear me but I can't make myself sing any louder. The alphabet feels too long and then it's finally over. I still don't smile.

"Okay, thank you, sweetheart," the man says without even looking at me.

I know I didn't do a good job because Mother doesn't speak to me for the rest of the week unless we're in front of Richard.

Mother breaks her silence at bedtime to read me her favorite book about a bunny and its mother. She tells me she loved it as a child because she always wanted to run away, but I don't like that book at all. I keep that to myself, but I think somehow she knows and reads it to me anyway. Almost every night. That bunny tells his mother he is going to run away and turn into all sorts of things to stay away from her, but she promises she will find him no matter what. Why does he want to run away from his mother? I don't think I could ever run away from mine. I can't imagine running away from Mother, even when she hurts my feelings, but maybe if I run away, I could get all of her attention for once.

But I don't know where I would go.

And I don't know if she would come find me.

Her bunny.

Richard is gone by Father's Day. The house sells quickly and I'm angry with Mother because I don't want to leave. She says we have to, but it feels too soon and it feels wrong. I don't really understand what's happening. What about Grandma Lois? I tell Mother I will miss her and Richard and my school and the house, and to shut me up Mother scoops me in her arms and jumps right into the swimming pool with me with all of our clothes on. She's finally in the pool with me.

Mother and I scream and laugh and splash each other. My skirt floats as I move my hips from side to side and it makes me giggle. She reaches out for me and I go to her, arms first. "How can you miss anyone or anything when you're with me?" she asks, pulling me close. Then she cradles me like a baby. "You'll always be with me, bunny. Right?"

I tell Mother I can sing like Princess Ariel when I'm under the water. Would she like to hear it? She actually smiles at me and says she does. We hold hands and count to three and jump up and then down under the water. I watch the bubbles come out of her nose as she watches me sing, garbled and giddy that Mother is finally in the pool with me. She lets go of my hands to clap when I finish. We're almost out of breath and I wish we were actually mermaids so we could stay there longer.

Before popping back up to the surface we smile at each other again. With our teeth. When I feel the sun on my face again, I'm still smiling and feel so happy and forget that we have to leave, but Mother's face has already changed. Her smile is gone. "The next pool will be better," she says. I'm cold again. Mother hoists herself up out of the pool without looking at me, her jeans soaking wet, and walks back into the house.

When she shuts the door behind her, I fall back under the water and cry.

Chapter 3

The Case Company was a huge get for the ad agency, so I was flooded with constant praise by all of my superiors and, begrudgingly, by my peers. I could feel another promotion was imminent as long as I delivered on what we promised the Case Company. The agency wasn't aware that I was offering my pussy on a platinum platter to the family's default golden boy, but that was neither here nor there. New business had closed and then Collin asked me out, so I hardly saw the correlation. I knew the office would be shortsighted about our burgeoning relationship, so I would have to keep it under wraps until we were engaged.

Another day, another dollar, and I had to answer my own phone at work since my assistant was late coming back from lunch. Unacceptable, but I rather enjoyed chewing her out because she looked like a distressed amphibian when she was upset and it made me laugh. Cheap thrills. Per the incoming number on the screen, I fully expected Collin's voice on the other end, relatively deep with a dose of that mysterious mid-Atlantic about it. Instead, a timid female voice was on the line.

"Hello, is this Bea?"

"Yes, and who is this?" I raised an eyebrow, suspicious. I never liked an unexpected conversation with a stranger.

"Oh, I'm sorry, I should have said!" the mystery woman replied, shaken, with no confidence to speak of. "My name is Sylvia Austin. Syl, actually. I go by Syl. I'm Collin's new assistant."

Hmm. I had a vague recollection of Collin telling me he was in the process of hiring someone, but I had wrongly assumed he would hire an Ivy League bro, some new grad whose father was cashing in a favor from Collin's father so the nepotism cycle could continue indefinitely. I waited patiently for Syl to say what she wanted, but the silence went on for far too long.

"So does Collin wish to speak to me, *Syl*?"

"No, no! He's in a meeting. Actually, I was just making some updates at my desk and I was wondering if you could share a few preferences with me?"

"Preferences?"

"You know, what you like. Favorite color, favorite flower, favorite jeweler. Things like that so I can stay ahead of it for when —"

"Did Collin tell you to do this?" I interrupted her, since I was very busy and important.

"No. Just something I'm grabbing in advance of important holidays, milestones, anniversaries and things of that nature."

So he hired a smart girl. I appreciated her proactivity, but I didn't appreciate the assumption that I would be available at her leisure. It was improper.

"All right. Blue — cobalt, royal or navy, generally, but never anything resembling turquoise or teal or a robin's egg. Peonies, especially the blush tones. Never a tropical varietal of any kind. If there is ginger or heliconia to be found in an arrangement, I'll throw it out. My taste in jewels can range from Catbird to Cartier, I'm open-minded. Dainty and delicate usually, but the gem itself can be obscene. That said, I don't do statement necklaces — my neck is too thin to carry one so I make statements in other ways. I have a meeting now myself. If you need anything else, please send a calendar invite to my assistant for a future discussion."

And I hung up on her.

I wanted Syl the Assistant to fear and revere me in equal measure, so that would be a good start. I immediately wondered what she looked like and if she was younger than me. I started to poke around on the internet, but I was only finding Sylvias that were women of a certain age. She didn't sound like she was in her golden years, and before I could dig any further, I was startled to see my boss come into my office without even a knock.

Len.

Len Arthur was the picture-perfect archetype of an adman from days gone by, who yearned for the eighties, when Campari and cocaine reigned supreme on Madison Avenue. He exclusively wore gray sport coats, when black or blue would have been much more flattering on his near-translucent skin tone. He looked very stern when he entered, his eyes were nearly crossed as they zeroed in on me, and I had no earthly idea what the pressing issue could be, much less one that warranted such a rude entrance. I had no choice but to greet him with my tits up and legs crossed, assuming the position to be admired.

"Hello, Len. How's your day going?"

"Bea. I'm just going to come out and ask you." Oh God. Was he going to ask me out?

A true nightmare, for me and HR. Sure, Len could be on the lascivious side at a work-mandated happy hour, but he knew the boundaries as well as I did, at least while we were in the office with everyone in full view. No one could have an affair in that office with all of the glass windows and doors.

"Are you engaging in an intimate relationship with a client?" he asked me.

"Excuse me?" I was incredulous. How the hell did he know that?

"I received a phone call from Collin Case's assistant. She was updating his files and contacts and mentioned she had spoken to you earlier today as the other point of contact on the Case Company account. I thought nothing of it until she mentioned she was 'killing two birds' by updating her professional *and* personal records for Collin as his vendor and, ahem, his girlfriend."

"Len, I completely understand your alarm, but I can explain the situation. And please know that this isn't how I wanted you to find out about —"

"I'd guess you didn't want me to find out at all," he barked. Len's salt-and-pepper mustache danced around in a manner most grotesque when he was upset, like it had a mind of its own. Appalling.

"Collin and I have been see—"

"This type of conduct is *very* much frowned upon at our agency, Bea."

"I realize that, but I can assure you —"

"I will have to make a recommendation that HR —"

"Len, please." I stood up now, using every tactic I had to snap him out of the constant interruptions. He looked me up and down, he couldn't help it, and I knew that would be the case. I finally had his full attention. "Like I was saying, Len, I can assure you that this isn't some silly little tryst between client and vendor. Collin and I are in a very serious relationship."

"Well, I should hope so, Bea. The Case Company is one of our highest profile clients. The optics of this are, well, frankly, they're indecent."

"Indecent," I scoffed at him, briefly indulging in the insubordinate. "Len, I apologize that I didn't disclose this to you before, but I can promise you that there will be no conflict whatsoever —"

"No conflict?!" The man was red in the face. I couldn't stand it. I excelled at my career, and it was important to me, because it was my very own that I had built and always had under control. Now a simpleton like Syl had put it all at risk. I took a deep breath, choosing to be direct, so I could prepare for the worst.

"Len, is my future at the agency in jeopardy?"

"I'm not at liberty to discuss that further until you've spoken with HR."

"Len, are you *terminating* me?"

"Bea. That's enough. You'll be receiving an invitation shortly to meet with Rhonda, and we'll get this all sorted out."

When he left, I spotted Jessica McCabe in her cube, quickly looking back at her computer, acting like she had been the whole time, but I saw the corners of her mouth turn up in delight. Surely her only triumph for the entire week. *Good for her.*

To say a meeting with Rhonda in HR was less than ideal would be an understatement. She had never been a fan of mine, all decked out in discount designer outfits from outlet stores with a heinous perm she'd likely been sporting for thirty years, grimacing at me whenever we crossed paths. She'd been in HR at the agency probably longer than I'd been alive. This was all so frustrating. Surely Collin had communicated to Syl that our relationship was not for public consumption at our respective workplaces? How could she make such an enormous mistake in her first week? And who else might she have blabbed to on the phone while "updating her files" that day? I called Collin immediately, all while keeping a watchful eye on my inbox for Rhonda's forthcoming wrath.

"Collin Case's office," Syl practically sang through the phone.

"It's Bea for Collin." Suffice it to say, the tone of my voice didn't match her own enthusiasm.

"I'm so sorry, Bea, but he's in a meeting right now."

"I do not care. You need to get him on the phone with me right now. It's urgent. We have to clean up a mess that you made today."

"What?!" Syl was completely mortified.

"Didn't Collin mention the terms of our relationship to you?" I asked her.

"Terms of your relationship? I'm sorry, I don't know what you mean."

"Get him on the phone."

"Yes. Um, ri-right away," she stammered. I could tell she was about to cry. I heard the click of the phone, and ambient music began to play. She had the audacity to put me on hold. Before I could hang up and ring her again, Collin was on the line, frantic.

"Babe, what's going on? Syl said it was an emergency and she was crying."

"She should be crying. *I* might be crying soon."

"What happened?"

"Your new assistant told Len Arthur about us this morning. I just had him in my office reading me the riot act about my indecency and poor judgment, and now HR will be reaching out to me to discuss my uncertain future with this agency."

"Shit. I'm sorry, Bea. It's one hundred percent my fault. Don't blame Syl. I must have forgotten to tell her," he admitted, an imbecilic move on his part. I wanted to shout at him as well, but that wouldn't behoove me, particularly if I'd be getting sacked by the end of the day. Rhonda's request had just come through with a proposed time to meet within the hour. This was a disaster. My résumé had not been updated nor my network sufficiently fluffed for maintenance. I was in no position to be seeking both new employment and a new boyfriend, so I remained calm with Collin. A show of temper could only be deployed in a relationship at moments when the other party would find it endearing and cute, believing their partner is a spitfire or a spark plug or a pistol or some other terrible turn of phrase reserved exclusively for women who openly share their opinions.

"Well." I turned on a crack in my voice so Collin would feel appropriately contrite but no one in the office would see any tears. "I'm not really sure what to do now." Collin loved when I pretended to need his help, but this time I feared I really did.

"Okay, babe, don't worry about it. I'll take care of it."

"You will?" I asked him, pitiful on purpose.

"I'll call Len right now and clear things up. Everything's going to be okay, Bea. I love you."

Another immediate illustration of Collin's appeal, despite his affinity for Top-Siders. One phone call from him to my boss about the issue and the whole thing would disappear. It was a reassuring feeling, but also unsettling. I didn't like to rely on others for my own well-being, but in this instance, it couldn't be helped. I had failed in talking Len off the ledge myself, so Collin would take care of it because Collin cared about me. I was delighted and embarrassed.

Moments later, Rhonda from HR rescinded the email invitation to meet. Len came by my office once again, explaining that he had misunderstood the situation and all was well, they were proud to have me as a part of the agency. What an emotional roller coaster of an hour. It was maddening, and despite Collin's admission of guilt, it really was all Syl's fault, so something would have to be done about her.

Collin wouldn't have it in him to punish her, but I would.

I arranged to have lunch with Collin the next day, meeting at his office first, an attempt to make my personal attack on Syl as organic as possible. It was also my first appearance at the Case Company openly as Collin's girlfriend, so in addition to terrorizing a potential new foe, I made sure to look my absolute best for all the members of the peanut gallery. My ensemble leaned pleasure over business. I left my blazer at work so I could show off in a formfitting blue sheath, minus a bra. It wasn't crass due to the dress being tight across my chest, limiting any untoward motion, but an air-conditioned office would prove my point. I felt all eyes on me as I entered the Case Company, heading straight for Collin's office, just as I had hoped.

But there wasn't even a moment to revel in the attention because I could not look away from Miss Sylvia Austin. I had wrongly envisioned Syl as a mousy little thing. Fresh out of college. Pretending to be an adult in

Ann Taylor LOFT, black-rimmed glasses and a poorly constructed lob from a newb at the Aveda Institute. So imagine my surprise when I saw a grown woman behind the desk in possession of beautiful, enormous breasts, albeit displayed tastefully, along with cheekbones sharp enough to stab and these pillowy pink lips that brought only one thing to the imagination. She was tan and blonde and fit. In a word, exquisite. Yikes.

"You must be Bea!" Syl exclaimed, getting up from her chair, sporting a violet dress with a modest hemline that still highlighted her legs. Her calves were lean and toned. She obviously worked out. Syl started to hug me like an absolute freak show, but I was able to artfully dodge her advances, holding out my hand for her to shake instead. She did so, and I noticed it was medium-firm compared to mine. Her first and only sign of physical inferiority.

"Syl. Nice to meet you," I said. She covered my hand with her other hand while we shook them, a method far too intimate for strangers, but I could tell that was just the kind of person she was. Warm and engaging. How irritating. I noticed immediately that she had an engagement ring on her finger. It was a mere chip of a diamond, but it definitely signified her betrothal. That took the edge off a bit.

"I made a reservation for you two at Hillstone. I know it's one of Collin's favorites."

"You know everybody's favorites now, don't you?" I cooed.

Syl broke eye contact with me, hanging her head in embarrassment. She looked like a small child with such submissive body language. It was unnerving. I thought she was a bit older than me, but I couldn't tell by how much. Razor-sharp cheekbones or not, her skin suggested she spent significant time in the sun, so her age was difficult to decipher. At any rate, I wouldn't comfort her about her mistakes. Not my job.

"I really am so sorry about that, Bea," Syl said, finally looking back up at me, with far too much sorrow in her eyes. "I had no idea it was going to cause a problem. I just didn't know it was a secret. I hear that Collin took care of things with your boss, but is there anything I can do to make it up to you? I'd really like us to be on good terms. Again, I'm so, *so* sorry."

She was so apologetic that I decided she was too pathetic to punish. What would be the fun in that? Also, the poor girl was clearly marrying a pauper and obviously had some career misfires, too, taking a lowly assistant job well into her thirties. While I wasn't pleased with her professional faux pas from the day before, I'd let it go. But still, she was a very pretty girl. Magnificent, really. So even though I was relatively sure that Collin would never dabble with someone like her due to her station in life, and already being spoken for, I'd still have to keep an eye on the matter. He was a man, after all.

"It's been taken care of, Syl. All is well," I told her, refocusing my ire on Len Arthur and the agency instead. "Thanks for making the reservation."

"No problem," she said, with a sigh of relief. "I'll let Collin know you're here."

Syl summoned Collin from behind closed doors, and when he appeared, I noticed a slight flutter in the pleats of his trousers when he laid eyes on me. No, no, I thought to myself. Syl would be no one to worry about at all.

"Hi, honey." I kissed Collin effusively, knowing we had the whole floor's attention, and away we went. "He'll be back," I said to Syl.

"Have fun." She grinned. "Really good to meet you in person, Bea."

"Likewise," I said, giving her another gentle once-over with my eyes.

■ ■ ■ ■

I clucked my tongue at Collin when we were alone in the elevator. "So. Where did you find Syl?" I asked.

"Oh! Yeah, her résumé came through HR and, uh, she just seemed like a good fit after her interview. She's a little green, but learns quickly, all things considered. I like her," Collin said, watching himself in the mirror as he put on his aviators. Not his best look. He didn't have the bone structure in his face to support a rounded frame.

"What did you think?" he asked.

"Seems sweet. She's quite charming in person. *Very* attractive."

"Bea."

"What? I'm just stating facts here."

"I didn't hire her because she's hot."

"*I* didn't say she was hot. You just did."

"You're a trip." He laughed, putting his arms around my waist. "You know you're the hottest girl in any room anywhere." True.

"Well, you're such a darling man, looking out for a girl like that," I fraudulently commended him.

"A girl like what?"

"Just, you know, probably down on her

luck a bit."

"How so?"

"Isn't she a little old to be your assistant?"

"What? No way. You should see my dad's EA, Connie. She's ancient. And great at her job." I was surprised to hear someone like Mr. Case favored loyalty over legs. "Being an EA is a lot of work, sweetie," Collin continued. "A different path than ours, but honorable just the same." The Honorable Syl Austin. It was such a preposterously endearing proclamation from Collin that it just made me want to marry him even more.

Sweet men rarely sour.

The two of us walked into Hillstone and they rolled out the red carpet as per usual. Freshly poured Perrier for me. An ice-cold beer for Collin. The server awaited our order with bated breath. I was all ready to launch into a friendly trash-talking session about Len Arthur, but it quickly became apparent that Collin had his own agenda for our luncheon, holding my hand from across the table with a decidedly anxious energy. It felt like he was going to dump me or propose to me, but instead he brought up the subject of his family.

Excellent. Nearly four months in. Right on schedule. It was go time.

"Since we're basically out in the open

now, between Len and my friends, you know, I figured it was time to tell my family about you, and so I did. And they want to host us for brunch on Sunday. Are you free?"

"I am. That sounds great." I sipped my sparkling water, keeping my composure, but I was squealing internally. Once I had Collin's family on my side, a proposal would be on the horizon shortly. A Sunday brunch in Connecticut would progress to a country club golf outing in the coming weeks, all leading up to a soiree at one of the summer houses to celebrate our engagement.

I was that much closer to becoming Mrs. Case.

I could leave everybody else behind forever.

Especially her.

Chapter 4

I knew exactly what I was up against with the Cases. It would have been much simpler to set my sights on someone with an easier family to charm, or even better, someone with no family at all, but the Cases offered a forever type of security, the kind where I could stop being such a cunning little vixen for good. Nothing worth it comes for free. But I was an unknown entity to the Cases. I knew they must have held a deep-seated belief that their only son would ultimately marry into another family like their own, allowing some young society journalist the opportunity to craft a wedding announcement for the ages, one that would both impress and infuriate the Cases' elite social circle because the match was so favorable to both families.

Mr. and Mrs. Hayes and Haven Case were the quintessential American couple with cash. Consummate hosts of parties and luncheons and galas. Golf and tennis and equestrian enthusiasts. Philanthropic. Personable. Presbyterian. And in possession of absolutely no edge to speak of unless you count watching Fox News behind closed bedroom doors with two glasses of brandy *each.* Married for thirty-five glorious years, in addition to prodigal son Collin, they also bore two hellacious daughters, Chloe and Calliope, born as bookends to Collin, paraded around like a couple of bootleg Bush twins. Chloe was the eldest and looked up to her mother, while Calliope brought up the rear and idolized the likes of Tinsley Mortimer. Both were single, which put me at an even further disadvantage with them, especially Chloe, who I'm sure would have liked to be married before her younger brother.

The Case family compound was in the Golden Triangle of Greenwich. A historic Georgian mansion with all the bells and whistles and servants' quarters that purposely stood atop a gentle hill so they could always look down on their neighbors. The gated rainbow driveway and six-car garage was host to many a classic car per the patriarch's preference, but also a ridiculous red Ferrari. I made a mental note to ask Mr. Case for a pleasure cruise to take an interest in his hobby and to garner favor with harmless flirtation via one-on-one face time.

The vast interior of the home was soaked with various shades of beige and ecru and eggshell with a smattering of crimson. It was fully staffed, as were all of their residences, and those employed were always silent unless spoken to. Tennis courts. A greenhouse. A fitness studio. A screening room. Nine bedrooms. Twelve bathrooms. A pool that existed purely for decoration over recreation. It was resplendent. A marvel of a manse. I would have felt instantly at home if Collin's family were to give me a warm welcome. Opulence soothed me. That feeling of undeniable security was intoxicating.

Collin fetched me from the front of my (well, Morris's) building in a black Range Rover, which was a thrill, since we were usually carted around by a driver on the Case payroll. Collin thought it would be fun to drive us himself, like it was a novel thing to do. I hadn't been in the passenger seat of a vehicle in quite some time, so I enjoyed our leisurely journey to the suburbs, basking in the rays shining in from the window. SPF 100+ applied to preserve the moneymaker.

Calliope Case was waiting for us just

outside the entrance, eager to pass judgment on her older brother's new companion. She waved nonchalantly, nibbling on a small packet of sunflower seeds in bare feet, not quite smiling, but a warm enough reception for Connecticut. She wore a short-sleeved white T-shirt, sheer enough to see her white underthings, and a long blush skirt made of tulle. The ballet boho babe vibe was unexpected, but it suited her as the youngest of the clan with her long and wild strawberry ringlets.

"Hi," she buzzed in that odd East Coast accent of theirs. "Wow, Coll. She's gorgeous." It was definitely a compliment, but more for Collin's benefit than my own.

"It's so nice to meet you, Calliope." I held a tasteful bouquet of peonies for the lady of the manor, a gesture that was well-suited to my fabricated upbringing in the South, but Calliope snatched them from me.

"Mm-hmm, how was the drive?"

Collin and I followed Calliope into the house, the two of them making idle chitchat about traffic and the annoyance of other drivers on the road. She had the kind of skinny ankles with a protruding Achilles tendon that suggested Calliope toed the line between naturally thin and disordered eating. She led us into the front parlor and took a big whiff of the flowers before she flopped onto a cream chaise, her skirt flouncing along with her.

"Mom and Dad should be out in a sec and Chloe isn't even here yet. She's *always* late," Calliope explained to me, finally making direct contact.

"Sounds about right," Collin said. I noticed he already slipped off his loafers and sat cross-legged on the couch in his socks, slouching forward. Ick. It was fascinating to see these adults ease into such childlike behavior in the home of their parents. It would almost be charming if I didn't find it so unattractive. I wanted Collin at my side, staking his claim, proud of his prize — me. Not curled into a ball on the sofa like a little boy. I remained upright in a wingback chair, tilting a bit forward myself, with one leg crossed behind the other like Princess goddamn Grace to make a good first impression on my future in-laws.

"I think she was picking up Gale as a favor for Mom. I guess she wanted to join in the fun." Calliope sneered. While I hated the surprising revelation that Gale would be there for a milestone moment in my relationship with Collin, I was happy to observe that Calliope seemed to share my scorn for the woman.

"Oh, I didn't know she was coming," Collin said, clearly surprised, too. "Are Royce and Nora joining as well?" Those had to be Gale's parents. The *names.*

"I don't think so. Haven't seen those two around much in the past month. I think there was a little falling-out over some silent auction item at the NYSCF thingy they all went to. Mom was going on and on about it, but I wasn't paying close attention because who cares?" Calliope laughed and then turned her attention to me. "Bea, how's *work*?"

Calliope said *work* like it was a foreign word to her, in that same patronizing tone Gale had at the trivia night. Whatever affection Calliope had earned from me was swiftly tossed aside.

"It's fantastic," I lied. I had really fallen from grace in Len's eyes since he had found out about Collin and me. It was subtle, but I could feel it and I wasn't pleased about it. "I really enjoy my work. I'm competitive so it scratches that itch."

"What do you like about it? Besides working for *our* company?" She rolled on her side and extended one of her legs up, taking care to hold on to it through the skirt. I knew I was having a conversation with a woman in her twenties, but I felt like I was being interrogated by a precocious toddler.

"Obviously the Case Company *is* one of my favorite clients."

"I bet." She grinned.

"Collin!" I heard a woman's voice bellow down the hallway. Sultry with some texture. Like someone who smoked in the eighties and still engaged in the occasional cheeky ciggy when no one was watching. This was the moment. And there she was. Mrs. Haven Case, a vision in daytime pastel Chanel with a bronzed precision bob, sharp green eyes and not-so-subtle Botox. The archetypal old-money mother. "Sweet-heart," she purred at Collin. I stood up to greet her, but she breezed right past me to embrace her baby boy. Even so, I noticed her maternal touch was still quite removed, with plenty of space in between their bodies. Her kisses were in the air on either side of Collin's cheeks. She gave him two stiff pats on each of his shoulders. Finally, she twirled around to face me, scanning me up and down with a robotic smile.

"So this is the infamous Bea." She clasped her hands together, but didn't reach for me, not for so much as a handshake. "Dear, come and meet Bea," Haven called out behind me, and Hayes Case rounded the corner.

I had seen Mr. Case before in passing at Collin's office, though we had not yet formally met. He was still technically the CEO of the Case Company, but he had a slim presence at the office, once or twice a month, preferring to take meetings on the golf course or at the Metropolitan Club if he happened to be in the city. He was a man of average build, shorter than Collin, but broader overall. Still had his hair and embraced the gray. It also looked like he maintained an exercise regimen, absent of a paunch, but he was certainly not ripped. He had a presence. Hayes Case looked like he was somebody. He approached me with a hand held out and a closed-mouth grin. His shake was firm, almost painful, but he released my hand quickly.

"Welcome to our home," he said.

Neither Hayes nor Haven offered air-kisses or half-hearted embraces to me, so we all took a seat in the parlor. Calliope continued to snack on those infernal seeds with a satisfied smile, like a demented little chipmunk, clearly loving the awkward energy in the room. Staff quickly popped in with mimosas and small breakfast items, miniature croissants and egg bites.

"A vase!" Calliope called after one of

them, waving the peonies around like a lunatic.

"Don't fill up," Haven said, her eyes on me as if I would actually put anything with bread in my mouth, even diminutive in size. "We'll have a whole spread in the dining room when the girls arrive."

"You didn't tell me Gale was coming," Collin said to his mother.

"Didn't I? It's all right, isn't it? Gale mentioned to her mother that she was such a treat so I thought it might be nice for your new girl to have a familiar face on such a momentous occasion. Meeting the parents can be stressful," she said only to Collin, as if I weren't there.

"It's fine," Collin said, but his tone suggested otherwise. He winked at me. It seemed like Collin also wanted this moment of ours to be private. I smiled at him and looked forward to our eventual gossip sesh on the drive home, provided he was game to talk shit about his family, which most normal people are after a get-together.

"Hi. Sorry we're late," another sultry voice announced in the entryway. Must have been genetic. Chloe Case entered the room with Gale Wallace-Leicester in tow, looking like total opposites. Chloe was the spitting image of her mother, all prim and puckered, though she had the same chestnut hair as Collin, expertly balayaged for dimension. She possessed a definitive youthful glow suggesting a lifetime of shunning the sun, and donned all-black attire, tailored to perfection. I knew she was in her mid-thirties but her buoyant skin didn't let on. Severe and chic, she would be one to impress and it wouldn't come easy. She also worked at the Case Company, in public relations, but like her father, was also rarely in the office, so we hadn't met yet either.

Gale lumbered in after her, draped in a shapeless shift the color of old concrete, and began the requisite greetings around the room. I was last in her receiving line.

"Surprised?" She smiled.

"And delighted," I replied. I went in to give her a hug and she stumbled slightly, taken aback. We both laughed, knowing that the energy had shifted with her presence. I was coming alive. What little traps would Gale try to set for me in this house of horrors? I'd have to sniff them out at every turn, refusing the lure of any bait. She'd expect nothing less. Nor would I.

"Shall we go to the dining room?" Haven suggested, leading the way, and we all followed, Calliope practically skipping along in her ridiculous skirt. Collin grabbed for my hand as we joined in the perverse parade. Perfect. Everyone needed to know that he was crazy about me. Brazen in-house hand-holding would surely send a message to that crowd, people who merely grazed one another with their lips and fingertips to show any semblance of familial tenderness.

The dining room was as grandiose as expected, with floor-to-ceiling windows offering striking views of the grounds and the pool. Taper candles had been lit by unseen staff, and a harpist resembling a young Stevie Nicks strummed contemporary tunes in the corner, dressed all in white like an angel.

"She's like part of the family," Haven whispered, awaiting my reaction to this over-the-top display. I knew it was all meant to make a point about how I was different from them, but I wouldn't give Haven the satisfaction of appearing dazzled. I belonged there because Collin belonged there and we belonged together. We all sat down around the table, and Collin put his warm hand behind my neck, giving me a few gentle squeezes. I rubbed his knee in return and kissed him softly on the mouth.

I could make points, too.

"You have a lovely home, Mrs. Case. Thank you both for inviting me," I said.

"We couldn't go on much longer without meeting. You've clearly cast quite a spell on our son. He's usually very professional."

"Mom," Collin gently scolded her.

"I adore Collin," I interjected, taking control. "You know, initially when he called me, I hesitated to accept his invitation because of our established business relationship. But he was such a gentleman, and so handsome and funny, that I just couldn't resist his request to take me out." Flattering Collin meant flattering his mother, but I also wanted to set the record straight that *he* pursued *me*. I wasn't some two-bit temptress with no class.

"We're all very tickled that Collin snagged himself a career woman," Chloe said between bites of arugula. "Thankfully, society girls are starting to fall out of vogue, though nobody's shared that with Calliope."

"Oh, please." Calliope snorted. "As if your job is real."

"Anyway," Chloe continued, not taking the bait for a sisterly row. "Gale tells us you're from *North Carolina*?" Chloe said *North Carolina* like she was saying *New Jersey.* "I don't think we've ever been. Do you visit often?"

"No. Both of my parents have passed," I said, taking a sip of my mimosa.

"Bea is absolutely crushing it at the agency. She's going to be running the whole show in no time." Bless him. Collin attempted to take the heat off me with a non sequitur, but I knew any praise in my direction would fall on deaf ears. They would require all the details of my past and not a minute too soon.

"I could totally see that," Calliope said. "She looks like she doesn't take any shit."

"Calliope, not at brunch," Haven said, teeth gritted. "We're so sorry to hear about your parents, Bea. That must be awful to be without family when you're still so young. Tragic."

She was painting me as some kind of hillbilly orphan girl, just grateful for the opportunity to be in their presence. Gale was noticeably silent, likely because the Case women were doing all the work for her. She must have been getting a real kick out of it, too, not that she would let on. A front-row seat to my dressing-down could be squandered with her involvement. Could be seen as out of turn. She was in the circle, yes, but she wasn't in this family. So Gale remained perfectly still for the time being. Watching and waiting.

I'd have to go on the offensive, treading lightly, to keep up.

"I've managed, but I do miss home sometimes. Speaking of home, how's it been going here for you, Calliope?" Per Collin, I knew that Calliope had had a recent messy breakup with a live-in boyfriend. She was nursing her wounds back at her parents' home. What was supposed to be a few weeks had turned into a few months and she wasn't on the scene as much as she had been previously. What would she have to say for herself about that?

Turns out, not much, since Haven took over from there.

"Oh, Hayes and I absolutely love when our children are home, so her stay has been a welcome distraction from the regular grind. Calliope and I have even been taking American Sign Language together. She recently joined a junior board for the cause, so we thought it would be prudent to better acquaint ourselves. Our tutor comes to the house twice a week."

"Can we see a demonstration?" I asked earnestly. I had a few signs of my own I wanted to share with them, but I thought putting them on the spot like that would be a better use of my time.

"Maybe after brunch," Calliope said, clearly mortified and hoping I would forget.

"Do you speak any other languages, Bea?"

Gale asked me, finally chiming in.

"Just a little high school French, I'm afraid," I said, and before she could say anything further, added, "And please don't test me. I would need a refresher, as I'm sure you're fluent, aren't you?"

"We actually did Mandarin immersion as children," she said, looking at Collin adoringly.

"Better for business," Hayes declared, and Haven nodded along.

Gale said something to Collin in Mandarin and he replied, instantly annoying me. Chloe started to add to the conversation, but then Calliope cleared her throat.

"This is really fucking rude."

"Calliope!" Haven exclaimed.

"Well, it is. I didn't go to Mandarin immersion."

"You didn't have the attention span for Mandarin," Hayes mused aloud. "She knows French," Hayes said to me, as if I gave an actual shit.

"Barely," Chloe added.

"*Casse-toi.* French enough for you?" Calliope hissed at her sister.

"Oh, real nice." Chloe rolled her eyes.

"That's enough," Haven barked.

As obnoxious as they were, it was amusing to see a real family's dysfunctional dynamics emerge right in front of my eyes. It was like watching a play. I could find myself a role in this theater of the absurd, I was sure of it. Just as I'd always suspected, all families are a few snide comments away from a full-blown feud, in front of guests no less. Long-standing rifts always bubbling to the surface, all members dying to tell the others how they really feel. I wanted to get involved, egg them on, take sides, play favorites, keep secrets for years on end, let one blow at an opportune moment years down the line and —

"Did you go to France in high school, Bea? To study?" Gale asked me, yanking me right out of my reverie as the new rabble-rouser of the kingdom.

"No, but English has worked out for me, I suppose. I've managed to find my way in the world just fine," I said to her, looking around the home that I wanted to make my own someday, putting a hand on Collin's shoulder. "I'm having such a wonderful time, Mrs. Case. You're an incredible hostess."

Gale took a frustrated bite of brioche.

"Thank you, Bea. It's quite an operation, but I take a lot of pride in keeping this home afloat." God, she meant it, too! What a laughable estimation of her so-called responsibilities. How could she even say those things aloud when we could see all the people working for her, not to mention those that were behind the scenes?

"Mom does a great job with all of our homes," said Collin. "I was actually thinking about taking Bea to the Southampton house for Memorial Day weekend."

Haven looked at Collin, puzzled. Hayes cleared his throat.

"I heard Chloe was using the Southampton house for Memorial Day weekend," Gale said knowingly.

"That's true," Chloe said, slightly annoyed that Gale made a revelation that wasn't her own. "I'm hosting a mixer to kick off the summer."

"A mixer? Were you going to invite us?" Collin asked her, slightly annoyed.

"It's a singles mixer," Chloe replied. "So . . ."

"This is the first I've heard of any mixer. Who's doing your list?" Haven asked, clearly offended she wasn't involved in the party planning.

"I have the list under control, Mom."

"Are *you* going, Gale?" I asked, testing the waters for general knowledge about her alleged lover, Luke from Duke. Chloe openly grimaced. Not that Gale would want to go to Chloe's mixer, lest it take away from time better spent pining after Collin, but she obviously wasn't on Chloe's list.

"I have plans," Gale said, offering nothing further. Chloe looked relieved.

"Oh! With Luke?" I grinned.

"Who's Lewwwww-k?" Calliope trilled, tapping her toes under the table.

"Gale's new beau," I announced joyfully.

"You have a boyfriend, Gale? Have you brought him home yet? Your mother said nothing to me about this," Haven said. "Collin, have you met him?"

"I have not, but I'd be happy to." Collin smiled at Gale.

"Oh, yes. We're just dying to meet him," I added, giving Collin a few affectionate scratches on the shoulder. "A double date needs to happen as soon as possible."

"I haven't told my parents about Luke yet," Gale said to Haven, ignoring me. "It's still pretty new so I didn't want to jump the gun with meeting the parents," Gale said, suggestively in my direction. "We'll just have to see how things play out."

"Still, it must be going well," I continued. "Memorial Day weekend plans and all. Where are you two off to?"

"I don't know yet. It's a surprise," she replied, fully committing to this invention of hers. Boo and hiss. I wanted her to step up harder. She must have known I'd bring up the faux boyfriend. Get in the ring, Gale. Don't hold back now.

"If it turns out to be Southampton adjacent, maybe you could swing by Chloe's party after all," Calliope encouraged, getting on board with needling Gale a bit.

"I already said it was for singles," Chloe huffed.

"Do keep us posted, Gale. We're looking for a getaway ourselves, apparently." I smiled at Collin.

"I will," Gale said to me, jaw clenched. Had she had enough for today? Or was she still lying in wait?

"A weekend away *is* rather serious," Haven said. Initially, I thought she was talking to Gale about Luke, but I quickly realized she was talking to Collin and me.

"And?" Collin pressed her, albeit with caution. "What's wrong with that?"

"Seems a little fast." Haven dabbed the corner of her lips with a beige linen napkin.

"We're here, aren't we?" Collin was visibly perturbed. I had to let him take the lead now.

"Well, you're here because we invited you. Considering what happened at the office, we had to see her for ourselves." There she went again, talking like I wasn't in the room.

"Haven," Hayes said, pursing his lips, shaking his head slightly. "Not the time."

"Not the time for what, Dad?" Collin raised his voice.

"Not the time," Hayes replied firmly. Collin didn't say another word. Ah, there's the man I was marrying. I knew this was going to be an upward climb with his family, but I did not expect to be on the receiving end of such flat dismissal this early in the game. I was convinced it was Gale Wallace-Leicester's doing, but what had she told them? Or had they done a background check? Hired a private investigator? My credentials were all verifiable, but the Cases weren't just any family. Could they dig deeper than I could hide? Did they know the truth about me? About *her*? I had to forcibly remove the paranoia from my mind. Another sip of the mimosa would do.

"Maybe a quick jaunt to North Carolina should be in the cards for you guys," Gale said, thrilled by all the simmering drama, ready to prowl, potentially pounce. "You could show Collin where you're from, Bea! Bittersweet, but I'm sure he'd love to see your hometown."

I wanted to fling my shrimp fork directly into Gale's face. She was so smug, prodding the Cases' inquiry into my past, knowing it was my fatal flaw in their eyes. Well played, the evil tart. But none of them would ever know where I actually came from.

"I'm sure we'll think of something," Collin said, putting an end to the conversation. He placed a hand on my thigh under the table in reassurance, moving it back and forth. He slid up even farther than was appropriate at the brunch table, just for a moment. Not terribly discreet. What an interesting development. It appeared his family's disdain for me only made his heart grow fonder and cock grow larger — a dynamic I wasn't expecting from a man like Collin but would now fully exploit to my own advantage.

"Please excuse me. Sorry, I just get a little emotional when I think of my parents," I said, getting up from my seat, weeping ever so softly for effect as I left the dining room. I knew they wouldn't feel bad in their heart of hearts, but I did want them to feel embarrassed by their behavior toward me in front of Collin. They were crossing a personal line with him, and with me, and so soon. It was time for them to back off. I waited for a beat in the hall when I was out of sight, hoping to hear Collin scold everyone and then follow me out, but it didn't happen.

Hmm. All thigh rubs, no action apparently. He was still Collin, after all, but that was why I wanted him. Any acts of rebellion against his family would be small and largely undetectable. Save up for the real betrayal — marrying me. He needn't worry. I would get us both to the finish line.

They continued to eat in silence, so I thought I might as well take a lap. The house was predictably very stuffy and not quite to my taste — I leaned Regency Moderne myself — but I could appreciate the overall aesthetic. I had seen homes with horrendous taste, despite tremendous wealth, but it appeared Haven had the good sense to lean on traditional home decor design principles, nothing overstimulating to the eye. Clean lines, no tchotchkes to speak of and a natural color palette in every room. Sure, she was a beige bore, but at least she wasn't some Marie Antoinette maximalist with an offensive gallery wall complex. Could you imagine?

"Bea." Haven appeared at the other end of the hall, her voice neither warm nor cold. "Come with me." She was trying to intimidate me with commands in lieu of requests, but unlucky for her, I already had a mother from hell. What was one more?

"Where to?" I asked her, walking with purpose in her direction. She pursed her lips in return, performed an about-face and so I followed her into another room. The study. All books and banquette seating along the sides. An imposing desk in the center. And far too many lamps, but I kept my mouth shut about that.

"Let's not keep Collin waiting. He clearly dotes on you." Haven slithered behind me to slide the doors shut.

"He's a wonderful man."

"Mmm. A real catch. Especially for you." Instead of sitting behind the desk, Haven perched on the banquette nearest to the window, one heel crossed behind the other just so, and firmly patted the open spot next to her. "Right here, dear."

I did as she asked without breaking eye contact. I would be respectful, yes, but certainly not meek.

"None of us meant to offend," Haven said. "It's not personal. It's just that you don't quite fit, so cutting to the chase, Hayes and I are willing to make this all as painless as possible. Perhaps even a preferred outcome for you."

I remained silent, not because I was shocked by her candor but because silence is an underrated power move during a negotiation, which is obviously what this was.

"So what would it take?"

I was still quiet, but kept up the eye contact.

"Hayes and I are willing to pay you to break it off with our son. For good."

"I heard you. What would Collin have to say about that?"

"Nothing. Because as part of the deal, you wouldn't tell him."

"You've done this before." I smirked.

"Well, Collin always seems to be lured in by . . . the unfamiliar, and we're just keeping watch. So what do you want?"

"I want to be with Collin."

"A million? Two million?" She would have raised her eyebrows like a movie villain if she could, but alas, she was beyond the baby-Botox years. Zero movement up there. Meanwhile, I pretended to be impressed by those figures.

"See?" She smiled smugly, prematurely satisfied with herself. "A preferred outcome."

"I don't —"

"FIVE million dollars," Haven declared. "Best and final and you should take it."

She really thought I would take it. It was a considerable amount of money. If I was anyone else, I'd have considered it, but I was my mother's daughter.

I stood up to gaze down at her.

I didn't want five million dollars.

I wanted all of it.

"No," I said. A complete sentence now, per the Olsen twins, have you heard? I headed for the doors, my back to Haven, doubling down on disregard for her offer. "Don't worry. I won't tell Collin. It'll be our little secret." I turned to look at Haven once more as I slid the doors open. "Free of charge — *Oh!*"

Well, if it wasn't the little It girl herself, Calliope, listening to what I can presume was the entire conversation. Haven scurried between us, fleeing the scene without another word, but Calliope lingered with me for a moment, not at all guilty about being caught.

"Good for you," she said, sincerely amused and impressed. I just cleared my throat.

"Collin will be wondering where I am."

"He's not the only one," Calliope replied, whistling softly and walking next to me as we made our way back to brunch.

The main takeaway from the day was that Collin seemed *very* enthralled by the whole "girl from the wrong side of the tracks" perception of me, clearly aiding in his efforts to establish independence from the family he'd always hopelessly be dependent on, for better or worse. It wasn't an ideal scenario, but it was perhaps the most realistic. I had known the Cases were unlikely to receive me with open arms, the payout offer from Haven all but confirming the uphill battle, but perhaps I didn't have to try so hard at all. The more they openly disapproved of me, the more Collin wanted to push back, even if it was discreet. He liked the way it made him feel. The way *I* made him feel. Now this was a dynamic I could brandish in my favor. I had to keep pushing the Cases, but just enough to ensure Collin's continued loyalty to me. Make his family the bad guy, the bully, and I was their undeserving victim. So Collin could be my hero.

I returned to my seat in good spirits, with a quick readjustment of the décolletage for the men to appreciate and to add further fuel to the fiery feminine energy in the room. They all noticed, but Calliope was the only one who smiled at me devilishly.

"You look *refreshed,* Bea." She stifled a laugh. "Coll, maybe you could take her to the Newport house for Memorial Day?"

Gale's eyes widened at the thought, and she jumped into action.

"I think Bea would be so bored in Newport. Just spring for a hotel somewhere fun. Miami, Mexico, whatever. I mean, the family homes are for, you know, special occasions." She smiled at Haven, who nodded in approval. "It's just Memorial Day."

"Nah, she'll love it," Collin said, seemingly emboldened by Calliope's suggestion. He threw a lanky arm around me in a grand showing of possession. Of me, but also of himself. "It's a great idea, Cal." Collin smiled, happy his sister threw us a bone.

"But we haven't opened the Newport house yet," Haven said sternly, her cherry-red fingertips clutching the stem of her champagne flute all the more firmly.

"That's all right. I'll give the staff a call later today. There's plenty of time to prepare," Collin replied, as steadfast as I'd ever heard him. It was almost hot.

I saw a crestfallen Gale, frantically racking her brain for another move to make, determined I wouldn't spend a single night in a Case family home. The homes she thought rightfully belonged to her in the future with Collin. Homes that certainly didn't belong to anyone like me. But before she could say anything, I took the opportunity to accidentally spill a carafe of ice water that sat between us in her direction. She stood up with a frightful yelp, as if it were acid — *if only* — and I delivered the compulsory apology, but not without stealing a furtive glance at Chloe and Calliope, who were both trying desperately not to laugh.

Laugh it up, girls.

I would get them on my side.

I would get all of them on my side.

MOTHER

LOS ANGELES, CALIFORNIA

Something's wrong. I look all around me. This isn't our kind of place. I trace the cracks in the green floor with my eyes and then with my toes through my flip-flops as far as my leg will stretch, trying to stay out of her way. It smells like burnt coffee and cigarettes. *The Price Is Right* plays silently on the TV hanging from the wall in the corner. Someone just won a car. The man behind the desk wears round glasses and a Grateful Dead T-shirt. I don't know what that is, but he's giving Mother a hard time. She can't stand it. Her nails clack against her bag, soft taps on the leather. Impatient. Annoyed.

"Try it *again.*" Mother whips her credit card so hard at him that it bounces off his chest and falls to the floor. When I watch him pick it up for her, I feel like washing my hands.

"We're only going to be in this dump a

week, max," Mother barks. "You should be so lucky."

"Ma'am, your card has been declined," he says, and tries to hand it back to her. She ignores him, so he slides it across the desk in her direction.

"I said you need to try it again, asshole," Mother hisses.

"Okay, I'm going to have to ask you to leave."

"We're not leaving until you try the card again." She slides it back to him and bares her teeth. *"Please."*

"Miss, you have to leave," he says, softer this time. I start to feel sorry for him until he locks eyes with me and I realize he feels sorry for me, too. I don't like it so I look away. "Look, you have a little girl, and I don't want to have to call the police." Mother grabs the card and shoves it in her bag, not bothering to put it in her wallet. I don't often see Mother not getting her way and it makes me anxious. I want to ask her questions but I know she's in no mood to answer any so I just follow her outside as she huffs and puffs.

The weather in Los Angeles is perfect. Sunny, warm, a cool breeze. She had told me we were going to see the ocean soon and it feels like this is a good day to do it, but I don't think that's her plan right now. Mother lights up a cigarette, furious. I know I shouldn't speak, but I'm really hungry and I hope we can solve whatever problem we have over breakfast somewhere.

"Screw it," she says, and she starts to march down the street. That's my cue to follow her. I wish she'd just hold my hand.

On Hollywood Boulevard, we pass all kinds of weirdos and life-size versions of cartoons that would only be in my nightmares. Mickey Mouse. Superman. But they look off to me. People stop for photos with them, and I don't know why. It's so obvious they aren't the real thing. I avoid disappointment when I can see it coming.

Mother starts to walk faster. I keep up with her as best I can. She finally slows down when we are in front of the Hollywood Roosevelt hotel. Now it feels like we're in the right place. I know we'll go straight for the elevator. I like this game. It makes me feel important to her. A good opportunity to get her to like me.

"Go ahead," she says, allowing me to pick our floor. I push 8 and up we go, no stops on the way. "Take a look." She prods me in the back when we get there. I stick my head out of the elevator and look both ways.

"I don't see anyone," I say. She rolls her

eyes. I've disappointed her.

"My turn," she grumbles, and smacks the 12 button. "Money's on the high floors anyway." We exit the elevator, since Mother chose correctly. There's a housekeeper at one end of the hallway and we go quietly in the other direction. Mother stops in front of the last door on our end. There's a room service tray waiting to be cleared. Mother puts her ear up to the door and listens for a few moments until she finally erupts into an "Oh, no!"

Another cue for me. I skip happily all the way down the hallway to the housekeeper and flash her a winning smile, just like Mother taught me. I twirl a piece of hair in my fingers and say, "Excuse me, miss. My mother and I were about to go get lunch downstairs, but she left her purse inside with the key. Could you please open it back up for us? See? She's just down there."

Mother waves, smiles and then throws up her hand, doing all the right things.

"I'm sorry, honey," the housekeeper says to me. "I can't do that. You'll have to go to the front desk."

"Please? It would only take a second of your time and we would really appreciate it!" I know how cute I am and that it makes me hard to resist. Mother says that people always trust a pretty girl. She's right. Like clockwork, the housekeeper smiles back at me and follows me down the hallway. I skip every few steps in front of her, leading us back to Mother. "This nice lady is going to let us back in, Mommy!"

Mother smiles again and puts her hands over her heart. "Thank you *so* much, you're a lifesaver, really! We're already late for our reservation and by the time we went down and up again, I mean, you get it . . ." Mother trails off, but the housekeeper doesn't really seem to be actively listening to her. She smiles and nods and opens the door for us. A cute little girl and her mommy. Mother and I go inside and the housekeeper follows us. Mother's eyes go dark. I know this look.

"Oh, I'm sorry, ma'am, I'm just making sure that —" the housekeeper starts to explain herself, but Mother blocks her from coming any farther.

"Ex-*cuse* us!" Mother says, her hand on the doorknob, ready to slam it in the housekeeper's face.

The housekeeper nods and backs out of the doorway.

"See to that, too, will you?" Mother commands, nodding at the dirty room service tray. Then she shuts the door. Confidence is always the key, Mother says. Believe you are who you say you are, and they will, too.

We hear the housekeeper take the tray away. It's time. Mother starts at the walk-in closet, flipping the suitcases open. I go to the bathroom and go through the toiletry cases, looking for cash or jewelry. Instead, I find a fancy face cream I know Mother likes so I grab it for her, hoping for a hug or a kiss in return.

"No money, but here," I say, handing the small tub of cream to Mother. The corners of her mouth turn up a little bit. She's happy with the find. Thank goodness. "Did you find anything, Mother?"

"Nothing good." She sighs. "But I'll keep this as a souvenir. Nice work. Back downstairs."

Mother grabs a red swimsuit from the suitcase and stuffs it in her bag.

"Are we going swimming?"

"No."

"I need a swimsuit, too."

"You don't need anything," Mother says. "Let's go."

It feels like she already forgot about my gift.

She leaves me in the lobby and tells me to wait for her there. I look up at the ceiling and it reminds me of a church. I look at the newspaper. Mostly everything is about politics and the election. The weather is going to be the same as today for the next week and I think that sounds great so I wouldn't mind staying in LA, but I don't think we'll be here very long at all. When Mother's wild like this, that's when we're on the move the most.

Once in a while, her plans don't work out.

Three women over the hour stop to ask me if I'm lost. They all have the same question. Where is my mommy? I'm used to strangers talking to me when I'm alone and I don't mind it. I like the feeling of someone being worried about me. Sometimes men stop, too, but a woman will always interrupt. They just know. They watch out for me because I'm just a little girl. Alone. In a hotel lobby, on a park bench, outside a restaurant. I look for the women. They will always keep an eye out for me.

When Mother comes back for me, she's in the red swimsuit from the hotel room, no cover-up. Everyone is looking at her. All of the men. All of the women. Mother looks more relaxed now and she loves the attention. She's always the most beautiful woman in the room. I can tell she's been drinking because she's loose when she walks. Her hips sway more from side to side. She's putting on a show for everybody and now I'm mad. She was at the pool having fun and I was stuck in the lobby all alone. She can tell I'm upset.

"Oh, come on, bunny, you'll swim next time. This is all temporary. I'll even get you some new suits soon enough. You might be old enough for a bikini now. Would you like that?" I don't say anything. She's so embarrassing. Everyone is still looking at her. "Jesus, I thought I had a few more years until you turned into a surly teenager. Look. I brought you some fries!" she practically sings, handing me a brown paper bag, and my eyes get big as I yank it from her. She never brings me snacks like that so something really good must have happened at the pool. I'm almost never allowed to have french fries. She tells me all the time she wants to keep me lean. Keep me pretty. "I'll get dressed and we'll get going. We're done here."

"I thought we were going to stay," I whine, and immediately regret it. I know she hates when I whine, but Mother's in too good a mood to notice.

"Not this time, bunny," she says, sweeping a piece of my hair from the front of my face. "But don't worry. I always take care of you, don't I?" I put my hair back so maybe she'll do it again, but she leaves me for the ladies' room. I dig into the fries and enjoy every bite, knowing it'll probably be the only thing I eat all day. I scan the room for a water fountain because now I'm dying of thirst and I'm not sure where we're going next.

When she comes back, she's in her jeans, still wearing the swimsuit as a top. Her hair is still wet, but it looks good. We take a cab from the valet stand and in minutes we're back at the place we were before. I should have known. This will be fun.

The bell on the door rings as we step back inside. The man behind the desk looks right at Mother's chest. Men can't help it, she tells me. Mother hands him a new card, this one thick and black, the very best kind. "Use this one. My boyfriend's," Mother purrs at him. "But just one night. We're moving on tomorrow."

"Yes, miss." He puts his head down and tries not to look directly at her. I know he's not worth our time, but Mother still likes to play. She always likes to play and sometimes I like to watch her play, like I do now. The card goes through and we head straight for the pool. It's big and empty and in plain view of the office. Mother faces the window where the man watches her and shimmies out of her jeans. She stretches out on a pool chair, puts on her sunglasses and fires up another cigarette.

She wants him to watch her.

She wants him to regret how he treated us.

She wants him to be sorry.

I know we can stay anywhere with that black card, but Mother wants to make him feel bad for turning us away. He could have looked at her all week. What a fool he is. Mother doesn't stop there. When we leave the next morning, there's a different man at the reception desk. "Is there a suggestion box, sir?" she asks the new man.

"You're looking at it. I'm the manager." He's amused by her and crosses his arms, ready to hear what she has to say.

"Excellent. Then you should know that your employee from yesterday made me extremely uncomfortable. What's his name?"

"Burke." He grins at her. He has no idea what's coming. I stay close to her. She likes to know I'm paying attention to the game.

"Is that his first name or his last name?"

"I don't see how that's important, miss."

"Well, let me tell you that he was leering at me by the pool all afternoon, and I worried for my and my daughter's safety all night when we were in the room." Mother's voice gets louder as the smile falls from the man's face. "I barely slept! He's unfit for customer service and I'd like to file a formal complaint against Mr. Burke. *That's* why it's important."

"I apologize, miss. I'm very, very sorry that happened. That's completely unacceptable behavior. His name is Burke Tollackson, and I will be having a serious conversation with him today. I can promise you that."

"Good," she says.

But that wouldn't be enough for Mother. She continued to call that motel in Hollywood every few weeks, under a new name, to make a new complaint against Burke Tollackson, until she found out that he was no longer with the motel at all.

That's just the kind of woman Mother was.

But petty revenge was the least of her sins.

Chapter 5

"He's in with his *dad,*" Syl whispered at me from her post in Collin's office. Collin and I had a standing lunch date on Mondays at one. Our routine rarely experienced a shake-up. A meeting with his father after our family brunch was alarming. I had held my own with Haven, but would Collin be able stand up for me to his father? I was also very perturbed to be kept waiting in front of his assistant. She should have proactively phoned me about the delay. "They've been in there for about an hour. Do you want me to check in?" The high-pitched intonation of her voice suggested she wanted me to say no for her sake, but yes, obviously I wanted a status update immediately.

"That would be great, thanks," I said, taking a seat in one of the club chairs, crossing my legs. Syl winced at the task at hand.

"Honestly, I thought they would have

been done by now or I would have called you about the delay," she said, picking up the phone with trepidation, essentially reading my mind.

"Not a problem." I smiled, urging her to hop to it.

Syl cleared her throat. "Yes, ahem, hello. Collin. I'm so sorry to interrupt. I know you said that I shouldn't, but Bea is here for your lunch."

Whatever. I could handle a gentle toss under the bus to get the answers I sought. Syl hung up the phone and Collin poked his head out the door. "Babe, I have to rain check today. I'm sorry." He really did look sorry. Under extreme duress, too. Was their meeting about me or perhaps unseemly business dealings? A lawsuit? Dire financials? Or was Mr. Case merely following his wife's marching orders to trounce me after I rebuffed their offer? I was miffed but didn't want to make a scene with the patriarch present. Especially when I wasn't exactly sure where I stood. I'd have to wait it out before deciding on my next move.

"Of course, babe," I said to Collin in my sweetest voice. "Is everything okay?"

"Yeah, everything's fine," he said. It definitely *wasn't* fine. His face took on the flushed hue of a small child who was in trouble for being naughty. "I just can't leave right this second, but I'll call you later, okay? Love you." He shut the door. A monstrous display of disloyalty and right in front of Syl. It was embarrassing. I suppose Collin and his dad could have been discussing any number of line items as it pertained to the Case Company, but I couldn't shake the feeling that I was the subject in question.

"Hey. Bea. Are you okay?" Syl asked, alluding to knowing more than she let on, so instead of barking at her about professionalism in an assistant role, I maintained a soft approach to peel the layers even further.

"I'm fine. It's just a lunch."

"Would you maybe want to go to lunch with me?"

What a bizarre creature Syl was. An executive assistant asking her boss's girlfriend to socialize? No, I didn't *want* to go to lunch with her, but I had a feeling she was privy to the conversation behind closed doors. I was practically salivating over whatever intel she possessed. She could be an asset to me. So the two of us popped into a nearby Pret for a salad and a sandwich. I got the salad, obviously.

Syl leaned in toward me at our table; her tone was hushed and exuberant. She really couldn't wait to spill and I loved that energy from her. This is how we would bond, but it was good to know she wasn't someone who could keep a secret.

"I don't even know if I should be telling you this, but I feel like I owe you one after that whole thing with your office," Syl said.

Yes, accurate.

"Okay, now you have to tell me," I urged, perhaps too eagerly. She sat back in her chair a bit, enjoying the upper hand.

"I'm pretty sure they're discussing you." Syl smiled at me with the straw of her Diet Coke between her teeth.

"Oh? What about me?"

"Well, I couldn't hear *everything,* but Collin was basically defending you to his father. He said that you're like no woman he's ever met before and that you're ambitious and beautiful and not like the other ding-dongs they wanted him to settle down with."

"He said *ding-dongs*?"

"He did. It was cute."

"Right." I shrugged, not really agreeing with her. So I was with a man who used the word *ding-dongs* in regular conversation? Well, there were worse fates.

"What did Mr. Case say?" I asked Syl. "He barely said two words to me when we finally met yesterday. He didn't even give me a chance. Neither did his wife."

"All I heard was something about growing up, being a man and not screwing around with the people who work for them."

My mouth fell open. My future father-in-law had placed me in the same bucket as the help, not beguiled at all by my southern belle backstory. Unfortunate, but not entirely unexpected. I just had to keep working Collin. That was the move, but was it enough to go against his family's wishes when it came to marriage? Was I enough?

"But Collin defended me?"

"Oh, absolutely. He's obsessed with you, Bea. Honestly. I'm with him all the time. I would know."

"This is wretched," I lamented, laying it on thick, wanting to keep the lines of communication open between us moving forward. Syl was a gold mine. "I don't want Collin's family to dislike me, but it's like they've already made up their minds."

"I wouldn't worry about them," Syl said, smiling again, a piece of tomato lingering in the corner of her lips. She licked it away mischievously. "You can work on the family later. Terrible in-laws are a tale as old as time. You have Collin by the balls and that's what really matters. You'll see."

I laughed out loud. Syl was a character. "See what?"

"I think I've said too much."

I playfully pushed her from across the table. "You can't do that!"

"I'm sorry! I'm trying to put myself in your position. You might not wanna know."

"Of course I want to know. Wouldn't it drive you absolutely mad if I told you I had a secret and then declined to share it with you, all in the same breath? That's monstrous, Syl. You tell me right now."

Was it possible the two of us were having fun together? I never had any fun with women, except for the unhealthy kind wherein we engaged in duels of the mind. No, Syl was no Gale. Syl was putting me at ease. Entertaining me. A new sensation across the board.

"I know, I know. I just think I might be crossing a line here. I'm sorry. Really." Syl started giggling now. "I *so* want to tell you, though!"

"If you ever want to get lunch with me again, you better start talking," I said, dangling a carrot of perceived friendship. I could tell she liked me as well.

"Okay. If you're sure. And you promise you won't be mad?"

"I can't promise that if I don't know what it is."

"At *me,* I mean. Promise you won't be mad at me?"

An interesting development. Syl was acting as if we could become true friends when I would always clearly have the upper hand as her superior's significant other. Regardless, I leaned into the false intimacy. It would only benefit me.

Sure, Syl. I'll be your friend.

"Mad at you? Does it have anything to do with you?"

She paused for a second, sincerely wondering if it did. "No. Not really," she decided.

"All right then. Out with it!"

"Okay." She inhaled dramatically for effect, speaking slowly. "Earlier today. As in this morning. Collin asked me. To make a list of jewelers. That specialize in engagement rings. In the seven-*fucking*-figure range."

"Shut up!" My eyes went wide with the win in sight. An engagement ring already? I thought I had at least three more obligatory months lest we seemed too hasty to the adoring public. Incredible. And in the face of parental rejection? My allure truly knew no bounds. I wanted to openly rejoice with

Syl further, but my mind immediately went back to *her,* wondering if she'd be proud of me.

Of what I became. Of where I went. Of whom I'd aligned myself with.

And then I chastised myself for caring at all about what that woman would think of my life after her. It wasn't for her at all. This was all mine.

"So what did your research entail?" I asked Syl, wanting to get to the good stuff.

"I mean, it's not exactly *research,* is it? We're talking about Cartier. Tiffany. Harry Winston. Van Cleef. The staples," she said, as if it was the most ordinary thing in the world, which surprised me. What would someone like Syl know about classic diamond houses? "But did you want something more eclectic?" she continued. "I could easily drop a hint and send him some specific designers, they'd likely just have to source a bigger diamond —"

No, no, I thought. Eclectic wouldn't do and it had nothing to do with my taste. I wanted the kind of undeniably and quintessentially classic engagement ring that would hold some value should something go awry one day. Always advisable to have a Plan B. One of Mother's better mottos. Her gifted jewels often came in handy when we were in a bind.

"No, you were on the right track with the others. More my speed. Are any family heirlooms in contention?" I asked her.

"I think that might be part of the issue between Mr. Case and Collin," Syl admitted.

"Right. You know, I really don't think it's his father. It's his *mother.*" Saying that word aloud always made me shiver.

"You know what, Bea? Who fucking cares? A new ring is way better anyway. You don't want anyone's bad juju, especially in a crazy family like that. Who knows what kind of marriage Grandma and Grandpa Case had?" Syl was trying to butter me up. And the answer was "a rich one," but I agreed with her. Gimme something fresh. "Gum?" she offered, popping a little white cube of Trident into her mouth. "Sugar free, obvs." I took one from her and let her continue.

"He's standing up for you, to his *family,* and I think that says a lot about a man," Syl added. I nodded at her for the sake of appearances, but I disagreed. I thought it said more about *me* and *my* effect on Collin, someone who had probably never taken a stand against his parents about anything before in his life. I had truly enchanted him.

"They're being ridiculous," Syl went on.

"You're an accomplished woman in your own right and they're acting as if that's a bad thing. Please. It's just hard to be girls like us sometimes." That declaration startled me. Syl thought we were similar? *Really?* Maybe I wasn't a full-fledged member of the Case family just yet, but I could have been associated with the nouveau riche or at least a wealthy generation or two before my own. She didn't know anything about me, but as if reading my mind, she added, "Collin told me about your parents' passing. I'm so sorry."

"Oh. He did. Well, thank you," I said, because it's what you say, no matter how odd.

"I don't really have my parents either," Syl offered to commiserate with me. "It's hard." I went silent. I assumed she was hoping I would pry further into her life, but I didn't see the point. I could handle awkward silence no problem, but most people couldn't. Predictably, Syl changed the subject after a few more seconds. "I should get back to the office, but I'll keep you posted on ring things, if you want me to?"

"Only if it seems like Collin is getting derailed with the proposal. If he's staying the course with everything you already told me, I don't need any further updates. It might be nice to be surprised about the ring itself and how he'll decide to pop the question."

"Totally agree," she said, back to her bubbly self. "So you're not upset that I told you?"

"Not at all." I smiled, touching her on the shoulder. It was definitely wise to keep her close, especially if I could keep her flapping those fangs about the things I cared about. "Thank you, Syl. I really enjoyed our lunch. I'm glad you asked me."

"Me, too," she said, spitting out her gum into a napkin. "So we can do it again sometime?"

"Sure. I'd like that," I said, and I meant it. She held out another napkin for my gum and gathered all of our trash to toss, just to be nice apparently. As we walked out of the Pret, another question occurred to me. "How often would you say Gale calls Collin at the office?"

"Gale?" Syl looked perplexed.

"Gale Wallace-Leicester. She's a close friend of Collin's?"

"Oh, right," she said, still a bit flustered. "I recognize her name, but we haven't really spoken too much. I'd say she's called a few times since I started. Nothing excessive."

"All right. If that changes, I'd be curious

to know. That is, if you were comfortable sharing. No pressure, you've already given me so much."

"Sure," Syl said. "But she rarely calls as it is."

"Okay. Then I'll see you later."

Syl went in for a hug like I knew she would, but this time I accepted it. Passersby probably thought we were genuine girlfriends. A thing like that. But it didn't mean I could trust her. It probably meant I needed my guard up around her even more. A delicate dance. Lure her in, without revealing too much of myself. Story of my life.

I practically floated back to the agency, high on the engagement news that fully allowed me to plot my ultimate revenge on Len and company. It wasn't quite the moment to pull the trigger yet, but all in due time. Collin's proposal was officially pending, bypassing the all-important step of moving in together, which would surely follow, if not precede. Frankly, it couldn't come soon enough. I needed to get out of Morris's place as soon as possible. I could tell he was tiring of my lingering presence without any benefit to him. I knew Morris would never throw me out on the streets, he wasn't that kind of man, but I also didn't want to be badgered about earning my keep through anything unsavory in the sheets. He *was* that type of man, so time was of the essence.

Collin and I had plans to go to the symphony that evening, something I found dull in practice but refined in theory so I had to go along with it and pretend I enjoyed it. An excuse for a new frock was welcome, but more so the adoration of anyone we passed throughout the course of the night. We were a very attractive couple, though I was pulling most of the weight in that regard, no surprise there.

Before the music began and idle chatter swept through the concert hall, Collin revealed to me that the Cases' Newport home would be ready for us come Memorial Day weekend. Excellent news. He had taken care of business. Collin gave my left hand a squeeze, an exhilarating tell, and I thought about texting Syl to inquire about any ring updates during the intermission, but I stopped myself because I deserved the surprise. Why not? I wanted to start reveling in momentous occasions, instead of constantly looking over my shoulder, waiting for the letdown.

Once I was married to Collin, I would never be let down again.

CHAPTER 6

Newport, Rhode Island, reeked of old money, which, while obnoxious, I honestly preferred because I knew what to expect. Everyone waxed on about the Hamptons, which provided lovely ambience, minus the rampant banter between finance bros or star-fucking bimbos stalking celebrities. It was all so showy. The concentration of rich idiots in the Hamptons was much higher, especially of the new money variety, whereas Newport had a distinctly more laid-back vibe, since the crowd had little to prove in the wealth department. A welcome respite for both Collin and myself. It could be exhausting performing for someone all the time, and while I was always in a mild performance mode to keep Collin secure, I felt more relaxed than I had ever been with him when we chucked our bags into the master bedroom. So much so that I was the one to initiate a daytime romp simply because I felt like it.

I wasn't naive about my feelings for Collin. I knew I didn't love him in the way a normal person loved their partner. The Hallmark definition was simply not a priority for me because it didn't seem to result in anything worthwhile, much less tangible. Feelings were fleeting and fickle, with no guarantees. Belongings, assets and money had staying power if you played your cards right. I would have put up with far worse. Any affection for Collin was due to the affection I had for the life he could provide, but he was a genuinely sweet man, buck teeth and lack of bravado and all, so I counted myself lucky in that regard. That's not to say Collin wasn't without his faults. He could be secretive and quiet. He was not a gregarious man, similar to his father in that respect. I wasn't always exactly sure what Collin was thinking, but he likely felt the same way about me. While his every thought may have been unknown to me, his behavior was almost always predictable, and that was what really mattered. I believed he would always choose me and that was reason enough to stay with him forever if he asked.

When he asked.

"Did you want to go out or stay in for dinner, babe?"

"Let's go out!" I cheered at Collin, eager to frolic about town in my glory. If he was gearing up to propose as expected, I decided I wouldn't mind a public display as long as it was tasteful, resulting in polite and genuine applause from onlookers along with a bottle of the restaurant's finest champagne sent to the table.

"Really? I thought we might stay in," Collin said, instantly annoying me. If he didn't want my opinion, why bother asking? "I thought it might be nice for our first night to settle into the house, dine alfresco on the terrace, get a fire going, put some cozies on." Oh God. I cringed. When Collin said things like *cozies* it made me want to slap a diaper on him and send him on his way to his mother. His vernacular left much to be desired, but like I said, he wasn't perfect.

"All right, whatever you want is fine with me," I told him, before making tracks for the wine cellar.

"Well, I can put in requests? What sounds good?"

"Lobster," I replied, because it was what you ate in Newport and it was rich, even though I couldn't think of a more overrated star of seafood. In my estimation, lobster had absolutely no flavor unless it was slathered in butter of all things. Horrendous.

"Great idea. Gale loves lobster, too."

"I beg your pardon? *Gale* is here?"

Christ. Would I get no rest on our little lovers' getaway? The abject cruelty of it all. I rightfully expected some hard-earned PTO, a weekend of my own wherein I wouldn't have to be so "on," but I reminded myself there would be no time to relax until Collin and I were married. Don't get comfortable, Bea. No sick days. No weekends. No summer fucking Fridays.

"Bea, come on, I told you on the way up that we're going to host Gale and Luke, too."

He most certainly had *not.* This was one of his well-trodden tricks. Collin would frequently drop unpleasant social plans on me, swear hand-to-God he'd told me about them previously, and then it would ultimately be *my* fault that I was in a sour mood about it. It was so routine at that point that normally I just nodded along, but this was beyond offensive considering the person in question. Our special weekend away and I had to spend it in the company of Gale Wallace-Leicester? A regular girlfriend would lay into Collin, huffing and puffing about the wildly inappropriate choice of guest considering the circumstances, derailing the entire weekend, potentially the whole proposal, at least for the moment. But I didn't want Collin to be cross with me due to an extemporaneous outburst no matter how good it would have felt. I wanted him to feel bad of his own accord. Because of his own poor decision-making. His own idiocy.

"I thought this was *our* weekend?" I whined, but only slightly, at the pronoun specifically. This was a very valid question, but the desired result would be all in the tone and the delivery.

"It is, babe! It totally is. I'm sorry you're disappointed," he said. Hmm. Getting closer. "They're staying at the house, but we won't be attached at the hip or anything. I just thought it'd be nice to have dinner together one night to meet Gale's new boyfriend. They have their own separate plans, too."

I didn't say anything. I merely sighed. I wanted more.

"I know," Collin said, right on cue. "I shouldn't have agreed when she asked, but she's my friend. And a friend of the family. She's always loved our Newport house, more than her parents', and honestly when we have guests here, it's like ships passing in the night so I didn't think it was a big deal. I can call her and say that we'd rather she —"

"No, no!" I interrupted, ready to ascend to beloved martyr status. "You've already invited her. It wouldn't be right to rescind. I understand. We'll have a lovely dinner tonight, all together."

"Thanks, babe." He kissed me. "You're the best." Too right, you ass.

I wondered what sort of troll Gale managed to scrounge up for this charade. There was no way in hell she had a legitimate gentleman caller. The reasons were twofold. The first, she was utterly repellent, and the second, she was so hopelessly in love with Collin that she wouldn't seriously consider anyone else. But perhaps I could lean into the silver linings presented. I knew I'd be anxious in anticipation of the proposal. Gale would be a good receptacle for any potential nervous energy. Keep it off Collin and foist it onto her. Something to do to keep my mind off the clock. She could obviously handle it. I continued to be impressed by her persistence to ruin me. Of course she asked Collin to stay at the Newport house, because she knew he wouldn't have the balls to say no to her. But who would prevail as the true puppet master that evening? It would be me, but I wanted to observe her efforts. And just who was the man she was bringing? The curiosity element beckoned greatly. So I'd run with it. See? An attitude adjustment can change the whole game.

Mother taught me that, too.

The staff set out a magnificent tablescape on the east-facing deck, overlooking the sea. Fairy lights and candles and hydrangeas and expertly placed pieces of white chiffon all really set the mood. Gale and Luke had arrived seemingly under the cover of night, retreating to their bedroom without greeting us first. She must have wanted to freshen up before competing with the likes of me, as if she could compete at all. Bless. Would she remain laissez-faire about appearances now that I was officially in one of the Case family homes, not merely as a guest, but as a hostess? If there was any time for her to step it up, the time was now. She must have known that. So what was she going to bring to the table in an attempt to throw me off my game? I was dying to find out. And I truly couldn't wait to catch our first glimpse of the illustrious "Luke from Duke."

Collin and I were having a predinner cocktail — old fashioned for him, a gimlet for me, I was on vacation — adorably hand in hand in a couple of Adirondack chairs, gazing upon the Atlantic, when the French doors swung open to reveal the gruesome twosome.

Luke was about six-two with sandy blond hair, impeccably dressed in classic American prep attire with loafers, and had a smile so bright he could start a fire. He had a hand, arm or finger touching Gale at all times.

"Hello, you two," Gale crowed in a printed muumuu of a dress that required belting for any semblance of style, but it was clear that she was trying to level up there in her own misguided way. I threw back a big gulp of my drink and linked arms with Collin to approach them up at the dining area.

"Welcome!" I said, firmly latching onto the lady-of-the-house role. "I hope your accommodations are to your liking. This must be Luke."

"Great to meet you both," he said, holding out his hand, first to me and then to Collin. He made pointed eye contact and said both of our names aloud with each shake. Okay, Dale Carnegie. I saw exactly what he was doing while Collin remained oblivious.

"So happy you guys are here." Collin grinned. The poor sap looked genuinely happy for Gale, it was all over his face, dimples popping, teeth shining. I was so disappointed in Collin. How could he not see that this coupling would not happen in a frozen hell on any planet in the universe? Part of his charm, I suppose. An oblivious man makes for an ideal husband. I'd always have to keep telling myself that, wouldn't I?

"Gale tells me you went to Duke," Luke said to me warmly, clearly not wasting any time executing on his marching orders.

Oh, Gale. This man was clearly a paid escort.

"Yes. That's true, Luke." I smiled, making an effort to communicate that I saw him. I *also* knew that a person loved the sound of their own name, except that certainly wasn't his real one.

"I can't believe we didn't cross paths. What dorm did you live in?" he asked me, refusing to stray from Gale's goals. Fair enough. Everyone's got to make a living. I tried to exchange a look with Collin, but I knew he wouldn't get on my level even though we were now adults discussing dormitories and it was all so dreadfully boring, but I had to shell out my prepared answers knowing this exact situation would arise.

"Trinity." I smiled at Luke.

"My college girlfriend lived in Trinity. Do

you know Eleanor Whittier?" Luke slow-blinked at me with a smile like he was battery operated, still with his hands all over Gale. She was reveling in her handiwork. They must have practiced.

"Can't say that I do," I replied. "What year were you on campus, Luke?"

"Oh, I graduated in 2012," Luke said. I could not have been more pleased with the revelation, but I was also offended. Gale must have thought I was *their* age, but how could she assume I was in my thirties considering my practically poreless complexion?

"Oh, we must have just missed each other," I said, snapping my fingers. "I didn't get to campus until that fall."

"You graduated college in 2016?" Gale nearly growled at me.

"That's right," I said cheerfully as the staff came out with the first course. "Oh, I'm starving!" I exclaimed, purposely jutting out my clavicle in Gale's direction.

"So where did you two meet?" I asked Luke, holding up my glass for a refill.

"Through coworkers, remember?" Gale pointed out.

"I know, but I want all the first-date details." I rested my head on my hands in anticipation. Collin even caressed my back as a cherry on top. Luke matched the gesture on Gale, but I noticed she shrugged him off ever so slightly. He acquiesced and cleared his throat.

"I took Gale to Eleven Madison Park," Luke said, not offering much more.

"Very nice," I nodded.

"And then we went to a gallery opening," Luke finished, almost with the cadence of a question, looking to Gale for approval.

"Which gallery?" I asked.

"Uhh." He fumbled, but Gale picked up the ball.

"Mishkin. You wouldn't know it."

"Oh, you're right. I'm hopeless when it comes to art. Collin handles all of it for the house," I said, twirling a finger through his hair. "He has such good taste."

"That's debatable," Gale said. "Sorry, Coll, but your eye isn't the most evolved."

Collin shrugged. "I like what I like."

"Are you in the art world, too, Luke?" I asked him.

"No, I'm in finance." Typical. The age-old, no-further-questions-necessary career. Perfect cover for an escort.

"Hedge fund, tech or —"

"It's boring, I assure you," he said.

"So who introduced you? Which co-worker?"

"One of my buddies buys art, is into art," he said, more firmly, not missing a beat, but obviously getting annoyed with me.

"But Gale works at a publisher, not a gallery. What do you mean?"

"Luke's friend is one of the photographers," Gale said curtly.

"Right," I said, skeptical. Even Collin's brow was furrowed in confusion.

"Let's talk about something else," Gale said, clearly upset that whatever she had planned with her hired hand for the night went completely out the window. My time at Duke was not brought up again.

I continued to make plenty of conversation with Luke, purely to antagonize Gale and honestly Luke, too, because I was insulted that he thought he could pull the wool over my eyes. I asked him more questions about everything. He performed his duties well enough and doted on Gale in the way a new boyfriend is supposed to in front of friends. But even Collin gathered something was amiss, not that he'd ever admit it. He stayed quiet, letting me drive the bus. Part of me wanted to dish about it with him later, but I knew he'd say I was being unfair to Gale, and I didn't want to disrupt any proposal plans over a silly lovers' quarrel, with my nemesis as the kindling. Besides, now Gale was planting the seeds of doubt in Collin all on her own. I admit her plan with Luke had the makings of a good one, but she underestimated her opponent when it came to the execution. With someone else as the lead, she couldn't adapt, be flexible or light on her feet.

She knew it, too, which is why she implemented a Hail Mary next.

Solo.

We were all set to retire for the evening. The lobster and liquor had been consumed. There was nothing left to say or do. We could finally put ourselves out of our goddamn misery. When I returned from the powder room, ready to bid good night to our guests, Luke was already gone. I silently observed that Gale stood closer to Collin on the veranda, watching the night settle in farther along the seaside.

She wasn't cuddling him per se, but she was close enough that it could be construed that way from the right angle. It was easy to see their lifelong dynamic at play, just in the physical proximity they shared. Gale repeatedly brushed her elbow against his side, she'd look up at him with hope he'd return her wanton gaze, bump her hip into his, accidentally, on purpose. How many times must she have done such a thing? Any vim or vigor she possessed around me completely vanished when she was alone with Collin. He truly was her weakness. It was pathetic so I enjoyed the show and listened in, staying hidden from their line of vision.

"Ah, Gale, I really wish you would get on board with Bea," Collin whispered, taking a peek over his shoulder to check for my presence.

"I'm not *not* on board," Gale said, her voice an octave higher than normal.

"I'm not an idiot, Gale. I know you don't like her, and I don't need more of that bullshit from the people in my life. Especially not from you," Collin huffed. "We're supposed to be friends."

First his father and now Gale. I had ignited some sort of fire in this man, so much so that he would stand up to lifelong friendships and family traditions in my honor. I felt all-powerful. Before me, Collin Case was like a sad grilled cheese sandwich of a man, but I had transformed him into a proper croque monsieur courtesy of my homegrown wits and wiles. He should be so lucky to become my husband. I brought out the real cock and balls in Collin Case, and no one was more shocked than me that I actually found it a genuine turn-on. Hmm. Stranger things.

"We are friends! I don't know what you want me to say. I think Bea's fine," Gale said.

"She's fine?"

"By all means, feel free to sell me on her, Collin. Why do *you* like her?"

While I found her candor irritating, I also really wanted to hear his response. A relationship performance report in real time could be priceless.

"Gale, come on, I shouldn't have to *pitch* you on my girlfriend. I *love* her. Are you that surprised? I mean, Bea is exactly the kind of woman I've always wanted to marry. She's the woman of *my* dreams, but like every guy's dreams, too. She's perfect." It was an A+. He knew he had a real prize. He also revealed that it was important to him that I was coveted by others. Noted. "Luke obviously excluded," he added, for Gale's benefit. What a guy. Never wanted to hurt somebody's feelings, even if they deserved it. I would be the first to admit that the whole display was incredibly romantic of him in general, but to say all of these wondrous things about me, and to a woman who so obviously had the unrequited hots for him for their entire lives? Pure magic.

I'd never been more turned on by him before and an evening seduction later would be a well-deserved feather in his cap.

"*Every* guy's dream? In what way exactly?" Gale pressed even further, the jealous hag. Her voice returned to its naturally lower octave, but at a much quicker cadence. She was panicking. I imagined her face, all scrunched up in feigned confusion about why Collin could possibly be attracted to me. Those well-worn 11s must have been popping out of her football field–size forehead like goalposts. "I know she's like, hot, or whatever, but what else is there? And to your point, it's not just me. I know your family isn't wild on her either."

"That's because they don't really know her yet." Collin groaned. "Look, dating outside of our circle is always scandalous with families like ours, but that's so old-fashioned. And you know that. I mean, are your folks thrilled about Luke? Where'd he come from?" Of course they weren't, because Luke wasn't a real person, certainly not the man in the guest bedroom, and someone they would never meet, but that was beside the point.

"Look, Bea is *it* for me," Collin continued passionately. "I mean, yes, she's beautiful for one." An obvious check. My hard work was paying off. Abs don't come for free.

"She's smart," he added. Also very true, smarter than he even realized. "And honestly, Gale, the thing is, Bea really *listens* to me. She understands me. I don't know how else to explain it. She's the only one who really wants to hear what I have to say." Perfect. That's exactly what I wanted him to think. I impressed myself for pulling this off with Collin fucking Case at such an astounding pace. Post-engagement, it would only be a few more months to seal my fate for good. I *had* this, whether Gale believed it or not.

"But *I* listen to you, too, Collin," Gale whined, mustering up some sort of confessional confidence. She was really going to do it. Even though I was in the house. Incredible and impressive. I could appreciate a direct hit. Such a thing took gumption and guts. As far as I knew, Gale had never made an outright plea for Collin's affection, always hoping, in vain, that he would come for her. Poor Collin. He would hate to reject her, but that's what he would do; I just wasn't sure how.

"I know that, Gale. That's why we're friends," Collin said, letting her down almost too gently, but I could see her heart was breaking. She could read between the lines. "But I've never had a *girlfriend* like Bea before. It's just different with her."

"Oh, *please,* Collin!" Gale raised her voice, startling him. "*All* of your girlfriends have been *exactly* like Bea." Well, well, well. Now we were getting into some very juicy, uncharted territory. Collin would barely speak about his past lovers with me, which was probably for the best. I didn't want to tell him about any of the monsters I previously had relations with either, but the curiosity remained.

"That's not true at all. Bea is completely different from my exes. They're not even on the same level, Gale. Bea is, just, everything that I've been looking for. *Everything.*"

"Oh, the hell she is, Coll!" Gale wailed. "I'm sorry, but I need to say this to you. Bea is just another opportunistic blonde with fake boobs who wants your money. She knows *exactly* who your family is and what that means. How can you not see that? She can't be trusted."

First of all, my breasts are incredibly symmetrical and pleasing to the eye, but they're not surgically enhanced. In all honesty, they're probably the only *good* thing I inherited from my mother. Technically two good things. Second, I was thrilled she said it. All about the money. It was only going to make Collin more loyal to me. He didn't want to believe he was like the rest of them. I could relate to that, even though I thought he was ridiculous considering his privilege that he rarely recognized. He still thought he was better than most, just different, simply by virtue of loving someone like me, an outsider. Someone from the "fringe." Benevolent Collin who could see beyond the bank account. Bravo, buddy. But of course he could. He could afford to. I didn't have that luxury.

Look at us, a regular twenty-first-century Romeo and Juliet.

"I gotta be honest, Gale." Collin took a deep breath. "I don't think this has anything to do with Bea." Was he going to *go* there? Was he going to say what had long gone unsaid? I could hardly breathe.

"What do you mean?" Gale asked Collin, knowing exactly what he meant.

I really thought he was going to tell her the truth. That he knew all about her feelings for him, for all of those years. And to *finally* reject the notion, reject *her,* to her face and put an end to it all. Part of me was disappointed. I wasn't ready for the game with Gale to end. I thought it was just beginning, but she had brought this on herself. It should have been Collin anyway.

He should have been the one to finish her.

"Never mind," he whispered.

I wanted to watch him be ruthless with her, but that's not the kind of man Collin was, for better or worse. Gale didn't push him any further. She knew it wouldn't end well for her. They shared a few more silent moments, Gale backing off, creating physical distance between them. "Good night, Collin," Gale said, morose.

"Hey, Gale." Collin's tone was softer. Sweet. Supremely disappointing to me. It appeared my pleasurable little popcorn moment was over, goddamn it. Why couldn't these two WASPs just go for it and deliver the drama we all craved as chaotic human beings? Ah, well. I had better get used to it. That was the life I was signing up for, and while painfully dull, I knew it would be worth it in the end. I could no longer see what was happening. I had to hide elsewhere with Gale on the move, but I listened closely. I imagined she turned around to look at him, hope in her eyes, wondering if he had changed his mind.

"Yes, Collin?" Gale said his name, almost breathless.

"I'm going to ask Bea to marry me this weekend. I thought you should hear it from me first."

Ears all the way up! Well done, Collin Case, my future *husband.* Way to stick the landing with the surprisingly understated final stake to her heart. A slow burn that truly paid off. A kindness in Gale's direction, laced with poison, at least from her point of view. How I yearned to see the astonishment on her face. I wanted to scream at the news with unbridled enthusiasm. Naturally, I bit my lip and stayed put, but on the inside I was soaring. Flying high, just hours away from an unprecedented victory. Sweet relief, utter joy and rarer still, some well-deserved peace in my heart. I did it.

I *fucking* did it!

Gale didn't say anything in response to the information, leaving the scene to return to the guest room she shared with her employee. Hopefully whatever she paid "Luke Dunne" included intercourse of some kind because she'd be in dire need to shake off the embarrassment of the evening.

We didn't see Gale or Luke for the rest of the weekend. Collin never told me what had gone on between the two of them that night. He said that Gale and her beau probably had other plans in town, but that we'd all see each other back in the city soon enough. Collin did indeed propose to me that Sunday night. We were out on the lawn at the romantic restaurant of the Castle Hill Inn. Fellow diners applauded, genuine smiles across their faces; it's always fun to see someone get engaged. The best champagne was sent to the table and popped with delight. The bubbles were crisp and festive. And the sparkler in that red velvet Cartier box was so enormous, so positively gargantuan, that the white diamond solitaire covered the entire area of my ring finger below the knuckle.

Well, Mother, I must have done something right.

Dean

SAUSALITO, CALIFORNIA

My bedroom at Dean's house feels like it was given to me by mistake. I perch every night in an ivory canopy bed, the room itself taking up the whole of the turret, accessible only by a single winding staircase from the end of the hallway, away from the rest of the house, away from her, with views of the whole city and the Golden Gate Bridge from the bay window, stacked with fluffy pillows atop a built-in bookshelf of young adult books. And *The Runaway Bunny,* but I tuck it away, spine facing in, not out. I want to throw it out the window, but I can't. She told me she loved it so I keep it for her sake.

I don't understand how I can be so lucky, not that I would ever share such a thing out loud. I don't want to jinx anything, but I'm already sad to leave and it isn't even time to go yet.

I read constantly, anything I can get my hands on in the library at school, now that

I'm in school again, but I let Dean read to me because he seems to enjoy it so much. He'll read anything I ask him to, even Sweet Valley High, my latest discovery from a bygone era that makes me wish I had a twin of my own. Dean does their voices to make me laugh out loud and it works every time. Elizabeth's is prim, Jessica's is wild, both hilariously too deep because Dean is a grown man, enormous really, with puffy hair, big cheeks and a broad smile. Tall and wide. He could be mistaken for a football player even though he's in tech finance or something; I don't know the specifics of his work, that's Mother's job. To me, he's an in-house comedian who's nice to me and lives for getting our laughs. Even Mother laughs at Dean's jokes and over-the-top theatrics, with this crazy snort I've never heard before, so I think it might be genuine. I don't think Mother would snort otherwise; the behavior is unbecoming.

Maybe she really likes Dean, too. I don't want to jinx that either, but everything is just better when Mother's married.

The only thing Dean loves more than cracking jokes is eating rich food. Though he's a self-proclaimed master of the grill, he doesn't bother cooking much, since he has the private chef come in pretty regularly.

Her name is Beth and she wears pearls and talks to Dean about the Giants. Sometimes she cooks for some of the players. Mother doesn't cook. She eats like a little bird, tasting everything, only swallowing the smallest amounts of the decadence on the table, and I follow suit, mimicking her every bite, but I always want more. So much more.

"Go on then. Another scoop. Boys like a little meat on a girl's bones," Dean booms at me, and he winks at Beth the Chef to put a little more food on my plate. Mother clears her throat, objecting as passively as possible. "Come on, Denise, lighten up," Dean says. "She's still growing. You don't want to give her a complex."

Dean has just told Mother to lighten up and I slink down in my chair, making myself smaller, excited to see what might happen next. The look on Mother's face can't possibly match how she feels inside. She pretends to take it in stride, forcing a thin-lipped smile in Dean's direction as he chews with a grin of his own, completely unaware of who he married. I'm jealous of how Dean can be himself around Mother. While he still can, anyway.

"But she's not that hungry." Mother makes her stance known once more.

She's talking to Dean, but the message is for me.

I am actually starving, but my body's used to it by now. Dean doesn't see that I already have the complex in question, by virtue of being her daughter.

"Oh, knock it off." Dean chuckles. "There's truffle in this. Get your money's worth, kid." Dean winks at me and I want to please him, so I take a few more luxurious bites of Beth's truffled potatoes. I don't even know what truffle is, but I like it.

Mother grimaces at the sight.

"Attagirl, Dani," Dean praises me.

"Don't do that again. You'll get as big as a house and then what? We're a team, aren't we? Or must I do everything myself forever?" Mother calls to me later, watching me head down the hallway to my winding staircase. She's never said anything to me like that before and I feel my cheeks get really hot. I don't dare say anything back. I wish Dean heard it, but he's in his office. I imagine him scolding her like he did at dinner. So free to speak his mind in front of Mother. He stands up for me. Like he wants to protect me.

It makes me want to protect him, too.

■ ■ ■ ■

Dean's fun and he likes to go out on the weekends, "go on adventures" he calls it and, when appropriate, he insists on taking me with the two of them all over the Bay Area. I'm sure he adores having Mother on his arm, to show her off, but I believe he's just as tickled to be in my company, too. I can tell that he likes that I'm precocious, in the same way that my teachers seem to appreciate it, using that word specifically.

I'm a novelty to them and I don't mind the role.

"You're a real hoot, Danielle," Dean says. "I get a kick out of you." He sings the last part because, well, he's Dean. "Get two scoops of the chocolate," he urges me at the ice cream parlor. "It's the best. You're still a kid, you know," he reminds me. "Enjoy yourself." He grins, but I shake my head at him politely. Mother waits outside to see what decision I'll make without her physically looking over my shoulder, but it doesn't matter where she is because she's always in my head. Yes, I want the chocolate ice cream with hot fudge and rainbow sprinkles, like a normal girl, but I want Mother's approval more. I want her to want me on her team.

"I'll have the lemon sorbet," I tell Dean, because I ache to pass her tests, every single one.

The longer we live with Dean, the guiltier I feel, which helps with my hunger level. I have a hard time eating when I feel like we're getting to the end. I think about telling Dean the truth about who we are all the time, but I can't.

If he believes me, what would happen to Mother? Nothing good. And if Dean *doesn't* believe what I tell him about Mother, then what happens to me? I don't even want to think about how Mother would react. Betrayal by her own daughter? And even if Dean promises not to tell Mother about our conversation, I know she'll find out anyway. She knows everything.

What would I even say to him?

Dean, my mother is not Denise.

Dean, I am not Danielle.

Dean, you are in serious danger.

Dean, I do not think I am like her, as much as she wants me to be.

Dean, maybe we can help each other.

Honestly, I just want to stay with him. Mother can go on without me and I think I can go on without her. Then it'll just be me and Dean, eating ice cream together in Sausalito, no sorbet. Mother will find a new family, and another one after that, and another one forever, wouldn't she? But would she find another teammate?

I hate the thought so I make myself stop even *thinking* about telling Dean the truth. I decide to be grateful for a second school year ahead in the same place, sort of in disbelief that it's really happening. I've never had more than one school year in the same place before. Mother's snort-laughs continue, making me wonder, does she really like Dean, too? I can never ask her; I'll just have to wait and see.

She keeps up the snort-laughs for a while longer.

But then I hear Dean tell her that he likes them, thinks they're cute, those snort-laughs, those ugly snort-laughs, and I realize it must not be the first time he's said that to her. The snort-laughs aren't real after all, they're just to keep it all going, she needs more time, but I don't know how much more. She never tells me.

Dean gives Mother a sports car for their first wedding anniversary, a big red bow atop the hood, like a commercial coming to life in our driveway.

"It'll be your turn when you get to be

sixteen, Dani," he whispers to me. "Don't you worry. Dean's always gonna take care of his girls."

I believe that he believes such a thing, so I just smile at Dean, receiving his arm around my shoulder, a gentle, paternal squeeze on my arm.

Mother is becoming more irritable with me than usual, picking at me more aggressively, right in front of Dean. She never does that in front of men. Constantly poking and prodding me about my weight, even though I hardly indulge in anything, even when Dean insists. I don't want to eat at all in front of her anymore, not even a salad. When we all eat together, instead of matching her bite for bite, I alternate, to get her off my back. I see her notice my efforts. Dean doesn't like any of it. A chill between them is growing. The warmth is leaving the house.

"You're still thick in the middle," she says to me after dinner, entering my bedroom while I put on my nightgown. I race to get the silky fabric over my body, fully taken by surprise. "I just don't understand why you haven't had your period yet."

She's right. I'm the right age.

"I don't know," I mumble, feeling like I've

failed her.

"I was eleven when I got mine. I figured you'd be around the same time," she says, not realizing what she's just given me. She offers so little of her past that a casual drop about her first period is irresistible. I hardly ask her questions anymore, but I'm dying for more details about my mother's youth.

"Eleven," I whisper. "Did your mother help you?"

"I didn't tell her anything," Mother scoffs. I'm stunned she even acknowledges she has a mother of her own.

After a moment, when I realize she won't give me any more, I ask, "Does it hurt?"

"Don't be such a baby," she says, rolling her eyes at me. "You'll be fine. You're growing up, but this in-between stage isn't ideal for us. You're not young-looking enough to be cute anymore, but you're not old enough–looking to be enticing. When you get your period, your weight should start migrating to the right places and we can finally move on."

But I don't want to move on.

"I guess we'll just have to stay here a little while longer," she continues, voice full of disappointment, to make me feel ashamed. I am ashamed, but also relieved because I want more time with Dean.

"Where are we going next?" I ask her, not sure I really want to know the answer.

"Don't worry about that, bunny, just focus on your health," she says, starting to soften, right in front of my eyes, pushing a strand of hair away from my face. I pull away from her. Instinct. She hasn't touched me in a long time. "Are you stressed out at all? What are you eating at lunch? Are the girls mean to you at school?"

I love when Mother acts like this so I scoot closer to her again, asking for more. I know it never lasts, but I soak it in when I can, these moments when she likes me. If I say the right thing, maybe she'll stay close to me for a little while longer. I think hard about what she might like to hear from me. How can I make her like me?

"I'm mostly friends with the boys," I finally admit to her, hoping she'll be proud. The boys at school don't talk much, they just want to play sports, and I'm good at soccer and basketball so they let me play with them during recess. The girls are into gossip, and while I find the camaraderie appealing, telling secrets to each other before school, whispering by the swings while I hang back with the boys, passing notes during class, it still seems too risky to me.

I can't tell them anything real anyway.

The boys are easier. Sure, they talk a lot about boobs, sometimes snapping my bra from behind, and they sing aloud to "The Whisper Song" like they aren't all still virgins and they talk about which girls they want to "bone," but that's all simple enough stuff to fend off. I make fun of their mothers while I kick a goal, or their sisters while I shoot the ball, or their dicks before I sprint to the other side of the field, faster than all of them, and they laugh and get back in the game.

It's so easy to be a guys' girl.

"The boys at school are your friends?" Mother asks me, more interested, more curious, but not exactly impressed.

"*Just* friends, Mother."

Truth is, I don't want a boyfriend in junior high. I don't see the point, especially after closely observing other relationships all year. They hold hands at school for a couple weeks, the boy feels up the girl in his garage and then tells all of his friends about it the next day, just to dump her a few days later, becoming the only topic of discussion in school for at least twenty-four hours or until the next breakup of some other doomed couple.

There's nothing to gain there.

Still, Mother asks me about the boys at

school almost every day after that conversation. She never asks about my grades or French Club or the soccer team, like Dean does. She only wants to know if I got a boyfriend yet.

No boyfriend.

No period either.

Thank God.

For my thirteenth birthday, Dean gets me a fancy chocolate cake with two whole tiers. It's soccer themed. Black and white and green, vanilla frosting. They sing the song to me. Dean practically shouts it at the top of his lungs. Mother merely mouths along. I smile because I do love the attention.

"Being a teenager is a pretty big deal, you know." Dean beams, handing me a small wrapped gift. The paper is silver foil, really pretty, I think he paid extra for a professional to do it. "That's from me and your mother. We love you."

No one has ever said that to me before.

My mouth falls open the slightest bit. I'm shocked, dying to say the words back to him, to *them,* but I close it back up and immediately start to cry instead. It's so embarrassing, and Dean rubs my back sweetly while she watches. Mother doesn't touch me. I wish she would, but she scratches the back of Dean's neck adoringly. She knows I love him, too, and it delights her for all the wrong reasons. Dean can tell this is an important moment for me, but he thinks it's because it's the first time he's said it to me. He has no idea it's the first time I'm hearing it at all and that I'll always remember it and I want to tell him how much it means to me that he loves me, how much *he* means to me, but I'll never be able to say any of that to him.

"Okay, Miss Waterworks, you don't even know what's in the box yet!" Dean laughs good-naturedly, soothing me with a small squeeze on my arm, helping me through my emotions in the best way he knows how. "Go on, sweetheart, open it."

Inside the silver foil wrapping paper is a tiny black velvet box. Jewelry. I crack open the top lid to find two diamond solitaire earrings, sparkling. They're pretty, too, and I wonder if Mother helped to pick them out. Probably not.

"See?" Dean said, proud of the gift, and maybe of me. "Big deal. Happy birthday, honey."

A week later I get my period and it feels like a death sentence.

I mean, I guess it was.

You know.
For Dean.

CHAPTER 7

My overall treatment at the agency was markedly improved when I started swanning about the workplace with that offensively large rock on my finger. I was officially engaged to Collin Case, heir apparent to the agency's biggest client. They would have been fools to cross me again and they knew it. Oh, how they all tried to make me forget.

Len Arthur hosted a catered luncheon in my honor the Tuesday after the Newport weekend. Nothing says "We're sorry" like an assortment of flavorless sandwiches from Au Bon Pain. It was unclear who tipped them off to my marital success. My best guess was Syl, wrongly assuming I would relish the attention, but the last thing I wanted to do was spend a free hour with a bunch of idiots I had to look at all the time anyway. The hideous event was essentially a pseudo–bridal shower wherein I was bestowed with midlevel to up-market wines, gift certificates to department stores and a fair amount of tacky household items I'd never use, like coffee mugs or pillowcases, etched with MR. & MRS., BRIDE or TAKEN. And I had to sit there and smile with a miniature veil atop my head in the middle of the day like an absolute loon. Alas, I supposed I'd just have to get used to this sort of thing for the foreseeable future. It was sure to be the first of many parties in celebration of my forthcoming nuptials.

Jessica McCabe stewed in the corner, which brought some joy. In fact, most of the women in the office were stewing, being forced to celebrate *me* of all people. They didn't want to be there any more than I did, but their foul moods were obviously due to my enduring retention of prime position in the agency, as far as Len and the other head honchos were concerned. If I was a treasure to them before, I was absolutely irreplaceable now. They wanted to keep the Case Company happy? They needed to keep *me* happy.

Speaking of, Syl had sent a small floral arrangement to my office, peonies and ranunculus, about twelve blooms or so, with a thoughtful card. All it said was "You fucking deserve it! xo Syl" — a boldly familial move, but I didn't mind that she was taking big swings, even if it was self-serving. If Syl was in my good graces, surely she'd be in Collin's. It's all politics at the end of the day. Syl was an ally, as far as I was concerned. And if she had anything to do with Collin's ring selection, which I strongly suspected, I should have been the one sending *her* flowers. Was it possible Collin had such pristine taste all on his own? I doubted it as much as I doubted that he'd asked the women in his family for their opinion on the diamond. I likely had some overzealous shopgirl to thank as well, but her sizable commission would have to be thanks enough.

Morris Haley III took the news of my departure from his digs swimmingly, even bidding me adieu with a sincere hug that didn't feel lecherous for once. I felt his hot breath on my neck, a bit wistful, but he didn't cross any lines, thankfully. I figured he was just about ready for my exit, since I had stopped sleeping with him weeks ago. I'd miss his divine shower room, but little else. Our time together had run its course.

I packed everything up myself. A simple task. I didn't possess many belongings, beyond designer clothes and bags and jewels that had all been gifted to me over the years by various men, things that could be sold at a moment's notice if needed, nothing I purchased for myself. I kept my earned money in bank accounts, foreign and domestic, and in the stock market, right where I liked it. I preferred having a light footprint when it came to material goods. Easier to make moves if necessary.

Collin didn't say anything when my things arrived at our now-shared town house in Chelsea. Men never said anything when I pulled the ultimate power move without any prior discussion. I was skilled at selecting the perfect moment to force cohabitation with my mate. An exercise in stealth. A time when I knew it would make perfect sense, a time when it seemed inevitable, a time so perfect that the man would look like a real jackass if there was any protest. Besides, I traveled so light, used to leaving everything behind. Stuffed animals in Atlanta, Barbies in California, any gifts for me from any of her men that couldn't later be sold. So I kept up the habit as an adult. I wouldn't attach meaning to anything at risk of not being permanent, which was just about everything. Cash in the bank, and under the mattress so to speak, that's what it was really about. I didn't prioritize stuff. So what could Collin say when I waltzed in with a couple of wheelie bags and a few bankers boxes? As far as he knew, I had been living with an eccentric roommate he never met. We never spent any time there because of said roommate, after I painted a picture of an obnoxious homebody — which honestly Morris totally was. Now Collin and I were engaged. I was moving in. End of story.

I adored the Chelsea town house. All that space. True luxury. The whole place felt different when I moved in, compared to the numerous times I merely slept over as Collin's girlfriend. While I appreciated Collin's decorator's taste prior to our being affianced, I was ready to do some strategic revamping so that when visitors arrived, they would remark on the much-needed woman's touch. More than that, I was finally ready to let myself fall in love with a place I could make my own permanently. The intoxicating allure of *stuff* began to call to me, the stuff that makes a home, that I staved off acquiring for so long. I wanted to flounce about in long silk robes while I sipped on artisanal teas and read fine literature on the chaise in the library. I was ready to stock a walk-in closet of my own with hordes of shoes and gowns and lingerie, all on Collin's dime. I planned to run up and down the stairs to get some cardio in on the weekend while also relishing in the fact that I lived somewhere with *multiple* private staircases in Manhattan.

I had really done it. It was *my* house, too.

And unlike her, I'd never plan on leaving it.

After I was all settled in, Collin invited his family over for dinner, in the spirit of uniting us all, and to break the news they must have known was coming. Channeling Haven and her harpist on tap, I arranged for a pianist to join us so they could all find some ease when awkward silence would inevitably prevail over polite conversation. I still had to be nice to the Cases, despite my true feelings.

"Will Gale be joining us?" I asked Collin, fully expecting a response in the affirmative, but he shook his head.

"Nope," he said, giving me a quick kiss. *That* put a spring in my step. I was actually looking forward to the visit from the Case family. When they arrived and we told them the news, the wedding planning would officially begin, whether they liked it or not. It sounded relaxing to plan a wedding, comparatively speaking. Most of my plans thus far had required so much foresight and forgery. It could get exhausting. Sorting out seating charts, a live band and a color scheme? Bring it. I was happy to finally take up residence on Easy Street, also known as West Twentieth.

Hayes, Haven, Chloe and Calliope filed into the town house knowing exactly what the night would be all about. They all wore shades of black to prove it to me, except for Calliope, in her signature baby pink. "I wanted this one," Calliope said to me out of the corner of her mouth as she looked around the foyer. "It's the best one. Collin always gets the best."

"Thank you." I smiled, and she almost laughed. I suspected Calliope enjoyed having me around because I made things interesting, but she couldn't let her family know that. Predictably, their overall reaction to our engagement news was ho-hum and borderline offensive. "Congratulations," they all said, practically in unison, unable to force even small smiles.

"Hayes, I suppose we should phone Marcy?" Haven said, her voice dripping with defeat. Poor ol' gal. Haven didn't want the ball, but now that it was in her hands, she had to run with it. People would be watching, and she cared what people thought. "She should have the engagement party planned for this month or everyone will start asking questions. Bea, I assume *we'll* be taking care of everything considering . . ." Haven trailed off intentionally, so I finished for her.

"Considering my parents are deceased?" Collin wrapped his arm around me with a small smile, squeezing my shoulder affectionately. He beamed when I took his parents to task, something he almost never did himself. That is, until he met me. "I'd be happy to contribute myself, of course," I added, knowing the response in advance.

"Nonsense!" Hayes barked. "It's our pleasure, Bea." Haven nodded in agreement, tight-lipped, emanating no pleasure whatsoever, but if word got out that the bride was contributing to the wedding with her own salary, marrying into one of the richest families in the country, it would be embarrassing for all involved. The engagement news was already running rampant through their social circle, all eyes were on us and the forthcoming event, so there would be no going back now.

There's nothing more superfluous than an engagement party. Between multiple showers, a bachelor and bachelorette party, a rehearsal dinner, a welcome cocktail, the ceremony, the reception, the after-party and the post-wedding brunch for good measure, it's like *enough* already. I've always found the pomp and circumstance of wedding celebrations to be outrageous and hardly romantic, but I wouldn't be so lucky as to get to elope with my betrothed like I would have preferred. All of the events would be part of the so-called privilege of becoming Mrs. Case. I was sure most women would be thrilled, but I wasn't *that* excited about all of the parties.

I'm sure it comes as no surprise, but I didn't have a lot of friends. A dynamic mostly by my own design, since I preferred to keep people at arm's length unless they would be of real use to me. More men than women fell into that bucket. I'd argue that men are relatively easy to read, but women have real depth, and darkness, to the point that you never really know what we're thinking. Women have actual *layers* under our societally mandated glossy veneers. So many unknowns, which is why female friendship had mystified me my entire life. No, thank you. It's not like Mother attended book clubs or wine nights or Pampered Chef parties and led by example. She knew better than to get involved with women and so did I. So in my case, it was actually helpful being very fit and sinewy and beautiful because very few women wanted to be, or tried to be, my friend. I'd wager that was to avoid any comparison or competition that they couldn't win, but I also knew that looking like I do made me seem intense and no fun, like someone who worships at the altar of Goop. I didn't, but I fastidiously maintained the appearance intentionally. Perhaps if my circumstances in life were different, I could have been a fun person, but no, I was not about to risk losing face so I could tie one on during girls' night out at some club over bottle service and then get cheese fries afterward. I would *literally* never.

The Cases hosted our engagement party at the Musket Room, which took me by surprise considering it was contemporary and chic while Haven Case's style leaned severe and stuffy. That said, it was their *first* wedding as parents so any event less than astonishing would not stand. I'm certain they relied heavily on Marcy, the heralded wedding planner, and her team for the latest youthful hot spots for premarital gallivanting. After all, personal feelings about me aside, the next few months would check a lot of their boxes when it came to their favorite hobby: showing everyone how much money they had in a completely acceptable fashion. What would the neighbors say if the Family Case didn't parade around the newly betrothed like a couple of Shetland show ponies?

Haven lent me a family heirloom for the occasion, a beautiful, but thinly veiled insult. A diamond necklace that had been passed down, generation by generation, to the wives of the firstborn Case sons. I noticed that she didn't just give it to me outright, lending it to me instead like some first-time starlet at the Golden Globes with only her first hundred grand in the bank. The dazzler was dreadfully heavy, but worth the trouble. Call me crass, but dripping in diamonds did feel like sin in the most satisfying way. I was only human. Mother would have been jealous.

The occasion practically demanded I wear white, but I wouldn't be caught dead in some dowdy lace shift that covered up all the goods. I opted for a sexy ivory jumpsuit with tasteful draping and silver accents, an Edie Sedgwick–inspired ensemble but with considerably less dilated pupils. In a small personal victory, I did catch Hayes Case taking a cheeky peek down my top when I leaned over for a veggie canapé. Men are all the same. He'd be on my side soon enough.

In a thrilling turn of events, the party was instantly more invigorating when Gale Wallace-Leicester managed to show her face. A true delight and a bit of a shock, since she'd been maintaining a low profile since our couples retreat in Rhode Island. Luke was not present, so I assumed she took him off the payroll. She must have been a glutton for punishment to accept the invitation, having to watch Collin and me glide about the room, hand in hand, while everyone ogled our happiness and hotness. It had to sting, and I was pleased to have a front-row seat. What daggers would she throw at me that I'd have to maneuver around? Give me something good, Gale. I was begging her. Make this last hurrah really worth my while before I hung up my hustling hat for good.

The lighting scheme was doing all sorts of favors for me. My engagement ring was repeatedly struck at the exact right angle, to the point where it seemed like I was shining it intentionally into her beady little eyes at every opportunity. Okay, fine, I *was* doing that on purpose, and not being very subtle about it, goading her to engage with me. Let's play!

"I *know* what you're doing, Bea." Gale smirked, the creases of her lips caked in matte red lippy. She didn't properly prep them prior to application. But still, what a long-awaited turn from my nemesis, who'd had her tail between her legs for the past several weeks. The bitch was back and we were both in heat.

Gale was dressed like an old oak tree in a pine green column gown. Cap sleeves. Not remotely flattering. A wintry color scheme in the middle of summer? A cry for help! She clinked the ice around in her tumbler of whiskey. Brown liquor? I also noticed her attempt at a winged eyeliner was atrociously uneven. A social media tutorial gone awry? It irritated me that she didn't just spring for a professional to do it for her.

"I'm sure I have no idea what you're talking about," I replied, taking a small sip of my champagne, flinging the shine of my ring into her eyes once more because I felt like it. "Thank you so much for coming, Gale. It really is great to see you. Been a while since Newport. How's Luke doing? Is he here?"

"We broke up," Gale managed to say with a straight face, looking me right in the eye.

"Oh." I clucked my tongue. "I'm so sorry to hear that."

"I bet," she scoffed. "It's fine. We were ill-suited for each other and besides, I've been busy."

"That's great. Staying busy after heartbreak is essential. Work going well?" I smiled.

Gale pressed her lips together, physically vexed by the pleasant conversation.

"Just who exactly do you think you are?" Gale's hand was gripping her glass so hard, I thought it might break. I loved it. She was openly challenging me at my own retirement, I mean, *engagement* party. Maybe I would end up having a little fun at this dull affair after all.

"Why don't we go get some air?" I suggested. She paused before answering. I don't think she was expecting such an invitation and perhaps she was weighing the odds of actually getting clocked in the middle of Elizabeth Street. As for me, I'd been salivating over getting another moment alone with Gale Wallace-Leicester since our showdown in the restroom at trivia night.

Gale and I stepped out of the restaurant and began to walk around the block in silence. I towered over her yet again, wearing my red bottoms, a gift from Collin. Gale was in mules. All heft, no height, true to form. I decided to speak first. "To answer your question, I am a lot of things, Gale, but as it pertains to you, I'm Collin Case's fiancée. And you need to come to terms with it because soon enough I'll be his wife. And there's no coming back from that."

"Oh, right. Hence the need for the prenup."

"What do you know about it?"

"Haven tells my mother everything and my mother tells me everything. We're *close.*" Gale cocked her head to the side, examining my face, seeking a reaction, a tell. Was she gloating about her relationship with her mother?

"A prenup is completely standard," I said, though I wished in vain that Collin would have thrown all caution to the wind. Not on Haven's watch. "I don't need to talk about this with you. What kind of person attends an engagement party to harass the bride?"

"I'd hardly call it harassment, but a confrontation has become necessary. I tried to be kind about it with you, but you've left me with no choice, since you've come this far and did not heed my advice to retreat. Don't you think the Cases have a right to know exactly what kind of woman their son wants to spend the rest of his life with?"

"*Collin* loves the kind of woman I am, and frankly, that's all that matters."

"That's romantic, but unrealistic. The

Cases have a sterling reputation in our circle and you're quite a mystery, hmm?"

"I have it on good authority that Collin *prefers* that I don't hail from your incestuous little East Coast dynasties. I excite him."

"And does he excite you?" Gale asked, as if she knew the truth, tapping her fingers alongside her cheek in faux curiosity.

"Collin and I are in love."

"Well, *I* have it on good authority that the Cases expected their son to end up with —"

"You?" I interrupted, allowing a single guffaw to escape my lips. She was not pleased. "Gale, before you go any further with your little tirade, I *know* you're in love with Collin. Everybody knows. It's excruciatingly obvious and I'm sorry that your biggest secret isn't much of a secret at all. I'm sure it must be uncomfortable to feel so exposed now, but 'your circle' has been well aware for quite some time. And yet, no arrangements were made to push it forward by Collin's parents, or yours for that matter. Didn't you say you were close with your mother?" I went for the jugular, yearning to throw down. I hoped she would take the bait.

"I bet they're all regretting that now, since they left him to his own devices and he wound up down your dark alley," she hissed. "Never mind *my* secrets. What about yours?"

I was momentarily stunned. Gale had this aroused look on her face, like she knew something about me that she shouldn't. That she *couldn't.* She wasn't quite smiling, but there was something unseemly about her. What did she know and how could she know it? *How* could she possibly know? She couldn't pose a real threat to me, could she? This was supposed to be fun, but now I wasn't so sure, not that I would let her see me sweat.

"Collin and I don't have secrets." I smiled.

"I could tell them, you know? At *any* time," she replied cryptically. Tell them what? My tracks had been covered. I made sure of it. Didn't I?

"Like I said, we don't keep secrets from each other." I had to stand my ground. It was the only move to make until I was able to gather more information. Gale's body appeared to be humming in anticipation; she was practically shaking. I could see the vibrations via her matronly displayed arms. Cap sleeves flatter almost nobody. Certainly not Gale.

"Let me put it this way. The Cases don't want someone like you on their family tree.

It's only a matter of time before they all find out the truth and the whole thing gets called off." Gale sneered.

These *people*. Their *legacies*. Their *traditions*. All for what? A perceived sense of superiority to lord over the rest of us? How jejune. The Cases should be so lucky to have someone like me in their family. Couldn't they see I was a star? I could be a real asset to them. But they would always be blind to that, wouldn't they? The only language they spoke was money. Meanwhile, Gale truly believed Collin was her birthright. Her imagined stake in Collin wasn't just personal, it was practically patriarchal, running deep in her bones. Not only would she not have Collin, but someone like me was going to get him. An affront like no other.

I hated to admit it, but perhaps I'd underestimated her.

How far she might go . . .

"So why haven't you pulled the rug out yet, Gale? What are you waiting for?"

She smiled at me. I instantly knew why. She was having *fun*. She wanted to draw out our feud as long as possible. Torture me. Screw me over at the last possible second.

Right before the wedding?

"Well, I do want to be involved in all the

festivities," she admitted. "Watch it all go down in flames in real time. The shower, the bachelorette party. Ooh! In *Las Vegas* perhaps? Have you been?" Gale pursed her lips into a perverse sort of self-satisfied smile.

Were those rhetorical questions? Oh, she thought she was so cute, managing to warp my innate confidence into major doubt. Insidious. Anyone could mention Las Vegas for a bachelorette party, but the *way* she said it. *How* she said it. Like she knew something. The conversation had to end. I thought fast about what to do next, and while it was kind of a long shot, I knew it would throw Gale off her game, which was the point for the time being.

I burst into tears.

Yes, a bit reductive as far as manipulation tactics go, but it turned out to be a very well-timed strategy because predictably, Collin was searching for me. He was jogging over to us in his tailored suit and shiny shoes. My very own knight in Giorgio Armani.

"Bea! Hey, what's the matter? Are you okay?" And then Collin's tone changed, in Gale's direction. "What the hell is going on?"

Collin always looked for me when I was

out of his sight at any event we attended together, even for a few minutes. He was territorial. I liked the feeling. Some women found such a thing boorish. To me, it signified safety. He enveloped me in his arms and I continued to cry into his chest.

"Gale, I asked you a question." He hugged me tighter, but I took an opportunity to look out at Gale, making teary eye contact. She didn't know what to do.

"Ta-take it easy, Collin!" she faltered. "We were just talking about our families and —"

"Well, that's enough. Whatever you're talking about, whatever you've been talking about, Gale, it has to stop. Right now." I relished his verbal lashing of Gale. "I'm serious, Gale. It's over," he added.

Gale was woebegone at Collin's tone with her, but any response would be insufficient. What could she say? Gale had made the bride cry at her own engagement party. That's never a good look on anyone. She offered a small nod of understanding his request. He was her weakness. Then the three of us headed back to the Musket Room in relative silence, save for a few sniffles from me, you know, for effect.

Collin held me very close the rest of the evening, more than usual. I suspected he was tiring of the lack of support from everyone in his life. Perhaps he was nervous he would lose me. That would only strengthen my position. "I think we should talk about what happened with Gale," he whispered into my ear, "but let's wait until tomorrow. This is our party, Bea. Enjoy the moment."

Our intimate stance spurred on a sprinkle of clinking glasses, most partygoers jubilant at the sight of us, and so we kissed to appease the crowd's demand for it. I saw Gale wincing at the sight.

"I enjoy every moment with you," I purred into Collin's neck. "And we don't have to talk about it, babe. Seriously. It's already forgotten."

But I wouldn't forget.

Gale Wallace-Leicester lingered for a little while longer at the party, out of duty to the optics. Eventually, she left, relatively unnoticed. But I noticed. I would have to notice everything going forward. No excuses. She had lit a new fire in me, one that had the potential to become a wildfire if necessary. We could all burn if she wasn't careful. I didn't want to be like her, like Mother, but I knew what I was capable of when my back was against the wall. If Gale knew something, anything, I had every reason to be shaken. She was clearly on the offensive and even if she lost this battle, I needed to get ahead of her for the sake of the war. That settled it.

I'd just have to grant her wish and make that bitch a bridesmaid.

Chapter 8

Gale would certainly be thrown for a loop when I asked her to stand next to me as I married the love of her life. Good. I wanted her on defense moving forward. I could always survive in that role, but I thrived when on the offensive, and if there was ever a time to tap into such aggression, it was now. Throw my opponent off course. Be unpredictable. Don't let her see me coming.

Certainly no one had ever asked Gale to be a bridesmaid before. Though, of course, I had never been a bridesmaid either, always destined to be a bride. Now I had to rise to the occasion. I had a good idea of what it all entailed considering modern society's obsession with wedding culture. I knew that as a newly engaged woman it was expected that I would conduct some sort of "bridesmaid proposal" to between four and seven lucky girlfriends who would be at my beck and call, completely against their will, for the next nine to twelve months. Women always seemed to do this to each other. Stuck in a cycle of expected performance and for what? The sake of tradition? We all know what that means. Keep the women busy with all these silly little things. Keep them jealous of each other. Keep them in constant competition. And they don't even know it.

But I knew it. So I'd work with it. Like I always did.

Chloe and Calliope would both be a given as sisters of the groom. I was actually grateful because it was an easy way to up my numbers when my prospects were slim due to my lack of friends. Collin wanted to have his whole bevy of bros by his side on our big day, but lucky for me, his mother thought anything more than four per side would be crass.

For my third, I decided to ask this horrid woman from spin class who thought we were friends because she followed me to get green juice after class a handful of times. Wren Daly was a fitness influencer — I know, shoot me — and a social climber targeting all of the new money circles. Basically, desperate for attention at all times. I figured she'd be entertaining to terrorize with all the over-the-top finery that would surround a Case family bride like me. Another cheap thrill, and I needed somebody who wasn't already in the circle.

And the fourth slot would go to Gale Wallace-Leicester. Keep my enemy close. I couldn't wait to see the look on her face when I popped the question. I knew she'd be perplexed, but excited, too. Surprised by my gall and filled with dread, but thrilled all the same. She really thought she could best me, but so what if she knew about Morris or Philip or Dan or any of my former conquests? So they all had money. So. What. We all have exes, for God's sake. Collin would understand that. What else could she possibly have? Something about my early, *ahem,* entrepreneurial days in New York? No. There was no record of such a thing. Potential fabrications were the more likely culprit with Gale. I had to ensure that they wouldn't be convincing. Call her integrity into question should any opportunity arise.

A small part of me entertained asking Syl to stand up with me, since I was genuinely starting to enjoy her company, but it seemed like too low of a bar, socially, and undeniably improper, as she was Collin's assistant. Still, the thought was appealing if not altogether insane.

Once I sent my list over to Haven, and she approved it, she suggested an afternoon tea in Connecticut. I could ask everyone in person and we could begin the planning process as a unit. The whole thing sounded completely terrible, but I agreed because it was all part of the gig. Smile, girls! Parade yourselves around for others' amusement. This is how things have always been done. Women supporting women. *Please.* We would all hate it and pretend we loved it. And the vicious cycle continues. The cursed event would take place the coming Saturday, which left me plenty of time to begin my personal and thorough investigation into Gale Wallace-Leicester.

My reconnaissance into Gale was so important that I took a personal day from the agency, knowing that Gale would be at an office of her own. It had been some time since I engaged in old-fashioned breaking and entering. Online and digital were largely the way I conducted such business for the majority of my adult life under regular circumstances, but Gale was proving to be anything but regular, so I hopped back into the proverbial saddle, well-worn and comfortable no matter how many years it had been. Sometimes the old way is the only way. Mother would be amused. Maybe even proud.

After Collin left that morning for work, I rummaged through his closet, his nightstand and his desk in search of a spare key to Gale's apartment. It sickened me that he would have one, but I knew it would be true. Collin was enthralled by an exchange of keys. He had asked for one of *my* keys when we were dating and I still lived with Morris. I had to come up with a whole story about a neurotic roommate who was uncomfortable with strangers, which wasn't too far from the truth, but it was a bump in the road in our relationship. He was upset when I denied him, but in a good way. The way that left him wanting more.

Anyway, an exchange of keys *meant* something to Collin, and since Gale meant something to him, for reasons beyond my comprehension, I knew that a key to her place would be somewhere in our home. It didn't take long to find a ring of unfamiliar keys, tucked away in a small drawer in the interior of his desk. They weren't labeled, but were all I had to go on. If none of them worked, I wouldn't be deterred. There's a myriad of ways to discreetly break into a person's home. I'd be rusty but competent enough to do what was necessary.

Gale Wallace-Leicester lived on the Upper West Side, in the West 70s to be precise, like the septuagenarian she truly was inside. Why a single woman in her early thirties, arguably the sunset of her *prime* — or as prime as Gale would ever get — chose to settle in a neighborhood where there are almost zero single romantic prospects was just beyond me. My guess was that the apartment had been in the Wallace-Leicester family for some time, but surely she could branch out after dipping into the family trust for something more desirable? Oh well. Her body, her choice, I suppose, but her choice was a puzzle to me.

The building was still a beauty despite its decrepit inhabitants. Naturally there was a doorman, which you'd think would be a problem for prowlers when it came to security, but when you look like me and the doorman looked like Frank did that day, well, it was not exactly difficult to gain entry.

"Hello there, Frank!" I called to him, making note of his sterling silver name tag, stepping out of a cab in a crisp white blouse, the top third unbuttoned. "I just need to run a lip gloss up to a girlfriend of mine. She left it at my place after our slumber party the other night." I winked at him suggestively and applied a quick coat on myself in the event he had an oral fixation. Most men do. Sweet Frank looked so provincial that I assumed a bit of subtle lesbian imagery would also help with my admittance. "I shouldn't be much longer than an hour or so," I continued. "Sometimes we girls get to gabbing and other fun stuff. I'm sure you understand." Frank promptly turned the color of a beefsteak tomato and he let me up the elevator, unable to utter a single word, much less clear his throat.

Soon I was in front of Gale's door, complete with a festive Independence Day wreath with red berries and a blue ribbon. Please rest assured that by *festive* I mean *absolutely hideous,* not to mention completely age-inappropriate. Why didn't she just accept her imminent spinsterhood already?

I took the key ring from Collin's desk out of my bag and began the process of sampling each one into the lock. There were about eight keys and the third one actually did the trick, but when I pushed the door open, I was stunned to find the dreaded interior chain as a barrier to entry, along with the disturbing knowledge that someone must be inside.

"Hello?" an unfamiliar male voice called

out. "Gale? Sorry, hold on, I'm coming."

Excuse me, there was a *man* in Gale's apartment? It was distressing and perplexing at the same time. I tried to yank the key out of the lock so I could bolt down the stairwell at the end of the hall, but the damn thing was stuck. Keys or no keys, I would have to promptly get out of there. I was startled by the mew of a feline below me and watched the little creature dart out from the crack of the door.

I dashed in the opposite direction. Luckily, each of the doors in her hallway had a small alcove in front of them. Nothing extravagant or terribly roomy, but for a waif like me, it was easy to back up against a neighboring door out of sight. Well, for the most part. My one physical flaw is that my feet are enormous. One of the very few drawbacks to being a striking five-ten is that you typically have to browse the mutant section of the shop for shoes. The silver lining is that your gargantuan size is almost always available.

I remained hidden in the alcove, my toes peeking out ever so slightly, waiting for the chain to unlock. Seconds later I heard the unknown man head in the other direction, shouting out for Hemingway. The cat, I presumed. A surprise to me. Surely Gale was a Virginia Woolf or Emily Dickinson fangirl by the looks of her. To be clear, the name was a surprise. *Of course* Gale had a cat.

I needed to remove Collin's keys from the door as quickly as possible, but not before taking a cheeky peek into the apartment of Gale Wallace-Leicester. It was enormous, outrageously so, with probably everything she could ever want in there. Well, everything but taste. French country and earth tones? Honestly, Gale.

I managed to extricate the keys with a firm tug and went on my merry way back to the elevator, careful to avoid Cat Man, who was making kissy sounds for Hemingway at the other end of the hallway. The curiosity about his identity was killing me. Did Gale have a new boyfriend she wasn't telling anyone about? That seemed highly unlikely. Or was it possible that she was so unhinged, not to mention so frivolous with her cash, that she hired a cat sitter for regular working hours?

The elevator doors started to close and then jerked open again. A frenzied hand found its way inside. It belonged to Cat Man. And my God, was he handsome. He looked like a younger Al Pacino or an older Timothée Chalamet. He was all hair. A swarthy fellow with luminous olive skin that suggested a robust moisturizing regimen. Or fantastic genetics. His whole demeanor could only be described as smoldering; sex exuded from every pore, not that you could see his. Exquisite skin. Exquisite specimen. That settled it. Cat Man and Gale couldn't possibly be sleeping together. He was way too hot for her.

"Sorry," he apologized to me. "It's just, uh, have you seen a black cat?" His voice was raspy and deep and sexy. His dark eyes were wide with a sweet panic over the missing cat. His dick was big, it had to be, no question. Wow. It was rare that I immediately wanted to have sex with someone purely for my own pleasure. I didn't trust that feeling, I had to stay the course, but it was too tempting to resist. I flirted shamelessly.

"A black cat? What, do I look like a witch to you?" I smiled. Unfortunately for me, he was too frantic to nip back at me with any quips of his own.

"My friend's cat just got out and like, hey, did you see someone, I don't know, strange or odd? In the hallway? The weirdest thing just happened —"

"Sorry, I don't live here," I interrupted him. "I was just dropping off a few looks for a client. I'm a stylist," I explained, never missing a beat when it came to a cover. I had several professions on hand to throw out should a situation arise. Stylist was always one of my favorites. Flashy and fun.

"Okay, thanks anyway." He slapped the archway of the elevator doors on either side in frustration and then he was gone, completely unimpressed with me and my fabulous made-up career. The elevator doors began to shut again. I was furious he didn't hit on me. What in the world? Perhaps he was gay, which would make a lot more sense in regard to the Gale of it all. It wasn't any of my business, but Gale had been meddling in my business with Collin, so all sense of propriety was officially out the window.

I was getting distracted. I needed to focus on the task at hand. If this man was going to be busy looking for the cat, and was potentially a frequent visitor of Gale's, this could be my only window. Now it was my frenzied hand reaching through the elevator to stop the doors.

I had to go for it.

Risky, for certain, but my breath quickened. How exciting. A ticking clock. A much larger margin for error. I could get caught by my new crush. What a turn-on. So few opportunities for excitement lay ahead post-marriage. The prospect of a caper in the moment was irresistible.

Cat Man had left the door unlocked, and he was nowhere to be seen, so I slithered in with ease, eager to explore the dwelling of Gale Wallace-Leicester. A green gingham sofa was the centerpiece of the living room. Yes, I'm serious. I wouldn't dream of joking about such an atrocity, clearly inspired by a childlike fascination with Laura Ingalls Wilder that must have stayed with Gale into adulthood. Why on earth did she not hire a professional designer?

Gale's home was dripping in literal green, from the sofa to the window dressing to the old-fashioned library lamp on her desk in the study, complete with a gold pulley chain. And sure enough, an eyesore bolted to the ground next to the desk, a large green safe that looked like it could have sunk with the *Titanic.* What was Gale's obsession with green? Were the rich really that obtuse? She also went heavy on the framed photos. Dozens of gold frames. With her family. With Collin's family. With Collin. Of her mother, her father, her grandmother, her grandfather, even older vintage photos of her great-grandparents, perhaps beyond. It was endless. She was committed. Old family values indeed.

I shuffled around the desk first and didn't come up with much beyond a checkbook, miscellaneous office supplies with monogrammed stationery — she *would* — and an obscene amount of mints. She had reserves. How curious. Seemed more appropriate for someone with a line of Casanovas running out the door, but I imagined it had more to do with her specific brand of neuroticism. At the very least, I could appreciate when someone cares about the precarious state of their breath. Not enough people do.

I thought about turning on her computer next, but I was dying to know what was in that hideous safe. Was it the Wallace-Leicester family jewels? A Fabergé egg or two? A stash of narcotics? As if Gale was fun enough to do drugs. Or perhaps that's where she kept the alleged ace up her sleeve about me. I had to get inside and examine the contents thoroughly, or as thoroughly as time would allow. I was insatiable. What did she have? Photos of me via a private investigator? With Morris? Or the others? That didn't prove anything. Copies of my identification documents — perhaps she was reading them closely in search of forged elements? They were undetectable, though. Weren't they? And she couldn't have anything from before Bea. *Nobody* did. But what *if*? I needed to work quickly, since Cat Man's resurgence could happen at any moment, but I locked the door just in case. Any jostling followed by muffled cuss words would let me know to opt for the fire escape in a pinch. Wouldn't be the first time.

To crack the combination, I started with Gale's birthday, easily located on her social media pages. I wagered she was the kind of person who looked forward to banal well wishes from acquaintances, past and present. March 1. Of *course* she was a Pisces. Shifty people with little control over their emotions.

I didn't really think the code would be as basic as her birthday, but I did my due diligence. Alas, I was denied. Another birthday came to mind. Collin Case, born on September 8. A Virgo man. My kind of guy. A crushing need to be seen as perfect, which is exactly the type of pressure I wanted a man to feel in my presence. And the safe opened right up. *Gale.* Using the birthday of her unrequited love as the gateway to her most precious artifacts? She could be such an old woman, but also such a *teen*.

I rifled through as quickly as possible. All the usual suspects were there. Her passport. A safe-deposit key. Her birth certificate and other health records. But then I came upon folders upon folders upon folders, alphabetized and meticulously curated, each one labeled with the name of someone in her social circle. A folder for each parent, each friend, each parent of each friend, each friend of her parents.

What a freak!

Naturally, I went for the Cases' files first. They *all* had one, some thinner than others. Calliope's was rather thick, and when I peered inside, there were a fair number of medical records that involved stomach pumping plus minor arrests due to public drunkenness and/ or recreational drug abuse in her early twenties. Her mug shot was cute, though. As for Collin, his file was the thickest of them all. It appeared I didn't have my own file. Rude. Gale likely didn't want to admit that I was significant enough to have a file of my own in her creepy records, but what kind of psycho kept organized files about her friends and family at all?

If *I* kept files of everyone I knew, which I wouldn't as it's all in my head anyway, I would have them digitized, password protected with double encryption and securely stored on the dark web, where absolutely no one could find them without the established protocol that only I would know along with the trusted hacker I would definitely hire with gobs of money to secure their loyalty. Yes, I have a trusted hacker in my network. I'm not some kind of rube. I would *also* keep hard copies of the files, but not in a safe that *looks* like a safe in the center of my apartment, just begging to be ravaged in broad daylight. My chosen vessel for hard copy storage would be hidden away, out of sight in a closet or under a floorboard, secured with fingerprints and facial recognition technology.

For God's sake, this wasn't *hard,* was it? Especially if you had money, which Gale did. Meanwhile, I had to learn this all on my own. Not from her. Mother's forte was not in technology, but obviously she had other merits when it came to conning.

Wrapping things up, I would be taking Collin's file with me. Cat Man had yet to return with the escape artist, so I managed to slip out of Gale's as easily as I slipped in.

But I ran into him again in the lobby. Chatting away with Doorman Frank, Hemingway the Cat purring in his gorgeous arms, biceps bulging. He worked out. No question. Cat Man stopped talking mid-sentence for a moment, presumably to look at me, but I didn't dare make direct eye contact. He didn't say anything to me, carrying on his conversation with Frank, so I smiled politely in their direction before heading out the door.

I did notice that when Cat Man clocked the file I held in my hands, he bit his lip, and it was *so* outrageously sexy. I could be in big trouble if I wasn't careful.

But I had been careful for so long.

Mike

KENILWORTH, ILLINOIS

Mother Yanks the hot-pink gown from my closet, and it reminds me that I want to get a French manicure of my own for the big day. French manicures look so chic next to hot pink. I'll have to make an appointment at the nail salon soon. They'll be busy with all the girls.

"What is *this* monstrosity?" Mother asks me with disgust in her voice and I can't even believe her. Is she fucking blind? My prom dress is bejeweled, strapless and the it-silhouette right now. It's gorgeous and I look gorgeous in it and she's just trying to hurt my feelings, but the dress is too pretty for her tricks to work on me. She's jealous again, but I'm used to it by now.

I waited in line for almost two hours at Peaches for the dress. Mike dropped me off and I went by myself. Other girls were there with their mothers or friends, trying on gowns, laughing or crying depending on the critique. Another reason to shop alone. The salesgirl asked me where my mother was and I told her she was dead so she wouldn't ask me any more questions. I didn't need any company. I knew what I wanted. I wanted this dress.

"It's my prom dress, Mother. Mike bought it for me, didn't he tell you? A boy asked me to prom," I tell Mother, knowing she'll be floored. Truthfully, I've been waiting for this moment.

"The *high school* prom?" Mother practically chokes on the question. Fair. I'm only in eighth grade, but I know I look older. Brendan James, a junior at New Trier, asked me. I know his sister, Jess, from school. I wouldn't say we're friends, but all the pretty girls stick together, more or less. Brendan picks up Jess from school and about two weeks ago he got out of the car and asked me to go to prom with him right in front of his sister. I said yes because Brendan is hot and older and I think maybe I'll get along better with high school kids than the kids my own age. I'm nothing like them.

"Yes," I clarify for Mother. "The *high school* prom."

"When is it?"

"Next Saturday."

"Hmm, looks like you'll be able to go." I

can't tell if she's impressed that I'm going to the prom and I'm only fourteen. "That was lucky," she adds.

"Oh," I say. I know what that means. "Are we leaving soon?" I ask her, not sure how I feel about it. I don't love Kenilworth, but I don't hate it either. The winter is brutal, but I like taking the train into the city and pretending I'm somebody else for the day. I go into shops at Water Tower with Mike's credit card and buy myself clothes and shoes. Sometimes I take things if I know I can get away with it. I feel a little bad when I take, but I think Mother would be proud of me, so I keep it up.

I don't have a lot of friends and my teachers don't pay much attention to me anymore, like they did when I was little, even though I'm still one of the smartest kids at school. It just seems like most women avoid me now. I know it's because of the way I look. I look just like Mother, but the younger version, so the sight of me triggers her now. Another bull's-eye on my back. It doesn't help that Mike looks at me all the time. I don't feel like I'm in danger, not from him anyway, but it definitely doesn't help with Mother, even though I thought this is what she always wanted. A teammate. An equal. Finally on her level.

But Mike should be looking at her.

I do love that Brendan James has a crush on me. It makes me feel powerful. In control and normal. Like a regular teenage girl with a maybe almost boyfriend.

"Do I get to meet him?" Mother asks me, looking positively thrilled by the prospect.

"I don't know. Probably not, it's nothing serious. Just a dance."

"It's your *first* dance. And the prom."

"Yeah, but he's not my boyfriend or anything."

"Do you want him to be your boyfriend, bunny?" she asks, moving a piece of hair away from my face.

"I don't know. I'm probably too young to have one, right?" I want her to say yes. Yes, I am too young. Freshly fourteen is way too young to have a boyfriend. At least in a parent's eyes. A good parent.

"No, not really," she says. "Look at you. You've grown up, just like we knew you would. You look older than you are. You must know that and what he's going to expect from you. Don't you?"

"Brendan's not like that, Mother," I say to her, and she laughs out loud. A big belly laugh. Honestly, I don't think he's like that, but I don't know him. Not really.

"*All* men are like that," she says. "But you

know how to use it to get what you want, like I do. Right?"

"But I don't want anything."

Mother slaps me hard, right across the face, and I'm stunned. She almost never hits me. Now I know we're leaving soon. She gets *edgy.*

"Remember. We want everything. All of it," Mother growls at me before leaving my bedroom.

I'm at Brendan's friend's house. I think his name is Matt. There are a few Matts here. The party bus waits for us in the driveway, lights flashing, music playing. We take group photos in the backyard. The boys. The girls. The couples. I have the best dress, but I knew I would. The girls don't really talk to me and I don't care. Brendan tells me they're a little annoyed he's bringing an eighth grader to their dance. Whatever.

"You're an interloper," he jokes.

"Something like that," I say in return. I know what he wants to hear. But I didn't know I needed to bring a boutonniere. He presents me with a corsage that matches my dress. Two small blush roses and one big hot-pink one. I feel dumb because the other girls' mothers must have told them about boutonnieres for their first dances. Now they all knew what to do every time. I didn't know I was supposed to order one at Jewel-Osco a week beforehand. I would have done it. I want to do the right thing here.

"Doesn't matter," Brendan reassures me, and I'm relieved. "I've got the best girl on my arm."

He's saying all the right things.

He knows what I want to hear, too.

Brendan's parents are nice enough. They look normal. Joyce and Steve. "Mackenzie, you look absolutely radiant," Brendan's dad says to me. He doesn't say anything like that to any of the other girls and I notice.

I'm sure Joyce notices, too.

We all have a few beers in the party bus, courtesy of someone's "cool" parent, I don't know which one. Maybe one of the Matts. I already know what beer tastes like and that I do not like it, but I nurse my Coors Light anyway to keep up appearances for the journey downtown. Brendan keeps an arm around me the whole time. We're off to the Adler Planetarium.

I decide to bask in the attention I get all night. Might as well. The girls talk about me behind my back. The boys do, too, but in the good way. Brendan loves it. He never leaves my side. We pose for a photo with a starry backdrop, his pelvis poking into my back, arms wrapped around my front. We laugh. We eat Chicken Vesuvio and potatoes and a vegetable medley with his friends and their dates. Silver balloon centerpieces are on the tables. The DJ plays Frank Sinatra songs while we dine, and we all feel older than we are in a fun way. Brendan gives me quick pecks on the cheek all night. Longer kisses on my neck, on my lips, on the dance floor. We move to every song. Rihanna. Maroon 5. Kanye West. We're hungry for each other. We can't help it.

The party bus takes us back to Matt's house and Brendan says he'll drive me home. He drives an Audi that his father bought for him. He asks if I want to stop by his house first and I say yes because that's what I'm supposed to say and also because I really want to. Brendan leads me into the finished basement. There's a wet bar, a pool table, an entertainment center with a projector. The sofas are cream. Italian leather. It's nice. His parents don't come downstairs at all but they must know where we are. Brendan puts on more Maroon 5 with a remote because he's trying to set a mood. He unzips my dress and I can't believe this is happening.

"Pool table?" he asks me. I know what he's really asking me. I say something about a

Tiffany bracelet, since every girl at school has one. The silver bangle with the heart charm. Mother says I'm supposed to want everything. It's the only thing I can think of. He says that when I'm his girlfriend, I can have anything I want. I believe him.

I love the idea of having a real boyfriend.

I love the idea of Brendan.

He might end up being a summer romance that breaks my heart, but it would be worth it to feel what all the other girls feel.

Or maybe I'll break his heart first.

His chest is smooth and small above me, back and forth, back and forth. I look at his sternum pretty much the whole time. He looks at the wall behind me, grunting softly. I don't make any noise because I don't want his parents to hear me, but I breathe softly on his body because I know he'll like it.

It doesn't hurt as much as I thought it would.

It doesn't feel as exciting as I thought it would either.

It's over very fast.

Brendan asks if I want more to drink and when I decline, he says he'll drive me home and I know I've said the wrong thing. Now we're in his car, holding hands, heading to Mike's house. He kisses me good night, long and slow, and he waits for me to get to the front door.

Then he drives away.

There are only a few days left of the school year. The whispers around the halls are constant and everyone thinks they're so slick as if I don't hear what they're saying about me, but I know that they all know. Brendan doesn't call me anymore, and when Mother asks me about him, she pretends like she doesn't already know what happened.

She just wants to see my face when she brings him up.

"Not anymore, but I'm fine with it," I say to her, but I'm not fine with it at all. "I didn't really want him to be my boyfriend." I'm lying.

Mother laughs at me. A chuckle. A crinkle of her nose. It's harsh, like she's enjoying my pain. She likes when I learn lessons the hard way.

"Hmm." She pauses at the door. "Whatever you did with him, you must not have been very good at it."

I didn't respond.

I thought she was right.

She would know.

"But don't worry, bunny, practice makes

perfect," she added with a smile, before leaving me alone once again.

CHAPTER 9

Gale's file on Collin was so enormous because she was beyond obsessed with him. Most of the information was rather innocuous because Collin was Collin, but apparently she wanted all of it in one place. Every single magazine and newspaper article about him was in that file. Not just the recent profiles from *Forbes* or *Fortune* or *Town & Country,* but even brief mentions, dating back to the early 2000s, that outlined his efforts at prep school lacrosse games, for example.

The file also contained the information about his episodes of clinical depression, formally diagnosed by the Case family doctor when he was a teenager. Collin had actually been up front with me about it when we started dating. He had been on and off various meds over the years but had yet to see a behavioral therapist about it. Likely because people like Hayes and Haven

Case didn't actually believe in therapy, they believed in prescriptions. Regardless, I wasn't deterred. I actually liked that he was a modern man, disclosing the state of his health with his future wife. I could handle it. Who among us hasn't had a bout with mental illness?

As it turned out there also were a few bits and bobs about me within Collin's file. Brief mentions in the ad trades, a basic printout of my former addresses dating back six years or so, not just my PO Box — so she *did* know about Morris and company; fine — and a few of my headshots printed out from the agency's team page. That was it? Gale. You have nothing!

Saturday arrived and I was off to Connecticut. I had never been to Collin's family home without him before. I was dreading it, since I would have no one on my side. Well, except for true buffoon Wren Daly. Haven sent a car for us; a tortuous forty-five minutes awaited me. I'd be forced to make idle chitchat with someone I usually spent time with soaked in sweat on a stationary bike, rarely speaking much at all. My preference. Chloe and Gale would already be at the compound, under the guise of preparing for the afternoon tea, but I knew it was because neither wanted to traverse alongside me. A silver lining.

Wren practically climaxed when the car arrived, manned by a stout, mustachioed gentleman. He donned a little hat and everything. Her ballooning lips fell open at the sight. "Oh my God, *look at him*! Bea! I thought we were just Ubering!"

"Collin's mother insisted." I smiled. Wren took my hands, squeezing them. I counted the seconds until she finally let go.

"I'm dying to meet her. I bet she's fabulous!" Wren crowed. I knew Haven would absolutely loathe Wren Daly and take as many subtle jabs aloud in her direction as she saw fit. Though she would likely, but incorrectly, put Wren and me in the same social bracket, I hoped Haven would ease up on me with some fresh blood to suck instead. A break in the clouds for the day ahead, for both of us. Because I knew Wren and I were not the same. Not in the slightest. Wren Daly could *never.*

A bottle of bubbly had been popped for us in the rear of the vehicle, compliments of Collin, and allegedly Hayes, though I'm sure he had no idea the tea was even occurring. But I wasn't above a cheeky noontime tipple, so I nodded when the driver asked if he could pour us each a glass before we set off.

"Cheers, girl!" Wren clinked her glass against mine and took an aggressive first sip of the champagne. Here we go. I had a feeling that the day was going to be extra difficult for Wren, since she was freshly dumped by a software engineer she had met on Hinge the year before. "I swear I thought he was gonna be good for me! I thought he would broaden my horizons, like, beyond the fitness sphere." When Wren said *sphere* her lips looked especially outrageous. A botched job she probably received gratis in exchange for a social post. Tragic. "Braden said all we had in common was sex, like that was a problem?" Wren droned on and on. "And like, isn't sharing your *different* interests part of a healthy relationship?"

"He's a loser, Wren." I had to humor her. "What man wouldn't want to be with an absolute goddess like you?" Speaking Wren's language was easy enough for me. I just didn't want to actively have to do it. Wren was beyond dull, but she was desperate to be my friend and I happened to have an opening so I prepared myself to listen to her insufferable chatter. She was a woman who fully subscribed to being a "girl's girl" in the emptiest way possible. She proclaimed about wanting to lift women up, called them *queens,* preached being "healthy" over "skinny" as if her clavicle wasn't a lethal weapon, love and light. *Always* love and light. I refilled her glass so she would keep drinking and keep talking. Then I only had to half-heartedly listen with a fake smile smacked upon my face for the duration of our journey.

"That's right." She grinned as I poured. "I don't think I could get serious with another man in tech again. Too in their heads, but like, weirdly shallow at the same time. I just wanna have fun and find my best friend. Like you and Collin!"

"That's sweet, but you know a man can't be your best friend, Wren."

"What are you talking about, yes they can, that's the whole point!"

"Collin isn't my best friend," I said.

"I bet you're his best friend."

Oh my God, could we please stop saying *best friend*?

"I'm actually not," I corrected her. "But you're going to meet her shortly."

"STAHP," she honked, her jaw going slack, resembling a sex doll.

"Seriously. Gale is his friend from childhood," I said. "She also just went through a breakup and I know it might seem unwise under normal circumstances, but trust me, you should totally ask her about it. You know how good it feels to bitch about your exes with someone else feeling just as miserable as you are." Wren nodded along, downing even more champagne. Perfection. Gale would hate Wren, too, but I suspected the feeling would be mutual and I was eager to see their meet-cute in real time.

"So who *is* your best friend?" Wren asked me, eagerly hoping for reassurance it was her. As if.

"She's dead," I said, my default reply to such questions. A normal person would give their condolences and move on, but it slipped my mind in the moment that Wren was anything but normal.

"Oh my God, Bea, I'm so sorry. What happened to her?" Wren was actually summoning tears for my loss. Awful, but I shouldn't have been surprised. I was in the presence of someone who openly referred to herself as an *empath,* a woo-woo self-diagnosis that is meant to herald emotional intelligence, but it really means the empath in question centers themselves in whatever tragedy or drama is at hand, instead of the person it's actually happening to — classic narcissism in my opinion.

Sure, I could have just said that Wren was

my best friend, avoiding the dead friend conversation entirely, but then she would have been insufferable about it all throughout the wedding planning and I'd rather spin incessant lies than seal *that* dark picture as my fate for the coming months. Why not lie? I was very good at it.

"She was murdered in my hometown," I whispered, a hush in my voice, really turning it on.

"Oh my God, are you serious, by *who*?" Wren drunkenly smacked me across the arm. I shrugged at her before looking out the window, wistful.

"The police never solved the crime."

"You mean her killer is still *at large*?" Wren exclaimed.

Ah, so she was a true crime fanatic like so many of her peers, a hobby I never understood. Grisly business that could happen to any one of us, at any time. I don't think most women realize how close we could all be to death at somebody's hand. Instead, they all seek out sordid stories for entertainment purposes, salivating over them, lapping up every horrifying detail. A false, not to mention sick, escape. But a breakup with tech bro Braden and consuming brutal murder investigations from the sidelines were probably all Wren's brain waves could handle on any given day. She was a fool. Mother would have thought so, too.

I nodded at Wren, solemnly for effect, and looked out the window again, signifying I wanted a change in subject, but she kept on talking. "Jeez. Remind me never to go to Wilmington."

I looked at her, raising an eyebrow.

"What makes you think the killer stayed in Wilmington?"

We rolled up to the Case compound and it was enough to send Wren into absolute hysterics again. The sheer size of the home was admittedly an arresting sight, one that I had gotten used to by then, but I delighted in her amazement at the grandiosity. Sure, I was equally agog the first time I saw the Case manse myself, the 1 percent in all its glory that very few are privy to, but I didn't let on externally. I pranced in there alongside Collin like I already belonged there. Another lesson from Mother. One of the most, if not *the* most, valuable. Meanwhile, Wren Daly had no earthly idea how to behave socially. For my purposes, she was perfect.

"So does she like to be called Haven or Mrs. Case? Are his sisters nice? Oh my God, I just got so nervous. Why am I so nervous?"

She had every reason to be nervous. She would not receive a warm reception.

"Just be yourself, Wren," I said, purposely giving her terrible advice. "They're all going to love you. Relax, this is going to be fun!" I grabbed her hand as we walked up to the door. Once again, Calliope was on greeting duty, radiating her hippie harlot energy, in a pale-yellow off-the-shoulder frock, bare feet and hot-pink toenails.

"Here comes the bride," she sang, a tinge of taunting in her voice. "Hello, I'm Calliope Case." Calliope held out her hand for Wren to shake, her signature saucy grin growing even larger at the sight of a stranger. Who did I bring to the lion's den?

"Nice to meet you. I'm Wren Daly." Wren waited a beat, as if Calliope would recognize her from social media. It took everything I had not to laugh out loud.

"Okay, come on in. All the ladies are eager to hear what the bride has to say today. Especially Gale. Were you at the engagement party, Wren?"

"Oh, I was in Ibiza," she said, exactly how you're hearing it, with the lisp. "I had to go for work, but yes, I was invited." She actually wasn't, but I could blame the guest list on Haven if it came up later.

"Let's get a look at that thing in the light

of day," Calliope said, snatching my hand to inspect my ring more closely.

"Isn't it fabulous?" Wren stuck her nose in next to Calliope's. "Did you post it on IG yet, Bea?"

Calliope scoffed at Wren, answering for me. "Not unless she wants to be robbed. Never post the family jewels online. Amateur hour."

Calliope openly laughed at her and I could tell Wren was embarrassed. I nearly felt bad for the girl, but I had wanted the sharks to attack someone else in that house for a change. It was Wren's whole reason for being as far as the wedding party was concerned.

Wren and I followed Calliope through the halls and out to the back terrace that overlooked the pool and the gardens. Wren could hardly form words at the sight of it all, which was probably for the best. The words would come eventually, I was banking on it. Haven, Chloe and Gale were seated outside with drinks. "There they are." Chloe sighed, sporting dark sunnies, a big hat and a red lip.

"Hello, girls," Haven chimed in, cracking only the smallest of smirks, alluding to being on her second G and diet T.

"Hi, everyone! I'm Wren Daly!" Wren felt

the need to announce herself again and at a much higher decibel, digging her own grave even further in Calliope's estimation, who snorted to herself.

"Come join us." Haven motioned to empty seats.

"I was just admiring Bea's ring in the sunlight," Calliope said as I took an open seat next to Haven, asserting myself once again to my mother-in-law-to-be. I noticed she did a once-over on it and nodded in approval. A hard-fought acknowledgment considering they wouldn't bequeath the family heirloom. Gale was in a floral sundress, shockingly appropriate for the event, and it made me wonder if Chloe had given her some guidance, and if so, *why*? Was Chloe in on whatever Gale was scheming? I was wary, but I greeted both of them with sweet smiles.

"Did Sylvia help him pick it out?" Gale asked, that venom in her voice again.

"Who's Sylvia?" Chloe asked.

"Coll's new assistant. Apparently she's super hot. I heard Dad use the term *leggy*, so we know what that means." Calliope grinned, but Haven didn't look amused by that at all.

"You've met Syl?" I asked Gale, remembering that she hadn't made much of an impression on Syl.

"Just on the phone." Gale shrugged. "She's sweet. So . . . what is everyone *reading*?" Gale asked the group, livening up the place as usual, but I knew she was trying to rile me up about the stolen file.

"God, nobody cares, Gale." Calliope dismissed her with a flick of her wrist, flouncing down in a chair.

"Sit, sit," Haven commanded Wren, who was completely out of her element. The staff handed us glasses of champagne, Wren grabbed one before anybody else, and the afternoon tea was in full swing with canapés and caviar and cunty behavior.

"This is a *vibe,*" Wren said out loud, taking snaps on her phone, mortifying everyone. I thought Haven might have asked her to stop taking unsolicited photos of the grounds, but she felt like playing with Wren instead.

"Wren, where do you hail from?" Haven asked.

"Oak Park, Illinois. Just outside of Chicago. But I've been in New York since college."

"Columbia? NYU?" Haven's nose turned up ever so slightly at the latter.

"FIT," Wren replied. Haven would have furrowed her brow if she could, but her daughters were excellent at deciphering her frozen expressions by then. I was learning, too.

"The Fashion Institute, Mom. We've been to some of their events. It's a good school for that type of thing," Chloe explained.

"Ah," Haven mused. "And how do you know our Bea?"

That was a first. It was odd to hear Haven claim me as one of their own for the first time. I felt strangely proud and wished Collin had been there to hear it, too. That said, Gale definitely heard it. I watched her openly shudder. *Heavenly.*

"We work out together." Wren grinned.

"I see. How nice. You are both very fit. Toned. Not just naturally thin. It shows that you work at it. Kudos."

Haven, petite with minimal effort, smiled slyly, taking another sip of her drink. Well, that was one way to burn a pretty girl. Impressive.

"Chloe got a little fat when she went to college," Calliope declared, firming up her position as my favorite. Chloe was irate. "What?" Calliope asked her sister. "It all came off when we went to the Southampton house that summer. Mom saw to that."

"*Yes,* I did," Haven said. "Oh, Chloe. It's all right. It's very easy to go off the rails after leaving home for the first time. All of those snacks available at all hours of the night. It could happen to anybody."

"And the beer!" Wren added. "At least that's what I imagine with the traditional college experience. My college wasn't really like that, since it was so specific to fashion. Sometimes I regret not going to a Big Ten school or someplace like that. I think I would have loved it."

"I went to *Yale,*" Chloe said definitively, slow-blinking in Wren's direction. Wren took a submissive bite of her lobster quiche in response, so I thought I'd take the heat off her momentarily and really get things going. Gale was suspiciously quiet and I wanted to poke the bear. It was time. I licked my lips.

"So, I'm sure you're all wondering why Haven is generously hosting us here today, and the reason is that, well, you're all very special to me, and to Collin, and so I wanted to ask the four of you to be my bridesmaids for the wedding."

"Yay!" Calliope cheered, genuinely happy at the request. "Nobody's ever asked me to be in their wedding before."

"I wonder why." Chloe took the opportunity to bite back at her sister, tapping the side of her nose out of Haven's sight.

"Bitch," Calliope muttered under her breath, but didn't deny the accusation.

"Of course we will, Bea," Chloe said, nonplussed. "It's an honor."

"On that note, who is the maid of honor?" Haven asked me.

"I don't want to play favorites. It's not really necessary," I replied. It seemed old-fashioned to denote a maid of honor, plus I wasn't actually close with any of these women. It didn't make any sense, but I had a feeling Haven wasn't going to let me off so easily.

"*Someone* has to be your maid of honor, Bea. It's tradition," Haven implored.

"I'll do it!" Wren offered, a bit too eager for everyone's taste. I realized I wasn't going to get out of making this decision so I went with the obvious choice.

"While I appreciate the enthusiasm, Wren, I'd like to ask Gale," I said without a moment's hesitation. Gale just about choked on her pâté. "Well, you are the closest to Collin. That's very obvious," I challenged her. "I'm sure it would mean a lot to him. And to me. You know him better than anyone, right?"

She *blushed.* How embarrassing.

"That's sweet," Calliope said, albeit skeptically. "Isn't that sweet, Mom?"

"Very. Nora and Royce will be touched, too."

"I cannot wait to meet your parents, Gale," I said to her. "It will be so nice to get to know each other better through this experience." She still hadn't uttered a word or formally accepted my invitation.

"Marcy and I already got started on the guest lists for the shower and the wedding. We can review them together soon," Haven said to me.

Gale's lips parted. She was about to speak. Something had compelled her. *Finally.* Where was my girl?

"Are you inviting the Bradfords?" Gale asked Haven, but she was looking at me as if the question were a mysterious trump card, ready to play when the moment was ripe. This was the first I'd heard of the Bradfords, but by the way she said it, I knew it wouldn't be the last. Haven looked deep in thought at Gale's question. It was clearly controversial.

"Hmm, we should probably discuss that with Collin before making a decision."

"I agree it should be run by him, but I don't see how you could omit the Bradfords from the guest list," Gale said to Haven. "It's Collin's *wedding.*"

"It's not Mr. and Mrs. Bradford that she's

worried about," Chloe said cryptically.

"Who are the Bradfords?" I asked, taking the bait.

"Friends of *our* families," said Gale, accentuating the pronoun in an attempt to hurt me. "Were they on the list for the engagement party, Haven? I noticed they weren't there."

"Alan and Pippa were in Europe for weeks at the start of the summer so we didn't formally invite them, but they know of the engagement. I didn't think to include David in their absence and Collin didn't correct me when he reviewed the list."

"The boys definitely won't want Dave at the wedding. The *girls,* however . . ." Calliope erupted into laughter and Chloe joined in. Gale remained stone-faced, laser focused on me.

"Calliope, stop that right now," Haven chided Calliope.

"I know, I know. I'm just saying. Come on, Mom. You know I'm right."

"It's not the boys' weddings, though," Gale said. "It's Collin's. It won't look good if the Bradfords aren't invited. It won't look good at all."

"I suppose not," Haven agreed.

"There's always the possibility that Dave might not even come. He's always traveling," Chloe said.

"Dave *always* comes," Calliope said, adding quickly, "to parties. Events. Weddings. If he's invited, he'll make it a point to be there."

I was getting supremely annoyed that I wasn't in the know about this person, but I couldn't let on and give Gale the satisfaction. Luckily, Wren did my dirty work for me. "Who's Dave?" she asked, then hopefully added, "And is he single?"

"*Perpetually,* and that's on purpose," Chloe said.

"I think you'll really like him, Bea." Gale scrunched her nose at me.

"Gale," Haven said under her breath before taking another sip of her cocktail.

"He's betting on it, I'm sure. Going four for four." Calliope giggled.

"What will I like about him, Gale?" I asked her outright.

"I just think you'll get a kick out of him, that's all." She grinned.

"She means Dave's a bit of a lady-killer," Haven said, which made Chloe and Calliope laugh out loud, splashing some of their drinks.

"That's putting it mildly! Dave's a total manwhore," Calliope said. "He got around with some of the boys' wives and girlfriends, and at this point nobody is friends with him anymore. Well, except for Gale."

"That's only because he doesn't want to sleep with her," Chloe pointed out, much to my delight.

"I don't want to sleep with him either," Gale said, defending her honor. "Look, say what you want about Dave Bradford, but he's one of us. That means something and Collin knows that, too."

"And you think he'll want to sleep with me?" I asked them all, emboldened by their salacious chatter.

Calliope was uproariously laughing now. "Yeah, duh!"

"Girls." Haven snorted, just as amused. "That's enough."

"I'm sure Bea has had a line out the door her whole life, but she has selected our dear Collin," Chloe said, slurping her drink. Wasn't that a compliment? So she couldn't be on Gale's side, could she?

"Don't worry, Bea. We're just teasing you," Gale said, no trace of a smile at all.

"And Gale is right. Dave and the Bradfords are a part of our lives, so . . ." Haven said authoritatively, to the point that I knew this illustrious Dave Bradford would be at my wedding. "That's enough of this talk now. Those indiscretions of Dave's are all in the past and have nothing to do with Collin or Bea."

"A bit of a lady-killer," Chloe repeated, still giggling. "Honestly, Mom."

Haven began to discuss color schemes and the shower and flowers while I put two and two together. I caught Gale staring at me, swirling a straw around her glass, looking quite pleased with herself.

Of course.

Dave Bradford was Cat Man.

Chapter 10

Dave Bradford. How anticlimactic, unlike the recurring sex dreams I had been having about him. I was hoping for a more fanciful moniker like Pacey or Dylan or Xander, but I suppose life wasn't a salacious teen soap for my viewing pleasure. What I really craved were the details about his alleged affairs with his friends' partners — Hannah, Elizabeth and Paisley, I presumed, the Tory Burch Trifecta; who knew they had it in them? — but it was far too inappropriate an ask in front of my future in-laws.

However, with that revelation, it was even *more* infuriating that Dave hadn't hit on me when the opportunity presented itself in Gale's building. But I suppose he didn't know I was Collin's fiancée. He was a man who loved the forbidden. How delectable for me, but I would have to slap my hand away should it get too close. A tawdry affair with a man like that for the sake of the thrill was a little too much like Mother for my taste.

But that didn't mean I couldn't have *any* fun with it. I was hoping Collin would be up for some goss when I arrived home after tea time. He had to know the scoop and if I poured us a drink or two, he'd give me the goods. "Babe?" I called out for him, surprised he wasn't waiting in the wings, anxious for my triumphant return. I had texted him that I was on my way back and that it went quite well, all things considered, so I was insulted when he didn't respond immediately.

"Collin?" I called out again. Nothing.

I went upstairs to find him fast asleep in the middle of the afternoon. Let me tell you that the sight of a grown man in the center of a king bed, curled up in the fetal position like a little boy, was not what I had hoped for when I was all riled up about Cat Man. I didn't want to outright wake Collin like some sort of harpy, so I slithered into the master bath and shut the door just loudly enough to rouse him and regain his focus.

"Bea?" I heard, muffled through the door.

"Just a minute! Sorry, babe, didn't mean to wake you," I lied. I took a few seconds to primp in the mirror and rejoined Collin in the bedroom. "You were fast asleep! Are you ill?" I asked him.

"No. Just tired. How was it?"

"It was really great! Everyone's excited." I sat down next to him on the bed, animated and adorable. "Even your mother. I can tell. We shared laughs! I do believe I'm winning them over. No surprise there, right?" I went in for a kiss and he met the bid for affection with little enthusiasm. A mere peck. The way you'd kiss a dowdy old aunt with a goiter on Easter Sunday. Well, excuse me.

"That's great," he said, his eyes closing once again, leaning back into the pillow. Now he was really irritating me, so I wouldn't dance around the subject of Dave as initially planned for the fun of it. I needed Collin's full attention at all times so I could use him appropriately.

"Dave Bradford came up in conversation."

"Oh yeah?" He sat up quickly, visibly perturbed. Excellent. "What about him?" Collin asked.

"There was a bit of debate about his rightful place on our invite list."

"Rightful place?"

"That seemed to be the consensus, particularly where Gale was concerned. Your mother initially said she'd talk to you about it first, but then my maid of honor basically declared that it was nonnegotiable due to his notable stature amongst the in-crowd."

"I like Dave," Collin said. I could tell he meant it, but he was looking at the ceiling, conflicted. Then his eyes were back on me. "Wait, *Gale* is your maid of honor?"

"I thought you'd appreciate that. I know she's very dear to you, and I couldn't pick between your sisters, that wouldn't be fair. And Wren, bless her, would be too hands-on for my comfort level. So yes, Gale seemed like she might be a good guide through the madness. I really think she's come around on me anyway." Laughable, but I sold it.

"Cool," Collin replied, completely convinced. "I'm glad you guys are bonding after everything. And she's right about Dave. He should be there."

"Well, great. I can't wait to meet him," I said, only slightly concerned by the thought of Dave bringing up our elevator rendezvous on the UWS, when I pretended to be a completely different person, at my wedding.

"You love me, right?" Collin asked me, curling his knees up to his chest, looking like a small child again. I didn't care for it at all.

"Collin! What kind of question is that? Of course I do," I said, waggling my bedazzled ring finger in his face. He often enjoyed the playful side I presented, but this time he wasn't cracking a smile.

"I know that. I love you, too." He took my hand. "This is going to sound a little weird, but would you mind keeping some distance from Dave? For me? I mean, say hello, be polite and all that, just . . . don't get too close. I like the guy a lot, we go way back, but he can be kind of . . . I don't know how to put it. A troublemaker, I guess."

"Well, I hate trouble," I lied, kissing Collin on the neck. "At least any trouble having to do with you." I moaned a little, signaling I was in the mood for some hanky-panky, expecting a warm reception from my fiancé.

"I'm still pretty tired," he said, rubbing my back. "Do you mind if I get a few more winks in?"

"Sure," I said, pulling away and picking up on the hint that he wanted me to leave my own goddamn bedroom. I was incensed. Why was *he* so tired? I just spent what should have been a leisurely weekend afternoon to myself with literal hellhounds in the suburbs. But I'd let him sleep. It would be of no use to me to pick a fight. Eye on the prize.

I settled into the living room sofa with my laptop and shifted focus to my career to take the edge off. I hadn't lost sight of raising a little hell with Len Arthur and the agency after the Collin kerfuffle. Some casual petty revenge laced with genuine career progression. After all, staying anywhere too long is just leaving money on the table. I gussied up my résumé and LinkedIn profile. I went through pending contact requests and accepted the ones I deemed appropriate, although most were from odd-looking men in middle management all over the country. A fact of life as a woman with an attractive online headshot.

I accepted Syl Austin's earnest invitation to connect without any hesitation and then began to peruse the litany of vacancies at advertising agencies across the city. One of them would be so lucky. In the midst of hunting, I was surprised to receive a text from her. Strange, especially on the weekend.

Are you looking? I won't tell anyone, the message said. So she kept up with the lurkers on her LinkedIn profile? Same, honestly.

Won't confirm or deny, I responded, imagining her laughing.

If you are, I can email you a list of internal no-go agencies. Hayes has a known shit list. I'm assuming you'll want to take us with you wherever you go? She ended the message with a smiley face.

I do love a long-standing feud. Yes. Please send, I replied.

How about that? Sweet Syl was looking out for me. My initial instinct was suspicion, but that was just my nature. I reframed my thought process, leaning into the logic over general mistrust. My fiancé was Syl's boss. She wouldn't screw me over.

Soon enough Syl inboxed me the rather robust list of agencies the Case Company refused to work with or had already worked with, unsuccessfully. Still, that left plenty for me to prospect, and I prepared twenty-seven emails to be delivered directly to the hiring manager of each agency on Tuesday morning around 11:30 a.m. Engaging in new business on a Monday was a fool's errand. Tuesday late morning would be prime time. I assumed I'd have a new offer in hand within three weeks at the most, following several rounds of interviews. I practically foamed at the mouth, envisioning when I'd give my notice to Len. The devastation that would surely sweep across his wizened face would be such a lovely sight.

I was so productive that I deserved a reward.

Dave Bradford's social media profiles were sparse, which I respected on a personal level, but selfishly, I wanted to waste away the remainder of the afternoon scrolling through his Instagram. I wanted all the fun of analyzing posts from years gone by so I could rip apart his old girlfriends and scan for visual evidence of his family wealth in the background. But he didn't even have an Instagram. Just an old Facebook account that was relatively locked down, since we were not friends.

Hmm, no matter. I'd just pop onto Collin's account to check out Dave's profile. I'd been regularly hacking into Collin's online accounts since our third date. I had wanted to know what I was getting into socially, plus it was useful to gather a few grenades to toss at opportune moments, getting him to believe we were "meant to be" based on mutual interests. Collin publicly adored the Yankees, *Peaky Blinders* and the ASPCA, so I did as well. His bank account balance obviously checked my boxes and his social accounts were full enough to pass judgment: Collin Case was a nice man, but not a particularly interesting one. Ideal for Bea.

Meanwhile, Dave's Facebook profile was practically an artifact from the golden age of the platform. It was a hotbed of photo albums from years gone by, mostly highlighting innocent debauchery from his years at university, but in that charming way you're allowed to be when you're in your early twenties and white and male. The only somewhat recent update was a job change.

Self-Employed/Angel Investor.

Well, if that didn't just scream independently wealthy?

The most current photos of Dave were tagged by other people, mostly women, women I assumed he had been romantically involved with at one time or another due to their close proximity in the images. Dave was supremely photogenic, always smiling with his pristine teeth, the perfect size for his perfect head, unlike *some* people, and he was always touching the waist, bum or just under the breast of every woman in the frame. Lady-killer indeed.

Dave Bradford's allure was becoming much too great for me, so I logged out and joined Collin in the bedroom, hoping the tides had turned for some afternoon delight. Dave was exactly the type of man I could have a very good time with, but at what cost really? I wasn't in my early twenties anymore, cavorting with every bad boy with BDE in a band on the LES in my off time. That had been only temporary until it was finally time to focus. And grown men don't *marry* twenty-one-year-olds unless there's something really wrong with them, and I certainly didn't want to end up with any of that clientele on my then-roster. That was just the day job of my youth. I didn't start the hunt in earnest until I was an age-appropriate twenty-five. And look at where I was now. I couldn't derail my plans for a tryst with Dave Bradford, no matter how satisfying it would be.

I tried to arouse Collin, hoping I could coax him from his slumber, making it obvious I would be on top so he could still relax, yearning to scratch my own itch, but he still wasn't having it. It was disconcerting to say the least, very unlike Collin to rebuff me. I didn't appreciate it. Literally hot and bothered, I left him in bed and took a shower instead. I'd recently had multiple heads installed.

As predicted, I received three offers of employment from highly acclaimed advertising agencies within weeks. One was boutique, the second was enormous with thousands of employees globally and the third one was somewhere in the middle. It had a firm hold in the tried-and-true advertising tactics, but still looked to the future without being considered "too modern" for the old-fashioned clients, not unlike the Case Company. They also gave me the highest offer, so I closed the deal with them after a confident negotiation, nearly doubling my current salary.

Now it was time for the best part.

"Rhonda. Len." I was holding court in my office with the two of them, ready to perform the song and dance wherein I would give the requisite two weeks' notice, knowing that I would be dismissed immediately. It was the advertising way. "I have decided to move on from the agency," I continued. "I thank you for the opportunities you've given me during my time here and I hope we can stay in professional touch. I have a letter for you, in writing, outlining my resignation with two weeks' notice, and I wish you both the best. I'm happy to be as helpful as I can during this transition."

The little color he had drained completely from Len's face.

Rhonda from HR cleared her throat. "We appreciate the notice, but per our policy with the nature of our business, we will have to ask you to leave immediately after relinquishing your computer and building identification," she commanded robotically, as an HR professional is prone to do.

"Now, hold on a minute there, Ronnie,"

Len said, waving his hand in her face dismissively. Oh, what a thrill. He was going to grovel; I couldn't wait to hear it. "Is there anything we can do to get you to stay, Bea? I assume you're going to another agency? You don't strike me as the type of woman to ditch her career once she lands a husband."

"Obviously not, Len. This isn't the 1960s."

"Right. So would a counteroffer be of interest to you at this juncture? We will make it worth your while, I can promise you that."

"I appreciate it, Len, but I find that after loyalty has been questioned, all bets are off in the future. How could you trust me again with one foot out the door? It would become a festering problem, I'm sure of it. I'm sorry, but I just don't see it working out."

"This is business, Bea. I think we can all handle a frank discussion about money. Can't we?"

"Len," I said, summoning my most patronizing of voices. "I think it's best for both parties if we call it a day."

"But there are three parties to consider now, aren't there?"

Well, he wasn't being subtle about the Case Company. I loved watching him scramble, grasping at straws, all to keep me at the agency.

"That's true, but I'm no longer considering your party, Len. Thanks for everything." I grinned, standing up from my chair. I already had my desk cleaned out, computer and badge ready to submit, so I floated on out of there with my head held high, wearing a short skirt that would have been wildly inappropriate without nylons. Still, it was a subtle invitation for Len and the rest of them, Jessica McCabe included, to kiss my ass.

The Case Company would call to cancel their contract the next day.

Syl and I had made plans to take a long lunch together to celebrate my new job. Collin was invited, but he had taken the day off, citing he wasn't feeling well and needed rest. I'd have to address it later. I was all too ready to toot my own horn. I deserved it. My new office was much closer to the Case Company, a few blocks away, so when Syl asked me to lunch on my first day, I figured it was harmless enough, since I enjoyed her company.

"My boyfriend and I are thinking about moving to Queens," she shared with me over fast casual sushi. "After we get married, we want to have a baby and I don't think we could afford Brooklyn anymore. Oh, hold on." Syl pulled a small brush out of her bag and gave my front tresses a quick once-over, gently grooming me like a mother would a child. "Windy today, just a little knot. I got it."

"Thanks. Well, what does John do?" I asked, slightly jarred by her touch, but also oddly grateful. "I don't think you've ever told me." Most of our conversations thus far had revolved around me. I *was* the more interesting one, bless her.

"He makes pizzas at his family's restaurant. They're actually pretty successful, but John is kind of a, uh, wild soul, God love him, so I don't see the D'Attomos giving him any real responsibility soon. They have other favorite sons, older ones. I'm sure he'll get a piece, but we won't be able to rest on our laurels. So we're relying on *my* successful climb up the corporate ladder."

"What were you doing before the Case Company?"

"Retail. I was a manager at H&M."

"And you didn't want to climb their ladder?"

Syl popped a piece of a California roll in her mouth, talking as she chewed. "Meh, retail is a thankless job. Everyone treats you like you're a piece of shit, especially when you're the manager. So when I heard about this opportunity, it seemed like it might be less of a headache. It's about the same pay, but better hours and better benefits. And I only have to deal with a few assholes instead of a lot of them." She snorted and then stopped herself. "Not that Collin's an asshole! He's actually a very nice man, Bea. All things considered."

"What kind of things?"

"You know. I mean, no offense, but you guys are fucking rich people."

Oh, how I *loved* hearing her say that, but I still wanted her to be able to relate to me. I wasn't like them, that had been made abundantly clear, even if I still wanted to join their club. Regardless, I inexplicably wanted Syl to be my friend. Maybe it was the caring, maternal energy she gave off, being a few years older than me, but I found myself liking the way she made me feel. It made me want to share things with her. Not *everything,* but something. "I guess so," I said, "but I don't come from the kind of money that Collin does. Come on, you saw how his family was about our engagement."

"Pretty cold."

"Downright subzero," I said, swallowing some sashimi.

"Where are you from, Bea?" Syl asked me

in a way that was so sincere, so genuinely curious. Her voice was soft and she looked me in the eye. She wasn't just making polite conversation. She really wanted to know.

I gave her the North Carolina spiel. She hung on every word like she was memorizing it. I adored having her full attention. We were bonding, even if it was under false pretenses, at least on my end. I wanted to know more about her, too. She was so pretty and despite the frequent cussing, she was obviously intelligent. So how did she end up in such a humdrum life? Why didn't she strategize better? Who'd raised her? So many missed opportunities, and the fiancé? Surely she should have dumped him. He wasn't even fit to inherit a pizza parlor.

"What about you?" I asked her.

"I'm from here, but I was a foster kid," she told me. "I went into the system as a four-year-old."

Well, that explained a lot. It endeared her to me even more. She didn't have anybody. Yes, I had a horrible mother, but at least I had somebody.

"My dad is in prison," she added, a tinge of embarrassment in her voice. Poor thing. But we all had *something,* not that I could tell her mine.

"Oh, Syl. I'm sorry to hear that. Do you

speak to him?"

"Oh, yeah! He's great. Like, the best guy I know. I miss him all the time."

"Is he nearby or anything?"

"Upstate." I noticed Syl's responses were getting shorter. I could hear the pain in her voice. The last thing I wanted to do was comfort a woman crying in public about her incarcerated father, no matter how much I was starting to like her, so I changed the subject, bringing it back to number one.

"Families come in all forms, Syl. I miss my parents, too."

"I bet," she said, but the tone in her voice had changed. It was cutting. Dark. Different. We locked eyes, but she looked away first, out the window, going somewhere unknown in her mind. I had never recognized a piece of myself in Syl before that moment. I almost reached out to touch her, but thought better of it. I still wanted to take it slow. A few seconds more and she noticed that I noticed the change in her demeanor and ended her thought on a lighter note.

"But, Bea, the good news is that you're gaining a whole new family soon!"

"Ah, yes, as the newest member of the Case dynasty, I'm sure I'll be privy to all of their centuries-old secrets and charming quirks. Come on, Syl. They won't let me in. Not really. Collin seems to, though, and that will be enough for me."

"You're a lucky girl, Bea." Syl grinned and snapped her chopsticks at me, but I actually couldn't tell if she was being sincere or not.

It made me like her even more.

Francis

NEW YORK CITY

Mother tells me that Francis is a very nice man who will provide a very nice life for us. I've never been to New York before. I always thought she was avoiding it. It feels different this time. She feels different. She's fussing with me in the back of the car. Fluffing my hair. Picking at my dress. Like she's nervous. But Mother never gets nervous.

"You have to look perfect," she says.

I catch the driver looking at me through the rearview mirror. Mother hasn't stopped talking the entire time about someone like Francis being unprecedented for us. A whole new ball game. The school I'll get to go to is elite. I'll have every opportunity available to me.

We can't screw this up.

I can't screw this up.

If I love her, I won't screw this up.

Remember, bunny, we're a team.

■ ■ ■ ■

Francis is a man with staff. They dress in black. Quiet. The man who drives us. The man who answers the door. The woman who brings us tea. The other woman who talks to Mother privately, leaving me alone with another woman who dusts a nearby bookshelf, but I know she's watching over me while they're gone. I'm not an idiot. I can feel her eyes on me. She doesn't speak to me.

No one has spoken to me.

Mother returns with the woman and tells me to go with them. The woman is tall, she wears a long black dress with a white collar, and her hair is in a bun. She could be Mother's age, but it's hard to tell, since she hasn't faced me at all.

The house is enormous, much larger than it looks from the outside. We're led up stairs, down hallways, around corners. Everything is dark and wooden and old, but obviously expensive. Finally, the woman in black opens a door, a bedroom inside of it, and then stands a few feet away from the door, facing away from us. She clears her throat.

When I go to follow Mother inside, Mother stops me.

"You keep going," she says. The house is quiet. Too quiet. I want to ask Mother a hundred questions. She actually looks nervous and now I'm nervous and I have no idea why. As if reading my mind, Mother softens her tone, running a hand through my hair. "This'll be good for us. Don't worry. You're a star."

A star? A new compliment from Mother feels heavenly and frightening.

I do as I'm told and follow the woman back downstairs and down another corridor. We stop in front of a pair of double doors, one of them slightly ajar. She knocks loudly, with purpose, and it takes me by surprise. I flinch.

"Come in." The man's voice behind the door is low but friendly. The woman takes her post at the side of the door again, showing her back to me. I open the door and step inside. The room is an office and it reminds me of Dean's, and I'm stunned because I haven't thought about him in so long. A big wooden desk, a big leather chair, big bookshelves with big books, a big clock, everything is big.

Except for Francis.

He's behind the desk, fit and trim and tan and somewhat slight, in a navy polo. Casual and smart. He smiles at me. He could be someone's dapper dad. He's different from the rest. No gray in his hair. No protruding belly. No unsightly features. Francis is very handsome. A first for Mother.

"You must be Fleur," he says, standing up to shake my hand. We're nearly the same height in my sandals. He holds my hand tight and wraps his other hand over it, looking me in the eye, so familiar.

Like we've met before in another life.

Like we're friends.

Like I'm an adult.

"Welcome! Did you get anything to eat yet?" Francis asks me, and I shake my head. "We'll fix that. How was your flight?"

"Very nice," I reply, but it was so much more than that. Mother and I flew into New York on Francis's private jet. Incredible. The flight attendant even offered me a small glass of champagne. Mother said I could drink it. She had one, too. We both gazed out the window as we sipped. We didn't toast or clink glasses, but she said I should enjoy it and all that was to come because we were finally going to get everything we wanted.

"I like your dress, Fleur," Francis says, putting a hand on my shoulder, feeling the fabric between two of his fingers, just for a moment. The dress is black and white, from the junior's department at Bloomingdale's. It's my favorite. It makes me feel like an adult.

"Thank you," I say. I rub my right foot against my left ankle. An itch I need to scratch. I almost tip over in my sandals, but Francis steadies me, putting both hands on my shoulders now.

"You don't have to be nervous, Fleur," he says. "You're home now. I'm Francis and we're all just thrilled you're here. Your mother tells me you're very smart and accomplished already, so I'm sure your star will only rise here in Manhattan. It's very nice to meet you."

That word again.

Star.

All of a sudden I'm a star?

I'll take it.

Francis raises an eyebrow, looking behind me, and the woman has reappeared. "We'll get you back to your mother now," he says. "I'll see you later."

"Okay," I say. "It's very nice to meet you, too, Francis." I trip again in my sandals, they're probably an inch too high to be comfortable, and I immediately feel like an idiot. Why am I being so awkward? But he lets out a huge laugh and I'm relieved. Francis comes closer to me. He wraps his arms around me. He kisses me on the cheek. His lips are wet. They linger. He breathes onto my neck. Then into my ear. I don't move. Stay still.

"You're cute, Fleur," he says before returning to his desk. "Really cute."

Mother tells me all the time that she's proud of me. Francis adores me. His friends do, too. It's easy, isn't it? It's so easy to entertain a man, the right type of man, to get what you want. She always wants a full report and I provide it, proud of myself. She's been taking care of me for so long. It's time for me to return the favor, and she's right, it's quite easy. I wear little outfits at the parties and laugh and fill their drinks. I don't mind them looking at me. Not really. Men are always looking at me. At least I'm getting something out of it this time.

Francis introduces me to his friends at his parties and expects me to remember their names, so I do. He tells me later those aren't their real names. It's just for fun. It's all pretend. Just a place to blow off steam, an innocent gathering, something most people wouldn't understand, but I understand, don't I? Because I'm mature. One of the select few.

Of course, other girls are there, too. Some

of them look older than me and act like it, too, but Francis always says I don't have to do anything I don't want to do and that if anyone tells me differently, I should find him. That hasn't really happened yet. I don't mind being grazed by a hand here and there. It's just a hug, or just a little kiss. Whatever. It's nothing, just like Mother says. She says that's just a part of it. Means it's working, that I'm working.

She's proud of me.

Some of the other girls are there with their mothers. Some are even with their fathers, but I stay away from them. Something inside tells me to, and when I tell Mother, she agrees with me. Those are the type of men to be avoided. Most of the girls are with nobody and I definitely stay away from them. They like to go far, that's what Mother says. Alcohol and pills and powders in other rooms. I don't want any of it and I'm always told I don't have to, but it still makes my stomach turn. I see what it does to them. It feels like an alarm going off in my head. Francis asks me once if I want a little taste. He doesn't say of what, but I say no thank you and he shrugs, not bothered. Whatever you want, Fleur. Whatever I want? I feel fine and this is pretty easy, but I still wish I could pretend this is normal. I know that it isn't. At the house. On the planes. In other places. I'm never alone. I never feel in danger. It's just a touch. Just a hug. Just a little kiss. Just a massage. Mother is always there, or at least outside the door. Watching. Observing. Never engaging. She says she's there to protect me so I believe her. Hasn't she protected me my whole life?

So many men. Watching and looking and touching, just ever so slightly. Waiting for me to say it's okay for more, but I never do.

Leave them wanting more, Mother says. Always leave them wanting more.

I'm always returned to Francis.

I'm always returned to her.

"You're a star," she says to me. "Proud of you."

I don't try to make friends at school. They wouldn't understand. They're still kids and I'm an adult. I feel like one, anyway. Besides, my classmates are wretched. Uniforms accessorized with designer bags. I have the uniform. I have the bags. But who is my family? Where do they come from? New money or old money? I'll have all the wrong answers to the questions they'll have so I make sure I'm never asked them at all, staying far away.

When I have time to myself, I watch

television shows about normal teenagers. Girls from the wrong side of the tracks breaking the hearts of boys, with their hearts of gold, flip-flopping love stories with each passing season, blonde by brunette, in small oceanside towns where everyone is more than a little bit pretty, regular kids with summer jobs at seafood shanties delivering soliloquies to one another about the injustice of their adolescence, yearning to be adults already so their lives can really begin.

I'm jealous.

Francis watches his friend Diamond go too far at a party. I slap him on the hand. Francis immediately apologizes. To *him.* To Diamond. Then Francis grabs me by the wrist, snatching me out of the party. Mother watches but doesn't follow us. She stays still and stoic and calm. She looks disappointed in me.

"You're not a kid anymore, Fleur!" Francis barks at me in the hallway, just the two of us, alone. "What did you think was going to happen here? We let you take your time, you've had plenty of it, and if you want to stay here — if you and your mother want to stay here — you have to grow up. Okay? If she won't tell you that, I will, because I actually care about you."

My body feels like ice, but I cannot crack in front of him.

Or anyone.

I tell mother what happened with Francis later and she laughs at me. She shrugs and shakes her head. She knows this will get a rise out of me.

"But you knew that, didn't you? You're not an idiot."

"I thought I didn't have to do anything I didn't want to do!"

"Sure. But then you won't get very far, will you?"

"I thought I didn't have to be like those other girls."

"Bunny. We *all* have to be like those other girls. We just have to do it better."

I don't say anything in response. Do what?

"I don't want to leave yet," Mother adds. "Why don't you think about me instead of yourself for once. Isn't it my turn?"

Mother leaves me alone and I sit with that.

How could she say that when I'm always thinking of her?

But she never thought about me when I didn't want to leave all those times. Richard or Dean or Mike. Did she ever think about me at all or what I wanted? I always think about what she wants. What is she even talking about? *Her* turn? It was *my* turn, wasn't it? She could stay here with Francis, but I didn't have to. Maybe it would be good for us to figure it all out apart for a while. I don't know life without her, but I'm intrigued.

Sometimes the only team I want to be on is my own. At least I know who I can trust.

It's not like she would come find me.

I don't think so.

But I've never tried to leave her before.

I have $1,000 in cash in my hand from Francis after I ask him for it. After he bargains for it; I do what I have to do. Be like those other girls, but better. I am better. I think he knows I'm leaving. I think he's amused. I want to keep amusing him because I might need him later. I've been here for years now and I don't want him to be mad at me. What if I need his help one day? Especially without her.

I'll leave town. For a month, maybe a little more, maybe a little less. I take a train upstate. Everything gets smaller. I can do this, I tell myself. I can do this. I check into a small inn. Like something I've seen on TV. Like a regular girl. I pay in cash. I brainstorm in my notebook about what to do next, where I could go, what I can be. In the morning I apply to jobs in town. Like a regular girl, getting a regular job. Jobs that pay cash. I *need* more cash. I don't have identification. I'll figure that out when I go back. Francis will help me. Someone will help me. Look at me. I'm a star. Someone will always help a girl like me.

I'll fall asleep tonight dreaming about the future that will finally be mine.

But the knock on the door.

Fast and hard and full of rage.

I know who it is.

She found me.

Her bunny.

It sounds like she'll tear the door off the hinge if I don't answer it.

More knocks. No pauses. She doesn't stop.

Why wait?

Part of me is happy she came to find me.

Happy that I actually matter to her.

See, Francis? She actually cares about me.

Maybe we can go away together, Mother and me. Maybe she sees that I'm right. Maybe this is all I needed to do to get her attention.

I answer the door. I've never seen her look so angry with me in my life.

She cusses and screams and says we cannot go back to Francis's after this selfish stunt I've pulled.

We're in danger now and we have to leave New York immediately.

We've lost *everything* because of me.

She smacks me with full force across the face, more violently than she's ever hit me before, the crack of her hand echoing in my ears as I fall to the floor.

Mother bends down to look me in the eye.

She pushes the hair out of my face, hard, with the heel of her hand, not her fingertips, my head going right along with it. She tugs at my scalp.

"If you want to be a whore, if you *really* want to be an ungrateful little whore, so be it," Mother whispered to me.

A little incantation.

A little curse.

A little promise.

Chapter 11

The bridesmaids hosted my shower at Ladurée Soho. Yes, a French-themed bridal shower, truly the most cliché of selections, complete with a pastel macaron tower in my honor. Useless little things. Aesthetically pleasing to the eye but mediocre on the palate, and that's being generous. A waste of calories if you ask me, but no one ever questions the bride's refusal of dessert, as we're supposed to be watching our figure at all times leading up to the big day.

About seventy-five women I hardly knew were there for the intimate occasion. Haven absolutely refused Calliope's contemporary suggestion of a coed shower, bucking the latest trend. That was something we both agreed on, because a "couple's shower" should be the fucking wedding.

It was Wren's bright idea to have everyone wear shades of pink and red, in the spirit of love, so that all photos would have me, in white, at the center of them. A beaming ray of bridal light amidst a sea of adoration and support from the women in my life. I could just imagine Gale nodding along with the idea during their planning session, wanting to kill herself in the process, and definitely murder me first. I pretended to be excited about the shower, but the truth was that no one has ever been excited to attend a bridal shower. Including brides. Everything is little. Little sandwiches, little sweets, little favors, little brides — if they know what's good for them. And the bride must be constantly on and in a genuine state of surprise as she opens each gift, gifts that she literally selected and requested on a public registry that every guest has already viewed and passed judgment on, especially the chosen china pattern. And a bridal shower is not even an occasion where heavy drinking is encouraged to get through the two to three hours. See? Just a little party. Little sips of champagne only. Maybe Grandma gets a sherry. It's a stale tradition, but it was still tradition, something very important to Mrs. Haven Case.

I made sure Syl was invited. I thought it was appropriate enough to include her by then and I wanted a friendly companion nearby, especially if Gale pulled something like she did at the engagement party. Syl could be a stabilizing force so I could get my game face on. Our lunches were becoming more frequent and we had even indulged in a happy hour or two, sometimes with Collin in tow. He was supportive that I appeared to be making a real friend, something he hadn't witnessed before. Perhaps the professional boundaries were getting a bit muddled, but she was like my little pet, despite her years on me, always wanting to please me. I loved giving her advice about getting ahead at work and how to impress Collin. I could be a charitable person when it was warranted, unlike Mother. I genuinely wanted Syl to succeed! I wished I could give her dating advice, too. Maybe she would leave her unworthy fiancé and find an upwardly mobile man to exploit and also, for someone like her, to love. She would need both, I could tell that much. Essentially, I believed she could be more like me if she really set her mind to it. A little nudge here and there in the right direction could set her on course, unlike Wren Daly, who couldn't be course-corrected with a cattle prod she was so dense. I was even in Collin's ear about Syl sometimes, too. I asked him to look out for her career trajectory, without being too demanding. He would nod in approval, smiling, clearly tickled I was taking care of my friend. I shared that with her.

"You don't want to be an executive assistant forever, do you?" I asked Syl at the shower. We had managed to tuck ourselves away in the corner of the venue with champagne. "The possibilities are endless if you know what you're doing. You have real potential. I can see it."

Syl looked unsure. Maybe she was just not in the mood to talk about work at a party. Fair, but I didn't know why she seemed so distant. I was the bride, I should have had her full attention. "I don't know," she replied. "It's not a bad life if you have a good boss, which I do."

"Cute," I said.

"You look fucking amazing by the way," Syl said to me, artfully changing the subject with the highest of compliments, coming from the second-hottest person at the party. She looked amazing as well, if I'm being honest. Syl wore a shocking hot-pink off-the-shoulder bandage dress that made her fake tan really pop. She *nearly* showed me up, but I'd had professional glam done for the occasion, so fat chance competing with airbrushed skin and mink eyelashes.

"Thanks, Syl. I'm really glad you're here.

I barely know any of these people."

"Are you kidding? Thank you for inviting me! I'm dying to formally meet Mrs. Case and the wild sister."

"Calliope?"

"If you ask me, they were asking for trouble giving her a name like that!" She laughed, glancing over at Calliope, who was talking some poor woman's face off over by the macarons. A bump or two must have been had. "And I can't *believe* Chloe stuck to the dress code," Syl added. "I've never seen her in anything but black when she's at the office."

I laughed. "I'm sure it is painful for her to be shrouded in salmon right now, but familial duty calls. Can you believe I'm actually going to be related to these people?"

"No," Syl said, no longer laughing. "But here you are."

"I'll introduce you to Calliope. I suspect she might be a kindred spirit at heart."

"Oh yeah! She looks like she likes to party." Syl snorted. She was getting a little judgmental and I couldn't get enough of it. It was fun to talk a little shit with someone, and as if on cue to rain on my proverbial parade, we were interrupted.

"Well, you must be Miss Sylvia! Finally, we meet in person," Gale squawked. She approached Syl in a burgundy sheath with an unfavorable hemline smack-dab in the middle of her calves. *Burgundy.* Technically a shade of red, but surely she must have known that a frock the color of an aged wine was not really the vibe for a bridal shower. Nor was it remotely flattering on her dusty complexion. "We're so happy you could join us. I know Bea is very fond of you."

Gale pulled Syl in close, with her fingertips only. One of those half-hearted hugs reminiscent of Haven and likely Gale's mother. Syl fidgeted out of Gale's soft grasp, slightly taken aback by the maneuver. She must have been struck by the colloquial touch of a stranger, but I wasn't surprised. The gauge for Gale's social cues was almost always off-kilter. "Nice to see you," Syl said, eyes down at her feet. "Excuse me, ladies. I'm just going to run to the restroom. Does the bride need anything when I come back?"

"Oh, no. I'm just fine here with the maid of honor at my service," I said, noting the roll of Gale's eyes. Syl practically sprinted away from us and I couldn't blame her. I didn't feel like making conversation with Gale either. Plus, it would be wise of Syl to circulate and network a bit at the party. Perhaps she was taking my advice to heart.

"Are you enjoying yourself?" Gale asked

me, insincerity abounding.

"Immensely. Thank you so much for planning such a wonderful event. Now, where's your mother? I'd love to meet her." I smiled.

"I'm sure you'll cross paths. Haven will see to that." Gale sneered. "Are you thinking of your own mother today?"

"Of course. I wish she could be here," I said, shuddering internally at the thought. "I'm sure she would have loved the whole thing."

"You really think so?" She was laughing at me. "Perhaps." That was cruel. Even for Gale. Her contempt for me was growing, which could be good in theory. Typically, the higher the emotion, the larger the room for error.

"What would you know about it? I noticed you didn't have much on my lineage in your files."

Her eyes shifted from her mother at the gift table back to me. "I could tell Collin about your thievery," she hissed.

"Yes. You could, Gale." I brushed the side of her arm with my hand, wanting to feel the electricity between us. "But then he'd know you have a whole record of private information about him. And his entire family. And everyone else in this little perverse sect of society. And that might be kind of a turnoff, among other things. The Cases can be litigious." I pinched her full tricep, wanting her reaction to become more physical, but she didn't recoil at all. I should have done it harder.

"Assault?" She laughed. "My goodness, Bea. Someone's getting agitated. And it's still early!" She flashed her teeth at me, confident. "Don't talk to me about the Cases. You have no idea what people like us can do to women like you with a wave of our hand. One phone call. But you think you're special, right? I suppose in some ways you are. For example, I couldn't file away someone like you just like everybody else."

She had to be bluffing. I'd seen the files. Everyone was there. Even people I'd never heard of and of course I checked my former aliases — I covered my tracks just in case! I could have screamed. Gale should have been falling weaker with each passing day as the wedding approached, yet she seemed to be growing even more assertive. This grandstanding of hers felt like a tell, but Gale and I were not cut from the same cloth. Was she acting out due to losing or was she actually gaining on me? I looked around for Syl, in need of some grounding.

"I'm ready for a refill," I said to her, shaking my empty glass in Gale's direction. I needed her out of my face. She was right, I was getting flustered, and then there was no telling what I might do. Within reason — I wasn't my mother. I needed to keep my emotions in check. Always. Besides, Gale was the maid of honor. She was supposed to take care of me. At least in front of everyone at the party. She snatched the glass out of my hand with a smile and lumbered away, but I knew she wouldn't return. Not unless it was poisoned.

I glanced around the garden at the largely middle-aged crowd. They were all so similar. Haven Case. Nora Wallace-Leicester. Their friends. The women all wore Chanel or Diane von Furstenberg or Carolina Herrera, adorned with plenty of diamonds and assorted jewels from their husbands or families, possessing the type of glowing mature skin that only money and microneedling could buy. When they smiled, the skin around their eyes hardly creased, true age only detected by their hands. They all floated down from their ivory towers to attend the bridal shower of the country bumpkin about to infiltrate their personal Mount Olympus by marriage. Ah, well, have another, old girls. Cheers! A handful are always bound to get through over the years. Maybe even one of them, years ago, not that

I'd ever know.

Because once you were in, you were *in.*

Mother would have blown them all out of the water. She was always the most beautiful woman in the room.

I must have had an anxious look upon my face because Syl returned to my side with a bubbly beverage and a sweet burrow into my shoulder. A concerned friend. "Are you overwhelmed?" Syl asked me, stroking my arm softly.

"A little bit. It is pretty ridiculous, right? All of these people are here to celebrate me just because I'm getting married. They don't even know who I am."

"But you're not just getting married, Bea," she said. "You're getting married to *Collin Case,* perhaps the country's most eligible bachelor."

"How very *Tatler* of you, Syl." I laughed. I really did like her. And she was right. I *was* marrying Collin Case. No matter what. "I should have asked you to be a bridesmaid."

"Ha! I actually think it's better for our friendship that you didn't. Being a bridesmaid *sucks.*"

"Have you been one before?"

"Oh, yeah, more than a few times. Girls from my H&M days, a girl from the group home. Really, it's a punishment, which I know, I know, isn't *very nice,* but it's true. I mean, you know how it is."

"Not really. I've never been a bridesmaid before."

"Really?" Syl seemed genuinely shocked. Like I must have had scores of girlfriends over the years. She didn't know she was my first real friend.

"Well, I'm sure Wren will ask you when her time comes, and she'll pull every trick in the book," Syl explained. "She'll pick the worst color dress and make you go to Vegas for the bachelorette party and it'll cost a small fortune. All so you can share a queen bed with some weirdo she went to camp with when she was ten. Although, I guess *you* don't need to worry about the spending part." Syl started laughing. "She'll probably make you her maid of honor. Everyone always picks their richest friend so their parties are better. Hey, maybe *I* should ask you to be my maid of honor?" The way she rattled off all this information led me to believe she was a true authority on female friendship. I was agog. "I'm kidding," Syl continued. "I'm not doing bridesmaids. We'll probably just elope or have his family there. We'll see, we haven't planned shit yet. Anyway —"

"That's not why I picked Gale," I interrupted her, yearning to confide in her about the real reason, still unsure if I could.

"Obviously." Syl rolled her eyes. "So why *did* you?" Her voice lowered as if she was urging me to consider her a true confidante. I wanted to tell her secrets. Maybe this one was a good gateway to test the waters. It was such a mild bit of gossip, comparatively speaking. A reason that anyone could understand. And I knew that Syl would be supportive. That's just who she was. I could feel it, feel her.

"Gale's in love with Collin," I revealed, staying blunt about it, just in case. "So it's a keep-your-enemy-closer situation. And, truth be told, I think it's kind of entertaining to mess around with her."

"Hahaha, so you're a real girls' girl." Syl snickered, winking at me. I laughed along with her, not totally understanding what she meant, but it was exciting.

And a reminder that I should still proceed with caution.

I was forced to open presents in front of everyone, which I admittedly enjoyed. I appreciated undivided attention and uproarious applause for doing nothing but being Bea. Plus, Gale had to sit next to me and write down every single gift received, along with the name of the giver, so I could send the appropriate thank-you notes in a week's time. Frankly, I didn't know how she managed to do the job, particularly when the gift from her own mother was two sets of luxury bed linens. The imagery alone of my marital bed with Collin probably sent her into the dark web that evening, curious about the expense, both financial and social, of hiring an assassin.

I thought about what Mother would have given me at a party like this. Something expensive to please everyone else watching, but something impersonal to keep me at arm's length, like a vacuum cleaner or a food processor. I also thought about what a normal mother might give her daughter at a bridal shower. Jewelry, luxury pajamas, a new fragrance. Something special, handpicked for her taste, just for her. Just for the bride.

Thankfully, the shower was winding down, because I'd had enough adoration from strangers to tide me over until the wedding weekend. But I still had to make it through the bachelorette party that night. Oh, yes. We were doubling down on pre-wedding events, in a true act of torture, but also efficiency, so I was more than happy to oblige. By all means, let's get it all over with in one fell swoop.

Wren Daly had previously insisted upon planning a destination bachelorette party, but in a blessed turn of events, there wasn't a weekend everyone was available to travel at the same time, so I suggested a night on the town post–bridal shower in lieu of the Nashville bash Wren was dying to plan. Besides, not one of us would have appreciated a hootenanny at a honky-tonk, least of all Gale Wallace-Leicester. Though I did enjoy the idea of her sulking in a corner clad in country-western garb.

As the shower wrapped up and the guests shuffled out of the garden with their grins and goody bags, Gale pulled me deep into her arms so she could whisper in my ear, "I'm really looking forward to tonight." And she pinched me back. Hard.

Game on.

A few hours after the shower, I met the bridesmaids plus Syl at Le Bernardin for dinner. Chloe's edict for the night was that everyone wore black so that I would shine in whatever color I decided to wear as the bride. None of us would be caught dead in sashes, except for Wren Daly. I went with a gold lamé number that showed a lot of skin, sprayed with the requisite tan, a true showstopper. If I was going to have to have a bachelorette party, I wanted the spectacle.

Dinner got us good and sauced, with seemingly endless wine and cocktails, especially Wren Daly, who was gunning for the role of sloppiest bridesmaid, to no one's surprise. Conversation ran mostly polite, considering two of Collin's sisters were there, his assistant, and the woman who had loved him for the better part of twenty years. No one wanted details about our sex life except for, of course, Wren Daly.

"Where are you guys going on the honeymoon and when can we give you our prizes?" she slurred, leaning over the table, receiving major side-eye from the waitstaff. Our time would be almost up if she carried on that way. Fine with me.

"Wren, come on, I said no gifts," I protested, definitely wanting all the gifts.

"It's a bachelorette party!" she shouted. "You're supposed to get slutty things to wear on the honeymoon from your girlfriends. It's the *law.*"

"Wren's right." Syl laughed. "I brought you a gift, Bea."

"Oh, yay!" Wren clapped. "See! Let's do gifts now! Then you can get them sent home before we go on to the next mystery location. *Oooooh!*" Wren tried in vain to get the others to echo her sound.

"You guys didn't have to do that," I said.

"We got you gift cards," Chloe said, dry as a bone.

"Yeah," Calliope added. "Not really wild on picking out sex clothes for you to show our brother, but we know the drill." Calliope handed me a small bag from Agent Provocateur. Chloe placed a similar one from La Perla on the table. There was a brief tinge of embarrassment on Wren's face when she placed her bag from Victoria's Secret in view, but Syl had a similar offering, so she popped her own right next to Wren's in solidarity.

But nobody should have been more embarrassed than Gale Wallace-Leicester, who was empty-handed. She remained quiet. Either she did not realize she was supposed to get me a gift for this party, or she was boycotting the notion entirely, falsely believing Chloe and Calliope would have elected to do the same. Either way, now she was the only one, the maid of honor no less, who didn't come bearing a gift for the bride. What on earth was she going to say for herself?

"Gale?" Calliope asked her, taking on the role I could not in front of everyone. "What did you bring for our Bea?" *Our* Bea. There it was again, this time from Calliope. I liked it.

"It's fine," I said. "You guys didn't have to bring gifts. Your presence is gift enough. Don't worry about it, Gale." Oh, I wanted her to worry about it.

Her gaze met mine. "*Still* early. My gift comes later," she said. What could she possibly mean by that?

"Well, open ours now!" Wren commanded, but I was too distracted by Gale's proclamation to fully enjoy the moment, though I did what was asked of me. The gift cards were sizable sums from Chloe and Calliope. Syl's contribution was a hot-pink teddy with a matching robe, something she would wear, which endeared it to me. Wren's was an all-black garter ensemble. No creativity but good enough. I'd look great in all of it.

Being on the receiving end of gifts from sunup to sundown, from women no less, was a new sensation. I knew that they all *had* to do it, but it felt important. It felt real. Like this life couldn't be taken away from me somehow. I had to stop thinking that way. It was too naive. Anything could happen, particularly with Gale still circling.

I couldn't rest until the wedding was over.

Then and only then would it all be over.

“Want to pop out for a li’l smoke? It’s your bachelorette party,” Syl whispered in my ear, the thought simply marvelous, just a few innocent drags to take the edge off with a friend.

She was really so good at taking care of people. Taking care of me.

The next mystery location wasn’t mysterious at all. We went to a club. Pick one, they’re all the same, who cares, but we had the VIP table and the bottle service and we danced and we laughed and did a skosh of coke courtesy of Calliope’s dealer. Syl looked at me first for permission and I promised I wouldn’t tell Collin. This was an official GNO. Syl fit right in and noticeably kept her distance from Gale. Good girl. She was loyal.

But Gale couldn’t keep me away; I wanted to play. “So what did you get me?” I shout-whispered to her, the bass throbbing around us. I was feeling bold, like I could push her off the railing into the hoi polloi below us. If only.

“You’ll see.” She grinned. “Night’s not over yet.”

“Getting there,” I shouted, but Gale shook her head at me.

“You’ll never guess.”

"Don't make it too naughty. I tell Collin everything," I threatened.

"We both know that's not true," she said, the strobe lights flashing against her face.

Soon, Gale announced it was time to go to the next location. Based on the reactions from Chloe and Calliope, they weren't in on this plan at all. As for Wren, she had completely overshot her tolerance and wouldn't be able to go anywhere else, except potentially the emergency room. "Someone has to get her home," I said.

"I can do it," Syl offered kindly.

"Great idea," Gale said. Did she want Syl gone? That was unnerving. She must have picked up on our burgeoning camaraderie and Gale wanted me all to herself, no allies present. I was on high alert.

"Can't you meet us back out? Wren doesn't live far," I said to Syl.

"We can't. I'm not allowed to give out the address and everyone has to be with us when we arrive at the location," Gale said, upping the suspicious factor by about 1,000 percent. My heart was racing. Where the hell were we off to?

"I gotta get back to John anyway," Syl said. "He'll get pissed if I'm out much later. He always suspects the worst. 'Nothing good happens after two a.m.' and all that."

"He's right, though," Chloe said. "Where are we even going, Gale?"

"Let's get them in a cab," Gale said, motioning to Syl and a barely coherent Wren Daly. An amiable bouncer assisted us, and it was easy to have full faith in Syl for her mission ahead. She was so reliable. After Wren was essentially laid to rest in the taxi, Syl popped back out and gave me a giant good-night hug.

"Happy bachelorette, Bea. I had a great time. Have fun, and thanks for inviting me."

"Text me when you get home, okay?" Words I had never uttered to another woman before with any sort of sincerity, but with Syl, I meant it.

As they drove off in the cab, a black SUV arrived at Gale's behest. "Get in." She smiled at Chloe, Calliope and me.

The last ones standing.

The car took us from Chelsea to the Upper East Side. Very peculiar indeed. There were no bachelorette festivities to be had in that part of town. At least none that immediately came to mind, but I had to remind myself that Gale was a total weirdo and it was anyone's guess what she was planning. She was bubbly, which was a sight. One leg crossed over the other, her foot bobbing up and down, unable to sit still. The behavior didn't suit her, made her look like a child. My alarm bells were ringing, but I couldn't let on anything in front of my future sisters-in-law. Gale had me in her clutches for now.

Chloe and Calliope were fading fast, dozing in their seats. Sure, nightlife could be fun with the right crowd, but since all of us were forcibly hanging out together, I don't think anyone anticipated any sort of after-party attendance in the wee hours. I wished I could join them in their slumber, but I had to stay spry. And with good reason.

The car turned on East Eighty-First Street.

I immediately sat up straighter.

Hackles fully raised.

Focused and sharp.

It couldn't be.

But there it was.

I never wanted to see that house on East Eighty-First Street again.

The SUV parked in front.

It looked exactly the same.

Unassuming, but I knew what was inside.

Every single terrible thing.

Gale watched me take it all in, enjoying it, so I removed every emotion I could from my external body. Chloe and Calliope could never know. Or Collin for that matter. *How* did Gale know? The threat level from Gale had crossed into unprecedented territory. I felt sick.

"Here we are!" Gale chirped.

"What is it? Where are we?" Chloe asked, still half asleep from dozing in the car.

"I did some research. Nothing but the best for Bea. This is your gift." Gale grinned.

"I don't get it," Calliope said. The driver opened the door for us to climb out of the back. I followed them, calculating my next move in my head. I could not go back inside that house. Never. Ever. Again. Not when I finally understood what it really was. It was a trap. Always a trap. My whole life with her was a trap. But Gale couldn't know about this place. Gale couldn't know about me, the real me.

And Gale couldn't know about her.

"Everything all right?" Gale asked.

"Why wouldn't it be? What is this place?" I asked, keeping my wits about me. I needed to stay emotionless. Stoic and still. Like Mother.

"It's a party," Gale said. "I had to pull some strings to score an invitation. It's incredibly exclusive."

"What kind of party?" Chloe asked.

"Is it a sex thing?" Calliope was practically salivating with curiosity.

"My lips are sealed." Gale smiled, starting up the steps.

"What kind of strings did you pull exactly?" I asked. I needed to know how she knew, but she wouldn't give me anything. She had the upper hand and she knew it. We both did. She could read me, though I was trying my damnedest to be a blank page. I had to try harder.

"Why doesn't everyone stop asking questions and we head inside?" Gale said, leading the way.

Calliope swung an arm around me, urging me to follow Gale and Chloe up the steps. "Who knew Gale had it in her?" She laughed in my ear.

I did.

The door swung open and we were greeted by a tall man in a hood. We couldn't see his full face. I wondered if I knew him. If he'd recognize me. I felt like a different person by now, but did I look different? I'd thought I was an adult back then, but I was just a kid.

I kept my eyes down because I didn't want to find out what that man knew.

I'd let Gale do the talking. I didn't want to fall into any of her traps.

Inhale. Exhale. Just keep breathing.

"Guests of Hawkes," Gale said. "There's four of us."

Hawkes? That wasn't familiar, but the concept behind it was. Hawkes must have been somebody new, but code names were always a part of it. Some fun, some mystery, a game, it was all a game to them. Like little boys. But they were all grown men.

The hallway was dark, lit by candles. I remembered this particular theme. One of his favorites. Masquerade ball. I heard laughter coming from the great room to the right. The laughter was largely coming from the men. I slowed my breath. I had to keep my mind ahead of my body. It was taking more focus than I thought it would, but I never thought I'd be back here again. How could it look exactly the same? How could he still be doing this? Of course I knew the answer. Money. Power. Always money. Always power.

Inside I was crumbling. Remembering the ballroom. Being told to walk around, dressed in a skimpy silky pastel little thing made for a grown woman but I was still a little girl — a teenager is still a girl. Stop walking if one of the men asked me to. Talk to them, laugh with them. It was easy, she said. Didn't I feel powerful? Like a grown-up? Wasn't it only fair that I helped take care of her after she'd taken care of me for so long? It was fine until it wasn't. She wouldn't understand and I'd had to run away. But I couldn't run now. The stakes had never been higher. What was my whole life for if I couldn't handle this moment? Gale Wallace-Leicester could not see me falter. I would not allow it.

But still, all I wanted to do was run. Again.

"This is kinda creepy," Calliope whispered to Chloe. "Who the fuck is *Hawkes*?" Chloe shrugged. I wished they would say out loud that they wanted to leave. Gale might put up a fuss, but the Case girls always got what they wanted, more or less. I couldn't speak. I couldn't play into Gale's hands at all. My only move was to go with the flow.

I was in hell.

The man in the hood said nothing to Gale in response. He simply motioned with his hand over to the great room. "Come on, girls," Gale squealed, leading the way.

I felt nauseous. A familiar taste in my mouth, I could already taste the whiskey that wasn't from my own lips. A familiar scent in my nose, the black-dipped tuberose candles mixed with the smell of cigars. We weren't even in the ballroom yet, but it was all rushing back. The sounds of deep laughter, big booming guffaws when nothing about it was funny. The faces of those men, some with their masks down when they got too comfortable, flushed from the drink and what was before them, a feast not only for their eyes. We were their prey, but the easy kind. Just girls. Girls who mistakenly thought we were women because of the people around us. Girls who thought we were in control when we were anything but.

I don't know how I kept moving. My muscle memory wanted me to dissociate entirely but I couldn't. I had to look alive. I had to get through this. I had to follow Gale. I couldn't let on a thing. The fear was all-consuming.

Focus. Focus. Focus.

I wished that Syl was still with me. I would have held her hand.

Another man waited for us at the door, sporting a top hat, white tie and tails, with a small, handheld mask of his own and a self-righteous grin on his red face. I didn't recognize him, but he looked like one of them. In his forties, maybe his fifties. Taking his turn at the door. Leering. Checking. Approving. Just another monster.

"Pretty, pretty," he growled. "Guest of?"

"Hawkes," Gale said to him, though not quite as confidently as before. Any woman worth her salt would pick up on the sordid energy in that house, even someone like Gale. Clearly she hadn't really known the full scope of what she was getting us into, but she was going to see it through. Getting to me was more important to her, that much was obvious. She possessed that personality of pointed cruelty. Even when you think they won't go so far, they do. Some women are just like that, I guess.

Mother was.

I wondered if this party would be the same as the parties before. Probably so. Different men maybe, different girls for sure. Would some of their mothers be there, too? The second the door swung open, those long-buried memories clamored to the forefront of my mind, overlapping with everything I saw before me. So similar. The masked men. The women in lingerie. No, girls. *Girls* in lingerie. I was light-headed. Too much. Breathe in. Breathe out. I'd be okay. I had to be okay. I wouldn't let her get me. I wouldn't let anyone get me ever again. I steadied myself. Head over body always. Focus. Focus. Focus. I could sit there, have a drink, observe, be silent, until it was time to leave. I wasn't one of those girls anymore. I wouldn't let Gale prove that I ever was.

I felt a hand on my waist. Someone trying

to get into the room around us.

A man.

It was him.

I looked right at him.

Not very tall. But bold. With presence. Silver hair now.

He looked right through me.

I didn't register to Francis at all and yet I'd know him anywhere.

I'd have to remember him until the day I died, but he didn't even see me.

I couldn't hold it in anymore.

It all came up.

Fast and violent.

CHAPTER 12

We had been drinking all night. It was so late. It wasn't suspicious that I vomited. Not glamorous, but not unheard-of behavior for a bride at her bachelorette party. Chloe and Calliope insisted that we leave right away, so we did, but I knew we would have been escorted out anyway within seconds.

They never wanted the girls to be sick at the parties.

Gale didn't say anything back in the car. Whatever her plan was, it had been derailed by my outburst. And soon the wedding would be upon us. I was truly afraid of what Gale Wallace-Leicester might do. She was clearly very serious and I needed to stay ahead of it, but I was failing thus far. I should have started planning an attack of my own. After that display on East Eighty-First Street, she would deserve it.

But I couldn't. I was *too* close. I'd stay on the defensive for now.

I wasn't my mother.

I could play defense for one more week. Survival mode. I knew it well.

One more week and I'd be married and Gale wouldn't be able to do anything about it.

In the week leading up to our wedding, I noticed Collin's mood took a noticeable dive. He seemed different. Changed. Perhaps it was the clinical depression rearing its ugly head, but he had the medication to combat it, I assumed. Or worse, he was getting cold feet. Did Gale get in his ear under the cover of night? I was keeping close watch on him, but she was clever. No. That wasn't it. She couldn't have made any lasting impact, not without making sure I knew that she was behind it. Curse that beast, she was rattling me. I'd been thrown off my A game since the bachelorette party despite my best efforts. I needed to calm down but take extra precautions. So I decided to kick it up a notch at home, as far as domesticities went, going so far as to cook for him myself, instead of ordering in or making reservations, and I performed four nights in a row of enthusiastic fellatio. Still, he was rather vacant, even as he came. It made me anxious. Wifely duties were not checking the box, so I needed to dig deeper.

"You can talk to me, you know." I snuggled up next to Collin after a quick brush of my teeth and an Altoid. "I'm here for you. Always."

"I know. I'm okay. There's just been a lot going on."

Vague, but not altogether unexpected. We hadn't been the type of couple to really *get in there,* so to speak, emotionally. He seemed fine with that. Obviously, I was, too, but I wouldn't stand for this palpable distance. Not when there was so much on the line. Collin always maintained the appearance of having it all together, including me, but this retreat from my touch made me less confident. I began acting like the type of girl I loathed.

"I just wish you would tell me what's on your mind, baby. What are you thinking?" I asked him. Seriously, *shoot me,* but I was going to be with Collin for the long haul. I'd have to do plenty of things I didn't feel like doing. It was what I signed up for. That was the plan. The rewards would be worth it. Mother would never *really* talk to a man about his feelings. So I would.

"Okay." He took a deep breath. "Something has been on my mind."

"Go on," I prodded.

"Gale mentioned something about your bachelorette party getting a little weird," he said, taking my literal breath away. I had to tread very carefully.

"Oh? What did she say?"

"She seemed concerned about your behavior."

"Gale was concerned about *my* behavior?" It took everything I had not to scream. A pathetic power move from Gale. Our game was supposed to be between us. To flat-out tattle to Collin was beneath her.

She was playing dirty.

"Look, I know you don't really like her and that this maid of honor thing was a goodwill effort for me. Which I appreciate. But she said you guys went somewhere and that you already seemed . . . familiar with it?"

This was a conundrum. Had she told him the truth about me, or whatever she thought the truth was? What did he know? What did she know? I didn't want to offer any new information. I had to be very, *very* careful.

"Okay . . ." I trailed off, waiting for him to pick up the conversation. I needed to keep him on my side. Every moment mattered. Every word. Collin sighed loudly again. He was trying to find the right way to say whatever it was. Driving me crazy.

"She just said that you might have some stuff from your past that you don't want to share with me," he finally said. "And I thought we told each other everything."

God, could he really be that naive? *Everything?* If couples told each other *everything,* we would all most certainly be alone forever. Get real.

"Collin. Let me tell you what happened. Your best friend Gale practically accosted us with some weird sex club, *with* your sisters, mind you, and it was in really bad taste. Yes, I'd had a lot to drink that night and got sick, but who is *really* the sicko in this instance?"

"Bea, I'm not judging you. I wouldn't judge you. If you did have anything to tell me, well, you should." He didn't know the truth. If he knew, I'd already be out the door. The whole wedding would have been called off. Right?

But there was doubt present in Collin where it hadn't been before. She'd set it up so I'd have to lie to his face. Happy to do it, I had been already for some time, but something else was in his head now. A sinister seed she had planted about my moral character. It felt as if he was looking at me in a totally different way. No longer fully on a pedestal.

"Judging *me*? Honey, there's nothing to tell. You're making assumptions based on something Gale told you. Something that *she* instigated. She brought us to that place. I'd never seen it before."

"Bea . . ."

"What did she tell you, Collin?" I was afraid to ask, but I had no choice. I needed to know what I was dealing with so I could perform whatever damage control was necessary.

"She thought that it was a fun bachelorette place. Like a burlesque show. She said Dave told her about it, that some of the Harvard guys go."

The relief I felt was nearly orgasmic. Gale didn't know the truth. Not really. She was just trying to ruffle my feathers, stir up drama and involve Collin. It made so much sense. Dave? Harvard guys? Their recommendation? Yep. Of course they knew the house on East Eighty-First Street.

But then the thought occurred to me . . .

What if that was exactly what Gale wanted me to think? She wanted me eating right out of her hand, ready to crush me with those frightful paws of hers when I wasn't paying attention. I *had* to keep paying attention.

"Burlesque? Collin, please. I don't think

that's what it was," I said.

"Right. She agreed, but she said you seemed to already know that going in. Like you'd been there before."

So she *was* planting little seeds, the gardener of my nightmares. Was that it?

"I just told you I haven't."

"Right, but —"

"You think I'm lying to you? We're getting married in two days!" Collin didn't say anything. The panic resurfaced. Truth or not, he was questioning his faith in me. Exactly what Gale wanted in the end. "Aren't we?" I asked him. *Pathetic.*

"I just think we need to be honest with each other. If there's something that went on in your past, when you were fresh to New York or whatever, you can tell me about it. Okay? I'm going to be your husband. It won't make me stop loving you, but I don't want there to be any secrets between us."

I wanted to marry Collin, but that did not include telling him the truth about my mother or her husbands or the other men or anything else I had purposely concealed from him. That was the past and he was my future. They would not coexist. Why were modern-day couples so hung up on knowing every little thing about their beloved? It wasn't the key to happiness. The opposite. We're all a damn mess. Don't we deserve a little privacy in that regard?

I had to deliver the performance of a lifetime.

"Collin. There are no secrets between us. Please don't be upset. Now, I know you don't want to hear this, but Gale is in love with you, and she would say *anything* if it meant even the slightest chance that you would leave me. Whatever she thought about that house or my reaction to it, it really has nothing to do with me. She just wants you and she thinks she deserves you. More than I do, that's for sure. You and I don't come from the same world, Collin. We don't talk about that very much because it doesn't seem to be an issue for you, at least so far, but if you're looking for an easy out based on a hearsay gut feeling from a jealous foe like Gale Wallace-Leicester, maybe you're the one who needs to be honest with me."

A lone tear fell from my cheek.

My voice broke at the very end.

It was some of my finest work, with a supporting nod to my own sincere desperation at the thought of losing everything.

But how could Collin argue with any of that?

He couldn't.

"Oh, Bea. Please don't cry. I'm so sorry," he apologized, nearly brought to tears himself. "I really am sorry. I shouldn't have said anything. I don't know what I was thinking. Between work and my family and then Gale said that stuff. Shit, I'm sorry, I was just losing it. There's so much stress in my life right now, but you always stand by me with your full support. That's all I could ask for. You're a magnificent woman and I'm so sorry, Bea. So sorry. Do you forgive me?"

I didn't find his deeply apologetic display very attractive, but the sentiment was appreciated, since I was legitimately worried everything was about to fall apart. Did Gale really think I would come clean to Collin? Did she actually know everything and want to torture me? Or did she really know nothing and just want me to torture myself?

It certainly seemed plausible that Dave could know about East Eighty-First Street based on the reputation that preceded him. Told Gale about it. She took it and ran with it. But in my heart of hearts, it also felt like too much of a coincidence. But it was impossible. There was no trace. Was there?

I was questioning everything. I hated it. I hated her. I hated myself for underestimating her presence as sheer amusement and nothing more, because I was wrong. As it turned out, Gale Wallace-Leicester, mules, moles and all, was a worthy adversary indeed. Why had I wanted such a thing?

Especially when I knew what such a person could do.

It was a very lonely day. I was the bride, but I didn't feel particularly special to anyone there, except for Collin. No mother in the bridal suite to equal parts annoy and care for me. No father to walk me down the aisle. Bridesmaids who either actively disliked me, or were indifferent, or kissed my ass to the point that I disrespected her. Yes, I mean Wren Daly. It was strange because typically I never felt downright lonesome. My own company had always been enough, but there was something about that day and what it represented that vexed me. Perhaps it was that I was getting what I wanted at long last.

But then what?

The enormity of my greatest achievement being unlocked was overwhelming.

I was a true *Vogue* bride. Better. Truly stunning. I refused to wear the kind of dress that required help getting into and out of, as I preferred to piss in private. I opted for a sleek Galia Lahav gown that left little to the imagination. Strategic cutouts around my posterior and décolletage that would all but ensure the guests would be drooling. I donned a cathedral-length veil with pearl accents that shimmered when they hit the light just right. The combination would photograph splendidly. I didn't care much about our personal album, but there would be features in the society rags. I wanted them all to squirm at my beauty and grace.

I. Wanted. People. To. Talk. It was the only way to bite back at Gale, since I was moments from full possession of the one thing she couldn't have. She wasn't having any fun at all as we got ready in the bridal suite. None of us were really, except for Wren Daly. She was embracing the bridesmaid role to an obnoxious degree. I promised myself that after the wedding, I'd never invite her anywhere again. She just wouldn't stop *fussing* over me, touching me, primping me, fluffing me, taking selfies, posting on Instagram, tagging me, tagging Collin. It was too much and I hated it and wanted to scream at her to stop with all the theatrics, but I was the bride.

I was supposed to want all of that stuff.

I walked myself down the aisle. *Quelle surprise.* I suppose I could have asked

Hayes Case to be on my arm, in lieu of my nonexistent father, but that would have felt far too phony. No matter. In all honesty, I craved the attention. I wanted everyone's eyes on me and me alone. Bear witness to my greatest achievement. It was about to be over. I had won.

So Hayes walked Haven down the aisle. She wore silver because anything lighter would have been socially inappropriate, but she was sending a clear message about whose special day it *really* was. The bridesmaids and the groomsmen followed. Finally, a flower girl with her little basket of white rose petals. I don't remember who she was. Someone's child. We took a photo or two together. Her teeny-tiny fingernails were painted pale pink.

And then I made the journey alone, standing along the end of the aisle at the Rainbow Room. I locked in on Collin, avoiding Gale's hard gaze at the front of the venue. It was really happening. What could she do now that wouldn't mortify the entire family? Her fate was sealed and so was mine.

Collin gasped with his whole body at the sight of me in that dress. It pleased me, since we just had a hell of a week as a couple. His loyalty had come into question for the first time, but his public amazement at my presence washed it all away. I took full control of the moment, smiling brightly, enchanting the crowd. Everyone loves to celebrate love. I never wanted Collin to question me *again,* so I had to do my part. I allowed my eyes to fill with the perfect amount of tears, not enough for any to actually fall and ruin my makeup but plenty to show the emotion. They glistened. Collin began to cry as well. Perfection. Five hundred people were watching and everyone could tell he was completely obsessed with me. I did it. Here was a man who truly loved me and cherished me. A man about to promise that he would never leave me. I only broke our gaze one time to take a quick gander at the audience, to revel a bit in everyone's obligatory admiration of me. Amidst the largely unfamiliar faces, I was startled to see one that I recognized instantly.

Dave Bradford. The Cat Man.

He also recognized me, with that knowing grin of his, eye contact activated. Was it genuine? Was it menacing? It was difficult to say because despite my disgust at his potentially sleazy social circle, he looked like a cheat day snack in his suit, momentarily throwing me off-balance. I had to put my focus back on Collin, careful not to let my sights veer in Hello Handsome's direction again.

But I could not stop thinking about him.

The officiant was in the middle of reciting some meaningful passages about marriage that wouldn't offend anyone's respective religious sensibilities. And there I was tuning him out, plotting an opportune time to sneak another furtive glance at Dave Bradford. Incredibly fast and imperceptible to anyone else, except for him. He was grinning right back at me. It was unnerving and unsettling and hot and sexy and my mind immediately went to dark places. I wanted to be ravaged by him in the bridal suite at our earliest convenience.

Stop it.

Collin said I do. Seconds later I said the same. And when we kissed to seal the deal on our most blessed of wedding days, eyes closed, it was Dave Bradford I imagined on the receiving end of my lips.

Damn it.

Yes, he was hot, but he was also dangerous. A friend of my foe. In possession of a secret — he knew I had lied when we met. What would he say to Collin? What could I say if Dave told the truth? Why must I always put myself in situations like this? So precarious. So stimulating. Why?

Stupid question. I knew exactly why.

Despite trying not to think about her the entire day, and nearly succeeding, *that* was the moment. I reminded myself of her in every way and I was ashamed. I should have known there would be no escaping my mother that day.

After all, I was the bride.

Daughter

LAS VEGAS, NEVADA

Mother is punishing me. I am not allowed to have a life without her. How dare I try? What was I thinking? Not her bunny. So now she wants to show me what that could be like in Las Vegas. What our life could be if she doesn't work, if we don't work together, as a team. Mother and I have quickly become "off-Strip" in every way, and I hate it. She puts us up in a one-bedroom apartment in a hellacious building that looks like a motel. She has the money for more, even without Francis. She knows I know that, and it delights her to hurt me this way. If I want us to get out of this, it's up to me, she says. She will not lift one finger.

Didn't I recognize everything she did for me?

Didn't I realize the privileges that came with the life she gave to me?

Didn't I see that by putting us in front of the right men, we were able to cut the line?

Didn't I know that girls like us don't get nice things unless we make the right choices?

I meet Seamus at a cocktail bar in the Bellagio. I look old enough. I've always looked old enough. Meeting men is easy, but I'm looking for a specific type of man. I've talked to several men that night, but they were the wrong kind, the kind Mother hopes I'll find so I'll come running back to her.

But I'm starting to figure out that I actually kind of know what I'm doing.

Seamus is from LA, he tells me. Well, Manhattan Beach. It's fantastic, he says. He's in business, I don't know what kind and I don't care, but he loves to gamble and goes to high-stakes poker tournaments, likes to have a pretty girl on his arm, occasionally in his bed if he's in the mood, and I'm paid for my services.

The perfect part-time job.

Our relationship is pleasant. It feels transactional and I like that. We both know where we stand. It's good for him. It's good for me. If I keep this up, I could leave Mother. I come home with money, but not too much. The rest is in the secret bank account Seamus sets up for me. He knows I'm in trouble, he just doesn't know how much. I don't share more than necessary to get what I want.

Mother's mad that I'm succeeding, that I don't need her anymore. She's furious that she's the one who needs me now. Mother is getting older. She's still beautiful, but she's no longer young. What will she do if I leave? *When* I leave. I don't know. I pretend I don't care. I don't want to care. She demands to know my source, but I don't want to tell her. I want to keep Seamus all to myself. I also don't want to put him in harm's way. In *her* way.

"I'm giving you the money. Isn't that what matters? I'm doing what you asked me to do," I say to her. She doesn't say anything back to me. I'm starting to think I was set up to lose no matter what I did. I always fail her tests.

A man is in our living room. We never have men over when Mother and I live alone. We only play games in others' homes. But Mother explains that this man is here for a meeting, a potential source for us. He's absolutely hideous, not on our level, not on my level. It's not just how he looks. No trace of a neck, but also no trace of a soul. He's massive. Sinister. I want him out.

"I don't need another source," I say to Mother. The man licks his lips at me. He's disgusting. How could she let him into our home? She's so angry with me. He's wearing a gold chain, for God's sake. Something isn't right. She wants me to be afraid. Hurt. How much more can she hurt me?

My shoulders sit high, almost to my ears. I take a step back as he licks his lips again. I can't relax. He's revolting. I look at Mother. Okay, you've made your point. Call off the beast. Please, Mother. Please, Mommy.

She nods her head at him and thankfully, it's a signal to leave.

I was ready to run, but would she actually do something so evil?

"Could be good for you, you know," Mother says as he shuts the door behind him. "To be knocked down a peg or two. Maybe you'll learn to respect me and everything I've done for you."

Mother doesn't make threats.

Only promises.

I know her.

I have to leave, but she won't let me go.

I stay awake all night.

Dreaming of the future.

When I will be alone.

When she will be gone.

She has to go.
And so do I.

Seamus has the cash and the contacts for everything I need. Passport. Social security number. Birth certificate. All of it. He's the sole resource I have. I think he can be trusted. I have faith that he can. It's my only option. I have to get out. I also know about his wife and children and potentially unsavory business dealings, so he'd be wise to keep my secrets, too. The ask is easy. A naked man with a primal obsession with your body will give you anything you want if you know what you're doing. I'm learning it's not just about the sex with Seamus. Seamus likes to be heard. Likes to be seen. Likes to be understood. Seamus believes that I really care about him. That I have true empathy for him.

Like he needs it.

As if he doesn't have everything already.

The perfect mark.

This isn't really the challenging part.

That comes next.

It will have to be quiet and understated, but I have to move fast. That man was just a preview. She's planning something for me. *I'm* her target right now. Her mark. I know it. So I must plan in return. Play defense. Something that looks accidental when she's eventually found. Or purposeful, but at her own hand. Pills will probably do just fine. Mother's an occasional to frequent fan anyway. Xanax. Valium. Whatever takes the edge off. No brand loyalty. The execution will be simple. They'll be easy to find. I'm in Vegas. I can find anything I want to find here, especially things that are laced with the illicit or the fatal. I'm starting to sound more like her and that's how I know I will pull this off.

I'll be Mother's daughter for now.

I need to be.

Then I'll leave them both behind.

I put a few of the pills I bought in her own supply, a little tube in the medicine cabinet. Bases covered for any investigation should anyone care, but who will? I'm the only one who cares about her, but that ends tonight. I sit with her as she watches television. I'm not paying attention to the program. I only hear my breath. In. Out. Trying to slow it down. Does she notice? Does she know what I want to do to her? Fix us a drink, she says, like clockwork. I make her a drink, a gin martini, minus the goods. She'd taste it now. I use three ounces instead of one and a half. She won't taste it after this one.

Down the hatch.

An hour goes by.

I wait for her to ask for another.

But will anything happen?

Nothing ever happens to Mother.

Everything always happens to me.

It has to be her turn.

Another, she says.

I crushed two pills earlier that day and I wonder if I should have crushed three. Or four. Why did I still want to be gentle with her? Can't stop now. I fix the drink. I pour the powder. I shove the plastic bag into my bra. Fast, fast, fast. I do it all fast.

Did she see me?

I place the drink in front of her.

She smiles.

Thanks, bunny.

Sip, sip, another sip.

Time passes. I don't know how much.

And then, she looks sauced. She should. I made her that way.

I think I'll go lie down, she says to me. She says she's dizzy. She stands up and loses her footing. Unsteady. She laughs. You got me drunk, bunny.

Are you okay? I ask her. She doesn't look okay. She's not okay. I'm fine, she slurs.

She sweeps the hair away from my face.

Then she stumbles to the bedroom, giggling now.

Like a fool. It's working. Mother never looks like a fool.

She laughs even louder with a snort.

See you in the morning, bunny.

She holds on to the walls in the hallway for balance.

She falls to the side, sliding down the wall, all the way down.

She's so still.

Still breathing, but still.

I think about touching her one last time.

The last time. What have I done?

What am I doing?

Should I call someone? Ask for help.

Help.

No. No one will help me. No one ever helps. Not for free.

This is the only way.

To be truly free.

It was always the only way. I tried to get away. She didn't let me.

She'll never let me go.

So do I touch her one last time?

I don't wipe the tears from my face. Let them fall. I need to feel them. I need to feel this.

For her and for me.

I deserve this pain. We both do. Feel it. I feel it.

I know I am a bad daughter.

But what did she think she'd get?

She's a bad mother.

Maybe I'll brush the hair away from *her* face.

No. I won't do it. I can't.

My face is soaking wet.

I can hardly see. I rub the crook of my arm across my face.

I can see. I can see everything. All of it.

The black and the white and everything gray.

The future is finally mine.

What's another scar on my heart?

Do I even have one?

I take the glass, I leave the bottle of gin, I grab my bag and I go.

I look up at the door on the second floor. I stand in the parking lot. I wonder if she's still alive. I wonder how much longer she has left. The tears have stopped. Everything has stopped. Time. I wonder why I no longer feel any fear or sadness. Nor do I feel any regret.

I only feel free.

I'm free from my creator, I'm out from her enormous shadow that would keep me in the dark with her, only letting me in the light on the shortest of leashes, always wrapped tightly around my neck. Not quite strangling me, but close enough.

She would never have let me go.

I tell myself that over and over. And over again.

It had to be done.

I'm not hers anymore.

I'm not her bunny.

I'm not a fucking bunny at all.

Now I can be anything I want to be.

Not like Mother.

Not like Seamus.

Not even like Dean.

But like Francis.

Filthy fucking rich.

Because money is power.

Only then would I be safe, secure, untouchable.

I wanted it all and I knew how to get it.

She taught me that much.

I could do the rest alone.

So where would I begin?

Chapter 13

I was officially Mrs. Collin Case, but I couldn't stop scanning my wedding reception for Dave Bradford. I decided that we needed to meet again, to fully satiate my curiosity, and then this infatuation would have to end. *Permanently.*

I felt confident he wouldn't rat me out on my wedding day about our first encounter at Gale's, but the risk was always present. Hence the appeal. My primal instincts were always humming on idle, foot hovering above the gas, just underneath the surface. I couldn't accelerate, at least not aggressively. Maybe just a brisk pleasure cruise. What was the harm? Everyone was a little loose at weddings, why not the bride, too? The only minor annoyance leading up to my illicit reunion with Dave was Collin. He would not leave my side as per usual. I was his brand-new beautiful wife and he rightfully wanted to show me off to every bastard in the room. I acquiesced since I excelled at being paraded around like a prize. I didn't mind a build in the anticipation either.

Hand in hand with Collin, smiling so much my cheeks were in pain, we mixed and mingled our way through the reception. Table by table, I was introduced to cousins and coworkers and Calliope's ex-boyfriends, until we finally approached a well-dressed collection of bachelors at the singles table. A prime position for one Dave Bradford, still grinning mischievously in a way I found positively panty-dropping. And I don't say *panty* often because it's vile.

Gale was also assigned to the same table, but she was nowhere to be found, which couldn't have been good for me. I should have excused myself to home in on her location for my own sake, but I was completely hypnotized at the sight of Dave. He was delicious.

"Collin!" Dave exclaimed at my husband, not yet looking at me, driving me wild, doing it on purpose. "Congrats, man!" Dave rose from the table, his tie undone, running a hand through his curls, and the two of them did that boorish man hug where they instinctually smack each other a few times on the back with gusto, like a couple of apes.

"Dave, so stoked you made it!" Collin

said. I stopped myself from openly cringing. *Stoked?* I'd never heard Collin utter such bro terminology in my life. I wanted to comment that Dave must have brought out the frat boy in Collin, but of course they would correct me and tell me that they were in a "final club" at Harvard, not a frat, so I kept my mouth shut. Ideally, I wanted to stay at least somewhat attracted to both of them. "This is my *wife.*" Collin emphasized that word all night in a way that I actually found very charming. "Bea."

I smiled at Dave and he held out his hand for me to shake. He made no mention of our prior meeting. I received his hand. It was charged. And who can really say that about something as dull as a handshake, especially when we were giving off the energy that all we really wanted to do was hump each other? I pulled my hand away and fast. He called so loudly to my hedonistic side. A side that I had all but muffled due to Mother's influence. I didn't trust anything that beckoned on that primal level of lust, and I completely lusted for Dave Bradford. "Great to meet you, Bea." He grinned.

"This is Dave Bradford," Collin continued, not picking up any of the signals we were throwing down. "He's one of my oldest friends, but he's been back and forth to London these days, so we don't get to see him as often as we'd like. Glad you could make the wedding, bud. Means a lot." Well, that was a creative way to disguise the real reason Dave wasn't around much. Dave merely had business in London, not repeated torrid affairs with married women.

"Wouldn't miss it." He smiled, answering Collin, looking at me. "I won't be in London for too much longer actually. I'm moving some investments around. Planning to be back in New York the majority of my time with this new company I'm adding to the portfolio, save for some essential travel to Seattle, where the founders are based." How was this man making a conversation that would be so mind-numbingly boring with anyone else so completely riveting? "Congratulations on bagging such a fine fellow, Bea." Dave finally turned his full attention to me. "Collin Case is a true gem of a man."

I couldn't tell if he was being sincere or snide. "Oh, he's all right," I teased lovingly, squeezing Collin's hand tight for effect. As if that would make it any better about feeling outrageously horny for another man right in front of him.

"Well, go on and keep that newlywed party train moving. You have a lot of schmoozing to do." Dave shooed Collin and me away, his hands on the smalls of our backs, as we returned to the crowd. "Insane guest list. Good luck." Dave's touch actually made me sigh aloud. Drat. My arousal was becoming too palpable and it was not for public consumption. I needed to reel it in. "Bea, it was a pleasure. Coll, we'll catch up soon."

"For sure, man," Collin replied, leading me away to the next table. Thank God. I needed to get away from Dave and not a moment too soon. I spied Gale at the other end of the room, speaking with Syl, of all people. Syl looked miserable, the poor dear. Her neanderthal fiancé lingered nearby with a Heineken in hand, not even considering coming to her aid. No one wanted to be cornered into conversation with Gale Wallace-Leicester.

What the hell were the two of them even talking about? I didn't like it, but Syl would spill later. We were friends. Besides, Collin and I were married.

Gale had lost.

I stole away to the bridal suite for a breather, feigning that I needed a lip gloss touch-up, as if the makeup wasn't etched into my skin to last for a solid ten hours. The reflection in the mirror felt new somehow, the veil and gown notwithstanding. Who was this woman? Who was Mrs. Beatrice Case going to be? I had built her up for so long, a version of her, and now, here she was in the flesh. She officially existed in the world. Free to be herself, whatever that meant. She would never want for anything. She would always feel safe. Secure. She was a fixture. A full-blown member of the Family Case, a new branch on the ancestral tree, a new bullet point on their Wikipedia page, a blank slate ready to be written upon. Would she be the chair of a philanthropic board? Would she start a line of resort wear? Would she take on a senior role at the Case Company? Would she run for office one day? Jesus. She could do anything.

But I had no earthly idea what my actual interests were now that I was finally here with her, as one. What would we do with all of this free time? An intoxicating question and one that required careful thought. The boring and dull choices were always what I had envisioned. But a lifetime of that? Was it even possible for someone like me? If pre-marriage Bea got excited at the mere whiff of mayhem, what would married Bea do when something juicy presented itself, which it inevitably would? Such is life.

A tighter leash could be required.

In the midst of our continued greetings with guests, I idiotically turned around to sneak another peek at Mr. Bradford. He was *brazen.* A sensual lip bite in my direction with zero remorse. You know the kind. That subtle type of facial body language amongst humans that literally translates to "I can't wait until we fuck later."

I was in imminent danger if I kept it up.

But I wanted to keep it up.

Dinner was divine. Options of chateaubriand or lobster or both. The various speeches from our line of attendants went off without a hitch. I could not have cared less about what Wren Daly had to say about our pseudo–best friendship, but I smiled during her performance all the same. Soon it was Gale's turn to speak.

I bunched up my toes in my shoes with excitement. I yearned to hear her praise our union, but I also wondered if she'd try something. Something wild in the name of taking me down in front of everyone they knew. I'd have to think fast, spring into action, fix the problem immediately. It was the first time it occurred to me that this might always be how it was with Gale

Wallace-Leicester. On alert, feeling unwieldy, a threat. Married or not. She was here to stay, a fixture herself, not in the Family Case, but in the larger kingdom itself. We could always be connected if I didn't actively do something about it.

Gale Wallace-Leicester stood there in the mauve column gown I'd selected for her and raised a champagne glass. She almost looked pretty with soft tendrils coming down the sides of her face. Professional hair and airbrush makeup can make just about anyone look good. "Against all odds, I was chosen as Bea's maid of honor," her voice boomed. The room filled with polite chuckles. They all knew she loved him. How pathetic. Why was she leaning into it? "Collin is my best friend. I suspect most of you already know that. In particular, Bea knows that."

More laughs. Jesus Christ, was she going to try to *roast* me at my own wedding? I managed to exchange a glance with Syl, whose furrowed brow suggested she was also uncomfortable with the route Gale was taking for her speech. "It's not easy to have a third wheel in a relationship, but when the third is someone like Bea, it's a real treat."

Pardon? Was she implying that I was the

third wheel in *their* relationship? To a ballroom full of our wedding guests? "Bea has wisely never tried to get in between Collin and me," Gale continued. "She understands our history, like our families do, like you all do. And that's about all I could ask for in a partner for Collin. Someone who gets how important a friendship can be. That alone takes a really special person. I suspect that's why she asked me to stand up next to her on this occasion and why Collin asked her to be his bride. So I'd like us all to raise a glass to the brand-new Mrs. Collin Case, a woman who knows her worth, but also the worth of her husband, his family *and* his friends. To the happy couple!"

Everyone inexplicably raised their glasses at that sorry excuse for a toast. Collin and I were expected to kiss afterward. We did so. I was then expected to get up out of my seat and embrace her, but under the guise of tears of happiness, overwhelmed with emotion, I was able to stay seated. I didn't want to touch her. I didn't even want to look at her.

This was a *message.* My prophecy coming to life in real time. She wasn't going to give up. Ever. It wasn't just about Collin or her, but all of them. Citing the history, the families, again with the legacy. It was a clear invitation for more combat that I'd have to accept if I was going to stay. And I was going to stay, I had worked too hard to let this one go and start anew. It might not even be possible to find someone as suitable as Collin again. I would not leave. I didn't want to be like her, like Mother.

But perhaps some of her influence wouldn't be the worst thing where Gale was concerned. Nothing too dark. No. No. Never *that* dark. Not again. But I needed to start playing dirty, too. Gale's threat now all but demanded it. Cat and mouse was over. Time to go in for the kill.

Figuratively speaking.

Collin and I performed our first dance to a song he loved. "It's Always You," made famous by Frank Sinatra. It was a song with themes of overt obsession so I was delighted by his choice, even though Sinatra is rather pedestrian. Collin and his mother danced to *another* Frank Sinatra song with much less sexual overtones. I don't remember which one because I didn't really care. I even danced with my father-in-law, at his behest, since everyone would be watching. He chose a Dean Martin song to really mix it up. Way to go, Hayes. He finally got to put actual hands on me. I knew he'd been dying to do so, despite his initial protests of the marriage.

After a few of the old standards, courtesy of the live band, it was time to spice up the dance floor with the DJ. Everyone was good and sauced and rarin' to go by that time, including myself. I *thrived* when I got to dance, and at my wedding, I was going to steal the show, especially after Gale's moment in the sun. When there's a dance floor, I'm on it all night long. Seriously. I do not leave unless I absolutely must. I've always been good at it. Whenever I'd gone out dancing, I would get compliments from complete strangers about how great I looked. So yes, I was most certainly going to put on a show in front of my now-legal nearest and dearest. Truthfully, when I get the opportunity to dance, I take it, because it's the only time I feel like I can actually be myself. I'm not pretending when I'm dancing. I genuinely adore it. I don't have to think about anything. I just do it. And I look incredible.

I should have known it would be like a moth to a flame. Like clockwork, during a particularly pulsating Rihanna number that all but encouraged gyrating hips and ass, Dave Bradford found his way over to the bride. "Mrs. Case, may I dance with you?" he shouted at me over the music. A sly smile. His tie long gone. A sweaty brow. He was irresistible.

"I'll dance with anyone if they're good!" I shouted back to him. I wasn't lying. In my opinion, men should always learn how to dance if they want to get in with women anywhere, especially if they're hard on the eyes. I'd dance with the ugliest guy in the bar if he had serious moves. It's beyond fun to be twirled and dipped and tossed around by someone who actually knows what they're doing, even if they're ghastly by any other measure.

"I'm not very good." Dave grinned, but I didn't believe him. He looked like he'd be a phenomenal dancer, limber in the right places, but perhaps that was wishful thinking. He got closer to talk into my ear. "But I'll do it anyway because it's fun and I don't really care what any of these assholes think about me."

"I'll make you look good." I grinned.

Fate smiled upon us because the music slowed down to something undeniably sultry. I'm convinced the DJ had been observing our interaction. Perhaps she instinctively knew I wanted this man to put his hands on me. Maybe she thought we were friendly exes or people from each other's past who never quite got the timing right. Either way, she must have felt wistful about it enough to throw us a bone in the form of a slow song so we could enjoy the moment, but one that wouldn't be interpreted by anyone else as anything unsavory. She played a Tony Bennett and Lady Gaga duet of another old standard. It was the kind of song you'd dance to with your grandfather or a child or a slow uncle.

It wasn't amorous. The perfect disguise.

"A stylist, huh?" he whispered again in my ear, far too close. He then waved at Collin, who waved back, as if to give his approval for the dance. Curious. Collin knew this man had no problems encroaching on women who were spoken for. My husband must have been trying to play it cool. I wondered if I'd hear about the transgression later, considering he had made his wishes about Dave and me known, but I couldn't imagine Collin bringing it up while we consummated our marriage, which I was actually excited to do so I could further fantasize about Dave with no repercussions.

"I don't know what you're talking about." I smiled, pulling away intentionally to create space. I wanted him to work for it.

"You know *exactly* what I'm talking

about," Dave said. He gave me a quick twirl, tossing me out, before pulling me in close again. He *was* a good dancer.

"Why didn't you say anything when we stopped by the dreaded singles table?" I whispered back to him.

"Funny. But I don't find being single dreadful at all," he said, pleased with himself.

"So I've heard," I purred.

"You know, we all thought Coll would bag a socialite when his number was up. Not a career woman like you. It's impressive. My money was on Heather Concord. Easy on the eyes, low on the brains. But you probably keep him on his toes."

"You didn't bet on your friend Gale?" I asked.

"No." He laughed. "I did not bet on Gale Wallace-Leicester marrying Collin Case."

"Why not?" I asked, feigning innocence, which he caught on to immediately.

"You're bad," he replied. He liked it.

"So you're coming back to New York full-time?"

"Mm-hmm." He nodded, giving me another spin out and back in again. "Still figuring out where I want to land. Somewhere safe." He smiled.

"What about the Upper West Side? To stay

close to your friend Hemingway."

"So she's a comedian?"

"The observational kind. What were you up to that day?"

"When I'm in town for a quick trip, I usually stay with Gale."

"Why?" I couldn't hide my disdain and that made him laugh again.

"She doesn't ask questions."

"I think it's a valid question considering the existence of hotels and, I'm assuming, a fair amount of properties in the family?"

"Gale's an old friend and her place is nice. It's private. And I can be off the grid a bit," he explained. "See, Bea, I don't like my whereabouts widely known. I don't know if you know this about me, but I'm followed. Socially, that is." I snorted. "I know I sound like a dick" — he laughed, too — "but it's true. So I was in town for some meetings and I didn't want to see anyone else and I didn't want anyone seeing me. Fuck Page Six, you know?"

"Mysterious whereabouts. Hmm. Sounds about right."

"Oh yeah?" Dave was amused. He looked too hot. Too delicious. His dark hair slicked back for the occasion, a regular wolf of Wall Street up to no good, practically licking his chops as he grinned at me and my décolletage. "What have you heard?" I'd heard too much. Bad things that drew me to him, because deep down I was a bad person, too. I had to fight it.

"I know all about your contribution to my bachelorette celebration."

"What?" He looked genuinely confused. I refused to believe him. I had to. For so many reasons, largely because this information was what would keep me away from him. I wanted no part of anyone who went to the house on East Eighty-First Street willingly.

"You know what I'm talking about. Don't play this game with me."

"I think you're probably too smart for me to play games with, no matter what Gale says about you." He was trying to distract me with chatter about Gale. Smart, but I was smarter.

"I'm sure she has plenty to say about me. None of which I care to hear."

"I wouldn't stress about it. She's obsessed with Collin. We all know it. It's been that way forever. Kinda sad. Gale's all right. Just stuck."

"Are *you* all right?"

"Probably not." He grinned, getting closer to my ear once again. His beard brushed against my shoulder. It was impossibly soft.

His crotch grazed my thigh. A semi lurked, not surprising. "But neither are you, hmm?"

He saw me. The person I tried so much to hide. It was hot and hideous. I didn't want to be seen unless I allowed it, which I never did, but Dave wasn't waiting for permission. He was taking what he wanted, just like I did. A kindred spirit of the most menacing kind, akin to taking a shot. Hurts a little at first, in a fun way. A light buzz almost immediately appears. You want it again; you're having a good time; it feels like living on the edge. Too much, though, and it could all go dark. Very dark. A blackout.

"Careful," I warned. I couldn't go down that road no matter how much fun it looked.

"Being all right is boring. You're far from boring," he said.

"You don't know anything about me," I scoffed, jerking away from him, afraid he knew everything about me, could smell it on me. Collin was watching. So was Gale. Haven, too. Mother would have been watching as well. Gleefully, I'm sure. Dave jerked me back into his body. I allowed it so I could enjoy the last few seconds. The song had to be almost over, and after our dance I never wanted to speak to him again.

It wouldn't be worth it. Would it?

"I know you broke into Gale's apartment," Dave said.

"Who cares? Gale knows, too. Did you talk to her about it?"

"Nah. None of my business. I didn't even put two and two together until it came to me where I'd seen you before. Tagged in all of Collin Case's photos. A pretty quick engagement, no?"

"Just under a year is perfectly civilized for normal people who pursue monogamous relationships," I said, knowing neither of us were particularly normal. "Collin and I knew what we wanted. We're adults."

"But you can't *really* get to know a person in that short amount of time."

He dipped me next and I really went for it. Might as well. I threw my head back so dramatically that we received a smattering of applause for our performance. Dave whipped me back upright and we locked eyes again.

Okay, this had to end. I saw Haven gnawing on the straw of her diet G&T, watching us intently, probably frothing at the mouth at the mere glimmer of an affair, which would result in a swift kick of my ass right out the Case family doors if she had her way. I couldn't give her the satisfaction.

I looked again for Collin. He was having a

stiff drink at the bar. I'd clearly driven him to it, so I needed to get out of there and make amends with a cheeky public caress at the front of his trousers.

"Isn't that part of the fun of marriage? That's when you get to know each other. When you're *really* in it," I challenged Dave. "And you either make it or you don't."

"Isn't that playing with fire?"

"Maybe. But I'm not afraid of getting burned."

The song ended on my lie, and I left Dave on the dance floor.

Of course I was afraid of getting burned in my marriage to Collin. Sure, the prenup was favorable to the untrained eye, but it wouldn't mean hanging up my hat for good, which is all I wanted to do. I *had* to stay with Collin. I *wanted* to stay with Collin. If I played by the rules, there wouldn't be any problems, beyond extreme boredom, which was somewhat of an Achilles' heel of mine. I could see myself struggling with the rules. Gale provoking me, seemingly forever a fixture in my marriage unless I did something about it. A grim and yet somehow gripping prospect. Dave. Desiring a full-blown dick-down courtesy of the hottest man I may have ever laid eyes on. A disaster waiting to happen if I wasn't careful. Even

Syl. Perhaps I was cut out for a female friendship after all, I just hadn't found the right woman to convince me until her. But what if she couldn't be trusted? The temptations were firing from all angles, but I had told myself that after Collin and I were married, my rabble-rousing would have to come to a close. Stay the course. Be a good wife. Reap all the benefits. Lonely and boring, but safe, which was the whole point of the ruse anyway.

God. Mother would definitely be *laughing* if she could see me now. I was so irritated with myself for thinking of her at all on my wedding day. The opposite of my North Star. I would not go south like her. I needed to distract myself from such a depressing state of mind, but Collin was taking shots with his friends, already sloppy, singing along to Neil Diamond. He'd be of little comfort. I really wanted to talk to Syl. I didn't know what I could reasonably tell her, but her presence could be soothing. I scanned the room for my friend, noticing that Gale was still watching me. Observing me with a half smile and a half-drunk glass of champagne in her hand. Sinister energy as per usual. Did she know I was searching for Syl? Did she think I was looking for her?

None of it mattered because Syl had already left.

I was on my own. As always.

CHAPTER 14

Collin and I went to the Maldives for our honeymoon. We woke up every morning to a shimmering blend of teal, cerulean and turquoise waters, gently knocking against the dock poles of our overwater bungalow. I had a different bikini for every day — iridescent, animal print, floral, more animal print, of course. Giant hats and sunnies and constant SPF to keep that moneymaker fresh. When golden hour struck each evening, the pinks and the purples only emphasizing my outrageous tan, Collin was an excellent Instagram-husband, taking thirst-trap photos of me in front of all the breathtaking scenery. He took extra care to capture my essence from my best angles — not terribly difficult, as they're all pretty fantastic. I even allowed for a few newlywed selfies, since those would be obligatory to post as well. My caption game was on point, drawing near-constant DMs from people who wanted to "collaborate." No, thank you. Delete.

The point of it all?

I knew that Gale Wallace-Leicester would see every post on my feed — *and* in my stories, with a fake account so I wouldn't outright catch her stalking. Nothing felt better than that. I also innocently wondered if Dave was checking in, too. My dance with Dave at the reception aside, Collin and I actually had a wonderful time together on our trip, leading me to believe any foul moods or brain fog he had been experiencing was all due to wedding stress, like he'd said it was. Now the wedding was over so we could finally be ourselves.

Within reason.

Collin and I arrived back at our town house with a signature newlywed glow, physically manifesting in our enviable island tans. He even lifted me across the threshold like we were in the 1950s. Lovely. I had never felt so accomplished. Work was work, that was always a given, I'd rise to the very top in due time, now just for fun. But marrying into one of the richest families on the planet? That took true skill, and I'd done it, all while I was still shy of thirty.

There was nothing left to do except finally

take down Gale Wallace-Leicester for good.

Oh, no. I wasn't about to forget every stunt she pulled. Attempts to sully my reputation with the Case family. Her bullshit toast at the wedding. *East Eighty-First Street.* I couldn't forget. I wouldn't let her just slip away, lying in wait, rearing her ugly head into my marriage whenever she saw fit to do so, like I'm sure she was planning. I'd thought long and hard about it on the honeymoon. I wouldn't be like Mother, not this time, but playtime was over. I was Collin's *wife* now, a newfound power in our dynamic, and Gale needed to go. I was well within my rights. She was asking for it, and I would use Collin to do it. It was the best way to proactively protect myself *and* I wanted to make it hurt. Why not? She deserved it.

If Mother were in my position, I knew she'd have an entirely different outlook on the matter. She wouldn't give Gale the time of day. She probably would have drowned Collin in the Indian Ocean, after learning his net worth, taking him out on a catamaran at sea on the honeymoon, placing the blame on a feigned boating accident, fully milking the persona of a rich widow for as long as it behooved her. And then she'd be on to the next one.

See, we were *nothing* alike. Mother and me. I had done what I had to do to survive.

But Mother liked the chase. Mother liked the con. Mother really liked a long con, provided the stakes continued to grow. It was exciting for her. She relished seeing what she could get away with, and for a very long time, she got away with a lot. Mother was never about love or stability or finding a partner or trying to raise a well-adjusted daughter or anything a normal person would like to achieve. She wasn't a normal person. I knew I wasn't normal by the standard metrics either, I couldn't help what I inherited, but I knew I could be different from her.

I had to be, once I freed myself from her.

Would I have liked the opportunity to show a man the real me? Have a real relationship? Fall in love? Of course I considered it, a long time ago when I first returned to New York, but who in their right mind would want to deal with everything that I carried with me? What was inside of me? Who would *really* stay at the end of the day? No one normal, no one kind, no good man would cook breakfast for a girl like me, buy me flowers just because, introduce me to their own mother, knowing the truth about me. She took that from me. A girl like me would only attract the darkness, and she made me that way, with a smile, knowing exactly what she had stolen. In doing so, Mother unwittingly taught me that it was always better to leave than to be left behind. Better to be what others need, cater to their emotions, give them what they want, than focus on what I actually needed myself. And now? Now I didn't need what most people need. I worked that all out, cultivating it like a callus, training myself to be a predator, like a great white shark. Singular focus. They eat, fuck and sleep? Well, me fucking too. Get to the top of that food chain and stay there. Stay alive.

Of course I would have liked something different, but it was never going to happen and I don't dream for anything that I can't make come true. Not anymore.

So I intended to take my job of keeping Collin happy *very* seriously, which would prove difficult because his libido took a real leap off a cliff after the honeymoon. Don't get me wrong, our sex life was never *raucous,* but it was certainly consistent, and his sudden disinterest was baffling, particularly when we really upped the ante in the Maldives. We had been screwing constantly. It was the happiest I'd ever seen him. Worlds away from his dull family, his dull job, his dull friends. It was all Bea, all the time, for three full weeks, and he couldn't get enough of me. Hell, maybe I was just the littlest bit happy, too. A honeymoon has that effect on people. Everyone you encounter is just so thrilled for you, it's contagious. Little treats and surprises everywhere you go. It's their pleasure! Congratulations! Such a beautiful couple! Beautiful weather, beautiful places, beautiful food, beautiful drinks. It's just all so goddamn beautiful. No, I didn't love Collin, but the feeling of being there with him made me imagine what it would be like with someone I did love. Someone I *could* love, had my life gone a different way. What a fairy tale, but if not in the Maldives, where else could you fantasize about fairy tales?

But Collin was moody again a few days after our return. His whole demeanor had shifted. He had gone sullen, more quiet and cold. Collin was a congenial man most of the time. Nearly always pleasant. He was never wildly intriguing or the life of the party or the brightest bulb in any room anywhere, but people liked him, myself included, and that's because he gravitated to the sunny side of life. Until he didn't. Yet another wrench for me to contend with.

I wasn't sure how to broach the subject of depression with Collin. We had talked about it once early on and it never came up again because he said it was no longer a problem. Yet here it was. Sometimes I would hear him crying alone in the bathroom. On the weekends he would scarcely get out of bed. He was ordering multiple Oreo milkshakes to our apartment and asking *me* to answer the door like some kind of binge-eating freak show. He managed to keep going to work for the sake of his father, but it was clear he was phoning it in, which only strained their relationship even further.

Syl clued me in on that development. I hadn't seen her since the wedding. She had commented on social media a handful of times since, to compliment the honeymoon photos, but our text chain had run cold. I was sure she was giving me space to enjoy being newly married, but I was relieved she finally reached out. I actually missed her.

"Hey," she said on the phone, her voice an octave higher than normal.

"Syl, I've missed you! And our lunches —"

"I know, I know. I'm sorry. It's been a while, but you just got married and anyway, we should definitely do lunch soon, but I wanted to tell you about something that I think you should know," she said, speaking faster than normal, suggesting nerves about whatever she was going to tell me. "I overheard Hayes on a call this morning," Syl continued. "He was talking about Collin and his, um, performance at work. He's disappointed."

"Interesting. I've also noticed similar behavior at home."

"Collin just sits all day in his office. He barely takes any calls. No meetings. I don't know what he's doing in there. The door is always closed. And it's not my place, but —"

"I'm glad you told me."

"Well, you're his family now. And I'm worried, too. He's not himself."

She was right. I was Collin's family now and he was clearly struggling. What would a good wife do in this scenario? She'd put her husband first even if it was painful. So that's what I would have to do, too. Besides, once Collin was up and running again, I could shift our family's focus to the ruin of Gale Wallace-Leicester.

I decided to confer with Collin's mother as a first step. His medical files from years past only told me so much. A more robust firsthand account would be appreciated. It was obviously serious if I was willingly seeking out the advice of Haven Case, in a gesture of goodwill for my relationship with my mother-in-law, for Collin's health and ultimately my revenge on Gale. I made the trek to Connecticut under the guise of lunch, explaining that it would be nice to get to know each other better, one-on-one, but Haven Case was no fool. She knew I had an ulterior motive before I even stepped foot in the manse. It almost felt like she was expecting this sort of visit from me. Her smile was eerie. Knowing.

"Have a seat, dear," she said. Haven received me in the parlor, greeting me with an air-kiss when I approached her. We didn't touch. "I was delighted to see your request for company. And very surprised because it's such a sweet gesture."

I would have loved to spar with her, but that wasn't the point of the visit. I had to keep my eye on the prize. It was so difficult, her voice oozing with judgment. It infuriated me that I had such a hard time getting her to like me, despite my sparkling wit and undeniable charisma. I knew that Haven and I would have gotten along just fine if I had come from some family of consequence. No question. We were quite similar when it came down to it, but I feared that I would never be good enough in her eyes. She might never consider me one of them, merely pretending forever, always secretly hoping Collin would serve me my walking papers and my allotted millions outlined in the prenup.

And yes, she'd made sure it was just under $5 million to spite me.

"The pleasure is all mine, Haven." I smiled at her. "Thank you for hosting me."

"So how are we enjoying married life, Mrs. Case?" she asked me, as if my new name were a punch line. I had to cut right to the chase. Get in, get help and get out.

"You know that I'm so happy to be married to your son," I began.

"Oh, yes, *I know,*" she interrupted, sipping her tea, keeping her eyes locked with mine.

"But I'll be very clear with you. I wanted to ask you about something rather difficult. You see, since we've returned from our trip, Collin has seemed distant. I'd even go so far as to say unwell, and I'm not really sure what to do for him. To help. And since you're his mother, I wanted to come to you."

"For *help*?" She cocked her head to the side, feigning cluelessness.

"Yes. With *your* son." I had to swallow my pride. It was the best thing for Collin, so it would be the best thing for me.

"But you're his wife?" She was taunting

me. Enjoying it.

"Yes, which is a role in this family that I'm taking very seriously, hence my visit to see you today. I know we both want what's best for Collin."

"Do we?" Haven let the question hang in the air. I refused to acknowledge it. I had my limits. "So Collin's in one of his *moods* I take it?" Haven said, finally breaking the silence.

"Could you clarify what you mean?" I wanted specifics. I wanted to know everything that she knew.

"I assume he's getting a little insular? Withdrawn? Sad, basically?"

"Yes," I said, nodding my head as she rattled off symptoms like a Zoloft commercial.

"So he gets a little *surly* sometimes, Bea. It's not a big deal," Haven mused, completely nonchalant. "He snaps out of it eventually every time. You just have to let nature run its course. Be patient. It's really nothing to worry about."

"But I *am* worried, Haven." I was insistent, hoping she would suggest something tangible, like a refill or a shrink. "I've never seen him like this before."

"Bea, please. You've only known him, what, a little over a year or so? Isn't that right?" She played with the pearls around her neck as she played with me.

"That's right," I said with a pained smile. "Since you're so familiar with this issue, I gather that this is a recurring, um, problem?"

"It's not a problem if you already know the solution. And the solution is time. Collin will sort himself out. He always does."

"Okay. Does he have other resources available to help him with depression?"

"You say *depression* like it's something serious," Haven scoffed. "The Cases come from healthy stock. It's nothing, Bea. Completely normal. As for resources? Hmm. He has a wife, doesn't he? In sickness and in health, dear. You said it yourself."

She was reveling in my dismay over her own son's mental issues. No wonder Collin was so eager to get married to me, my charm and beauty withstanding. I actually made it a point to care about his well-being. I knew intimately that if you couldn't rely on your own mother, you're inevitably fucked-up forever about where to go for any sort of help. You just let any and all issues fester on the inside until you explode or melt down or spiral into a deep pit of despair, like Collin. Or use it as fuel, like I did, but most people weren't like me. At any rate, Haven Case was basically telling me that Collin was my problem now.

After a few more weeks of being patient and no improvement whatsoever, I realized I would have to speak directly with Collin about the issue at hand so we could fix it and I could get down to business with Gale. My previous soft attempts were always rebuffed. He was rather deft at changing the subject or he'd stonewall me altogether, retreating to another room without me. It was infuriating. I demanded respect and admiration at all times, especially this early. Our marriage was off to a pitiful start, which could make it easier for Collin to leave. Sure, a few years down the line, couples get ornery with one another. It could happen. It's normal. Every WASP probably stays in an unhappy marriage, or spells of one, regardless; no one wants to divorce after a certain amount of time. More discretion needed for any *extracurricular* activities perhaps, but they often learn to look the other way. Put up a front. It's fine. But that's not where Collin and I were. We were mere weeks in and he was already behaving this way? I was very concerned. With Collin being of a different generation from his parents, maybe there would be even more understanding that he made a mistake. A rash decision. Who among us hasn't fallen in love too fast before? Wrongly seduced by Cupid's wayward arrow. They could all look the other way as I was left out in the cold with nothing. A blip on the Case family radar. Break off my branch from the tree, let a new one grow in its place. I had to get ahead of this and figure out what was wrong with him. Primarily for my *own* mental health.

Collin was watching an animated show for adults, in pajama pants, housing ice cream from the carton. Dreadful. His poor diet was starting to show on his body. He needed me and I would have to be up to the task. "Hello, Mr. Case." I snuggled up next to him and went in for a kiss. He offered his cheek. Savage. I had to bring out the big guns. "I visited your mother the other week. As you know, I've been concerned about you."

Collin shot up from the couch and turned around to look at me, stunned by my revelation. "So you went to see my *mom*?" It was the most animated I'd seen him in ages. I stood up to meet his gaze.

"I had some questions for her about what's been going on with you. I thought she might be helpful, since it didn't seem like you wanted to talk about it with me."

"You went to my mom for help?" He laughed mirthlessly, his teeth taking center stage yet again. "Jesus Christ."

"I don't know what else I was supposed to do. You think I wanted to go see her? I'm trying. With your family. With you. Collin, I've been trying to talk to you about how you're feeling since we got back in town. It's been weeks. This isn't like you."

"I'm sure she had a lot to contribute. So what wisdom did she impart to you?"

"I thought I was doing the right thing. I'm sorry if I upset you."

"I'm fine."

He was lying to my face. Oh, we were married now, the dark side of it quickly emerging. But I had to stay sweet and concerned. Not for Collin, but for me. Eye on the prize. I'd watched Mother do it before. I could do it, too.

"She mentioned that this happens sometimes and that it isn't cause for concern. I disagree —"

"Like she'd know anything about it," he grumbled.

"Have you talked to anybody recently?" I had to tread lightly. This was a delicate subject. Clearly. "Like a professional?"

"No," he barked. "I know how to handle

myself."

Love is patient, love is kind, I thought to myself and scoffed.

Keep it up, Bea. Keep. It. Up.

"Okay. Well, maybe you could see a doctor. Just in case there's some new developments. There's no shame in taking care of yourself. We can get some referrals easily, I'm sure." I believed this to be a pretty mild request and one that should be nonnegotiable. Didn't he want to feel better? Besides, I needed him at his peak to finish off Gale.

"I see my doctor regularly," he said offhandedly. Collin sank back on the couch to resume his heinous program. I was losing him again. Now he was depressed and cross with me. A terrible combination.

"Okay, well, did you call him or her about what's been going on recently?"

"Him," he snarled.

"Did. You. Call. Him?" If he was going to take on the persona of a misogynistic ass, I could also rise to the occasion with some sass of my own. I wasn't a saint! I was being a very good wife to him and he was refusing all of my advances to help him. An outrage.

"This is my business, Bea. Don't worry about it."

So he was testing me. How positively

maddening. I wondered if Mother went through any of this with her husbands — surprise "quirks" postnuptials that could throw a marriage right off-kilter. Nothing that called for homicide, of course, but irksome all the same. I didn't actually worry about Collin, though I wasn't expecting such a dramatic turn from my mild-mannered man. Truthfully, I would have loved to spend some time to myself while he went through his episodes, occasionally and privately, but I needed him now to get to Gale as soon as possible. So I kept up the charade of aggressively caring.

"But I *am* worried about it. I love you. You could see a therapist, or maybe a psychiatrist could prescribe something else that would take the edge off a bit. Just until you're feeling back to normal. It's not a big deal. I know your mother may suggest otherwise, but I'm not judging you, Collin." I sat next to him on the couch, running my hands through his hair, wanting him to look me in the eye, hoping that if he truly connected with me, he would snap out of it. "It's hard to be a person sometimes, honey. I get it. It's okay."

"I *am* taking care of it!" Collin shouted. "Now lay off me, Bea, all right? Please? I know how to deal with this and you just have to let me be." And then he got up to get a beer from the fridge, which totally seemed like a sensible decision in the midst of a heated discussion with one's wife. Atrocious behavior, but I would not be deterred by his antics, no matter how exasperating. If he wanted to be an oafish husband, I would match that undesirable energy, channeling a stereotypical shrew of a wife.

"*How* are you taking care of it?" I asked. "With a doctor?"

"It doesn't matter! Bea, I'm sorry. I don't want to rope you into my shit like this. I know that I suck right now. I'm not an idiot. But it always goes away. It will go away again. I promise. Just leave it alone and trust me. Please?"

"Collin. I am your wife. You have to —"

"And I want you to *stay* my wife, so we're not opening this box today."

He stood in the kitchen, staring at me in between sips of beer. At least he was finally making eye contact with me, some life behind them, but I flinched at what he just said. Now it was out there. He could go at any time. How to play it next with so much on the line? It seemed to anger him when I wilted like a flower. That wasn't something he loved about me. He came alive when I got a little fiery. He liked reactionary Bea.

He liked the knowledge that something *he* did made me react strongly. Power. Of course. Okay then.

"Are you *threatening* to leave me? We've been married all of a few weeks. This isn't how a functioning couple should operate. We aren't communicating and I won't have it, and if you think you can just push me away, you've got another thing coming."

I was trying not to panic at his silence, but then he finally held out his hands for mine. I'd done it. Thank God.

"Bea. Stop it. Just stop. Please." I let Collin hold me close even though I was enraged by even the insinuation that he would leave me. How dare he frighten me so! He hadn't touched me at all in what felt like ages. Maybe I was in over my head. I wasn't cut out for this kind of life. Bored and married and having to deal with someone else's problems in addition to my own. Sharing a life. One heated argument away from losing it all. Yikes. Perhaps Mother was right. We weren't like them. We never could be.

I didn't want it to be true.

"That's not it," Collin whispered into my hair, taking a deep breath, in and out. "That's not it at all. I'm not going to leave you. I would never leave you, Bea. Never.

I'm terrified you'll leave me." His reassurance hit me like a drug. I still had the upper hand.

"Okay, babe. I'll trust you," I said. What other choice did I have?

"Okay," he agreed. We kissed properly. *Finally,* but still, it felt removed. There was a new distance between us. He was electing to keep something from me, and I would have to allow it.

"Collin. I hope you know that I'm never going to leave you either," I said, an attempt to comfort him after he'd gotten so upset. We managed to muster up the will to have sex. Bleak, but sufficient. For him. I was left underwhelmed. And anxious. I started making justifications in my head. If *this* was how it was going to be with Collin for the foreseeable future until he felt better, maybe I could have a little fun in the interim. It might be good for both of us, for our marriage. Well, mainly for me.

Collin wouldn't even notice.

Chapter 15

Christopher Underwood, my new boss, was similar to Len Arthur in nearly every respect. Average height, paunchy, thin lips and a weak chin that would do well to sport a beard, but he didn't have the good sense. Though he leered openly when I walked past his office, and I'll admit that Len was more discreet. It made me think that Christopher must be nearing retirement. He was of thc right age and he clearly had no regard for general propriety in an office environment. I *also* found myself having zero regard for my work, at least not in the way that I normally did as far as promotions, advancements and access to interesting projects went. The sad fact was that it wasn't difficult to impress Christopher, or anyone at the new agency, because I had brought the Case Company business with me.

I was already at the top with zero effort.

"I feel restless," I told Syl at happy hour, our reunion finally coming to pass. Her schedule had been a nightmare, apparently, so I let her take the lead, feeling pitiful when dates I suggested were not amenable to her. Irritating.

"Why's that?" she asked, glancing out the window behind me. Was she even listening?

"Well, I'm not having to work as hard."

"And that's a bad thing?"

"I just don't think complacency is ever a good thing for anybody. Idle hands and all that."

"Oh, but I think you'd be a fun plaything for the devil," Syl said, tossing back the rest of her drink. She was ahead of me by at least one. She seemed nervous. Fidgeting. Coping with cocktails. "What about any home projects? Could you take on some of those to pass the time?"

"There's nothing to be done. I suppose we could start exploring a new vacation house, just for us, but I don't know. Our home life right now is still a little fraught, as you know." I was unnerved by my candor with Syl, but I couldn't help myself. I was starting to trust her.

"Whatever, Bea, don't stress. Men are on their own fucking planet. He'll come around."

"Have you noticed anything else at the office?"

"I don't know much more than what I already told you," she said.

"Right. I'm sorry I asked. I know it's a weird line to cross."

"It's fine. We're friends," she said. That's right. We were. So we should act like it, too. I was tired of talking about myself anyway. A first.

"How's John doing?" I asked her.

"Oh, the same. Noncommittal about setting a date. My dad thinks I should break it off with him, too. He's on your side."

"Well, we are correct, but don't all dads believe their daughters are too good for their boyfriends?" I asked, not really having any firsthand knowledge about what dads are prone to do.

"Yeah, but I actually trust him. He's a good man. My dad." She stared at me intensely, willing me to engage further on the subject. I complied.

"I believe you, Syl." I sensed she might want to talk about her incarcerated father in more detail and that I should indulge her if I wanted to continue our developing friendship.

"He shouldn't be in there, in case you were wondering. He didn't do it," she said forcefully.

"Okay. I said I believe you."

"I'm serious, Bea," she said, her eyes growing wide. "It's actually fucking crazy that he's in prison. *My* dad. He's basically been there my whole life and I still can't wrap my head around it. He's the sweetest man. Just so fucking sweet."

"I'm so sorry, Syl."

She inhaled and exhaled quickly. It was bizarre to see her so upset. "What about your parents?" Syl asked in a more accusatory tone than I would have liked.

"I told you. They're —"

"Dead, I know," she interrupted, on a mission. "But what were they *like*?"

"Nice," I said, knowing how to weave this particular web without much thought. "Sweet, too. Older. Just sort of normal people. Their main hobby, outside of me, was ballroom dancing. They even traveled to competitions sometimes. It was cute." Specifics are always convincing, just not *too* many, lest you lose track in a future conversation.

"Were you close with them?"

"Close enough," I continued. "I was an only child so it was always the three of us. That said, they treated me like their child, not their friend. They had healthy boundaries, which I always appreciated." What a dream scenario that would be. I found myself daydreaming about what that would have been like. Healthy parenting from not just one, but two people. Syl didn't know either. Maybe that's why I felt so connected to her. I hadn't spent so much time elaborating on my made-up parents because most people didn't ask further once they learned of their deaths. But Syl wasn't most people.

"What was your mother's name?" Syl asked.

I never knew Mother's real name because she refused to tell me. Only the first letter. I asked her every so often, during the in-between times when it was safer, no man to overhear us, but I suspected she liked holding it over my head. A mystery, along with my own given name.

"Alice," I told Syl.

"And your father?" Syl prodded.

"Bob. Robert," I added, getting uncomfortable with revealing all of these details. I motioned to the server for another drink. I was feeling forlorn, sad for a version of me as a child that didn't exist, would never exist, and longing for people that didn't exist, would never exist. "What's your father's name?" I asked Syl, wanting to turn the tables on her.

"Giles. He just had a birthday. Almost thirty years lost inside."

"That's a very long time," I said, hoping it would put an end to the conversation. Some happy hour.

"Anyway," Syl said, clearly picking up on my signals. "I'm sorry you've been feeling restless at work. I'm sure things will pick up soon." Her tone was flippant, suggesting my problems were frivolous. Maybe so, but it was a nice change of pace. She didn't know what I had gone through, but I was dying to tell her. I dreamt about comparing dark family pasts with Syl. She would understand me on some level. Her father was in prison, leaving her to grow up in the system. Syl and I both had the same hard edges that we could soften on command to the untrained eye. Me with a made-up story. Syl with that sunny disposition. We let people think they had us figured out. It was a lot easier to be a woman in the world if you weren't a puzzle to be solved.

I stumbled home from the bar feeling unsettled. I needed some kind of release. Collin was nowhere to be found when I got back, a little buzzed, a little frisky. I should have been more concerned about his whereabouts, but I just wanted to shake off that abysmal happy hour with Syl. Collin was fine, I told myself. He knew what he was doing.

There was no work to catch up on. No scheming to be done. No revenge to plot, at least not until Collin was well enough for me to utilize him properly. I was well and truly bored, which was never a good thing for a girl like me.

I felt like getting into trouble.

Dave Bradford's number was easy enough to find in my regular hacking of Collin's computer, phone and tablet. It was just there, waiting for me to use it. We'd just text, I told myself. *Maybe* sext. Perfectly harmless.

Hey, this is Bea, I texted him. So thrilling. So dangerous. Somebody might see it.

I know who it is, he responded within seconds, with the little purple devil face emoji. Flustering. A tawdry retort. He was obviously game.

If you have my number, why haven't you used it?

Too bold. Dk if Coll sees your msgs or not.

Nothing to hide. It's just texting.

I settled into the bed, crossing one leg over the other. I was exhilarated. The blue dots came and went a few times on the screen. He was practically strangling me with suspense. Seconds passed, but it felt like minutes. He finally settled on a message.

For now.

I was wet. I did not respond further. Always leave them wanting more.

And I knew I wanted more than just texting.

Want to help me look at apartments? Dave texted me the following day. I scoffed aloud in my office. Real estate shopping was so intimate. It was a terrible idea.

When?

On your lunch?

I often take a working lunch, I texted, toying with him, having fun, the whole point.

Can you slip away on a Friday?

Maybe. But can you wait that long? Sounds urgent, especially if you're staying with Gale.

Not at Gale's. Four Seasons. I can wait. Dave Bradford at the Four Seasons sounded like the lunch break of a lifetime. I could not wait.

I can pencil it in for Friday under new business.

The blue dots again. Bated. Breath.

Great. Lk fwd to learning more about your biz.

Oh God. I asked myself if this was something Mother would do. The answer was:

not exactly. She didn't succumb to sexual urges like a regular person. Hers was more of a bloodlust. Money hungry. The con was her lover. Still, when I started to sense one of my wild streaks coming on, I really tried to keep a lid on it, despite my animal instincts. It wasn't behavior like Mother, but it was Mother-adjacent enough to give me pause. But it had been *so* long. The urges hadn't even really happened since I'd been with Collin, except for the rivalry with Gale, but that wasn't the same thing. I had found my lack of deviant behavior comforting. Boring, but comforting. I was hoping that side of me had been snuffed because this was *it* with Collin. He was the one. The person I needed to have. To feel safe.

But then I met Dave and now I was salivating over him. This bubbling feeling of just wanting to *see* what could happen if I did step a toe out of line or drive the train off the tracks. I often felt like I could burst if I didn't go after the bad thing that I wanted. Purely pushing boundaries for pure pleasure's sake.

The same kind of thing always got Mother going.

I wasn't proud of it, but the truth was that anytime I took a menacing turn, I never felt more alive. So I had a predilection for erratic behavior? Oh, well. I'm sure I'd inherited it from Mother. But I knew how to manage it.

Mostly.

I wouldn't actually let him touch me.

Would I?

The workweek dragged on, as I had almost nothing to do except eagerly await Friday. In retrospect, it probably wasn't a good idea to have all that anticipation built from our last correspondence. There was absolutely nothing in the interim. No chitchat. No confirmation the day before. Just an address in the East Village that came through via text that morning around 10:00. I was instructed to meet him there at 12:30.

A brooding Dave waited for me, just outside the building, smoking a cigarette, looking extremely hot. When I exited the taxi, the left corner of his dirty little mouth curled upward, the cigarette firmly in position on the other side. I wanted to ravage him right there in front of the doorman. Take out your phone and film it, buddy, I didn't care. Luckily, cooler heads prevailed when I approached him, since I shook his hand instead of mounting him.

"Dave. Nice to see you again." I smiled.

He didn't say anything in return. He

simply motioned with his head for me to follow him, tossing his cigarette to the side. We didn't say much in the elevator either, though it was clear our hearts were racing and our loins were quivering. He stood right next to me, our bodies softly touching, a physical heat building between us. It was erotic. Illicit. Mouthwatering. When we finally got to the correct floor and the doors parted, Dave opened his mouth.

"How's Collin?" he asked me.

Jesus. What a boner killer. If Dave wanted to start a full-blown affair with me, why would he bring up my husband? I was annoyed. "Wonderful," I replied. "The perfect husband."

"That sounds like Collin."

"Does it?"

"Gale's always thought so."

"Ha. Ha." He was teasing me on purpose. He liked that I was married. He liked that I hated Gale. He liked this game we were playing. Truthfully, I did, too. He put a key in the door. I noticed it was the only door on the floor. The penthouse. "So where's the broker?" I asked him.

"Not here," Dave said, walking in the door. I followed him inside, elated to be alone. The apartment was stunning. No town house, but nothing to sniff at either.

Three beds, three baths, and I wanted to have sex with him in all of them. Plentiful views through the floor-to-ceiling windows. Lots of concrete and metal and matte finishes. It was harsh and industrial. What we deserved.

"What do you think?" Dave asked me, looking around like an inspector.

"It's all right," I said, nonchalant. "Lots of hard edges."

"No children here. I don't see the problem."

"It's fine. If you like that sort of thing."

"I do." Dave leaned over the counter in the kitchen, looking like a real cad. "That's why I bought it. You were right. I couldn't wait until Friday."

"So you just invited me over to your *home*?"

"Looks like it." He grinned. What a brazen little hussy. I was gagging for him to make a move.

"Hmm. Well, it's definitely an upgrade from Gale's guest room."

"You girls and your beef." He laughed.

"She started it. I had no issue with her until she started meddling in my relationship. Tell me, why do you all have this inexplicable unfailing loyalty to her?"

"All of who?"

"The *guys,*" I replied. "Gale is the only gal in the bunch. So she's a real 'guys' girl,' right? As if there could be anything worse." As I said that aloud, it was the first time I realized Gale and I might have had something in common other than Collin. She didn't have any girlfriends either.

"Worse than having no friends at all?" he asked pointedly, opening the refrigerator. He pulled out two beers and I laughed out loud at him. Why didn't we just have a loaf of bread? I pranced over to him and took one of the beers out of his hand, delicately placing it back from whence it came.

"Quality over quantity is my policy," I told him, opening the freezer in search of vodka. As predicted, Dave had a bottle of Belvedere that beckoned. Good man.

"Allow me," he said, taking the bottle from my hands, pouring two fingers into a crystal lowball. "No mixer I assume?"

"Correct." Why hadn't he pounced on me yet?

"So does Collin think you're at lunch?" he asked me.

"Collin and I don't eat together every day like we're in the high school cafeteria. He has a job. I have a job. I often take a working lunch. I'm a very, very busy advertising professional. Why do you keep bringing him up?"

"Making observations."

"And?" The vodka was going down way too easy on that fine Friday afternoon.

"You don't seem that affected at all by my mentioning him," Dave said.

"You're testing me?"

He laughed and clinked his bottle against my glass. "I'm not, but if I were, you'd definitely pass."

"I always do," I said, no shame.

"So why'd you marry him, Bea?" Dave was getting closer again. He pulled out a barstool, urging me to sit down next to him. I perched on the counter instead, crossing my legs, leaning back on my hands, arching my back. A position of seduction. A total tease.

"He's perfectly marriable, don't you think? Checks a lot of boxes? A bachelor of the most eligible kind. He's a catch."

"That's true. I love the guy. He's one of the good ones. The rest of us? We all got something."

"Even you?"

"*Especially* me. Look at me. I'm here with you. You're married to one of my oldest friends. That's pretty messed up. Right? Kinda sick?" It absolutely was and I knew that's why I loved it so much. The shame would have to be dealt with later. It was nowhere to be found in that apartment.

"So why are you here with me?" I lowered my voice to a whisper, knowing it would drive him crazy. "Just because I'm married to Collin?"

"No. I like it, but that's not the only reason."

"So?"

"Look at you," he said breathlessly. Dave stood up from the barstool, putting his hands on my hips. God, he was so impossibly sexy. It felt like we were in an erotic thriller from the nineties. The best kind.

"Hey." I pushed his hands off me to keep dangling that juicy fruit. "I'm not sure I can do this to Collin, even though I've been terribly neglected in that area." I leaned to the side to grab my drink, finishing it, my lipstick lingering on the glass.

"If that's true, then Collin's an idiot." Dave clutched his beer bottle even tighter, viscerally irritated that my husband wasn't having his way with me on the regular. It was hard to disagree. "How he doesn't have his hands all over you twenty-four seven is insane. He doesn't deserve you, Bea. And hey, you know, I probably don't either, but I can guarantee that we'd have a good fuckin' time."

Yep. That would work.

I hopped off the counter and pulled my phone out from my handbag to save the recording. To listen to it later and furiously masturbate, sure. But also for safekeeping should I need it. Dave raised his eyebrows, either put off or intrigued by my basic espionage maneuver. I decided to assuage his potential nerves.

"Relax," I assured him. "It's an insurance policy. *You* are clearly coming on to *me,* which would displease Collin and the rest. I don't know you from Adam. How can I be sure you wouldn't turn this around on me?"

"I respect that." He really did seem impressed, even though it's a relatively basic method of blackmail. He must not have watched much television.

"So you understand that I need to be able to trust you if we're going to proceed —"

"To the bedroom?" he interrupted me, the tomcat.

"I haven't decided yet. Not much of a loyal friend, are we?" I was teasing Dave, but his expression changed after I said that. He was serious. About to get on a soapbox, chest puffed out like a gorilla. A ridiculously sexy gorilla.

"Hey, I know you're new here, but let me

tell you something. Our so-called group doesn't know anything about loyalty, you understand? Why do you think I'm hardly around? This is time-honored crap and old-money shit. It has nothing to do with loyalty and everything to do with the fact that we've always been so obsessed with our own success that we never made any effort to socialize outside of the friends we were given from childhood by our fucked-up loaded parents, who went through the same exact cycle in their own stupid lives."

Oh God. He felt so sorry for himself. What a clown. A ridiculously sexy clown.

"Except for you, Mr. Citizen of the World? Because you're different? 'Not like other girls,' right?" I laughed at him, but he was serious. Poor little rich boy.

"Bea, I don't have any friends either. Not real ones."

"Well, maybe we're going to be friends, Dave."

"Nah," Dave said, practically growling, shaking his head from side to side as he came close to me again, hands on my waist, then his mouth to my ear. "Friends don't fuck."

Chapter 16

I imagined that we would have banged with gusto, like wild animals. Very bad, but very good. Lip. Smacking. Good. God, why was I such a glutton for punishment? The proximity to him was nearly more than I could stand, but stand it I would. Such a shame. It would have been so satisfying. I could not remember the last time I'd experienced true pleasure. Sex was nearly always performative for me. Collin's quest to find my clitoris was hit-or-miss most of the time, and even when he managed to hit due to his dogged persistence, it was quite methodical. Like being treated for hysteria by a doctor in the 1800s. Very manual. Very matter-of-fact. With Collin, it was typically "check the box, then roll over and look at your phone" sex.

Dave, on the other hand? I knew he'd be an unhinged beast with no inhibitions whatsoever. The kind of guy that throws you over his shoulder, ready to lay you down *real good,* in a way that makes you feel light as a feather. The kind of man that makes for an absolutely terrible boyfriend, you'd never bring him home for Thanksgiving, but you'd still want to gobble his ass up on the regular. Dave was the type of man that could get you into *rimming,* for God's sake, and yes, I would have with Dave, no hesitation.

But it would be uncouth to say the least, so I got a full grip and got the hell out of there.

"Sorry, I have to go," I told him, laying it on thick with a full fan kick off the counter.

"The fuck?" he practically laughed.

"Thanks for showing me the place. It's great." I smiled at him, slinking toward the door. Down, boy.

"Bea, come on," he said, his voice returning to a sexy growl. "You never indulge in anything you actually want, do you? And I know you want me."

"Meanwhile, you indulge in everything." I rolled my eyes at him.

"Well, sure." He grinned. "Life's for living, baby." He looked really hot and I thought again about jumping his bones, but no. NO. I didn't want to go any further down the rabbit hole. That was enough fire play for the day. I wasn't like her. I couldn't be like her. And I knew exactly how to yank myself out of it.

"I want to know how you know about East Eighty-First Street."

"What are you talking about?" Dave looked very perplexed.

"I know all about how you got us on the list for my bachelorette party. *Hawkes,* is it?"

"Bea, I don't know anyone called Hawkes and I don't know anything about your party."

"I don't believe you."

"Hey," he said firmly. "I didn't have anything to do with that." I raised an eyebrow at him. He took a deep breath. *See?* I knew it. "All right, fine," he continued. "I'll be very honest with you."

"Out with it," I demanded, ready to cut him loose after he came clean.

"I know what's on East Eighty-First Street, okay? I know about it. I went once a long time ago and it's definitely not my scene. And furthermore, I wouldn't send a bunch of girls who are old friends of my family there for a fucking night out. That's too sick, even for me. What happened?"

"Nothing," I said, actually believing him. Not ideal. That would mean Gale found out another way, just as I suspected. But from whom? And what did she know exactly? I was supremely alarmed and wanted to leave. What if she was having me followed now?

"But *you* knew about it?" Dave asked me, in a way that made me uncomfortable. Okay, yes, it was officially time to go.

"I'm going to be late. You're not going to tell anyone about this?"

"No," he said without a second thought. "But I'm around if you ever want to —"

"I won't," I interrupted him, meaning it. Too much on the line and he would be too much of a distraction. I needed to focus on getting ahead of Gale and whatever her plan was. I shut Dave's door behind me, proud of myself for leaving.

It's what Bea Case would do.

And that's exactly who I was now.

I decided to leave the office a little early that day. I was still feeling the effects of my scintillating, albeit chaste, lunch hour and wanted to luxuriate in the tub with the faucet in the late afternoon to take the edge off. I knew no one would miss me at the office. I was anxious, after Dave's seemingly honest revelation, so imagine my surprise when I was faced with none other than Gale Wallace-Leicester in my home. I hadn't seen her since the wedding and the sight of her took my breath away. Her jeans were too tight and her hair was a mess and she was standing in my kitchen, pulling a Perrier out of my refrigerator, looking very pleased with herself.

"Bea. Nice to see you. How are you?"

"Gale. I didn't know we were having a guest for dinner."

"Oh, I'm not staying. We were just wrapping up." She grinned at me.

Collin appeared, exiting the restroom, stunned by my presence. "You're home early," he said like an absolute buffoon.

"So are you," I replied, maintaining rational behavior as best I could. I wouldn't let Gale get my goat unannounced like that.

"He's been taking afternoons off a few days a week," Gale said to me, the foul wench.

"Gale is who I talk to about things," Collin explained. "It's always been that way. She helps."

"*She* helps?"

"I didn't want to tell you. I didn't know how you'd take it. Gale doesn't make me feel weird or bad about it. Not saying that you do!" he added, recovering. "She's just always felt safe when I was an annoyance or embarrassment to my parents. Gale makes me feel normal. It's just our history. It's nothing else."

There was nothing normal about this dynamic and I was well within my rights to make such a declaration, but I had to go slowly with the barracuda present. Any sudden moves without thinking them through and she could bite.

"You *are* normal, Collin," Gale said to him, taking on the voice of a therapist, when she had absolutely zero credentials except as an absolutely conniving little cunt. I had to make a big move, but I couldn't predict the outcome. My least favorite type of situation. What to do?

"I'm sorry I didn't tell you it was Gale. I just know that it's been kind of tense between you two," Collin said. Gale and I stayed silent, perhaps both calculating how this would all play out.

"It was my idea to keep it a secret, Bea." Gale shifted her focus to me, playing the martyr for Collin. Well played; he enjoyed being coddled. "I know you don't like me very much, but this is what's best for Collin."

"Is it? Because to put it quite plainly I haven't seen much improvement. Are you feeling better, babe?" I asked Collin pointedly, staking claim to him as my husband, another feeling he thoroughly enjoyed.

"It's taking longer this time, but Gale says that's because we're getting older and —"

Put the blame on Gale, I thought to myself. Not on Collin. He can't handle any criticism.

"Gale isn't a doctor, Collin. A doctor would have proper therapy sessions with you and perhaps write you a different prescription —"

"But drugs make me a different person, Bea. I don't want to rely on them for the rest of my life."

Make him feel normal. This was normal. Drugs are normal.

"It's perfectly normal to take prescription medication responsibly when needed, sweetheart."

"But an all-natural approach is best," Gale said. "Don't worry, I consult with a holistic pract—"

"That's enough!" I barked, taking my own all-natural approach, a big swing. But truly, how dare Gale sink so low? Toying with Collin's health to further her own perceived gains? She had weaseled her way into his psyche as a support system when in reality she was chipping away at his very foundation!

"Bea, take it easy —" Gale began to say.

"*I* am talking now." I cut her off. "Collin, what do you tell Gale that you won't tell me?"

"Collin, you don't have to —"

"Yes. He. Does," I growled at her. If Collin needed a woman to take charge, it was going to be me. He liked a firm hand from the women in his life, that much was clear. Or at the very least, he responded well to it, from me.

Collin cleared his throat. "I talk to Gale about dark stuff. Like the stuff I don't want anyone else to know, especially my wife. She suggested that instead of blindly switching meds again with some doctor who doesn't even know me, I could work through it naturally. Together. Because she understands me. That I could get there. That if anyone could, I could."

If only Collin knew how much I was fascinated by the darkness in people, but I didn't think I could reveal such a thing to him. I was already pushing the boundaries of the picture he held of me in his mind with this fervent outburst against Gale. I had to be methodical.

"And I'm happy to be that person for Collin." Gale smiled.

"I bet you are," I snarled at her. "This is really unethical, Gale. To gamble with

Collin's health just to —"

"*This* is why we didn't want to tell you, Bea," Gale said, maintaining composure in her voice, that put-upon voice, that sickening voice. "But it isn't about you. It's about Collin. Can you understand that?"

How could Collin let this woman speak to me like that in our own home right in front of him? It was infuriating. I had had enough. Yes, it would have been fun to toy with Gale Wallace-Leicester even further, using Collin to dismiss her because of something I plotted and planned and devised and executed. But I couldn't wait any longer. I'd have to take the easy route. The window was right there. But if I opened it, would it go my way? It had to. At least then I would know for sure where I stood with Collin.

"Collin, I am your wife, and I cannot even explain to you how betrayed I feel," I said to him, completely ignoring Gale, tears filling my eyes. Guilt trips could work wonders in a man like Collin. I learned that from our last row post-honeymoon. "If this marriage is going to work, we need to be able to trust each other. Tell each other the truth."

"Oh, Bea, please don't cry." He came closer to me. It was working. "You're right."

"This *thing* between you and Gale cannot continue. I won't stand for it. It's not good for you. It's not good for us."

Gale scoffed, asking the question I knew Collin would not, falling right into my trap. "Are you giving him an ultimatum? Collin, I —"

"Gale, please," he said. The dark circles under his eyes. The extra pounds around his midsection. The pathetic look on his face. He'd do anything to keep me. I needed to finish her.

"Yes," I said. "You need to see a real doctor and you need to stop seeing Gale for whatever these quack sessions are. It all needs to stop."

"Okay," he agreed, and very fast. Gale's heart had been pierced, her eyes frantic, blinking fast.

"Fine," she said. "I can make a good recommendation and —"

"Collin," I said to my husband, not even looking at Gale. "I don't mean just the sessions. I mean all of it. All contact with her."

Gale gasped dramatically. "We've been friends for our entire lives, Bea, and you come waltzing in —"

"Gale!" Collin shouted. She shut her mouth.

"I'm serious, Collin. It's her or me and you have to decide right now."

"Collin!" Gale was beside herself. She

couldn't move. She was frozen.

Because she knew what was coming.

"It's you," Collin said to me, no hesitation, forlorn but accepting his fate. It was the right thing to do. I was the one he wanted. I had the power.

"Collin, you can't be serious! You're giving everything up for a girl like —"

"A girl like *what*?" he asked, challenging her to say it to his face.

"You'll see," she growled. "I'll make sure of it."

"Good-bye, Gale," I said to her, opening our door, wishing I could kick her square in the ass on her way out.

"I'm sorry, Gale," Collin said, meaning it, with that sweet familial tone he reserved just for her. But Gale could no longer speak. She couldn't move.

I cleared my throat aggressively. "We're both asking you to leave *now.*"

Gale looked to Collin once more, desperately trying to connect with him, meet his eye, willing him to say something, but he wouldn't look at her, much less speak to her. His focus was entirely on me. As it should be.

When Gale crossed the threshold, my hand on the door, she stared at me before leaving. A full five seconds. Enormous evil in her eye, possessing a callousness I had yet to see from her. She was no longer having fun. Neither was I. Gale smirked upon leaving, a small snort in my direction. A feeling of disquiet fell over me. Those eyes. Her eyes.

They reminded me of Mother.

Chapter 17

I received a phone call from Syl first thing in the morning at the office. Odd timing. Perhaps Collin wasn't handling the previous night's events very well. Even though he had done exactly as I asked, effectively banishing Gale from our home, I worried about the potential repercussions that could manifest in my marriage. My husband and I hadn't said very much to each other for the remainder of that evening after Gale left. Sharing dinner and tears and promises that he would seek help using the appropriate channels. Further, I wondered how she would retaliate. I knew she would. I just didn't know how. What other moves did she have to make? She could be desperate. And a desperate woman knows no bounds.

"Do you have lunch free today?" Syl asked me, a waver in her voice. Couldn't that have been a text?

"Is everything all right? You sound upset.

Is Collin okay?"

"Yeah, he seems fine. I'm fine."

"Okay, well, I don't think today works for lunch, but I could look to —"

"Actually, it's important. Can I pull the friendship card here? I really have to talk to you about something," Syl said.

"All right," I said, my interest fully piqued. The friendship card! "I can shift some things around. Where and what time?" I had no idea what Syl wanted to discuss, but the tone of her voice suggested something dramatic. So did the unfamiliar meeting place she selected. A tavern of some kind, poor signage, a place you'd walk right past. The interior was dark, not very crowded, but the crowd that had gathered was a bit rough. Very rough. It wasn't really a place to dine, more a place to drink. Or plan a murder.

Syl was already there when I arrived, sitting anxiously in the corner booth, her knee bouncing up and down underneath the table. She gave me the smallest of waves and the smallest of smiles. She was a bundle of nervous energy, unable to sit still.

"Syl, hi. Are you okay?" I asked her, approaching the table. "What is this place?" I laughed a little to lighten the mood, but she didn't join me.

"I know. I'm sorry it's a dive, but I wanted to go somewhere more private." Her voice was shakier than it had been on the phone. She spoke faster than normal. I sat down next to her, considerably concerned about what she was going to say.

"Is this about John?" I asked, wondering if she just needed a friend and a shot or two, post-breakup. And really, it was high time she dumped him. He had nothing to offer her.

"No, no. John's fine." Syl bit her nails. I'd never noticed her doing that before.

"Okay. Well, I'm here," I replied, unable to hide the minor annoyance in my voice. Out with it already! The suspense was getting to be too much and I was on edge as it was.

"I know, I know," she said softly, eyes down at the table, as if she was psyching herself up.

"Should I be afraid?" I took a seat next to her in the booth, but not too close.

Syl finally looked me in the eye. Hers were glassy, coated with tears at the ready to begin their descent down her cheeks. It was dire, and strangely, no, *impossibly,* I felt like I knew what she was about to say before she even said it aloud.

"I think you might be my sister," she

whispered.

I waited for a follow-up statement in sheer panic mode, bewildered at the thought. For a moment, my mind immediately went to Gale, but I couldn't connect any dots. Plus, Syl was legitimately crying. She was emotional and upset, but from where on earth did she pull such a ridiculous notion? How? And why did I think she could be telling the truth? It was a lovely and horrifying thought all at the same time.

Sisters.

"I think we have the same father," she sniffled. "And —"

"Syl, I think you have the wrong girl. I —"

"You're not from North Carolina," she said, with more strength in her voice. She was convinced!

"What are you —"

"Stop lying to me now. Just stop."

Commands? From Syl? I didn't care much for that at all. My guard was going right back up. This was too chaotic, even for me.

"I'm not ly—"

"You are!" she shouted, cutting me off. "But it's okay," she added, touching my hand sympathetically, rubbing her fingers across my knuckles in a way that I found supremely annoying. I loathed being patronized. "I know this must sound crazy because you probably didn't know I even existed. Right? *She* never told you?"

"Who?" I asked, my throat low. Again I heard her response in my mind before she said it.

"Our mother," she uttered. The word sent a deep chill down my body. But she couldn't know Mother. She was mine and mine alone. This wasn't real. Syl was mistaken. Wasn't she?

"Syl. I don't know what to say. You've got the wrong information or something, I mean, I'm not your sister." I laughed in her face, fully committing to being Bea Case, despite my inward spiral. I wouldn't show Syl anybody else. I wouldn't show anyone. "I'm sorry, I don't mean to laugh. Do you have someone you can talk to about this? I think the situation with your father is affecting you more than you realize. They say that trauma can manifest much later than —"

Now Syl was the one laughing. Cruel and cutting. Like a villain. Like *her.* "You're good, Bea. You are really, *really* good. And hey, I'm not calling into question anything about what you've done for yourself, I swear. It's fucking impressive. I bow down to you. I mean, I like you, too, genuinely.

We're friends, right? That we can agree on."

"We'll see," I said. I didn't appreciate her changing tone. It seemed erratic. Like an amateur. But still, how was she morphing into somebody else right in front of my eyes? How did she fool me? How did she find me?

"Just hear me out, okay? Aren't you curious? You must be." Yes, I was curious. I was dying to hear her story, even if it was frightening and could threaten my entire station in life. "Our father is in federal prison for a double murder he didn't commit," she said. "Our mother and you."

I didn't want to hear any more, but still, I wanted to know everything. Were we a part of a family after all? It didn't matter. Not to Bea Case. She had her own family now. "That is insanc, Syl. I'm not sure what kind of game you're trying to run on me or on Collin, but —"

"Let. Me. Finish," she hissed. Another shift in tone. "My real name is Jane Wink. When I aged out of the system, I changed it. I didn't want to be associated with those grisly headlines anymore. It didn't exactly do me any favors with finding a family to care for me."

"Give me a break, Syl. I'm very conf—"

"Our dad —"

"*Your* dad." I cut her off. I'd had enough. Even if what she was saying were true, I had to move on. Curiosity could remain, but I wouldn't indulge. It wouldn't lead to anything good. "Let's not jump to any conclusions, *Syl.*"

"*Our* dad is Giles Wink," she said forcefully, starting to lose her composure, crumbling. I immediately went to my phone to search for the name as she continued speaking, corroborating everything available in the public domain. Giles Wink was fifty-seven years old. The appropriate age. He was convicted on the double murder charge after a house fire that was deemed arson. The home was in Westchester. Jane and Giles were spared from the flames. The prosecution said that was intentional. Evidence was found that Giles's wife, Georgina Wink, was having an extramarital affair, leading to the conclusion that Giles had killed her and her unborn child in the ultimate revenge.

It was very macabre and very messy.

Kind of like Mother.

"I thought you could meet him," Syl added, back to her softer self. But I wouldn't be fooled.

"Absolutely not," I said.

"But you'll like him. I know you will."

"I don't care, Syl. I'm not going to meet your father. I'm not getting involved. This has nothing to do with me."

"Dad wanted to name you Charlotte," Syl said, nostalgia dripping from her voice. She held my hand again, but I wouldn't be manipulated by her attempts to tug at my nonexistent heartstrings. Good luck, babe.

"You've got the wrong woman," I said, yanking my hand away from hers.

"I remember her, Bea."

"Oh! What do you remember?" I challenged her, without admitting a thing. Because nobody knew Mother but me.

"Not a lot. I was only four when she left. But I remember that she was very beautiful. Like you. She had long fingers, and once in a while she would run them through my hair when she thought I was sleeping."

I shook my head at her, despite the horrified feeling inside that she could really be telling the truth. "I'm from North Carolina. My parents were Bob and Alice. Are you looking for money? You get this job with Collin, mess with his wife, collect a paycheck based on some bunk theory because you know the Cases will just pay up to avoid bad press. Well, forget it, Syl. I'm not giving you anything. None of us will."

"Hey! Bea. I'm still me. I'm safe. You're

safe with me. Do you need to hear that? You're safe. I know she could be really scary and say things that —"

Safe? What did she know about safety? And how hard I had worked to finally gain some of my own. What I had done to get there! How dare she talk to me about being safe! I wanted to scream at her to shut the fuck up, but that's not what Bea Case would do. Bea had to be cool at all times.

"That's enough now, Syl," I scolded her in the mildest of manners, channeling my own mother-in-law, my inspiration for the moment. Stern but serene, your message fully received.

"Bea, I don't want money," Syl said, her head shaking back and forth again. She was losing her nerve. Good.

"Then what do you want?"

"I just want my dad back," she cried.

"Of course you do. And I'm sorry, but it sounds like a lost cause based on his crimes. He's not my father. You're not my sister. And we definitely don't share a mother, Syl. My mother is dead."

Bea Case had spoken and it was unkind and I knew it, but there was no other option. Syl looked at me for a hint of remorse or genuine care for her, but she would find none. She was playing a dangerous game and I wanted no part of it, no matter how much I liked her.

Look at where female friendship got me.

I knew better. I had always known better. So why had I let her in? It was so foolish. Potentially fatal if I didn't play my cards right moving forward. The only family ties I desired were the ones I had finagled myself. Full control. Trust no one. This was the last thing I needed. And if Syl was my mother's daughter, that was reason enough to stay away from her and for good.

"All right. If that's how you feel, maybe you would still take a DNA test? To make sure? As a friend, it would mean a lot to me," Syl added.

"Syl." I shook my head. She was unbelievable.

"It could free my father, Bea. We could keep it confidential, I've talked to a lawyer, you wouldn't —"

"I am not taking a DNA test, Syl. You're mistaken. I am Mrs. Collin Case. I'm not Charlotte Wink." I laughed, standing up from the table to look down at her with a gaze so cruel, my eyelids low, reeking with disdain, that there would be no mistaking we were finished with each other. I had to sell it. "And if I were you, I'd start looking for a new job."

"Just. Sit — sit down," she said, stammering, but trying once again to build back up to that "femme fatale in a dark bar" persona she thought she so expertly executed. "You're really not going to help me?" She looked flabbergasted and completely betrayed. I guess we both had each other fooled when it came to our friendship.

"I'm leaving."

"But what are you going to tell Collin?" she asked.

I stayed quiet, thinking for a moment. Truthfully, I didn't know what I was going to tell Collin about this horrible conversation. I had already demanded he cut Gale from his life. Now Syl? It would look suspicious.

"I asked you a question," Syl said. "And you had better answer me because now this involves Collin, too. Both of you."

"Is that some kind of a threat?" I scoffed at her. She didn't know who she was dealing with. Not really.

"Collin has said things to me at work . . ." Syl's voice trailed off, she raised one shoulder to her ear, looking down at the ground like an innocent little doe.

"What kind of things?" I asked.

"He's *done* things, Bea."

Syl conjured these bulbous tears that fell

down her chiseled cheekbones, as if she choreographed them. She appeared inconsolable, but pressed on with her story. "After hours. When we're alone in the office. He makes me do things to him that I don't want to do and it's . . ." Syl started sobbing, unable to finish the sentence. It was ridiculous. Of course she was lying, just to get what she wanted. Relatable, but clearly not something she did often. She wasn't good at it.

"Oh, please, Syl." I laughed at her openly. "There is absolutely no way in hell that Collin would ever do such a thing. Try again."

Syl wiped her face and smiled at me, the femme fatale reemerging. "You know that, Bea. I know that. But nobody else knows that. I mean, what would the Case family think about their only son at the center of a public sexual harassment scandal?"

I grinned at her, partially enjoying this side of Syl. Maybe she was my sister, maybe that man in prison was my father, but I couldn't care enough to find out. That was never my life. She didn't know my life. I *made* my life, and I was going to keep it at all costs. "You go right ahead with your little story, Syl. I'm not going to give you what you want."

"You would do that to your own husband? But you love him."

"You're the one doing it to him, Syl. Not me."

"But you can stop it," she whimpered. The villain all but vanished again. She was actually confused about why I wasn't falling for her mediocre proposal. She didn't really know me at all. It was time to finish her.

I leaned over the table to face her head-on, practically within kissing distance, speaking clearly and slowly so she would hear every word.

"Syl, come on. Do you really think I'm afraid of Collin's name getting dragged through the mud for allegedly screwing his secretary? You think he's afraid of that? It would be a stressful few days, sure, but that's only in the unlikely event the story actually went to press. And I know you think the world may be on your side for this one, Syl, but your claim is pretty flimsy when we break it down."

Syl sat back in the booth, arms crossed as if nonchalant, ready to listen to me.

I didn't want her nonchalant. I wanted her afraid.

"Not only is Collin a Case," I continued, "and therefore protected by a family name and reputation, but he's kind of a pussy.

Now, I love him, as you know, but no one will believe he 'did things' to you without irrefutable evidence of said things."

Syl finally broke eye contact with me, looking away and down. I kept going.

"So you could go the route of surveying other women Collin has worked with, in an attempt to corroborate some of your accusations, which might also work, depending on who you manage to corral into lying for you. But those types of people usually require cash, which you don't have. And all of this isn't even considering the cease and desist that would likely come your way, along with an actual lawsuit, but that's not necessarily a bad thing for you. That could actually work out in your favor. It's very possible the Cases would offer you a hefty settlement along with an NDA. Fact or fiction, they won't really care. You said you didn't want cash, but that would be a really great way to get it."

Syl looked back at me, her eyes narrowed. I had offended her.

"I don't want cash," she uttered.

"Whatever." I shrugged. "So let's just say everything did go your way. Because, please don't be mistaken, in any of these scenarios, there's absolutely no way I'm taking a DNA test. So, we were fantasizing that you managed to successfully alert the world to Collin's predatory ways without any actual evidence. Okay. Say it happens. We get some mild family embarrassment. That's unavoidable. Haven definitely won't like it. Too tawdry for the woman. She'd be the most furious. Collin will be 'asked to leave' the Case Company. As a formality, of course. He doesn't have to work. Unlike you."

"Bea. Stop."

But I wouldn't stop.

"As for me, I wouldn't love people thinking my husband did such awful things, but I also don't really care. The circle I'm in now with the Cases? This kind of stuff means *nothing* to them. They completely disavow cancel culture. It doesn't affect them in any tangible way. For some of those men, they'll even see it as Collin's rite of passage. Pat him on the back. Happens to the best of us, son. Some of them will even think he actually did it and not give one single shit. I know, it's sick, but that's neither here nor there because what I want to talk about in this dream world of yours is you."

"That's enough. I get it. You're really not going to help me." Syl was starting to cry. She'd completely lost her nerve, but I had all of mine.

"Escaping one unsavory legacy for another? After everything you've been through as Jane Wink? That's what you want? Sylvia Austin, sexual assault victim, for the rest of your life? What would John say? Your dad? Everyone? You *have* to care about everyone's opinion, Syl. You don't have a lifeboat like I do. So it's in your best interest to maintain some decorum, even as an alleged victim. Look, I'm only saying all of this because I actually do care about you, even with your foul behavior today. I like you and I respect what you're trying to do here. We all have to look out for ourselves, but the only person this scheme of yours will reflect poorly on, if you even got that far, is you. So save yourself the trouble, Syl. Please. Don't give it another thought." I paused for dramatic effect, waiting for her gaze to meet mine once more. "I know I won't."

Syl's lips quivered as she looked up at me. She was about to say something in response, but it came out only as a stifled sob before she ran out of the bar. Mission accomplished.

I wondered if I'd ever see Syl again. Would she go through with it, despite my scathing yet likely true warning? Something told me she wouldn't. After that display of hers, it didn't appear she had blackmail in her at all. It wasn't like her. She was trying it out to get what she wanted, her venue an inspired choice, obviously meant to help her immerse herself in the dirty deed at hand. Fake it till you make it. Method acting. Anyone can play at being a shifty character in a seedy bar, but what about the follow-through? See, what most people don't realize is that conning and scheming and extorting and doing downright dastardly business is not for the faint of heart. Most people, suffering from a good conscience, cannot do it, and that's why the people who *can* do it are often successful at it. Put simply, it's hard for anyone to imagine they're being taken for a ride because who would actually do such a thing?

Most people are trusting. Their first mistake.

I so badly wanted to order a drink. I deserved it after losing my first real friend of my whole life, but it was time to go.

Girls like Bea Case didn't belong in seedy bars like that.

CHAPTER 18

My first response was "No, no, please God, no."

I said it out loud in the restroom at work, decorum be damned. Two women I hardly knew from Accounts Receivable were washing their hands, talking shit about Colleen's vegan brownies in the break room, cut short by concern for me in my stall.

"Oh, honey. Next month."

"Don't lose hope."

I didn't say anything, waiting for them to leave. After an excruciating thirty seconds, I heard them click-clack away in their sensible and hideous two-inch heels. They thought I was trying to get pregnant? I suppose that would have been the normal thing, being a newlywed and all, especially one in a family where legacy was the only thing that seemed to matter. But instead of being thrilled about the heir apparent in my womb, I was in utter and complete shock.

Collin and I hadn't even talked about children. It was never part of our premarital discussions, but I just assumed that Collin assumed I would want a child as well. When he'd realize that wasn't altogether true, we'd have to indulge in a heated conversation. I would push the envelope as far as I could, just to see what might happen, what I could get away with, but I envisioned myself being the one to ultimately relent. I finagled my way into the family to get everything I wanted, so I'd give him what he wanted in return without much of a fuss, but I would certainly not be the instigator. And a small part of me believed that perhaps I'd get lucky. Maybe Collin didn't really want to have children either and we could go on being one of those fabulous child-free couples that are well-dressed, well-traveled and actually happily married until their deaths.

I would not be so lucky.

I was pregnant.

How? It had happened so fast. So soon. Completely unplanned. I was firmly on birth control. I never missed a dose.

And yet, there I was . . .

The strangest feeling.

It's not like I grew up playing with baby dolls or babysitting the neighborhood children. I imagined what a normal mother might be like, but I knew I didn't have one. How could I become one? I was rarely around children at all as an adult and when I was, I avoided interaction as best I could. We didn't have anything in common. What would we even talk about?

I knew it was unsavory to resent children, but I did just the same. Privately, of course. Any child I came across with Collin, or the rest of them, had it made. Must be nice. Must be really, really nice. To have a childhood at all.

But I also knew I couldn't resent my own child.

Because I wasn't like Mother.

I went back to my desk to finish out the day, hoping to think about literally anything else, but of course the baby was all I could think about. I could *do* this, right? It's all focus. Just had to focus. I was excellent at being focused. What kind of mother would I be? A good one. It wasn't hard, was it?

Oh, please. Of course it's hard. It's all any mother talks about when in the company of other women. The hardest job in the world. No, thank you. Life was hard enough. And what if I ended up like my mother after all? Did having children make Mother who she was? I had no earthly idea what she was like before children. Do children make some women snap in some way? Would I snap like her? What would *she* have to say about all of this? What did I have to say about all this?

Could I even love a baby?

In theory, of course. When asked, always. But would I *really*?

I didn't know.

I tried to look on the bright side. A child would only increase my value within the Case family, per my prenuptial agreement. More security was never a bad thing. Having a baby was a sound choice, a solid progression even further into the family, and on that note, even more of a reason for Collin to never leave me. Now I wouldn't only be his wife, I'd be the mother of his child. That was forever.

Strangely, the first person I wanted to tell was Syl, but we were obviously on the outs since our last tête-à-tête. No scandalous story ever did come to pass. She quit Collin's office rather unceremoniously. When he asked me what I knew about it, I said we had kind of lost touch after the wedding. Drifted apart. Happens all the time. He didn't hear any alarm bells. Oftentimes, less is more when lying.

■ ■ ■ ■

Collin jolted up from the sofa when I casually dropped the news that day. We'd just finished dinner and were figuring out what to watch on TV, a whole production of at least twenty to thirty minutes before actually making the decision. A pregnancy announcement certainly mixed things up. He'd had no idea what was coming, and I admit that I enjoyed the element of surprise. The feeling of being in control, about to drop a real bomb, unbeknownst to others. Further, I knew Collin would be a good dad, able to pick up the emotional slack where I might not be able to so our child would have a shot in hell at feeling normal, like they had normal parents.

"Wait, are you serious?" Collin had a face like it was Christmas morning. How could our reactions be so opposite? Another reminder that I wasn't the normal one in the relationship. Too much like her at the core. I felt ashamed again.

"I am." I nodded at him happily because that's what Bea Case would do. He scooped me up from the couch like I was a baby myself, twirled me around and planted a huge kiss on me. "I know we weren't actively trying, but it happened. We haven't even talked about children. I take it you're interested?"

"Interested?!" Collin laughed, believing my blasé commentary was merely lighthearted jest. "I'm thrilled! You're going to be the most amazing mother." Collin said it with such confidence that I wanted to believe him, but how could he know? "I love you."

"I love you, too," I said automatically, as I always did.

"Do we have to go to the doctor, or how does this all get going? We have to call my parents. Oh my God, Bea. I'm so excited. Are you so excited?"

"So excited." I mustered up a smile, poking him playfully to put me down. I was looking forward to sharing with the family and the whole coterie of clowns, including Gale Wallace-Leicester. Surely a pregnancy would throw a wrench into any of her as-yet-unseen retaliation efforts. A baby really firmed up my stake in this new world. The mother of a Case child? Talk about untouchable.

Maybe this would get Gale to give up.

But it could also get her to try even harder . . .

No. Shake it off, Bea.

With a baby, you'll be golden.

"Wow. I mean, holy shit, Bea. I'm going to be a dad." Collin let the realization wash over him, sitting back down slowly as he said the most disturbing thing of all. "I hope it's a girl."

"Why?" I asked him.

"Because girls love their dads."

"And what about their mothers?"

"You know what I mean, Bea." He laughed.

I did.

I absolutely abhorred pregnancy. It truly was the most atrocious state of being. I was completely miserable. Between the state of my gigantic body and the seemingly daily expansion of my thighs coupled with my anxiety at becoming a real mother to an actual baby, I must have been a complete hell beast to be around. But Collin never faltered as the doting husband, eager to announce our happy news. It was decided by Hayes and Haven that a public spectacle would be the best way to move forward, addressing the idea with their old friends, Archie and Plum Gerhardt. Excellent. Archie and Plum were celebrating their thirty-fifth wedding anniversary with a party on a megayacht in the Hamptons. All of

Haven and Hayes's friends would be there. The hosts were thrilled with the idea. Not terribly surprising. The olds loved to be involved with the youngs and our happenings. Something to keep living for in their advanced age.

I was thrilled by the idea as well because I wanted to see Gale Wallace-Leicester's face when she received our happy news. There would be no avoiding her at this party. Sure, Collin wasn't spending time with her anymore, but I knew their paths would cross at social gatherings. And what a dreamy reunion this would be. Another stake in her heart. She might quite literally turn to dust. It wasn't a planned attack, but it would *feel* like one and I didn't want to miss her reaction in real time.

She had been so quiet the past few months.

Perhaps *too* quiet.

The Cases were sworn to secrecy about the pregnancy, and I believed they were taking it seriously. I'm sure it pained Haven not to share with Nora Wallace-Leicester, but I reminded her that it would be more prudent to announce after we had passed the twelve-week point. "I'm not superstitious," I told her. "But better safe than sorry."

"You're right," she said, giving me a brief caress on the shoulder, her tight lips turning up into a small smile. She was looking at me in a new light. The mother of her first grandchild. A baby to melt the icy exterior? How basic and boring to boot. That's all it took to get her to like me?

The party was decadent. Obviously — it was on a yacht. The dress code was garden-party chic. I wore a loose dress so as not to spoil the surprise, but I tucked another dress in my bag for a quick wardrobe change after the announcement. A soft pink body hugger. Not because I wanted everyone to touch my belly, I dreaded that even though I knew it was inevitable, but I couldn't miss an opportunity for Gale to behold my burgeoning baby bump.

She arrived a few minutes after we did, keeping her distance from Collin, but making the requisite greetings to his family. Polite and brief. Collin's parents were informed of the situation between us, my fervent decree that their close friendship could be no more, and didn't get involved, per their parenting style. They weren't the type to invite unnecessary drama into their carefully curated lives. I also assumed they thought we'd all work it out. It was just growing pains between friends going through a new stage of life. Regardless, no one mentioned anything about it on the yacht.

Haven took care to make sure my glass was filled with sparkling cider, which, again, was shockingly lovely of her. "We still want you to look like you're having fun, Mama," she whispered. I was surprised by how much her demeanor had changed toward me since she heard the news. All that for a baby. I didn't feel changed at all, aside from physically morphing into a buffalo and being terrified I would ruin the baby. Or that she would turn out like me.

Like *us*.

The time had come for our announcement. Haven stood in between Collin and me, taking each of our hands, preparing for the moment. She was glowing more than I was supposed to be, but I didn't mind. It wasn't exactly a bad thing to have her warming up to me.

Archie and Plum took their places at the front of the ship, Archie holding a microphone to address their esteemed guests. "Thank you all for joining my beautiful bride and me today," Archie barked, red-faced and grinning, drunk as a skunk. "It means the world to us that you are here to celebrate our love, thirty-five years young. Cheers!"

He hoisted his drink up into the air and everyone toasted the happy couple. Archie cleared his throat again. I scanned the yacht for Gale. Wearing black trousers with a black blouse, she wasn't difficult to find amidst the sea of florals and fascinators, but I nearly jumped out of my skin when I saw who she was standing next to.

Dave Bradford.

I needed to calm down. He was a guest. Of course he was going to be there. They had to be just chatting. Catching up. Nothing to worry about. Nothing at all. Would he tell her? No. He said he wouldn't tell anyone. Besides, there was nothing to tell. It was just real estate. Any New Yorker worth their salt had a passing interest in such a thing. Dave narrowed his eyes at me, full of lust, but I didn't return the gesture. That was done. Gale Wallace-Leicester clocked his wanton gaze at me before meeting my own. I smirked at her in kind, imagining how satisfying it would be to heave her overboard, but what was about to come was going to be so incredible to witness, she'd probably end up doing it herself.

I took a deep breath. I could relax, right?

I had won.

"In the spirit of that love," Archie continued, "we've just been told such wonderful news from longtime family friends. They asked if they could announce it here today among all of our mutual nearest and dearest." Archie passed the microphone to his wife, Plum, all collarbones and Cartier, baring those pearly whites, the type of woman whose mouth always seemed open, unable to fully be at rest.

"Haven and Hayes Case stood next to us when we married all those years ago," Plum chirped, a stark contrast to her husband's booming voice. "We've been present in each other's lives for so many milestones, and we're thrilled to hear that another is just around the corner. Collin?"

I smiled at my husband, watching Gale out of the corner of my eye. It was too good. She knew what was about to happen. I could practically feel the sizzle on the side of my head from the lasers shooting out of her eyes. Haven released our hands and put them together in front of her body, urging us to join Archie and Plum.

Collin took the mic from Plum. "Hello, everyone!" He was ebullient, full-on waving at the crowd like a camp counselor on his first day. "I'm very pleased to share with you all that my lovely wife, Bea, and I are expecting our first child!"

I smiled harder than ever before, my now-puffy cheeks rising up my face, and we shared a sweet kiss. The party erupted into uproarious applause; everyone loves news about a baby. I felt wonderful, with the expression on Gale's face a well-earned trophy. She went pale, paler than usual, zero color in her face. Not a smile, nor a frown. She was frozen with the face of the non-plussed, doing her best to give me nothing, even though this had to be the final nail in her coffin. And yet, something still felt off to me. Amiss. Untoward. I couldn't put my finger on it.

She still felt dangerous. Unpredictable. A threat.

Mother's intuition?

My wardrobe change was a hit. So many strange hands taking the liberty of rubbing my belly without a fragment of permission from me. I detested being touched by so many strangers, but it was a necessary evil. Gale never took her eyes off me throughout these encounters with strangers and acquaintances. Always circling. But I wouldn't wait for her to come to me. I had to take a stance. For me. For the baby. And partially, to gloat. I couldn't help myself.

"Enjoying the party?" I approached her with my hands carefully on my bump, not that anyone could mistake my weight gain for anything other than pregnancy.

"Enormously," she said, eyeing my body, throwing back a sip of her scotch.

"Surprised?"

"Not necessarily. Going two for one will certainly up your odds, won't it?"

Deep breath. In and out. Dave had been falsely gloating. Even more insulting, since it was never even consummated. That big-mouth, big-dick bastard. Never trust a man. Never trust anybody. Another misstep. Regardless, our innocent escapade was likely to be perceived as unsavory and really should not be communicated to the Cases. I had to play it cool.

"Two for one!" I laughed. "How did you know that Collin and I make love twice a day?" I asked Gale.

She cringed, but carried on. "And Dave?"

"Like every man on this yacht, he wishes," I cooed. This was a game of reputation now, and Dave had a bad one. Not only that, but I did have the truth on my side. Flirting was not fucking. "I can't help who yearns for me, nor can I help if said person spouts off lies to play into his own degenerate fantasy."

"Then why were you at his place?" she hissed.

"What? Gale, please. When are you going to learn that you can't just spread awful rumors about me and think Collin will believe you? It's so weak, Gale. Beneath you."

"I have the texts. Your little real estate rendezvous. You went there with him. And, Bea, you modern woman, you texted him first. Didn't you?"

"A text isn't —"

"Stop. Just stop." Gale was laughing hysterically now. I was supposed to be the one gloating and here she was, not a care in the world, a supervillain with mild rosacea. "That's not even the worst of it. I have it all, *Bea.* All of it."

It was the first time Gale had said my name with that intonation. Almost ironically. Like she didn't believe that was my name at all. But she couldn't know. Tracks were covered. Painstakingly so. I knew this to be true. Gale took another sip of scotch and cleared her throat. It didn't go down easily. I wanted her to choke on it. She was far too feverish, caught up in her own exhilaration.

"You have nothing," I scoffed at her.

But what if? *What if?*

Gale shrugged, drunk and mean, with a flash of her teeth. "That's fine. That's fine. Don't believe me. I thought it was quite kind of me to give you a heads-up. Because you won't know when I pull the trigger. Trust me, you will not see it coming. I'd rather wait. It's no fun to harass a pregnant woman anyway, particularly when the child in question is one of us. Well, half. I'll bite my tongue for now. For Collin's sake. For Baby Case. And for my own amusement."

"Are you okay, Gale? You sound like a crazy person." It was hard for me to not match her energy, but I didn't want to look wild or bothered or engaged. Bea Case was cool. I had to be cool, too.

"Do I?" she whispered again. "You think you're in the clear? That's ridiculous when I know what you really are, but I have you now and I'll take you down whenever I want to. Could be weeks. Months. Years. I will fucking do it and do it with a smile and I'll do it when it will hurt you the most."

Her drunkenness was getting the best of her. She was breathing heavily and raising her voice, receiving a side-eye from select partygoers within earshot. I smiled at them good-naturedly, scrunching my nose at them. A small wink. I knew Gale was unhinged, but I was okay, right? She didn't know anything. She saw how Dave looked at me and jumped to a false conclusion. But the texts? She mentioned the texts. Whatever. She must have gone through Dave's phone. He's likely the only one still speaking to her. And why? Loyalty. Legacy. All that hogwash. Who cares? She was so full of shit, wasn't she? She was only trying to frighten me. Goad me into unraveling myself. And I wouldn't do it.

Besides, if she knew anything about me or *her* or the past or about East Eighty-First Street, if Gale really knew, I wouldn't have come this far. Why would she sit on it? It didn't make any sense. She just wanted me uneasy. Paranoid. Stressed. And I wouldn't give her the satisfaction.

Even if I felt all of those things in my little bones.

I spoke louder so the concerned parties would overhear my next move. "Good question, Gale!" She raised an eyebrow at me, curious about the non sequitur. "Well, Collin wants a girl. Wants her to be just like her mama. But I want a boy. A sweet, loving, happy little boy. Just like my sweet, loving and happy husband." I smiled at the strangers listening to our conversation, admiring me from afar, tickled by the promise of new life.

"A boy," Gale said, quiet without expression. "Collin Jr.? Or a nod to Hayes?"

"We haven't talked about names, but —"

Gale shook her head and held up a finger at me. "Or maybe something new to the family. Something strong but unassuming." She smiled, pausing dramatically before speaking again. "Like Richard?"

A ringing in my ears. Coincidence. Had to be. Common name.

"Michael's nice, isn't it? Everybody likes Mike," Gale continued.

Another name that everyone knows and suggests. Aboveboard. Gale's smile loomed large, displaying all of her little teeth, jammed together in that foul mouth of hers.

"Or what about *Seamus*? That's a fun one. One from the old country. Like Collin. And you can always trust Seamus, right?" Gale's nostrils flared at me, her prey, finally recognizing the depth of danger I was really in.

Was I even breathing? I couldn't tell anymore.

"You know what name I've always liked?" she asked me. Rhetorically.

Don't say it. Don't say it. Don't say it.

"Dean!" she chortled, and clapped just the tips of her hands together, a prim and proper predator. "Dean is everyone's friend. Lovable and loving. Pure of heart. I mean, who doesn't love a Dean?"

I dropped my flute of sparkling cider and my whole body followed suit, knees buckling, vertigo settling in, falling in what felt like slow motion and wondering if anyone would catch me, anyone at all, until everything went dark.

Blackout.

Chapter 19

The party was fucking over. I was whisked home in a heli, airlifted back to dry land and promptly visited by the Case family doctor on speed dial, who assured everyone that my dizzy spell was likely an isolated incident. He ordered fluids, rest and a decrease in stress. Easy for you to say, asshole. Did your sworn enemy inexplicably uncover the long-buried secrets of your dark and shady past?

Gale *knew.* She really knew about my past and I had no idea how she'd found out. How could she have outfoxed me? Money. That had to be the answer. It always was. She'd pay top dollar for surveillance and investigation. The Wallace-Leicesters were just as monied as the Cases; if anyone could do it, it would be people like them. They could do anything and get away with it, including ruining my entire life. I was so stupid to get involved in the first place —

my eyes were bigger than my stomach, I had bitten off more than I could chew. But what could I possibly do next? I couldn't let Gale lord this over me, deploying it at her convenience, with me rolling over and taking it whenever she decided to drop the bomb. I would lose absolutely everything. The baby would only keep me afloat for so long, right? If the Cases found out everything about me and where I came from, they'd effectively have me erased. Take the baby away. For God's sake, they could have me assassinated and frame it as an accident. People like them did that all the time, didn't they? Gale said she was waiting for when it would hurt me the most? Well, someone was banking on the love I would have for my child. I suppose I should have been glad somebody had faith in me in that regard, but instead there was only one question on my mind.

What would Mother do in this scenario?

I knew the answer, but could *I* do it?

I was teetering on the dangerous, the dark, the psychopathic — everything I'd been so desperate to avoid, but was I not in the most desperate situation of all time? I was reeling. I needed a grounding force. A soft place to land. Someone who actually put me in touch with my true inner self, no matter how depraved at times, to help me figure out the best way forward.

I wanted to talk to Syl. Sweet Syl, who would never actually hurt me, she could *never,* even though I had hurt her by denying the one thing she wanted, potentially beyond forgiveness. But I yearned for Syl. I missed her. Her girl talk. The shit talk. Gentle reassurances I was doing a great job. That I would do a great job when the baby came. I could hear it all in her voice, and I'd believe it if it came from her. At least, as much as I could believe it. I fantasized about calling her so we could reconcile. I'd tell her about the baby and that I was sorry, maybe I could even tell her a little more, connect about my past, our past if it was true, which I was starting to suspect it was.

The photos I found of Giles Wink online suggested that he was certainly Syl's father. He was good-looking. She favored him, no question. Except his nose, with its slight bump, the attractive kind, and the upturned end. A bit small for a man. The perfect size for a woman.

I recognized it because it was my nose, too.

And Giles with Georgina? Another sucker for destiny.

I had to see Syl.

So, what would I have to say? News of the

baby would be favorable. Who among us can resist a pregnant woman in peril? I could cry, turn on the waterworks a bit, but would she believe me? Syl was definitely the type of woman who would appreciate an apology, so I could ease my way into that while we were on the phone. Yes, all of these tactics could get Syl to hear me out and let me seek her advice. I was sure of it.

But I didn't even have to use them.

Before I got two sentences out, she let me back in.

That's just the kind of person she was.

"You know, Bea, why don't you come over to my place and we'll talk in person?" she said.

It was miraculous. Despite everything I said to her after she'd bared her soul — and threatened me for good measure, her own desperate situation — she invited me to her apartment in Brooklyn to speak one-on-one. John wouldn't be home. It would be just the two of us.

"Come on in," Syl said at the door, with warranted trepidation in her voice, until she noticed my bump. I had declined to share such news over the phone. "Oh my God! BEA!" She wrapped her arms around my giant body. Syl's touch felt incredible. An invitation to relax, to feel safe and to be heard. She kept her arm around me to pull me inside.

Her one-bedroom apartment was unassuming but tastefully decorated, though I was certain most of it was from Target or Amazon. A bit twee, but quite charming. Like Syl. "I'm so fat," I said, not at all meaning it in jest, but she laughed anyway. She guided me to her baby blue sofa, handing me a colorful throw pillow for my back.

"You look great and who cares? It'll come off. We have good genes. Do you want something to drink? Water? Tea?"

"Water would be nice, thanks," I said, not addressing her comment about presumed shared genetics. That wasn't what this reunion was about. Was it? At least not as far as I was concerned. I simply craved that maternal energy of Syl's, hoping some of it could rub off on me in more ways than one.

"Be right back," Syl said before retreating to her tiny kitchen. I looked around the apartment. Lots of plants, lots of wall art featuring nondescript beaches or pretty girls canoodling or random city skylines; she subscribed to *Cosmopolitan* magazine and received the Madewell catalog, and she'd framed a photo of herself with John at Niagara Falls, another with her father —

Syl as a little girl, both of them in a front yard with a sprinkler going. From before.

I wondered if Mother had taken the photo.

I wanted to get a closer look at it, but I stayed put. I didn't want to invite the topic into our discussion any sooner than necessary, if at all. I was still undecided. As much as I wanted to know the truth, it could jeopardize so much.

"Here you go," Syl said, handing me the water. She didn't sit next to me on the sofa, opting for a gray club chair instead. She swiveled in it from side to side with a blank look on her face. I suspected the reality of my return was settling in, baby or no baby. She was still upset. "You said some really awful things to me," she declared. I would not be so lucky. We were going to go there. She was the hostess. She could run this however she wanted.

"I know. I'm sorry. I've been thinking about you a lot. Since all of this," I said, motioning to my behemoth belly.

"It's wonderful," Syl said. "Really."

"Is it?" I sighed.

"You won't be like her. In case you were worried."

"You didn't even know her, Syl. How can you be so sure?" I asked her, saying enough without saying it all.

"Because I know *you.* And you're here. You came back. But she runs away."

"Not from me." My voice began to break. "I wish she had." I swallowed my pending sob, nearly choking on the thought of Mother leaving me behind. I thought of Dean. He would have kept me if she'd left. Maybe he would have found me a new mother after she was gone. Why didn't she leave me? It would have been so much easier for both of us. Wouldn't it?

"No, you don't," Syl replied. "You say that, but trust me, being without a mother, without parents, is nothing to be jealous about." I knew she believed that, but I also knew she had no idea what my life was like with Mother. It wasn't a contest, our pain, but if it was, I would win.

"Tell me about her," Syl said, soft and cautious.

"Do you remember anything else?" I asked her, still hoping for more details. "You mentioned her fingers. How she'd run them through your hair," I said quietly.

"No. Not much else. Just what Dad tells me. He said that I wasn't drawn to her, like most kids are to their moms. I don't have a memory of it exactly. Just more of this feeling like I could watch her, but not necessarily be near her. What I can see of her in my head, she's always far away. And it's all jumbled. Sounds and images, just a mess in my mind."

The same, but different. Syl could look at Mother, but not get close to her. I had felt the same, but I pushed through it anyway. I always got as close to her as I could, even when it hurt, especially so.

"Her face is my face, but I think you have her nose," I told Syl.

"You have his," she said.

Fuck. It was real, wasn't it?

"Don't. I can't go this fast," I whispered. We couldn't keep doing this if I wanted to stay Bea Case, could we?

"Where did she take you?" Syl asked, moving from the chair to the sofa, closer to me. I debated telling her everything, telling everything to somebody would feel like such a release, but I had too much to lose.

"I don't think I can keep talking about this," I said.

"It's okay," she said, sensing my secrets. "We can take our time now. Another day."

Would we have more time?

"Why didn't you tell anyone your story about Collin? You surprised me. It was a side of you I hadn't seen before."

"It's a side I don't actually have." Syl laughed, almost mirthlessly. "Honestly, I couldn't do that to you. Or Collin, he's so innocent in all of this anyway. I just — It's not who I am." I was right. Sweet Syl.

"I am sorry about what I said to you. I was being cruel because I was scared you might be telling the truth," I admitted.

"I was telling the truth. But I'm sorry, too. I shouldn't have even tried to pull anything like that, I was just kind of desperate because all I want in this world is for my dad to be exonerated from this crime he didn't commit, and you can prove it. You made me so mad. I really thought you would help me." Syl believed in me, and I'd let her down. I'd have to keep letting her down to stay Bea Case. "Anyway, the blackmail thing wasn't even my idea. I mean, I had been trying to find you for such a long time because I knew the truth and I knew you were out there somewhere. I never wanted to hurt you, I just wanted to know you and when I finally found you —"

"Wait," I interrupted her, *catching* her. "*Whose* idea was it?" Maybe not in a lie, but certainly in an omission. How had she found me anyway?

"What?" Syl shifted, tucking her legs underneath her body, pushing a piece of hair behind her ear. She was trying to look innocent. She had said something she hadn't planned on saying. But didn't she know by now that I was always listening?

"You said it wasn't your idea," I reiterated, harsh in all the consonants.

"I was saying that I never wanted to hurt you. I just wanted to find you so I could know you and then maybe you'd take the test to help —"

"Answer my question right now," I demanded. My skin felt hot and cold at the same time. Goose bumps appeared on my arms; my face went flush.

"Bea, before you —"

"Tell me right now. Did she find you?" I asked the question knowing it was impossible. It had to be impossible. *"How?"*

"Who?" Syl asked.

"You know who I'm talking about!" I was shouting now, daring her to tell me what I'd long suspected. *She* was never gone. She was never *really* gone. I knew it. I always had. I'd never been able to leave her, it didn't work, and she was always watching me, waiting to get me when I least expected it.

"Bea, you're shaking!" Syl came closer to me even though I had gone completely feral. It was frightening but also liberating to outwardly show what I was actually feeling inside for once in my fucking life. I couldn't keep it in any longer. I began to pace around the room, tugging at my hair, looming over Syl, demanding that she tell me what I'd long suspected. *She* was still here.

"She found you?" I croaked, my throat having gone completely dry. I wanted to reach for the water but was afraid I wouldn't be able to swallow. I had lost all control of my body, literally fit to be tied.

"Yes," Syl confessed, closing her eyes in repentance.

"But you just said you didn't know her face!" I spat back, knocking the water glass over just to feel like I was still in the room. That I wasn't dreaming.

Syl looked up at me, completely bewildered by my unhinged behavior. "Bea. You have to calm down."

"How dare you tell me to calm down! How dare you trust *her*! You think she cares about you? She doesn't, I don't know what she told you. She told you she would help you if you helped her? Please. She doesn't help anyone but herself! Where is she? I *knew* she was here. I could feel her. I've always felt her around me. Hiding and waiting to strike when I'm not looking, especially now, with the baby coming. I haven't been able to sleep. Not without seeing her in my dreams, my nightmares, every night.

Everything could be taken away from me, don't you get it? Everything!"

Then I started to cry. The weakest form of release, but probably the one I needed most.

"No, Bea. No. You're misunderstanding me." Syl came forward to hug me, possibly to restrain me, but I pulled away from her reach. "Hey, everything's going to be okay, we'll figure this out together." It infuriated me that her tone was so calm. So patronizing. I wasn't a child. I never got to be a child. She couldn't take care of me. Nobody could. I was the only person who could take care of me.

"*Where* is she?" I growled at Syl. "How could you not tell me? What do you *really* want? What are you two going to do with me?"

"Bea. Listen to me. Listen. I have no idea where our mother is. No idea at all. She hasn't found me. Do you know where she is?"

Inhale.

Exhale.

Inhale.

Exhale.

Pregnancy was making me lose my mind.

Of course Mother wasn't around. She couldn't be.

"But then *who* were you talking about?" I asked.

"Gale," Syl whispered, a knife to my heart.

"Gale," I huffed in response, so betrayed, so incensed. All this time? Gale knew all this time. She always had. Syl? Sweet Syl? *My* Syl? Gale had strung me along the whole time with all of her plotting and planning. For what? To persecute me slowly, like a poison. Watch me make a life for myself, only to take it all away. Watch me make a friend, my first *ever* friend, and she's nothing of the sort. And Syl was just a pawn in Gale's game. A willing one at that. Gale had always seen me. Perhaps before we even met in the flesh. I was a moving target for her and she wouldn't shoot until everything was lined up just so. Where did I come from and how could she exploit it? She knew. Hunted me down. By engaging in play, the dark play I love, letting me believe I could win while she diligently kept digging my grave behind the scenes, waiting for the right time to push me in and bury me alive.

"She found me," Syl explained. "I had tried for so long to find you and then Gale came around, saying she was good friends with Collin and that you two were getting serious. She explained how the family was and that I'd have to tread lightly, so she would recommend me for the job with Collin. She knew I wanted to help my father and she said you would take the test once you got to know me properly. She just said I should follow her plan. That it would be good for everybody. And she said that if you didn't want to take the DNA test, that the sexual harassment threat about Collin would force your hand and you'd forgive me when the truth came out, which sounded like a really harsh Plan B, but you have to understand. I'm *desperate* to free my dad, Bea. If I could do anything to help him, I would do it. I'm sorry. I should have known better because Gale is so weird, and when I realized she was only trying to hurt you, I distanced myself from her. But I couldn't distance myself from you. You're exactly how I hoped you would be, and I just *know* you're my sister and we can be there for each other, if you would just trust me."

I listened. I tried to see her side of things, but how silly. I didn't have that luxury. Never did. I could only look out for number one. I wanted to believe that I could trust her, but all I felt was her treachery. I thought I could let a lot of things go for Syl, but a secret partnership with Gale Wallace-Leicester was not something I could abide, despite her remorse.

"How can I trust you when you've been lying to me since the moment we met?" I hurried away from her, heading for the door. She reached for my hand, but I yanked it away. I no longer craved her touch.

"Bea, I'm so sorry, but I'm not going to lie to you anymore." Syl was frantic, her voice taking on a high pitch of panic, practically a screech. "I promise. That's everything. All of the secrets. I kept the part about Gale from you because I knew you'd take it the wrong way."

"There's only one way to take it!" I screeched back at her, turning around to look at Syl one last time before I left. Her sweet face. It was over. "You lied to me and now I know and you will not get anything from me ever again. I will never take that test. I don't care about you. I don't care about your father. We were never friends!" I roared at her, welling up again, but I couldn't let the tears fall this time. I needed to focus. Warm up. Get amped. Ride this wave into my next destination.

Syl kept trying to hold me and hug me, but I finally pushed her off me with all of my strength. Perhaps a little harder than necessary, but she got the message as she fell onto the sofa with a thud, striking her elbow on the end table. She was trying to love me, but I would not let her. She was trying to be my friend, but I couldn't trust her. Syl was the truest example of the dire circumstances of my life. I couldn't afford to love. I couldn't afford to trust.

What was I thinking? I suppose I wasn't.

"Bea, please! Don't leave like this. You're pregnant. Let me help you. Don't run away. Don't be like her!" Syl sobbed at me, begging to connect but keeping a safe distance. She could sense I wanted to get violent and that perhaps I would if she gave me an excuse.

"I am more like her than you will ever know," I seethed.

Syl didn't say anything in return, remaining motionless on the sofa as she watched me go.

Outside, I hailed the first taxi I saw.

"Upper West Side," I barked at the driver, menace in my eyes, revenge in my blood and fire in my heart.

It was finally time to take care of Gale Wallace-Leicester for good.

Chapter 20

She was surfacing. Under my skin. Bursting out of every pore. The cruelty emanating all around me and inside me. Every dark thought or instinct or desire that I had ever pushed down since I left Mother was returning with a vengeance, I was burning from within, and I ached to take it all out on Gale Wallace-Leicester.

This bitter battle between us would never end unless I put a real hard stop to it. She had tried to undo me at every turn, and I had unknowingly allowed it. Through Collin, through his family and now through Syl. It was a sin that required an everlasting penance. The gloves were off, the claws were out and I craved her annihilation beyond all recognition.

I wanted to *wreck* Gale Wallace-Leicester.

I imagined storming into her apartment, with its hideous decor, tackling her on the wretched gingham sofa with every extra pregnancy pound I possessed. Wielding my big body like a lethal weapon. She'd be taken completely by surprise. No physical instincts to fall back on whatsoever. It's not like she'd ever have been in a fight before, much less one for her actual life.

She'd be unable to wriggle out of my clutches, rendered completely useless, my nails digging into her skin, her flesh, her face. I would scream in her ears as loud as I could, a piercing sound, a maleficent banshee, and then finally I would wrap my fingers, now thick as sausages, around her neck, my thumbs pressing further and further into her jugular veins, happily squeezing the literal life out of her, watching her choke and perish, gasping for breath in vain, until she moved slower and slower. Struggling less and less. Until there was no more struggle at all. And I would howl with laughter when she finally died, laughter conjured from deep in my belly, deep in my bones, and I would never, ever get caught.

I'd killed once before.

I thought I could do it again.

It had been necessary then and it was necessary now.

Wasn't it?

I had the taxi drop me off a few blocks away

from Gale's. While a pregnancy wasn't the best way to slink about with any subtlety, it also meant I was unlikely to be outright hassled by anyone, so it was helpful for my admittance to the building. I managed to wait patiently for Doorman Frank to address a task for one of the bevy of senior citizens in the lobby, allowing me to skulk in largely undetected. I shielded my face gently with one of my hands, making sure my protruding belly was the focus. He didn't even look up when I got in the elevator. As the doors shut, I carried on picturing all the different ways I could murder Gale Wallace-Leicester, but none of them excited me more than doing so with my bare hands.

I wanted to feel her pain through my fingertips.

Her door was ajar and I went inside.

Gale was in the kitchen, in an unsightly old terry cloth robe, the kettle about to reach its climax. She took it off the heat and poured water into two mugs.

"So have you found out if it's a boy or a girl yet?" She grinned. No greeting. "It's herbal," she said, handing me a cup of the tea.

"We're going to be surprised," I said, taking it from her, biding my time. The steam rising from the cup made me want to toss it right in her face. A scalding burn, but it wouldn't be enough.

"That's our Bea. Always full of surprises." Gale laughed, claiming me as her own, a sick little pet she was waiting to put down. Laugh it up, Gale. She'd never see it coming. She had underestimated me. "Take a seat," she urged, but I remained standing, on the offensive.

"I've just come from Syl's."

"Oh! And how is she doing?"

"She told me everything," I growled. My chest was rising and falling at an increasingly rapid rate. I was hungry for her fall. Starving. Gagging for it.

"But she doesn't *know* everything," Gale said, her voice now rising, taunting me. "I'm actually surprised it took this long for her to tell you. That was only a matter of time. She actually has a good heart, unlike some of us. But like I said, she doesn't know everything."

"Care to elaborate?" I hissed, swaying back and forth ever so slightly, like a prizefighter staying warm before getting back in the ring.

"I haven't decided yet." She grinned at me again. Keep it up, Gale. I wanted it again, the barbs, the banter, but it was no longer just for fun or to scratch a pesky itch. This was all fuel for my explosion ahead. "It's much more fun to engage in the element of surprise. Don't you agree?"

"It will only devastate Collin. How could you do that to him? You're supposed to love him. Allegedly. Isn't he the reason you're doing all of this? Honestly, Gale. It's pretty pathetic."

"Initially, yes. It was about him. But the more I learned about you, how dark your past actually is, it became about so much more than Collin. It became about our families. I don't care how beautiful you are, how much makeup you put on, how you dress in designer threads on some other man's dime, it's all a cover, Bea. You know what you are. Raised by a criminal, you're still a criminal. Trash. So I'm happy to wait for the perfect moment to expose you for what you really are. It'll hurt him, yes, but in time, you'll just be a memory. None of us will ever say your name again. And you'll go running back to her, just like we've planned. Exactly where you belong."

Her revelation hung in the air, sucking the life out of me.

The heat inside me was nearing critical mass.

My throat was bone-dry yet again.

I felt like I couldn't breathe at all.

Like I was dreaming, floating in a scene of my own subconscious, unable to flee or fly away.

Had she *really* said that? Go back to her? Her. *Her.*

I dropped the teacup. The glass shattered on the tile, but neither of us moved.

"Careful," Gale said.

"She's lying," I muttered to myself, not even looking at Gale, more like looking through her. I was possessed by what she had just said. How? "It can't be true. It can't be . . ."

"Why?" Gale asked, biting her lip in pure excitement. "*Why,* Bea? Why can't it be true?"

I could hardly hear her. All sounds were muffled. A slight ringing in my ears. Eyes out of focus. I barely registered my surroundings at all in those brief few seconds, until she asked me another question.

"Because you killed her?" Gale's lips curled, her nostrils flared; it was animalistic. She was turned on, a slow burn that was finally turning into uncontrollable flames. Everything she had been waiting for. She knew. She always knew.

"Shut your mouth," I hissed, forcing my body to go still, fists starting to form in my hands. “You think you deserve your life? You really believe that you’re be—”

“Better? Of course I do, Bea. Dynasties rise and legacies withstand the test of time because of honor and loyalty and a commitment to being the best. Collin wouldn’t listen to me or his family. I had to take more serious measures on my own. Dig deeper, use more resources. It’s more fun, too, isn’t it? The long game. It’s exhilarating. I can see why you enjoy it so much. And after all, I’m not afraid of hard work.”

Hard work? My mind was coming back and my body would just have to catch up. *Hard work?* I rolled my head from side to side. *Hard work?* My hands were now fully in tight fists against my body. *Hard work.* Yes. It was almost time.

“So yes, I know all about it,” Gale continued. “You. *Her.* And I’ve been doling out your punishment with her help. Slowly but surely, until you swallow every last drop.”

Finally, I backhanded Gale across the face with all of my strength. The cracking sound startled both of us and lit us up, the energy between us now crackling, too.

“I’m not surprised by the violence, Bea. But try using your words.”

“Fuck you, Gale,” I bellowed, a guttural exclamation of my derision for her.

"Despite your best efforts, though, you didn't manage to kill your mother," she said, caressing her cheek, now bright red from the impact. Weak capillaries. Weak bone structure. "She was difficult to find, but I have capabilities that most people don't. And, as you know, I had nothing but time. Your identity is generally rock-solid by most advanced measures, but you can find out anything for a price. Money talks. Not that I have to tell you that."

I backhanded her again, even harder this time, my rage building with every word she uttered. She fell to the floor. I wanted her to fight back. Give me a fight, Gale. Give me the real release I craved. The one that we both deserved. "You think this behavior surprises me, Bea?" She laughed. "I was expecting it. You'rc an animal. And you're cornered. Of course you're going to fight. You tried to kill your own mother."

"How did you find her?" I snarled, hunched over and ready to strike again.

Gale crawled over to her hideous green safe and opened it with my husband's birth date, careful to smile at me as she did so. She tossed a file in my direction labeled VICTORIA OSTHOFF. It must have been there the whole time. I flipped it open, completely rapt with the material. Victoria

Osthoff was a recent widow to an oil guy in Texas. Vincent Osthoff. Marriage certificate, a birth certificate, addresses to estates, bank account records, social security cards, but it was the photos that solidified everything.

She had found Mother.

She was older, yes. Her features now more feline in nature, an unavoidable side effect of the work on a woman of a certain age, no matter how well done. Fresh highlights. French manicure. Her perfect nose, sneering in superiority. Her eyes blazing with malice. It was her. She had never stopped her games. She just carried on playing them without me.

She didn't come and find me after all.

Gale had found her.

"Your mother told me about Syl," Gale said. "She always knew where you two were. She kept tabs from afar. When I found her and I told her what you were up to with the Cases, she was more than happy to work together. She told me what you did to her, told me everything. She frightened me, but she had the information I needed so I proceeded with her proposal, despite the fear. Because she's the only one who could really take you down, from your rotten insides out."

I inhaled sharply. "You ought to be careful, Gale. Your fear is warranted. You don't know her like I do."

"Clearly!" Gale exclaimed. "I thought she'd want to keep playing until we won. I really thought the only thing left for us to do was to have her come forward and tell the truth to the Cases about who you really are and where you come from, particularly East Eighty-First Street. I didn't expect her to tell the *entire* truth, surely the woman wouldn't want to incriminate herself about her own misdeeds, but I figured she would share enough. You know. To *get* you."

"She is not your friend, Gale. She is not your teammate. She's using you."

"We were using each other!" Gale shrieked.

"Well, then where is she?" I cried out. "Tell me, Gale! Where is she?!"

"She's gone. I don't know. She didn't want to tell the Cases anything. She said she didn't want to see you. So our coalition was called off. Just as well. I'm on my own now, but I know enough to finish the job. I know enough about her, too. I'm just waiting to pull the trigger. With the Cases, the police, the law. You won't escape it. Neither of you. The ones at the top are at the top for a reason. We don't get burned, but we'll burn the ones that try us. With pleasure."

I was silent. Thinking. Weighing my options.

Because Gale was wrong.

Mother hadn't *left.* She wouldn't. It didn't make any sense. Not without seeing me first and seeing this through, whatever this was. What did Mother want? Did she want me back? Or did she want to kill me? Either way, it was abundantly clear that Gale had no idea who she was dealing with. Not a clue or she wouldn't be so pompous, so confident, so sure that she had me in her crosshairs. Mother was close by and had been for a long time. I had felt her presence growing since Collin and I had gotten engaged. It wasn't paranoia, it was real. And she wouldn't take off without finishing the job. Unlike me.

She was still alive.

Gale finally got up from the floor to sit on the couch, lurching into the cushions, pleased with herself. She thought she had me, like I wouldn't fight for my life with everything I had. Like I wouldn't sacrifice hers for my own. Gale thought she was in control, and it was laughable. She could incorrectly underestimate me all she wanted to, but she was a fool to underestimate Mother at all.

Mother was not gone if the job was not done.

Was she watching right now?

"I suppose I'd have nothing to say either if my own mother never wanted to see me again," Gale droned on. "But in some ways you're quite lucky, Bea. I do hope you've enjoyed the ride. After all, you've gotten much further than your average whore, haven't you?"

I struck fast at Gale, like a cobra. I hadn't been able to move that quickly in what felt like ages, but the will to harm her and the adrenaline to do it came together in that precise moment. I tackled her mightily; again she fell to the floor, and she screamed, just as I hoped she would. *Was Mother watching now?* I muffled Gale's pathetic cries with an atrocious green sequin pillow from her hideous sofa, the weight of my stomach shoving into her own, making it harder for her to breathe. *Do you see this, Mother?* I tossed the pillow aside, wanting to do it myself, finally wrapping my hands around Gale's neck, just as I'd imagined. I squeezed it so hard, her eyes bulged in horror, her legs kicked madly to break free. *Are you proud of me* now, *Mother?* I pushed my body into Gale's even further, stealing all of the air from her body. She would not take my life. I would take hers first.

I wanted Gale Wallace-Leicester dead.

How dare she pretend like she knew my mother.

How *dare* she.

I'm the only one who knows Mother.

Was this what she wanted? Did she want me to prove I would stop at nothing to get what I wanted? That I was just like her all along? If I killed Gale to keep Collin, to keep Bea, was I really so different from her? Maybe we wanted different things, but if the means to the end were the same, all my efforts to be different from Mother would be in vain.

Different path, same result. A twisted circle. Her favorite kind.

Gale's movements were slowing. Her calf jerked once more underneath me and then stopped entirely. She looked up at me, but her eyes were distant, like she couldn't see me any longer.

Mother couldn't see me either.

She never could.

I released Gale from my clutches.

She gasped for air, launching herself back to life, placing her own hands around her neck, in disbelief she was still there. She burst into hysterical tears, looking like she had just seen the light and nearly walked toward it. I watched her dry heave on the floor, neck ragged and red.

I grabbed the file on Mother, Victoria Osthoff, and fled, in dire need of a Plan B. I had nearly killed Gale Wallace-Leicester. I probably should have killed her, but I couldn't finish the job. My whole life was in her hands, and still I left, unable to do what was necessary. A comfort in some ways, but maybe I was the weak one after all.

I walked the entire way home like a madwoman. That was too many blocks on a good day, much less when I was pregnant, but I had to keep moving to stop myself from screaming or crying or worse. I just needed to get home to Collin, if he would even protect me now. I had given Gale exactly what she wanted. More fodder for her files that would remove me from her life for good. I couldn't exactly blame a violent strangling on pregnancy hormones, even if I didn't go all the way, as it were.

And Mother was out there, still watching me, waiting.

When would she show herself?

The thought of Gale and Mother plotting against me for so long, even involving Syl in their dual mastermind, was beyond my comprehension. I was furious with myself for not seeing it sooner. But how could I?

Maybe if I had listened to the voice inside, the one that *knew* she was still here somehow, but I'd ignored it for so long, allowing it to drive me crazy without any meaningful result.

I had told myself it was impossible, but when it came to Mother, I should have known nothing was impossible.

She had always been close and now I wanted her to find me. Desperately. I needed her help now. I needed my mother. I didn't know what to do about Gale and what I had done to her. She could be in communication with the authorities already. I was so ashamed of myself. How could I be so stupid, so pathetic?

But I was never more pathetic than when I saw Mother as I arrived home, in our back garden, legs bare and still lean, crossed elegantly on the chaise, lips pursed and pink to match her dress. Like no time had passed at all, she beckoned to me with one long single finger, and I went right to her.

Sometimes, a girl just needs her mother.

Chapter 21

"You have a lovely home," Mother said, an unfamiliar crackle in her speech, no longer as crisp; her youth had vanished, though she was still beautiful. Many women her age would have developed a warble in their voice, like an aged bird, but Mother was always more of a lioness. She purred.

"Thank you, Mother." It was all I could think to say. I clasped my hands under my protruding belly and pointed my chin downward, taking the standard stance of obedience in her presence. I felt so silly and so frightened. I had imagined this reunion with Mother so many times. I had dreamt about it, vividly. I dreamt of her all the time. In some dreams I was tough on her when she resurfaced. A little brat. I would tell her she got what she deserved after what she had done to me. She didn't deserve to live; she deserved death at my hand. I should have waited and watched it happen and made absolutely sure she was eradicated from this earth.

But in other dreams all I did was apologize to her endlessly. To her face, on my knees, shouting it from far away, shouting it right into her face again, but she wouldn't look at me. She'd never look at me, refusing to see me or hear me or acknowledge me. No longer a team. She didn't want me anymore. *I'm so sorry, Mother. Mommy, I'm sorry. Please forgive me.* Louder and louder, as loud as I could. Or sometimes no sound came out of my mouth but it felt like I was screaming my apologies to her. She never forgave me in those dreams. She just walked away. Far, far away from me. She didn't like me. She didn't love me. My own mother.

Did she forgive me? Did I even want her forgiveness? I was falling right back into the little girl I was before. All those little girls I'd had to be, never allowed to be just one, just me. I was always somebody else, but always her daughter, even now.

"Quite a score. Old money. *Big* money. I'm very impressed," she said, standing up from the chaise, still maintaining a distance from me. "But it's always risky with a large family, isn't it? I looked for loners, but not you, apparently. The Case family. Wow, so well-known! But I think you and I had different goals we wanted to achieve. I liked keeping us on our toes, but you? You just *loved* knowing where your next meal was coming from. Still do, right? For now, anyway. You probably think you'd like to die in this house."

That wasn't a threat, it was an insult. I looked over my shoulder at the house and realized I wouldn't mind that at all. A permanent home. I couldn't think of a better place to go.

"Aren't you going to invite me inside?" Mother asked.

"No," I said out of instinct. She still felt like a dream even though I knew this was real. There was nothing hazy about her presence, it hit me like a shovel to my face, but it was difficult to reconcile that she was actually standing before me. I knew her so well and yet I didn't know her at all. So much can happen in ten years. "Collin will be home —"

"Home late," she finished with a grin, informing me her work into my life was far from over. "He's out. A family emergency. By the time he gets to Connecticut and back, we'll be gone. So why don't you give me the grand tour and show me what a big girl you are. Don't you want to parade around as the lady of the house? I promise to act very impressed. Make me proud."

Logically I knew there would be no point to such a charade, but there was still that little girl inside me that wanted to make Mother proud. I still wanted to make her like me, because when she liked me, no matter how fleeting, it always felt good. I had always wanted to be on her team. I could charm anyone at will, but with her, I really had to work at it. And even when I thought I had her, it wasn't really a win, was it? She always had the upper hand. With her, I always lost. Mother's game against me was the only one I never figured out how to win. It drove me crazy still.

A text from Collin demanded my attention before I could muster up a response in any direction. Be home later. Mother was right.

"How far along are you?" she asked, looking my body up and down, biting the inside of her cheeks.

"Almost five months," I told her. To hear her acknowledge my unborn child made me feel heavier with guilt. The child was so innocent and yet they had come from her, from me. Surely that would change. Wasn't it their destiny?

"I hated being pregnant," Mother sneered. "Both times. I don't know why I even did it a second time."

"You never told me about Syl," I said to her softly, letting the insult about me roll off my back as best I could, but I knew I'd feel the effects later when I would least expect it.

"She's not one of us."

"She told me about the fire . . ." I trailed off intentionally. I wanted to hear the story from her, if she would tell it.

"She told you about that, hmm?" Mother chuckled to herself, like it was old family lore that was a pleasure to periodically revisit when we all got together for the holidays. "Not my best work, but I was young and wild and impulsive. No precision. Not like what I could do now. I really thought I could swing that whole thing with Giles. Be normal, like what you're attempting here with Collin. I married the man, I had the baby, we had the house, we had money. Nothing like this, but more than enough. I had everything we were supposed to want. I think I always knew it wasn't for me, deep down, but I felt I should try for the so-called American Dream. Maybe I could be like everyone else if I applied myself, willing myself to want what I actually had in my hands. I wanted to be like everyone else, forced it on myself, until I couldn't take it anymore. Not physically. Not mentally. Not at all. And you'll get there, too, if you carry on this way. You're just like me, despite your best efforts. Look what you did to Gale."

"I'm different from you," I squeaked, clearly not believing it myself. It made her laugh.

"When I got pregnant the second time, with you, I had to get out at any cost. It was stifling and boring and I wanted no part of it anymore, but I admit that I didn't want them hurt. It was sloppy. I secured the cash and hatched a harebrained plan. They weren't even supposed to be home. Anyway, it wasn't my intention for him to end up where he did, or the girl for that matter. I just wanted them to think I was dead so they would never come looking for me. For us. I wanted them to think that *we* were dead."

"I don't believe you. You didn't care about them."

"I cared enough, didn't I? They're alive." She took a few steps toward me, but I took a few steps back. She snickered, but stopped moving, keeping her distance.

"Why did you keep me? You must have considered other options."

"Of course I did," she said coldly.

"So why did you?" I had always wanted to ask her, but I'd been so afraid to ask her anything when I was young. I was still afraid, with much more to lose, but if not now, when?

"I thought you would be a useful tool," she said matter-of-factly. "Something to make it more fun. More exciting. An interesting variable in the inevitable monotony of life. And we had fun, didn't we? I know we did. You can't say it was boring."

"No," I said, surprised by the conviction in my voice, but I didn't believe her. I believed that's what she would tell me, but I thought the answer was much darker. I wanted her to admit it to my face. "That's not it."

"Oh?" Mother was amused, crossing her arms in front of her chest. "What's your hypothesis then?"

"Syl told me that she wasn't close to you at all. The way other girls can be with their mothers. She found you frightening. Almost repellent. And I think that hurt your feelings, Mother. She hurt your feelings."

"She wouldn't remember anything about th—"

"She sees Giles. He remembers. And she remembers. Little girls remember their feelings. I do, too."

"Go on." Mother smirked, mocking me. "Say what you want to say. This is your moment, isn't it? How long have you been wanting to say all this to me?"

"She was his. And I think you wanted to see if you got one for yourself," I replied. She wanted her very own daughter. A little plaything that she pushed away and pulled in at will, thinking only of her own feelings, her own *sick* feelings, and never mine or what she was doing to me. But was that how she loved me? The only way she knew how? She left everyone and everything else but she never left me.

She kept me.

I was hers and she kept me.

She wanted to keep me.

I was always going to be the one who had to leave.

Run away.

I waited for her response, taking a deep breath in the silent moments that passed.

"If that's what you need to tell yourself, I won't argue with you," she said, looking above my head and at the house, refusing to connect with me on any honest level. The window to the past, open briefly, had been shut. It only confirmed my theory. It wasn't normal love from Mother, but it was something, like I suspected. She had always known exactly where I was, even after I did what I did to her. Watching and waiting. Playing and plotting. And here we were. Finally together again. Mother and daughter.

"We have a lot to discuss about your dilemma with Gale," Mother said, strolling past me toward the door to the house. "Why don't we go inside?"

I didn't protest, because she was right, and I followed her inside my own home. We sat on the stools in the kitchen around the island and I immediately offered her something to drink out of habit.

"I think I'll make my own drinks around you from now on," Mother sniped. I held my breath. I knew she'd bring it up, but what did I have to say for myself? It was unforgivable, wasn't it? "You almost had me. One more pill might have done it. Just one more." I was quiet and unresponsive, thinking it best to be nonconfrontational. Don't panic. But around Mother, I was falling back into an old habit, waiting for her to take the lead because I wasn't yet sure of her plans for me. "Aren't you going to apologize to your mother?" she hissed.

"But you wouldn't have let me go," I uttered quickly, no time for logic to enter my brain, talking back and justifying the unjustifiable. I was going to make myself say all the things I'd been wanting and waiting to say to her. I was about to lose everything anyway. The time was now. "I didn't have another choice. You didn't give me another choice."

"I'd say you had an alternative —"

"You're here, aren't you?" I barked at her, admitting defeat. "You won. You bested me, as always. You always beat me, Mother. You win. How? I really need you to tell me, because you got involved with Gale and now look at the mess we're in together. All so you could get your revenge on me instead of just letting me go. You had to keep me, the whole time, but now she knows all of it. She knows everything because of you. She has us, Mother, don't you get it? She has us because of what you've done to me."

"No, because *you* couldn't finish the job."

"If you hadn't orchestrated any of this with Gale and Syl and —"

"Don't you see that I was trying to help you?" Mother raised her voice and stood up out of her seat, edging closer to me with every word, believing all of it. "You don't belong with Collin or his awful family, stuck in a palatial prison of your own making. You'll hate it. Trust me, you will get bored and then you'll do something completely destructive, which you've proven you absolutely cannot handle on your own. You're better off with me, despite your best efforts. Aren't you exhausted living this way? Aren't you tired of pretending to be something you're not? You must be so tired, bunny."

"I *am* Bea Case, Mother."

"Sure." She laughed at me. The cruelest sound I knew. It used to make me wilt, but now it lit a fire. Mother had never seen me with the fire of my own so I would show her. Again, if not now, when?

"I *am,* Mother. And now I'm about to lose everything I've worked so hard for because of your foolish actions and trusting the wrong person when you could have just let me go. Why couldn't you just let me go?"

"Maybe you'll understand when you become a mother." She smiled, mocking me again, enjoying my pain and desperation.

"Gale has probably already alerted the police or the FBI or who knows what, some sort of private investi—"

"Oh, please!" Mother guffawed. "Gale's bound and gagged in her bathroom."

Mother delivered this news like a comedian delivering a punch line, awaiting my applause, my laughter, my delight.

"See? Mother always has your back. You need a push from me, I suppose. I'm happy to assist, but you're going to finish the job. You're my daughter. Always will be. So we can do it together."

She was correct that I hadn't been able to finish the job. It only proved I wasn't like her, right? I wasn't able to take someone's life after all. A sweet relief on a cellular level, a new awareness in my bones that I couldn't actually go through with it. I didn't take Gale's or Mother's. I was not a killer. I never was. But if I couldn't do it now, then what would this all be for? I didn't want to lose Bea Case, and it appeared the only way I could keep her was to kill Gale Wallace-Leicester.

"Together?" I asked Mother. "And then what?"

"And then you'll see how good it feels! To embrace the chaos, take risks, go wild. *LIVE.* And we'll be back together again. You're just like me, bunny. You can't run away. We're two of a kind. She'll be like us, too." Mother motioned to my belly, reaching out to touch it, but I stepped away to grab a bottle of water from the refrigerator.

"We don't know if it's a girl or a boy yet," I said to her, before downing the entire thing. My thirst was unquenchable. A sign of my own nerves.

"It's a girl," Mother declared. There was

no way for her to know, but I had a feeling she was right.

"I don't want to leave Collin," I said. "That's the only reason I'm even entertaining this —"

"No, it isn't," she interrupted me. "You still want Mother's stamp of approval, don't you?"

"Mother, I don't think I can do what you're asking me to do. I'm not like —"

"Maybe you were right," she interrupted me again, even faster, in a moment that felt honest, but also manipulative. The sweet spot in our performances for each other. "That other girl never felt like mine, but you? You're mine. You're all mine."

That was all I ever wanted to hear from Mother. When she said things like that to me, I would always do whatever she asked. She knew that, too. That was just the kind of woman she was. A monster. My monster. My mother.

"Oh, we used to have fun," Mother continued, laughing. "Don't pretend like we didn't. We were good-time girls and that familiar feeling never goes away, no matter how old we get. Despite what you may think, I know you will tire of this life. I wish you would just realize that and stop fighting it. You won't be able to get out of this unscathed, you know. I don't care what you two agreed on when you got married, but the house always wins, and the house of Case is very powerful. It's intoxicating, isn't it? The challenge it would be to take them on from the inside? We could do it together. I'll even let you take the lead, since it's *your* husband this time, but you have to let me in. We can take our time. Enjoy ourselves a little bit while we secure our treasure. You'll have the baby. You'll introduce me to the family. You'll remember how to play. It's our favorite game, bunny. The long game. Just like old times. You can even pick the ending. I know you're softer than me, no one else has to die. But first things first, whether you like it or not."

"Gale," I said, hushed, sitting in the gravity of the situation at hand.

"And it has to be tonight."

If it were any other time, before Collin, before Syl, before everything, I might have taken a bite of her apple, just to be closer to her, but now? I was repulsed by the thought. Letting her into the fold I had cultivated, allowing her to be a part of my child's life, working with her to con the Cases, as if we could? I found it so preposterous that I was relieved. I *had* changed, I wasn't like her and I made my life for me all on my own.

But Mother was absolutely right about Gale and it was torturing me. It was the only way to preserve the life I built. We had to do it. *I* had to do it, but I couldn't. I could do a lot of things, I had done a lot of dark and terrible and awful things in the name of self-preservation, but murder? That wasn't me after all.

Was it?

"What time?" I asked her, wanting to hear her plan as I made up my mind. If anyone could convince me, it was her, whether I wanted to or not.

"Wait until Collin comes home. Have a normal evening together. Ask him if everything's all right. *Make* everything all right. And wait until he's asleep. Should we say midnight? Behind her building, do not go inside. Wait for me and we'll go together. Remember, it doesn't get done unless we're together. Understand?"

She would not let me off easy. She never did.

Mother got up to leave, heading for the back door. She was ready to slip away the same way she'd slipped inside. She issued her orders and I was to obey them, just like old times. And of course, she always got the last word.

But not this time.

"Wait," I blurted out. She looked back at me with her pursed lips, still pretty and full and bright red. She was curious and amused at my defiance, throwing up her hands, awaiting what I would say next. "I want an apology. I deserve one."

She went quiet for what felt like a full minute, stoic and still, weighing not what would be best for me, but for her. So rarely were they the same, but in this moment they happened to be in alignment. Mother's eyes softened as they'd done in the past, only once in a great while, her sharp edges falling away. Her shoulders released, rolling down her back. She walked closer to me and slowly her arms reached out. I let her touch me; she gingerly placed her hands on either side of my waist, then she slid them to my stomach and finally up my body, brushing the hair along my face, sweeping it over my ears.

"You're right," she said. "You were just being a teenager and I took my anger out on you in an unacceptable way. I can admit that. But that man was just an empty threat, bunny. I would never hurt you or let somebody hurt you, you know that." She said all of this wistfully, as if what happened in Las Vegas was an isolated incident, like my whole childhood with her as my mother wasn't where it all went wrong for me. "And I'm so sorry," she finally said. "I'm sorry, Bea."

I wanted to believe her. Like a stupid little girl, I wanted to believe she was being sincere and wanted my forgiveness because she was a mother who had wronged her daughter. She even used my name, the name I chose for myself. But I knew it was a performance because she was Mother and when we were together, I was still me, we were still us, and we only knew how to put on a show. For the world and for each other.

She didn't wait for my response. I watched her walk out the door immediately after uttering the words and shut it behind her, fully expecting my loyalty and obedience in return.

Mother always did get the last word.

Chapter 22

Collin arrived home around eight o'clock. I had dinner waiting once he texted me he was en route back home. I ordered in, obviously — as if I was in any sort of mental state to prepare a sumptuous meal from scratch. I even allowed myself a piece of crusty bread with a pat of butter. I rationalized that if there was ever a time I deserved to indulge, it was now.

Collin mentioned that he'd received a strange phone call to his business cell — someone unfamiliar implying a security breach at the company, a threat of personal information leaking that would be a detriment to the family, and he was all out of sorts. It was the appropriate response for a man in his position, but I took care to assuage his fears with plenty of ego boosting, telling him that a man with power like his would never be fully infiltrated, it was likely a hoax. The security team had the details and they'd take care of everything as always.

"Everyone wants to be a part of your life, Collin," I said to him. "These things happen, but you're protected. We're protected. No one could ever pull a fast one on our family."

Was I saying it all for his sake or my own?

As we ate dinner in front of the television, my mind raced with musings on murder. Was this the eventual culmination of my life's events? The unavoidable ending? Was it fated? My mother wanted me to be a killer, too. She thought I had it in me. I know she did, but how could she be so sure? I had to do it if I wanted to keep Collin, his name, his security, his safety. But if I did it, my worst fears would be confirmed — I really was just like Mother — and wouldn't that be its own ghastly ending?

So, what if there was another choice, if I was brave enough to see it through? What if I was willing to bet on Bea Case and tell Collin the truth in the hopes that he would protect me from whatever Gale was going to do or say to take me down? We were untouchable as the Case family, weren't we? Money can make anything go away, even my past, but did he love me enough to know my truth? The real me? I didn't know the answer, so how could I risk it?

That scenario had an outcome much more difficult to predict so I started to envision the first, which was simpler, not on an emotional level but on a logistical one, on a basic level, especially with Mother at my side. How would I do it? How would *we* do it? If I walked myself through the steps, could I wrap my head around it in a tangible way? Distance myself from the heart of the matter and focus on the facts only. Yes, the facts would be a good place to start. Facts were facts. Facts were calming. Facts informed decisions. Okay.

There are a multitude of ways to murder someone, none of which are necessarily easier than the other. There's DIY — guns, knives, a blunt object, even hand-to-hand combat. There's no denying the person is dead because they were physically harmed to the point where they could no longer breathe, but it's imperative that absolutely zero roads can lead back to you until you yourself shuffle off this mortal coil. No easy task. That couldn't be the road we take. No. Check it off the list. Not happening. Next.

You could also hire someone to perform the murder on your behalf, but the trust level there has to be beyond compare, and who can *really* trust an assassin service, no matter who the referral is? Chances are, if you're looking to murder someone, you aren't the most trusted individual as it is, so how can you trust someone to do your dirty work when they inherently may not trust you due to the enormous ask in question? Mother never even considered outsourcing for that reason alone. We didn't trust anybody.

My greatest teacher. My greatest enemy.

And that's why she wanted *me* to do it and she wanted to watch. She wanted a show. Another show. Always a show for Mother. Always a show for someone. She was right. I was exhausted. I was tired. But wouldn't it always have to be a show, in one way or another? I couldn't see another way. Not without knowing what would happen to me.

Okay, okay. Another route, let's see.

Mother's preferred exit strategy for her husbands was always via a good old-fashioned poisoning. It's sneaky, understated. And mostly undetectable depending on the chosen substance and the speed at which it's distributed. Mother mixed it up in that regard, playing on a spectrum, from low and slow to instantaneous and painful, depending on her mood and general affection, or lack thereof, for the man.

Of course, Mother would have her own

suggestions, her own way of wanting to take care of our entanglement with Gale. She'd know exactly what to do, tell me exactly what to do, but would I do it? I didn't think poisoning was what Mother had in mind. She'd want us to make it look like an unfortunate accident or at Gale's own hand. I'd already nearly strangled Gale to death so perhaps she wanted to run with that. Gale couldn't handle Collin and me together. A bundle of joy to arrive in a few months' time. Our endless happiness was her cross to bear and she would not bear it anymore. But would someone like Gale feasibly end it in such retro, not to mention painful, fashion, her lifeless body adorned in her beloved Everlane, hanging from her marvelous, vaulted ceiling? That didn't seem right either.

Of course, an internal debate like this was futile because Mother would take the lead and I would follow. She knew I didn't have the strength to defy her when my only option was Gale's demise and she would not do it for me under any circumstances, even the most dire, because she wanted to teach me a lesson. Always the hard way. The lesson was that I needed her, that I was just like her, and once I admitted that, she'd take care of me once again.

She thought that was what I wanted, too.

She'd be in charge again. She said she'd let me take the lead with the Cases, but I was no idiot when it came to Mother's ways. She would know how to manipulate me, and through me, she would learn how to manipulate them. All of them. Would she hurt them, and not just financially? Would she hurt Collin? For her own thrills, to satiate her own sick appetite? When it came down to it, when I really thought hard about everything, for all of the Cases' faults, they didn't deserve that. I wanted to protect them from Mother, their demise too big of a price to pay for my own preservation.

Even Gale Wallace-Leicester's.

Right?

And what would be left of me to preserve if *she* was back in my life?

I studied Collin's face that night for hours. I wanted to memorize him, just in case it would be over for us. The cut of his jaw, the bow of his lips, the cowlick in his hair *finally* grown out to perfection. His eyes, always tender and loving toward me. Those teeth. Those gargantuan teeth of his showing out. He was jovial again, shaking off the day and its harrowing events. He had no idea. Openly adoring me as I put on my nightgown. Rubbing my shoulders. Rubbing my belly. Talking about baby names again. What would we call her? Or him? He reminded me that we were being surprised because he told me you don't get many surprises like that in life. The really wonderful ones. The kind when you're so utterly surprised and you're happy with either outcome. Why take that away from us? He didn't know I hated surprises. He was trying to be the man he thought I wanted him to be. He *was* the man I wanted him to be. Safe. Secure. Reliable. He really believed all of our worries were behind us and if anything else surfaced, we would be able to overcome it together, no problem, because our marriage had been appropriately tested in the first year thanks to Gale Wallace-Leicester. We had passed and now we could celebrate together forever.

I watched Collin through the mirror as we brushed our teeth at the same time. His taking much more effort of course. He smiled at me as we conducted this nightly ritual and I caught my own full-body reflection, one I'd been avoiding for weeks now, but why? It was Bea's reflection, and she was radiant. The pregnancy glow wasn't a myth. The bump, for all of its faults in my mind, looked, well, rather cute in the mirror. And my skin was downright ethereal, as if this warmth was emanating outward from deep within me, within the child. I hadn't really seen it before. Collin had always seemed to see it somehow.

I imagined Collin with the baby when they arrived. Their first moments together, father and child. I'd be watching them from the hospital bed, probably feeling absolutely horrendous, but Collin would look over at me and tell me I was beautiful. Look at our beautiful baby. Rocking back and forth. Coming together as three. A family of three.

I could see the whole thing.

And I wanted it.

Something normal, something nice.

Would I still be able to have it?

Collin thought there wouldn't be other surprises.

Neither did I.

And yet . . .

Collin's alarm went off the next morning at 7:25 a.m. We always woke up to his alarm; it was louder than hell, these aggravating, piercing chirps from his phone. He said a calming tone wouldn't be able to rouse him from sleep so it had to be the violent kind that was bad for one's cortisol levels so early in the morning. I loathed it but he never pressed snooze, which was the mark of a true keeper. Someone considerate toward their partner.

Collin looked very well rested, unlike me. He practically shot out of bed like a firework, ready to amble downstairs with a bounce in his step and pour us both a cup of coffee, the timer already set the night before. He really had no idea what was coming. I could scarcely believe it myself. I hadn't slept a wink, my mind elsewhere.

I had stayed up all night, mentally practicing what I would say to him and how I would say it, specific words carefully chosen, annunciations planned at opportune moments. When I would cry, when I'd be strong, when I'd make eye contact, when I'd look away from him. So much rehearsal, lying completely still in my marital bed all night long, preparing to tell him the whole truth. I was going to share everything, but it still needed to be a show. I didn't know any other way. Perhaps that's who I always really was and so I was going to go out with a bang and finally do what scared me the most.

Not just for Collin, but for me. For Bea.

And I kept watch all night long.

Was she coming?

Collin's phone rang before he left the

bedroom.

If I was going to do it, I had to do it now.

It had to come from me, not from her.

It was the only way we could make it.

Bea and me.

"Babe, wait! I need to tell you something. It's important."

I reached out for him in a panic. I wasn't ready at all, but I knew who was on the other end of the line. It had to be Gale Wallace-Leicester, released from Mother's clutches because I failed to do her bidding.

No, I couldn't go through with it in the end.

No, I couldn't go to Mother, like I had always done before. I couldn't be like her, not after all this time, after all this work. I would have to try to protect myself and my family, even with thc looming possibility of losing everything. I was going to face what I had done in my life, all of it, and I hoped and prayed that Collin would still be on my side. He was my only chance. I didn't want to start over again. I didn't love him, but I chose Bea Case with my whole heart and now I loved her.

I hoped I could keep her.

I hoped Collin would want to keep both of us, too.

"Hold on a sec, babe," Collin said, looking at the screen on his phone. I couldn't have stood up out of bed if I tried; I felt my whole body going limp, like I was melting. Dear God. I was going to be one of those women who gave birth in prison, wasn't I? I felt ill, bile forming in my throat. I swallowed it back down.

"But, Collin, I —"

He answered the phone and I wanted to scream, was going to scream, until I heard him speak.

"Calliope?" Collin said. "Is everything okay?"

Calliope Case was awake at 7:30 a.m. on a Monday morning? I would have answered swiftly as well. Something was up, that much was clear.

Collin's face fell, grave and serious. I managed to sit up in bed, my senses coming back, this time on high alert. Survival mode yet again. Instincts kicking in. I needed my wits about me, to be quick on my feet if needed, sly and cunning, how would I grapple with this if she had gotten to him first? Had Gale gone right to the Cases before Collin? That would be a move out of her playbook. What with the *legacy.* The *dynasty.* The *families.* The Cases would believe her without question, particularly if she had hard evidence of our crimes and our past. They had been waiting for a reason to banish me from the family. They would alert the appropriate authorities to put me away for years on end, perhaps the entirety of my remaining hot years, and all Collin would do is watch me go, standing idly by as the love of his life was ripped from his bedroom, crying and begging him to pay for my legal fees, for the sake of his child.

Silence hung in the air. I could hear the coffee machine percolating downstairs. Was this the last time I'd smell freshly made coffee in this house? Or any house at all?

Collin hung up the phone, still rendered speechless as he sat back down on the bed.

"I can explain," I started, all memories of my rehearsal had flown right out the window. I was operating on animal instinct only. Stay here, stay alive. But he wasn't looking at me. It was like he didn't hear me at all.

"There was a fire," he said.

Oh my God.

"In Gale's building."

She did it.

"In her apartment."

Without me.

"Gale's dead."

For *me.*

I was disoriented, closing my eyes, reaching toward the headboard for balance so I didn't tip right over. Was this an act of survival on Mother's part? Gale had her, too. But Gale couldn't *really* have had Mother, right? Nobody ever could. I had always admired that about her.

But I had betrayed Mother by reneging on our deal. I didn't show up for her like she asked. I did not do as she said. I made my choice, the wrong choice in her mind, and she could have run and left me holding the bag like I thought she would.

But no, Mother took care of it anyway because that was how she always took care of me. Showing me love the only way she knew how. The dark, sick love my mother had for her daughter. She had always killed for herself, but this time she killed for me.

Collin collapsed on the bed, tears falling at an alarming rate, and I leapt into action, wrapping my arms around his body as he shuddered into my neck. "I can't believe this," he sobbed. "She was my best friend. I'm sorry, Bea, but she was my best —"

"I know, I know," I comforted him, absolving him of his sin, his closeness to her. She was his best friend and I had taken her from him, in more ways than one, now in a way I never actually wanted. Not deep down. I couldn't do it. I wasn't her.

But I was still the sinner. I was always the sinner.

"I'm so sorry, Collin. I'm so sorry."

I cradled my husband, rocking him back and forth, running my hands through his hair, knowing there was absolutely nothing I could do to make him — or myself — feel better. It was all my fault and the guilt was manifesting as nausea, not morning sickness, but the pure desire to expel such evil from my body, rid Mother from myself. But I also felt so relieved, the tension in my neck and shoulders dissipating after a full night of clenching and flexing in anticipation, and that made me feel even guiltier and more physically ill, but the vomit would not come up. It would just sit there, making me feel uncomfortable and wretched, because I didn't deserve the release. I had caused this pain. I had caused this death. Gale's death.

But the problem was gone, just as I wanted.

Gale Wallace-Leicester, and all of her files, her intel, whatever she had on Mother and me, was gone. Mother had taken care of it, taken care of me, burning it all to a crisp, but I knew that wouldn't be the end of it now that she was really back. I knew she was alive, that she'd always be close and that she'd want something in return. I had made it more difficult for her, entwined with one of the most protected families in the world, but Mother thrived on a challenge. I had seen it in her eyes the night before. She would always find me. She'd never let me go. Not until she was gone for good and I would never be able to do that to her. The devil himself would have to take her because ultimately I could not.

"What were you going to tell me?" Collin asked, remembering my panic from mere moments before.

"I don't even remember," I said softly, lying to my husband yet again, just as I would forever. My past never to be shared with him. I joined him in his tears, and we clung together and cried into one another's arms about what we each had lost.

Epilogue

Nothing looked good on me anymore, but I'd rather openly display the outrageous bulge that was my stomach, to prove that I was indeed with child, than float around Manhattan like a giant parade balloon version of myself. I selected a formfitting off-the-shoulder dress for the baby shower. Appropriate for daytime. Floral print, hitting me just above the knee. Miraculously my calves were still enviable. Thank God. They seemed to be all I had left.

The sharp definition my face once possessed had been swallowed up by newly acquired buccal fat, my collarbones barely registered through my décolletage and my eyelids were getting puffier with each passing day. I could not wait for the baby to arrive so I could begin the long road back to my peak physical form.

I wondered what the baby would look like. I hoped it looked like me. It's easier to be pretty in this world, I knew that much. I also hoped the baby would be delightfully chubby. Everyone adores a big fat baby. *Their* buccal fat is celebrated!

I wondered about the baby's personality. What would they be born with? What would they learn? Would I see myself in the baby? What did I even have to offer? My child was going to have a completely different life from mine. Would we ever be able to relate to each other? Would this baby, who would always belong to me, I was the *mother*, would they ever know the real me if I never told them? Would they be able to sense it? Some primal biological force that would tell the child exactly who I was and where I came from? Where *we* came from? Could I hide it from them forever? I didn't know.

Would Mother find the child one day? I couldn't bear the thought.

Ah, that was it. There it was. That's what I had to offer the baby.

I would keep *her* away.

She'd always come back for me, for us, and I'd always be ready. Until she was gone for good. One day she'd really be gone. She couldn't live forever.

And then, only then, I could breathe.

Haven placed her arms on my shoulders

and shuffled me down the hallway toward the garden, taking full possession of the party and of me and thus the baby, a preview of what was likely to come. She went all out with decor. The florals were obscene, an abundance of peonies and ranunculus, some of them crafted into a full bough with greenery, affixed on a tasteful wooden arch, where a large white wingback chair awaited my enormous pregnant ass.

I perched upon the end of the cushion, shoulders rolled back and chin up, fully finding my light with a broad smile that everyone expected of me. The admiration from guests was near constant. It soon became a receiving line for hugs and belly rubs and warm wishes. All of them wanted to share tips with me about motherhood. They were all so giving with the information. They didn't want anything in return. Just recognition that I had heard them. Never mind that most of them raised their children alongside an army of nannies. I supposed I would do the same, but my eye would always be more watchful. My one job.

Nora Wallace-Leicester arrived. It was her first public outing since Gale's funeral about a month prior. She greeted me with an air-kiss, a gift and as much of a smile as a woman in her position could stand.

"Thank you for coming, Mrs. Wallace-Leicester."

"I wouldn't miss it. Congratulations," she said robotically, unable to conceal her enduring grief. I wondered if Gale had told her mother anything about me. Were they close? Did they share secrets? I looked Nora in the eye, but she seemed to stare right past me, vacantly smiling. She just wanted to get out of the house. Find the new normal. Show face. Stiff upper lip and all that. At a baby shower. Nora would never have a grandchild; her legacy would not continue. It ended with Gale.

Collin practically skipped down the staircase to the garden, waving at me, his eyes aglow with all the love in the world for the mother of his unborn child. His meds were working overtime that day. I don't think I'd ever seen him so happy. He had been so broken up about Gale's death for weeks, but — even though he would never admit something so distasteful — I often thought he might have felt a small sense of relief that she was gone. That tension was gone. The security blanket he no longer required. He could finally be happy with me.

Haven hadn't wanted a coed shower, such a thing wasn't tradition, but I coerced her into letting Collin make a cameo at the event. I preferred having him very close to me ever since the fire because I knew Mother would still be watching. Her eyes would always be on me, on Collin and the baby. I didn't know what action she would take next, or when. And Collin, bless him, could be an easy target. I'd always have to remain vigilant and protect our family's den.

"Hello, sweetheart," Collin whispered in my ear, giving me a kiss on the top of my head, and the women all applauded him on his successful implantation of his sperm into my egg. Collin, handsome enough but always a touch awkward, briefly bowed, almost like a curtsy. I had to laugh. He could be charming, and I definitely brought out the best in him. He was exactly the type of man that the girl I was always trying to be would want to marry. He'd never cheat on me. Never leave me. Never hurt me. Look at where we were. The baby shower of our first child. Hopefully our only — I didn't want to go through the misery of pregnancy again, but I knew I wouldn't be so lucky. Collin was one of three. He'd probably want three of his own. Oh my God. Would we have three fucking children?

Bea Case would, though, wouldn't she?

I promised myself I wouldn't hurt Collin

again, even unknowingly. For him, but also for our child. That much I could do. I already knew the baby would prefer Daddy to me. I had a strong feeling about it, but it didn't bother me at all because I wasn't like *her.* And I didn't even have to *love* Collin, at least not in the traditional sense, since I wasn't sure that I ever could, but I could care for him in my own way. I could be the perfect wife. Simple. I'd make him believe I loved him and our family. I could be the star of this show, as always. He'd given me what I wanted so I would do the same for him. Fair is fair.

And more importantly, I'd provide safety for them in a different way. It was the trade-off now that Mother was lingering. I hadn't heard from her since that night, but I knew it wasn't the last of her. She would be back, prowling and plotting, so I would keep watch for the family, be on high alert and make sure she never infiltrated our lives again. It was a new purpose for me, including others as part of my motivation, but the rationale was one that I knew well. It was all I ever wanted. To be different from her, have her out of my life, even if my heart eternally hoped she would change, but I knew better. She would never, ever change.

And so it goes, but now it wasn't just

enough to be different from Mother.

I didn't know if it was possible for me, but really, I wanted to be more like Syl.

Syl bounded into the party, beaming from ear to ear, looking every part of the mother-to-be's best gal pal. I had invited her to the shower in an effort to clear the air between us. A couple texts were exchanged to check in on Collin after what happened to Gale, checking in on how I was doing with my pregnancy. Surface-level interactions, but still, very sweet. I knew we had so much to say to each other, but would we actually do it now that we were face-to-face again?

"Hi," she said, approaching my maternal throne. I struggled to get up and Syl took my hands to help me, hesitating before launching into the warmest hug, her own animal instincts on display. "You look beautiful."

"Thirsty?" I asked, not knowing how to begin, if at all.

"Sure." She nodded.

Syl took my hand and we strolled over to the table of refreshments, which were basically untouched due to everyone's unhealthy obsession with their own bodies. In some ways, we're all the same. Women. Always careful, always watching something, always for the good of the show. The show must always go on.

Syl delicately took a champagne flute from the tower and helped herself to a sip. She looked at me intently. I knew what she still wanted from me. Oh, how I *wanted* to be more than her friend. I wanted to be her *sister.* I wanted to do the right thing for her, take the test, free her father — our father — but how could I open that door now? I took a deep breath and marveled at my surroundings. I never had to worry about money or safety or security again. It had almost all been taken from me once. I couldn't risk it all again. Not even for Syl. Before I could say a word, she took my hands.

"I know," she said. "It's okay."

Of course she knew, but it wasn't okay.

Sweet Syl.

"I took care of it," she said, with an air of authority.

"Took care of what?" I released her hands instinctively, but she grabbed one of mine again, slipping me a piece of paper. I opened it furtively.

A DNA test. With very high percentages.

Essentially, confirmed sisters.

I crumpled the paper immediately, terrified by what it meant.

"Relax," she said, taking it back from me to put in her purse, hidden away.

"YOU relax," I hissed. "How did you —"

"I'm not going to share this with the Cases, you have my word."

"But I didn't —"

"With enough alternative samples, they can often get a solid read."

"What the fuck are alternative sam—"

"Hair. Gum. Cigarettes. Lots of things."

Jesus Christ, she *was* my sister.

"From the very beginning?" I asked, hushed, feeling deeply violated but also filled with a new level of respect.

"I wanted you to take the test of your own volition. It's better evidence, but you didn't so I did what I had to do. This is a start. I told you, Bea. I would do anything to get him out."

"Holy shit," I whispered. What else could I say?

"It's not quite enough, though . . ." Syl trailed off.

"You can't tell the Cases. I can't be involved, it's not —"

"Bea. I don't want to blow up your life," she said, grabbing my hands again. All I could do was laugh. "Listen. The fire? Gale? I know it was *her.* So do you. She's close. She's watching."

I couldn't speak.

"You don't have to say anything," Syl said, dead serious. "But I'm going after her."

"After her to do what?! You can't —"

"I can and I will."

"You don't know her. You don't know what she can do."

"I'll take care of it," Syl said. "You don't need to worry. I'm going to take care of everything. I'm your big sister."

"I don't want her to hurt you."

Syl looked fearless and committed to her promise, but she really didn't know what Mother was capable of. Still, Syl laughed in the face of such a threat.

"I fucking dare her to hurt me again."

"Syl, you can't just —"

"One other thing." She smiled. "I dumped John."

I could only smile back at her. So she wanted to be more like me, too.

I watched Syl leave, on her mission, still flummoxed by her revelation and worried sick for her future. She didn't know Mother like I did, but if she continued down such a vengeful path, she certainly would. Syl would need me, no matter what she said about being the big sister. She wouldn't be able to take care of Mother alone. We would need to do it together.

We would need to be a team.

Collin and I began opening presents together. It was easy to get caught up in the excitement of becoming parents. It had been so abstract until that moment. Little miniature clothes and onesies and shoes, all sorts of blankets and cloths and towels and diapers in the faintest shades of yellow, green, pink and blue, bottles and pacifiers and sippy cups, soft and cuddly stuffed creatures, seemingly the entire animal kingdom represented. The baby wasn't even here yet and they were so loved. I had felt removed from my body for so long and I don't know what came over me, but I became just the slightest bit excited for the baby, regardless of my cellulite production being in maximum overdrive.

Calliope was in charge of gift time against her will and looked relieved that we were coming upon the last one. Petite and pristinely wrapped, the final offering was placed in my hands. Wrapped in silver with a little pink bow. It was small and thin. I opened the card first. Glitter. Pink. Little woodland creatures parading about.

The interior was unsigned, bearing only a small note in perfect penmanship:

For your own bunny.

I knew she'd show up that day. She always did. She always would. Until the end. A sharp pain flashed across my chest. Fleeting, but forceful. I let it be. Let it pass. A moment of pain. A lifetime really. My physical body had always felt that specific hurt from her so much harder, that Mother wound, that push and pull of my heart, that pernicious interpretation she had of love, but now my mind could overcome it with enough focus, with enough will, with enough strength.

I had it all.

So I proceeded to open Mother's gift.

Ah, yes.

Of course.

ACKNOWLEDGMENTS

Thank you to my incredible agent, Rachel Kim at 3 Arts. I've never had a creative partner quite like her. She knows exactly when to push and when to praise and she's without a doubt made me a better writer. Also, Luke Maxwell and Katie Newman at 3 Arts are an absolute dream team. I'm just delighted we're all working together.

Thank you to my fantastic editor, Jen Monroe at Berkley. She really understood Bea (and me) from the very beginning. It was such a treat to get *Stone Cold Fox* all sparkly and ready to go under her watchful yet loving eye. I knew Jen was the one when she had the most macabre guess about the mysterious ending. A girl after my own heart! Also, thank you to the whole wonderful team at Berkley, including Catherine Barra, Fareeda Bullert, Craig Burke, Candice Coote, Jeanne-Marie Hudson, Chelsea Pascoe, Claire Zion, and everyone who had a hand in getting this story into the world. I'm so very appreciative.

I saw the cover for *Stone Cold Fox* for the first time on St. Patrick's Day, a wink to how lucky I am. I literally screamed with delight at the electric chartreuse font, the chic mani and enviable profile with a full pout in front of me. It was Bea, and the cover is beyond my wildest dreams. Thank you to designer Vi-An Nguyen for making the book look so sexy, like a *Vogue* cover.

Thank you to all of these marvelous friends, early readers and overall hype men and women for their astute feedback and enthusiasm as I wrote this novel: Kit Koller, Jenny Gaiser, Sheila McCrink, Liz Mansholt, Michael Marino, Claire Burgart, Brad Milison, Maria Dirolf, Rachel Crouch, Ryan Wineinger-Schattl, Becky Flaum Del-Guercio, Nick Kilgore, Nina Steffel, Whitnee Ferrer, Spencer Berry, Dajana Buonaguidi, Michael Calabrese, Carli Haney, Karina Rahardja, Adam Schwartz and Ali Levin, Rozy Boswell and Julian Landau-Sabella, Coral and Eli Edelson, Nitasha and Sameer Patel, and Ryan "TR" Mansholt.

Special thanks to Kinsey Wilder and Jordan Fox for the fun and fabulous photo shoot. I'll never forget the mini–leaf blower moment for as long as I live.

Thank you to Mrs. Mary Foskett, the teacher who changed my life and always treated me like a real writer from a very young age.

Thank you to Dolores Koller for instilling in me a love of all things clever and to Gloria Lesniak for doing the same with all things glamorous. They are my two sweet grannies, who always made me feel smart, funny and cherished.

Now I must share that I have a whole wonderful family who have all been very supportive of my writing from the very beginning and always told me I was great at it and to just keep going. It's truly miraculous. I have zero impostor syndrome because of them. The "self-esteem team" remains very strong; we're a confident bunch! So thank you to the Kollers, Petrovics, Lesniaks and Tomasellos. And thank you to my new family-in-law, all of the lovely Landaus and Crofts, who go out of their way to make me feel like a star, especially Amy and Gary Croft.

My aunt, Carole Koller, always let me read books for adults at her house when I was a kid because she knew I could handle them. *Ellen Foster, She's Come Undone, White Oleander* and countless others, all technically age-inappropriate, made me want to be a novelist one day. Thank you for being a consistently loving force and positive guiding light in my life. I'm so lucky to have you, Auntie Carole.

My father, Don Koller, still brings up "The Story of Snow, The Arctic Wolf," a short story I wrote in fourth grade (under the tutelage of the aforementioned Mrs. Foskett) that won first place in a county-wide contest in Chicago. Suffice it to say, he's been telling me he's proud of me for a very long time. Thanks, Dad (and Dormie Koller!), for all of your encouragement, good humor and endless praise. I love you.

My mother, Christine Koller, started reading aloud to me pretty much right after I was born. And she prioritized getting me a library card ASAP and even secured special permission from the librarian so I could check out extra books over the limit since I would go through them so fast. And she loved hearing my own stories. My mother never doubted me or my writing once and seemed to always know this day would come. Thank you, Mom (and Merle Tomasello!), for always looking out for me, believing in me and making sure I had everything I needed. I love you.

I also have to thank little Junie girl, my magnificent brindle beauty and canine love of my life, who sat dutifully by my side while I wrote this novel.

And finally, thank you to my darling husband, Charles Croft. There's truly nobody better. What else can I say? As always, it's all for you. You're the best and I love you more than anything. Gee.

ABOUT THE AUTHOR

Rachel Koller Croft is an author and screenwriter in Los Angeles, where she has scripted projects for Blumhouse, Sony Pictures Entertainment, and Comedy Central, among others. She lives by the beach with her husband, Charles, and their rescue pitbull, Juniper. *Stone Cold Fox* is her first novel.

The employees of Thorndike Press hope you have enjoyed this Large Print book. All our Thorndike Large Print titles are designed for easy reading, and all our books are made to last. Other Thorndike Press Large Print books are available at your library, through selected bookstores, or directly from us.

For information about titles, please call:
(800) 223-1244

or visit our website at:
gale.com/thorndike